AN ACQUIRED TASTE

A NOVEL

AN ACQUIRED TASTE

A NOVEL

**Bitterroot Mountain
Publishing House**

Published by Bitterroot Mountain Publishing House LLC
P.O. Box 3508, Hayden, ID 83835

Visit our website at www.BMPHmedia.com

Interior and cover design by Studium Argiletum.

Library of Congress Cataloguing in Publication Data

Hardcover ISBN: 978-1-960059-29-1
Softcover ISBN: 978-1-960059-28-4
eBook ISBN: 978-1-960059-30-7

Printed in the United States of America

10 9 8 7 6 5 4 3 2 1

1.   Literary Fiction 2. Historical Fiction 3. Hollywood

To all those who have been chased by a dream only to find a nightmare, may you awaken to find a brighter dawn.

CHAPTER 1
TWENTY-FOUR HUNDRED
MILES FROM PRAIRIE RIVER

We are all tied to our destiny, and there is no way we can liberate ourselves.

— Rita Hayworth

APRIL 1948

"Hello, Mabs," she said lazily, as if only half paying attention. "Where've you been all my life?"

Of course, I knew Dagny lived here. After all, it was she who I followed from our home in Prairie River, Saskatchewan, albeit seven years after she left. Still, I never expected to see her walking down Sunset Boulevard that morning. More precisely, I never expected her to see me. It had been over a year since I moved. Because of nerves or timidity or who knows what, I never contacted her once I arrived and pushed my childhood friend to the back of my mind, as sad as that is to say. Yet here she was, a forlorn gaze in her eyes as if she was searching for me all this time. But, instead of being delighted to see me, she seemed crushed by the encounter.

We grew up together, two friends, sisters in every way but blood. Like Canadian versions of Mary and Laura Ingalls, we lived a plains life years before anyone knew of *Little House on the Prairie*. Times were different then, to be sure. Neither of our families had much. We used to line our shoes with cornhusks when we wore through the soles. And milk was a luxury. Everything was a luxury growing up in Eastern Saskatchewan, even life itself, with more than one in ten children dying before the age of two. Dagny and I made it out though. We always made it out.

Being the more handsome, she went first. *Oh, I don't say that with any sort of jealousy, only as a fact.* Most consider me rather comely myself, and my looks certainly helped get me out as well— or perhaps they got me in. I'll never truly know which. She possessed a more *classic* beauty, however.

I remember the day Dagny left quite clearly. The sky was a cornflower blue, like her eyes, and the prairie grasses had turned a golden yellow, like her hair. I accompanied her to the train station, and as we sat there, Kenny Baker serenaded us over the small wireless in the lobby with *Love is Here to Stay*. Now, here she was, standing in front of me, looking a bit out of place in her own life, out of place on this palm-lined street they call Sunset Boulevard.

The sunset. The end. But the end of what? A day? A lifetime? I thought little of Dagny or Hollywood, even though I was surrounded by it, until this moment. Something about meeting her on that spot and seeing the expression in her eyes, though, gave me a sense that this was not a chance encounter, at least not in the eyes of the Fates. Something gave me the sense that my life was about to drastically change. *Would the sunset lead to a new dawn or would we live in darkness forevermore?*

"Was it just yesterday we were playing with cornhusk dolls? Or maybe it was a lifetime ago. I seem to have lost my datebook." Dagny said these words in a sorrowful and slightly confused manner, like a lost child looking for her mother. Even though many years had passed since I saw her last, and many more since we played with cornhusk dolls; even though I never expected to see her that morning, I knew I needed to help her find what she was looking for. I knew I needed to help her find herself.

"Come on, Dagny." I took her arm in mine, in hopes of leading her to some place happier, some place with more humanity, as elusive as it was in Hollywood.

"No! I feel like being sad," she exclaimed manically, a large smile gracing her lips. *My, my. She was farther away from Prairie River than I thought.* I persisted and we made our way to a nearby coffeeshop to sit down.

It was a dirty place, but somehow that made it more real. Bleach can cover up all sorts of ills, but does it ever really eliminate them? I realize that more than ever now. We tried to escape the ennui of Saskatchewan only to find that the real boredom lived in Hollywood.

Perhaps it was Dagny's classic outer beauty that shielded her from the truth of what her inner self had become. Gazing into a mirror every morning and seeing something so perfect gazing back makes it easier to lie to yourself, to hide the real you with a wonderfully distorted reflection.

A woman walked by the window, dressed far too glamorously for the hour. As odd as it was for me to see the first few times, the fancy-dress-set now blended into the background, but not her. She outdid them all. With a gown of flowing satin, arm-length gloves, and a tiara and necklace that rivaled those at a Hapsburg Ball, her presence was glaring.

"I'll follow that one. She likes big diamonds!" Dagny's eyes flashed with a fire as she said this, possessed by the twin demons of jealousy and avarice. And like the desires of a demon-possessed soul, those diamonds were also an illusion. Nothing but gems made of paste that would melt when exposed to too much heat. Or too much truth. The shadows and the glass that lay before us, however, obscured them just enough to appear genuine.

"Oh, Dagny." My soul emptied completely as I witnessed her devilish hunger.

"Mabs." She got serious, folding her hands neatly in front of her, sitting up, and facing me squarely. "You don't have to worry about me. Truly. I've finally made it! All those things we dreamt about when we were little girls, this is it. All the good fortune, none of the regrets."

She'd gone from melancholy to manic to something in between all in the blink of an eye. I was having a hard time keeping up, and for a brief moment I believed her. After all, it would have been easier. Who wouldn't want the life of a glittering starlet?

At the time, Norma Jeane had yet to become Marylin Monroe, so there was no way we could know the tragedy that would befall her fourteen years later. Nevertheless, I had a feeling, one perhaps rooted in my staunch Midwestern upbringing, that the fame and fortune surrounding us would only lead to fatality if I didn't help Dagny escape. I knew it would be a dream morphing slowly into a nightmare.

"You know, I like to start my day off on a healthy note. Some whole-wheat toast with strawberry jam and a cup of English Breakfast tea." Dagny smiled as if quite proud of herself for this one moment of the day devoted to prudence. I could smell the gin she'd imbibed the night before wafting off her like a cheap perfume. Never mind, too, that it was almost eleven. This was the beginning of her day though, so I decided to indulge her.

"I'll have the same."

The waiter wandered over.

"What'll it be, ladies?" he said in a matter-of-fact way, a bit gruff but still polite.

"Two orders of whole-wheat toast with strawberry jam and two cups of English Breakfast tea," Dagny smiled at him. She had a perky air to her now, any shadow of despair disappearing in the light of a radiant smile, a completely different person. If I'd met her at this moment, if I didn't know she had run off to Hollywood to pursue stardom, if she'd ordered an egg salad sandwich or a bowl of soup—something a bit more appropriate for the hour—I would have thought her a housewife married to an engineer or doctor. Hardly the bohemian who sat before me now.

"Mabs, I'm attending a small gathering this evening at a friend's home in Elysian Heights. I'd love for you to come and meet some of my *coterie*."

She ended her sentence with a word that didn't seem to fit her manner, at least not the manner I had been accustomed to seven years before. I wondered why she didn't just call them friends. I wondered, too, if she always used words like *coterie* or was doing so now to put on airs. Maybe I was a stranger to her now. If she hadn't called me by name when we saw each other on the sidewalk, I'd think us quite literally strangers.

Had it really been seven years? Were we really that far from Prairie River? I'd followed Dagny to Los Angeles on somewhat of a lark, desperate to shake off the monotony of a small Canadian town in the middle of nowhere. It was something thousands of girls my age did and are undoubtedly still doing.

While I hadn't yet followed her all the way through the main gates of Warner Brothers, MGM, or wherever she was likely to be reaching for her star, I still caught enough of a glimpse of the world around me that I was beginning to realize the answer to those questions with every passing moment. *Yes, it had been that long and that far.* I also wondered how *elysian* this Elysian Heights she spoke of would be.

I should have left right then and caught the next train—any train—to get as far away from the dangers I saw before me. I've always felt a need to come to the rescue, though. One that has brought harm more than a few times.

When I was twelve, I wandered on the banks of the river and came across a baby muskrat. It was hurt, so I bent down to help it. Instead of being grateful, it bit my arm. I ran home, crying the whole way. My mother cleansed the wound, but in those days, in that place, even though it was not so long ago and not so far away, anti-septic was primitive.

My mother attempted a homemade Dakin's Solution, but I wonder if washing it with well water would have been better. The wound became infected, and a fever set in. It lasted for three days, and I nearly died. All because I tried to help a baby animal.

I knew I risked injury again by sitting here in front of Dagny. I knew that this injury could end up much worse than the muskrat's bite. I needed to try, though. Even if seven years had passed, in some ways no time had passed at all. I may have been a stranger to her now, but she wasn't a stranger to me. She was the girl I'd spent an entire childhood with and though so many years had passed since we'd last seen each other, we'd gone through so much together in our youth that I couldn't let her simply wither and die here amongst the palms.

At that moment, with the air outside a balmy seventy-eight degrees and the sun shining, I shivered and wished I were back home experiencing a frigid Canadian winter. I thought of my mother's quilt wrapped around me as I sat by the fire, sipping some of her crude tea, made from whatever leaves and fruit rinds she could find in the garden.

While I was envisioning that poor tasting, yet familiar tea, our waiter brought over ours with breakfast. Or brunch. Or lunch. Whatever one has on a mid-morning Tuesday on Sunset Boulevard. I took a sip. It certainly tasted better than my mother's tea, but I knew it wasn't as comforting.

"You'll simply love them. I know it." Dagny continued on about the friends she was meeting that evening. "Struggling screenwriters, actors and actresses, like me still waiting for their chance to shine like the stars we know we're meant to be. A few of the old guard, their days playing the lead behind them, but on to other things. They take the rest of us under their wings. Real people, Mabs. The best kind. You may think Hollywood is full of nothing but actors, both on screen and off, but so many of us enjoy the struggle. It's what gives us hope."

I smiled at Dagny. Not out of agreement or happiness or anything like that, but more so out of perplexity. She definitely wasn't the girl I said goodbye to seven years before. I wasn't sure who she'd become. I wasn't sure *she* knew who she was. Her mood flipped back and forth by the minute, like a child's seesaw. Up and down. Down and up.

She reached across the table and cupped my hands as they cupped my tea. "Oh, Mabs, you will come, won't you? You must start meeting people in this town, especially people who can pull you out of your current station, help you to live a little—or a lot. I just know there's someone inside you dying to break out."

Was there? But how did she know? How did she know my current station for that matter? After all, she had only run into me less than an hour before and I'd barely told her anything. Perhaps she was now yearning for a bit of her childhood as I was. Perhaps I provided the only connection.

Maybe she was right about the inner-me as well. Maybe it wasn't she who needed saving. Maybe it was me. In the last half-hour, my world had flipped. I suddenly had no sense of true north.

I thought back to the day I left Prairie River. I wanted adventure then. I even dreamed occasionally of the silver screen like Dagny had, although not to her extent. Yet, I'd lived in Los Angeles for almost a year, renting a small apartment in Santa Monica, and done none of it.

Sure, I had a lovely life, even if it was a bit quotidian. I spent evenings strolling along the pier, watching the sun sink into the Pacific. The location was everything I'd have hoped for when I was young, if I'd known what to hope for. But it also offered an interesting duplicity. Both feelings of discovery and nostalgia welled up inside me every time I gazed out across the waves. I never saw the ocean before moving to Los Angeles. At the same time, though, the great expanse of it all, extending flat out to the horizon, reminded me of the prairie back home. *A sea of water. A sea of grass. A sea of tranquility.*

Considering I'd lived here for as long as I had, considering the impetus that had pushed me on the train a year ago, Dagny was right. I really hadn't met many people, writers, actors, or otherwise. I really hadn't experienced any kind of adventure. The closest I ever came was sitting in the library devouring books like *Robinson Crusoe.* And at twenty-four, I wasn't getting any younger.

"Oh, why not?!" I exclaimed. The cheeriness in my own voice surprised me. As soon as I said the words, I knew there were several good answers to that question and likely a few bad ones.

"Splendid! Now, we simply must find something to wear!" My doubts about Dagny began to fade as she said this. She was so elated at the prospect of me accompanying her to this little soiree of hers. But was it truly genuine? Or, as the saying goes, was it simply a case of misery loving company? One thing I knew for sure, she didn't know herself, any more than I did.

CHAPTER 2
NEW SHOES AND NIÇOISE

It's a chain of accidents. When you step into Hollywood, you wind yourself into thousands of chains of accidents. If all of the thousands happen to come out exactly right—and the chance of that figures out to be one in eight million—then you'll be a star.

— Clark Gable

It was fun getting all dolled up that afternoon. I'd only ever purchased one piece of clothing from a store in my life, having sewn everything else myself. I suspect Dagny knew this too, for she didn't allow me to pay for a single thing that day.

We went from store to store, both trying on new attire for that evening. It was a whirlwind afternoon, and I allowed myself to be carried over to it. At one store, I tried on a dress while in a room walled with three mirrors. Three! I could see how one might get used to such a life.

Dagny's checks papered four different places, and I wondered if they were real. The salesgirls all seemed to know her well enough though, treating us both like the stars she, at least, wished we were. Perhaps she had all the right, or at least the money, to live as she did.

I would come to know the truth much later, when so much of our lives came crashing down like a condemned building. And like the dust that spreads out from such an implosion, so too did the effects of that lifestyle, covering all of us with a dreadful patina of despair. Unlike some truths, though, which can set us free, this truth became a prison—even a death sentence—for so many of the rest of us.

"Dresses. Yes. Purses. Yes. Shoes. Yes. Now, we must do something about our hair!" I briefly wondered again if this was the small gathering of friends she spoke of or a film premiere only she knew about; a film in which she was producer, director, lead actress, and costume designer. Again, I'm certain she didn't know either.

"I know. I'll give Charles a call. He works under Sydney Guilaroff. Do you know Sydney?" She was talking so quickly, I could hardly keep up, let alone respond. Even if I had been able to, I barely knew what a hairstylist was. "Of course you don't, poor dear. Well, you will soon enough. He occasionally lunches at Chateau Marmont."

I knew the hotel, but then again, so did everyone who'd ever set foot in Hollywood in the forties. Was this Dagny's way of telling me that she too lunched at a place where a roast beef sandwich cost the better part of my weekly paycheck?

We stopped at a phone booth, and she pulled a nickel out of her purse.

"Hello, Charles? It's Dagny. I'm wondering if you can fit my friend Mabs and me in this afternoon. Four o'clock? That will be lovely." She hung up the receiver and turned to me.

"Four o'clock. That will give us just enough time for a spot of lunch and time to get dressed at my apartment before Kenneth picks us up at six. I know it's rather an early evening, but Philomena likes her sleep. As it is, we usually end up chatting until way past midnight.

"Now, I was rather hoping for a swim but perhaps some other time. I like the pool at the Bel-Air. They have the most charming attendants. There's this one young man, Robbie Wagner. I just know he'll go on to do big things one day. Oh, Mabs, we will have so much fun now that we are together again!"

Sydney Guilaroff. Chateau Marmont. The pool at the Bel-Air. I wasn't sure if it was all the excitement or the fact that I hadn't eaten anything but a piece of toast since eight o'clock that morning, but my head was beginning to spin. Dagny's mention of lunch settled it on the latter.

We stopped into a cafe, much cleaner and more upscale than the last one, and she ordered us some Niçoise salads. Even that was a new experience. Until then, the only tuna I ate came from a can. I briefly wondered if the kitchen failed to cook ours before Dagny pierced hers with a fork.

"Oh, do look at me, Mabs! Here I've been carrying on all afternoon about my life, which must seem terribly boresome to you..." I suspect she meant *boorish*, not *boring*, but I found her mistake rather endearing. The veneer had come off her polished demeanor for a brief moment, and she was, once again, the schoolgirl I knew back home who always needed my help with her writing assignments. "Do tell me about yourself! What have you been doing these past few years?"

Was she being liberal with the word *few* or had the time flown by so quickly for her that she really thought it had been three years instead of seven? Did she even remember me or was there another girl out there named Mabs who bore a similar resemblance? Perhaps the name Mabs was shorthand for any girl she didn't know but should have, the same way some men call each other Mac or Buddy.

I decided to dismiss these thoughts, however. If anything, I could view this as some sort of experiment, a case study into the Hollywood starlet, or whatever she was—or *thought* she was.

"Well, I left home about three years ago but only made it as far as Vancouver the first time before turning back. I guess I'm not like you, Dagny. It took a lot of courage for me to set out from Prairie River on my own. Heaven knows the only time I ever ventured farther than Porcupine Plain was when we all went down to Regina when we were ten. Oh, Dagny, I've always admired how independent you are. I've always looked up to you!" I was beginning to gush and realized so. Steadying myself, I continued on with more composure, hoping she hadn't noticed my brief display of childish giddiness.

"I finally mustered up the courage last February to move down here and pursue those silly childhood dreams of fame and fortune. I suppose part of me didn't want to endure any more of those cold winters. When I saw an advertisement in *Chatelaine*—I don't even remember what it was for now—which had sunshine and palm trees, I knew I simply had to go."

"Hmm. You do have a point. The sunshine and palm trees are nice. I haven't paid much notice of them in years, to be honest. Rather like breathing," Dagny said a bit absent-mindedly as if she'd heard nothing I'd said but that last line.

"I packed a small suitcase that evening; said goodbye to Mother, Father, and Olivia; and caught the next morning's train for Vancouver. Then it was on to Los Angeles," I continued.

"It was foolishly impulsive of me, I know. After all, despite surviving almost solely on soda crackers nicked from the dining car, by the time I arrived, I had but ten dollars to my name, barely enough to pay for a week's rent at a boarding house. Undoubtedly, you encountered much the same predicament when you arrived."

In fact, I was rather certain that she hadn't experienced any predicaments at all. Firstly, she'd always been more brash and able to ingratiate herself into getting things for free. Secondly, unlike my impulsive departure, I distinctly remember Dagny had saved up for nearly three years before hers. I'd even contributed a few dollars of my own; a tangible gesture, not so much toward her, but toward myself. At the time, I never suspected I'd leave Prairie River. Living vicariously through her letters and the rare phone call would be the closest I ever hoped to get.

I really should have been hurt that those letters and phone calls lasted only four months. The thought of bringing it up did arise, but I quickly suppressed it, the anxiety of the possible tension it could raise between us being too much.

Dagny replied. "Mabs, darling, that's a wonderful story! I should be the one in awe of you. What you did took far more courage than I ever had. To board a train like that on an impulse? I may have gone first, but what did *I* know back then? I was a stupid young git, barely out of pigtails, pining after Tyrone Power. It was more recklessness than courage on my part." Then she suddenly turned morose once again. "And I never had your family…"

The last sentence hit me especially hard as it trailed off like the smoke from a just extinguished candle. Of course, it didn't come as the slightest surprise. Dagny was always my sister just as much, if not more, than my own sister. Dagny's mother had died while giving birth to what would have been her only sister if she, too, had survived. Her father, greatly impacted by the loss, turned so cold and distant he was dead himself, if only in spirit.

While we were both barely six at the time, I grieved alongside her. In the end, though, despite my family's care for her, she had to grow up more quickly. Maybe this is what gave her so much confidence. Maybe she wasn't putting up a facade. Or maybe, even though it had been nearly two decades since her mother died, she was still torn between the necessity of independence and the yearning to be taken care of once again.

At that moment, even though only four hours had passed since we'd met again after so long an absence, I felt I knew her better than I knew anyone.

"Escape to Hollywood. Star in your own life." The last of my thoughts escaped my mind as a quiet murmur from between my lips.

"What's that, Mabs? Who's life? Are you finally getting the acting bug? We all do, you know. I can introduce you to my agent. He's not the biggest player in town, but he gets me enough auditions that I can reasonably call myself an actress without having to withstand the snickers of too many people at dinner." As she spoke, she waved her fork about as if conducting the words from her mouth. I couldn't help but follow it back and forth.

"What? No. I'm sorry." She'd shaken me back to reality not so much by her words or even how she'd said them but more so by the way she'd once again gone from playing the part of the injured lamb to that of the lioness. She was back to being quite pertly.

"Oh, that's okay, dear. How do you like your tuna?" She said, half-smirking, as if the last few minutes of conversation hadn't taken place. "Do you remember that summer back home when we thought ourselves lucky enough to get a can of salmon? Quite a change now, isn't it?!" Her eyes lit up at both the reminiscence and the realization that she was so far beyond canned salmon now.

"But do go on with your story. You arrived last February? Why has it taken this long for us to connect? Had I not seen you on the street earlier, I wonder if we'd ever have met again. But that is my fault. I know I never wrote to you, never called. It's just this lifestyle down here. Always a dinner. Always a day at the beach. Always a screen test. There simply isn't time!" she chattered on breathlessly.

Following such a torrent of questions with such a series of excuses left me wondering if they were pat answers she gave to all those she jilted or if she truly was sorry to have let our parting be so prolonged. I wondered, too, if her wordiness was due in part to the nerves of someone putting on airs or if she just liked to talk. Or maybe her life was that exciting. I was suddenly drawn toward her, drawn toward the life she spoke of, but nervous about it at the same time, like the first time one walks out onto the end of a high dive and gazes down into the pool below. I decided to let these thoughts remain unspoken.

"It's okay. I understand." How else was I going to reply? "When I arrived in Los Angeles, I needed a job. As luck would have it, pasted to a wall in the train station was an advertisement for a secretarial position. Not knowing how to type, I was skeptical that they'd hire me, but I chose to apply anyway, and—what do you know—they did!"

I thought back to that day. I had been rather nervous. Of course, I knew later that the man who hired me cared more about the length of my hemline than the number of words I could type in a minute.

"I didn't really give thought to, well, much of anything on the journey down. I felt nothing but excitement until the reality hit. I had no job, no place to stay, didn't know a soul and…" I paused for a moment, realizing I was now the one who would have to come clean about my reticence to find her. "I had every intention of finding you when I arrived but was nervous about what our reunion would be like. Scared even. So, I put it off, telling myself I was just mustering up the courage to do so, telling myself I needed to get settled so you wouldn't think less of me or feel the need to take me in. Then the days turned to weeks and the weeks to months. I got into a routine that, honestly, I grew rather accustomed to. At that point, I believed the moment had passed."

"Mabs, I would have taken you in in a heartbeat. You shouldn't have been nervous about that. And it wouldn't have been out of pity. After all, you cared for me for so long when we were children. I could never repay that kindness in full." This time, she sounded truly genuine. I put down my fork and reached my hand across the table to touch hers.

"Thank you, Dagny. That means a lot."

She placed her other hand over mine and we sat in silence for a moment, each of us remembering how we'd cared for the other so long ago; how we'd sat together on the bench outside the drug store reading discarded copies of *Chatelaine*, wishing to be as elegant as the women in its pages; giggling at the pictures of men—boys really, but so much older and worldly than we ever imagined we would be. That is, until she dared to imagine. That must have been the beginning of it all. Her quest for stardom began on that bench with an advertisement for a *Fame and Fortune* contest.

As if reading my mind, Dagny lent voice to my memory. "Mabs, do you remember when we were schoolgirls, and we read old copies of *Chatelaine*? Do you remember what I said to you on one of those particularly warm afternoons when the thickness of the air felt like it was going to crush us out of existence? Do you remember what I said about moving away?"

I searched my mind, and it didn't take long before it settled on the memory I knew she was referring to. "There's nothing for us here, Mabs," I replied, hearing every word in my mind as clearly as if she said them for the first time right then. "The whole world exists outside this town just waiting to be savored. And I don't mean Saskatoon or Regina. I don't even mean Toronto, Montreal, or Vancouver. I dream of a place called Hollywood!" We were twice that age now but, at that moment, I was still just a naive twelve-year-old.

In my mind, the Dagny of seven years ago was the twenty-four-year-old who sat before me. I tried to picture us both then, but her face as it was now, even the dress she was wearing, remained as part of the memory.

She had always been the older one, even if she was three months younger. She'd even matured physically before I had, as if the gods knew she needed to be ready for the path she chose.

"How did you know so much about Hollywood back then? Our home was so sheltered. I barely knew anything of Regina, even less about Toronto."

"*Chatelaine* wasn't the only thing I read." She gave me a sly look but didn't reveal her secret. "But do go on! You must have entertained yourself with more than just idle chatter while swimming in the steno pool." She laughed, pleased with her bon mot. I didn't find it amusing.

In fact, I rather detested the other girls at work. Or perhaps I envied them. While they were no match for the woman seated across from me, they were infinitely more worldly than I was, even if they came from places as remote as Prairie River, places with exotic-sounding names like San Buenaventura and Santa Barbara. While I pondered this, I realized I actually saw more of the world on my two-week journey from the Canadian Plains than they had. I'd traveled more than twenty-four hundred miles. They'd traveled fewer than two hundred and fifty. Funny, it had never quite hit me until now, and the realization gave me confidence. Dagny was right. I *was* the more courageous one.

"Maybe all my courage was spent simply getting on that train to come here. Maybe I found comfort in my little apartment and the occasional walks on the Santa Monica Pier. Honestly, I can't say I did much else. Nor do I even now. I take in the occasional picture at the movie house, but that's it, really." I suddenly felt sad, ashamed even. Had I truly wasted the past year? How worldly could I claim to be if I'd seen no more of the world than those girls in the office, but for what was on the other side of a train window?

Dagny must have sensed my disappointment.

"Well, Mabs, that all ends today. We're going to get all dolled up in these new dresses, Charles is going to give you a wonderful new 'do, and then we're going to attend the most marvelous evening of your life. And I promise, this is only the beginning. Now, let's get the bill and be on our way!"

I should have been putty in her hands; she my Svengali, me her Trilby. But while I did feel myself falling deeper and deeper under her spell, something else inside me, that schoolgirl I thought I'd left behind in Prairie River, told me to be wary. I should have listened, but this lunch of raw tuna; the new dress sitting in a box beside me; this man, Charles, who was to transform me in less than an hour; even the fancifully dressed woman who'd passed by the window earlier and caught Dagny's eye; all of these things were conspiring to pull me into a place I wasn't sure I wanted to go.

"Do you mean it, Dagny? Do you really mean it?" I wanted her to say no. I wanted her to throw back her head and let out a big laugh; to tell me it was all a ruse. I wanted her to be someone else. Literally. An actress playing Dagny. I suddenly yearned for home and a cup of my mother's tea, as awful tasting as it was.

"Heaven's yes, dear! Now let's go!" Dagny exclaimed.

CHAPTER 3
HAIR LIKE LANA'S

In Hollywood, a girl's virtue is much less important than her hairdo.
— Marilyn Monroe

Twenty minutes later, I was seated in a red vinyl and aluminum dining chair in Dagny's rather spacious apartment, which had a lovely view of a garden court and palm trees. She even had a large, clawfoot soaking tub. In comparison, the only view I had from my window was of another apartment building, and I shared a tiny bathroom with the three other girls on my floor.

Better still, Dagny lived at the quiet end of Sunset Boulevard at the base of the Hollywood Hills. It was close enough to the action that one could reasonably stumble back after too many champagne cocktails, but far enough away that no one else would stumble by the window at an ungodly hour.

But what am I saying? At that moment, I was still three hours away from trying my first champagne cocktail, and I'd never even *imagined* going to a club, let alone stumbling back from one. The closest I'd ever come was one evening, several months before, when I lost my way while strolling around West Hollywood and found myself across the street from Ciro's.

I stood there in awe of all the stars dressed to the nines. I really didn't know of many, rarely venturing to the movie house, but I do remember seeing Humphrey Bogart as he walked out. I recalled feeling a bit naked at that moment, even though I was fully clothed in a rather frumpy coat and standing a good ninety feet away. I also felt like a voyeur for even taking the briefest of glances at him.

What right did a country girl like me have being this close to Hollywood's debonair leading man? I was fresh from a little town in Canada no one in the world knew existed. Ashamed, I turned on my heels and ended up walking—almost running—for more than a mile before finally catching the streetcar the rest of the way home.

I remember, too, that it rained quite heavily on the walk so that my hair became matted, and makeup ran down my face. I must have been a ghastly sight and that only added to my shame.

When I made it back to my little apartment, I cast off my heels, flopped down on my little bed, and sobbed for the next thirty minutes. *What was I doing here?* I had no right to be in Los Angeles. While Hollywood may have been built on the pretense of being someone else, I felt I was the one acting. The tears streamed down my face with such force, it wouldn't have mattered if I just walked through a downpour. I shivered, not from the dampness in the air, but from the dampness in my soul. At that point, my very spirit was drowning in the illusion around me. I gasped for air with each wave of uncontrollable sobs. Holding my pillow tight and curled in a ball, I yearned for my family back in Prairie River more than ever before, an aching desire that didn't fully abate until I fell fast asleep.

The following morning, the rain had stopped, and the sun shined brightly through my window. The droplets of dew upon the panes created a rainbow of promise and hope within the room.

I never was one to pay much attention in Sunday school, but at that moment, I remembered the story of God's rainbow shining bright after the forty days of rain. I picked myself up from the bed, washed the dried tears from my face, and vowed never to let myself be taken over by such feelings of self-pity again.

"Your hair is simply marvelous!" Charles, the hairdresser, exclaimed, bringing my mind back to Dagny's apartment and the present. She leaned against the wall, drinking a Coca-Cola, and gazing approvingly at the situation. For once, instead of being the actress, she was the director, feeding Charles—and me—our cues and approving or disapproving every cut and curl.

He bounced at my wavy locks with the palm of his hand. "It will be a joy putting it up, I think!"

I had no ear for accents. I only knew my native plains and the rare French Canadian I'd come across, but this man's was enchanting. I knew that. I figured he must have been from somewhere in Europe. *Maybe Paris!* A vision of the Champs Élysées from a postcard I'd once seen popped into my head.

Then my mind returned again to the girl crying on her bed and I wondered what he would have said to me then. Nevertheless, I smiled politely.

Another twenty minutes later, and I must say I was quite impressed at how he transformed my hair. I looked rather like Lana Turner in *Green Dolphin Street*, which pleased me a great deal. She was one of the few actresses I knew a little more about. Somehow—probably while reading some magazine or newspaper—I learned she grew up in Wallace, Idaho, which endeared me to her because I felt I could relate, both of us having grown up in small towns.

Of course, that was about the extent of our commonalities. Wallace was a hard-drinking miners' town in the mountains, famous for fast women and loose morals. Prairie River was, as the name denotes, a prairie town where the stiffest drink one had was during communion on a Sunday, and most of the marriages were arranged, at least in spirit if not literally. Lana's father had been mugged following a craps game in San Francisco. The worst my father ever fared was being thrown from his horse and cracking a rib.

At this very moment, he was probably riding back from town on that same horse. No danger of muggers in Prairie River. No danger of craps games.

"Oh, your first evening out, Mabs! I'm so excited!" Dagny exclaimed.

"I've been to the movies, I'll have you know," I protested cheekily, but I knew she was right and returned her smile. This *was* exciting! After all, the only thing waiting for me back at my apartment was a can of tomato soup and the latest Agatha Christie mystery, or if I was feeling especially in need of comfort, Nancy Drew.

At this thought, I realized it would be tragic to refuse Dagny's invitation. I wasn't even reading about the life Dagny was living. I was reading a book written for girls half my age. I imagined that even the other girls in the steno pool were doing something more exciting than *that*.

True to Dagny's word, her man Kenneth picked us up promptly at six. I assumed, like most men Dagny had known, even the boys back in Prairie River, she had him wrapped around her little finger. He'd probably been waiting around the corner in his car for the past quarter-hour, counting the seconds until it was appropriate to come to her door.

"Do come in, darling Kenneth! We're just finishing putting on our faces. But where are my manners? This is my friend Mabel Eriksson. She's from back home in Saskatchewan. Everyone calls her Mabs though. So then, must you."

"Good evening, Mabs." Kenneth reached down and took my hand, raising it gently to his lips. It was like something right out of the movies and certainly nothing I'd ever experienced or expected. Men were gentlemanly enough back home, but nothing like this. *Such class! Such grace!* And he made it all the classier by showing up in a dinner jacket, hair slicked back like Rudolph Valentino. I felt as if I should tilt my head downward and put on a coquettish smile, maybe let go a silly little giggle. Instead, I simply replied, "charmed," and left it at that.

CHAPTER 4
THE FLIRTY ONE AND
THE SNOBBISH ONE

If you stay away from parties, you're called a snob.
If you go, you're an exhibitionist. If you don't talk,
you're dumb. If you do talk, you're quarrelsome.
Pardon me while I change my nail polish.
— Lana Turner

I wasn't really sure what to expect from this party. After all, the last party I attended was more than a decade before, some silly little gathering of schoolgirls after church. The excitement there had been one of the boys in our class introducing us to a muddy toad he caught near the river. Now, for all I knew, *muddy toad* was the name of some libation Dagny would force me to drink.

We pulled up to a rather plain looking house in Elysian Heights just after six. It was plain, at least, from the outside. Before we even made it inside, however, I knew what lay beyond the door was anything but. Jazz music filled my ears as we walked up the path, and I heard a cacophony of clinking glasses, laughter, and voices having the most wonderful time. I tensed up with apprehension, my palms started to sweat. I rubbed them on my dress, hoping they weren't so sweaty as to make a mark.

It all seemed too much for my entrée into Hollywood Society. Couldn't Dagny have just revealed me to a nice little dinner party of five or six? Part of me wanted to turn around and call the whole thing off. *Would they take to me or was I still too much of the prairie girl I wanted to leave behind in Saskatchewan?* I swallowed my nerves and followed Dagny and Kenneth to the door. It was too late to turn back now. It opened before we reached it.

"Dagny! Kenneth! Two of my favorite people!" the young woman who opened the door shouted over the music. She had on a black skirt with three appliquéd dachshunds on it. *How curious.*

"Or should I say three people? Hello, I'm Philomena!" She looked to me and extended her free hand, the other grasping a glass of champagne.

"Hello." I took her hand a bit sheepishly, already feeling overwhelmed. "I'm Mabs."

"Phil, that skirt is a riot! Wherever did you get it?" Dagny exclaimed. The party had already started, and we weren't even inside. Maybe we wouldn't even need to go inside. I'd have been perfectly content for the four of us to stay on the stoop.

"Don't you just love it?! It's something that Juli Lynne came up with a few months ago. You remember Juli Lynne. She did the opening number in that ghastly Persian epic a couple of years ago," she said, rolling her eyes.

"What was it called? *Evening in Paradise* or something? Anyway, she's mostly given up the acting racket and now makes these conversation starters." Her face softened into a smirk.

"Apparently, this is a boy dog, and he's attracted to this one over here. She's supposed to be the flirty one," Philomena said, pointing to two of the dogs. "But the leashes are all tangled so he ends up next to this one, who's the snobbish one."

"Rather a good commentary on life," Dagny laughed. I wondered which of us was the flirty one and which the snobbish one. Maybe I was the snobbish one. At this point, Kenneth was standing next to me.

"Isn't it, though? But do come in. Have a glass of bubbly. Stay awhile!"

"Well, as long as the bubbly's still bubbly and the hors d'oeuvres are still, er, *oeuvres*..." Dagny bit her lip sideways, as if realizing the silliness of the word she just shoehorned into the moment.

"Oh, you are a *hoot!* Yes, the hors d'oeuvres are still very much *oeuvres*," Philomena laughed and then turned to lead us inside.

"Everyone! It's Kenneth and Dagny!" she cheered as we walked inside. I was definitely feeling like a third wheel. I gazed down nervously at my shoes—green leather high-heeled *Jacquelines* Dagny had purchased for me—and briefly thought about making a run for it. *Too late.*

The entire crowd cheered raucously.

"And this is Mabs!"

"HELLO, MABS!" the crowd cheered again. I wanted to hide. *Maybe there was a coat closet nearby. Or I could excuse myself and spend the rest of the evening in the bathroom. Oh, what had I done?* I felt so out of place, and I'd just arrived. No, I would stick with it. No Nancy Drew to run to this evening. I'd have to solve this mystery on my own. *The Secret of the Shy Party Guest.*

I trailed behind Dagny and Kenneth for the next twenty minutes. I was cordial enough to the other guests, but I was always just on the edge of the conversation. God bless, Dagny. She was doing her best to include me, but I was rather bound to my shyness, even though I didn't want to be. She clearly noticed and pulled me into a corner. I felt like an insolent child being taken for a scolding and turned my eyes downward, ashamed that I'd failed her.

"Mabs, what's wrong? I can tell you're not having much fun, but I so desperately want you to enjoy yourself. What can I do?" She let out a heavy sigh. I could tell she was growing exasperated. I was clearly beginning to spoil her evening.

It wasn't a matter of what she could do, though. She'd done so much already. I knew I'd have to be the one to leave the comfort of monotony. *And why couldn't I?* After all, I'd left Prairie River for the glamour of Hollywood. Of course, even with the best of intentions, I quickly fell back into a routine only slightly more colorful than the prairie grasses I'd left behind. I'd traveled thousands of miles, and now Dagny had pulled me the last few steps. *Why couldn't I just enjoy myself?!* Here I was, surrounded by beautiful people, wearing beautiful clothing, and having beautiful conversations—at least it was all meant to be beautiful; I wasn't sure I knew the difference—and I was wishing my dress matched the wallpaper so I could blend into the background.

"I just don't know if I like all this, Dagny. I'm just not sure it's *me*. Maybe I should go back home," I continued, still staring at my feet. "And I don't mean home as in my apartment in Santa Monica. I mean *home* home, Prairie River."

"Oh, Mabs, don't be such a cold fish." I knew she meant it as a friend, but she was still rather stern. I felt like I'd been slapped across the face by a cold fish—maybe the tuna we'd eaten earlier that day. I suppose I needed it, though. Nothing else seemed to be working.

"I know this life takes a bit of getting used to after growing up in Saskatchewan then spending your time typing away in a steno pool eight hours a day," she continued, "But you'll learn to enjoy it. I swear. Call it…" she paused, searching her mind for the next words, "an acquired taste."

"O-okay. I'll try," I stuttered quietly.

"There's my girl," Dagny replied, taking my chin in her hand, and raising my head. "Now, let's get back to the party."

As Dagny carried on, I half-listened to the crowd around me, their words fading in and out like a radio searching for a clear signal.

The phone rang and our hostess, Philomena, glided off toward it. "Well, my, my, my. Who could that be?" Her words came out in an excited staccato. She answered it, listened for a breath, then cupped the receiver in her palm and turned to a young, fragile-looking girl standing near her. "Why, it's Winifred Jenkins…You know, that mousy thing who threw that simply smashing party in the Poconos last fall?"

The other girl looked somewhat perplexed for a moment and uttered something back, but then her mouth quickly turned to a bohemian smile that didn't let on whether she was giddy, upset, or simply nonchalant.

Our hostess continued, ignoring the call in her hand. "What?! You weren't invited? Well, haven't I gone and committed the ultimate faux pas? I'm sure it was just an oversight on her part. But you simply must meet her! She married that charming young man, Augustine Caruthers. You know, Auggie? They moved to Savannah, Georgia. A nice little home just off Pierpont Circle, I believe. You really must meet her though. I know she'd find you the most charming girl."

She returned the telephone to her ear.

"What's that?... You're here?!... In Los Angeles?!... Now?!... That's splendid! I'm entertaining this evening. Just a small group." There were more than thirty people in the room; hardly what I called small.

"Don't worry about dressing. Just come as you are. It will be a delight to see you and Auggie again! The address is 1543 Avalon Street... Yes. That's right. The same place. Elysian Heights. Come enjoy a bit of heaven!" She let out a decadent laugh as she uttered this last sentence then hung up the receiver.

About thirty minutes later, the doorbell rang and the most stunning couple I ever laid eyes on walked through the door. If this was what they considered dressing down for the evening, I wondered what they'd consider dressing up.

They were both a bit older than most of the crowd, in their mid-forties perhaps. Maybe this was the *old guard* Dagny had referred to.

Auggie was tall and thin with a square jaw and sleepy eyes. He dressed in a smart, black, pin-stripe affair with a wide collar and a wide, black-and-white tie that looked like it had been painted by Kandinsky.

Winifred, true to Philomena's comment, was a rather mousy woman with a very slight frame, piercing eyes, and a small mouth. She wore a sleek, black cocktail dress that sparkled like her eyes. Around her neck, she wore a diamond necklace with a ruby pendant. Her hair, ash-blonde, almost white, was styled in a

Castle bob and seemed to shine as brightly as her dress. The ensemble was completed by a black band around her forehead. Both a perfect picture in black-and-white, they looked as if they'd stepped off the Vaudeville stage.

Little did I know then, she had. Winifred had been one of the last of the Vaudeville Girls and had a small part in *Ziegfeld Girl* before leaving the trappings of show business behind to entertain in a different manner. Her parties were legend amongst the East Coast set. With her mannerisms, of course, none of it would come as a surprise.

She made the rounds and seemed to know everyone in the room. More than that, everyone seemed to gravitate toward her, like leaves being pulled toward a whirlpool. Even I was strangely attracted to her. *Just who was this woman and what was she doing in Los Angeles unannounced?*

CHAPTER 5
THE SILENT FILM
STAR WHO SPOKE

I am intrigued by glamorous women... A vain woman is continually taking out a compact to repair her makeup. A glamorous woman knows she doesn't need to.

— Clark Gable

"Dagny Lundberg! You gem. It's been too long." Winifred's speech was as elegant as her dress. She sounded quite like Katherine Hepburn.

"And who is this charming young thing?" she said, turning toward me and extending her hand. I felt uneasy, like I was having audience with the Queen. Had it not been for Dagny, I probably would have spent the rest of the evening mute.

"This is my friend from back home. Mabs."

"Saskatchewan! Lovely! I once took the train between Ottawa and Vancouver and saw much of the prairie. A ghastly journey, to tell you the truth."

"If you've seen one prairie, you've seen them all," Dagny quipped. I continued to stand there in silence.

"Too true, dear. Too true," Winifred laughed, then set her eyes on me once more.

"Tell me, Mabs, how do you like Hollywood? Have you been here long? I'm rather surprised we haven't met."

"I've been here about a year," I gulped, still nervous, although I'm not sure why I had any need to be.

"And who have you slept with since you've been here?"

I must have turned redder than the ruby hanging around her neck.

"Oh, Winnie, do stop," Dagny laughed, waiving her hand toward Winifred. "We've only just begun to bring her out of her shell, but not yet to that extent!" she added, saving me from having to say anything further.

"Oh, I'm sorry, dear," Winifred said, placing her hand on my shoulder, then quickly pulling it away in what was clearly an insincere apology. "But you really must. You really must. Plenty of eligible men in Hollywood. Of course, I always preferred the ineligible ones myself." She laughed and I wasn't sure if she was being serious or not. I continued to stand there, frozen, my mouth slightly agape, and wondering again if I shouldn't make a run for it and hide away in the broom closet.

"Mabs, dear, are you quite well?" she added.

I wasn't sure I was. What had been mere shyness was now causing such unease I felt close to fainting. I still couldn't utter a word.

"Come, let's get you a drink, and then you can tell me all about yourself."

I didn't have a chance to protest. She grabbed me by the hand and led me to the makeshift bar set up near the kitchen. Dagny moved in the opposite direction, deserting me and by the smirk on her face, no doubt loving every moment of it. She was now free to mingle. Perhaps she even enjoyed the thought of me squirming under the influence of Winifred.

"Let's see. Champagne? No. This definitely calls for something stronger. Jimmy!" she said to a man who just happened to be standing near the bar. "A martini! This poor thing is about to faint, by the looks of it."

"Winifred Jenkins, you old devil! I didn't know you were in town," Jimmy replied.

"Well, the devil part is accurate, but don't tell anyone else I'm old," she laughed.

"Not a day over twenty-five, Winnie. Not a day over twenty-five," he said, handing us each a martini glass filled to the brim.

To say I was a lightweight when it came to alcohol would have been an understatement, and I wasn't sure drinking a martini was the best cure for my state, but I was powerless in the hands of this woman.

"Well, are you going to drink it or just stare at it?" she chided, downing half her glass in one gulp.

I did the same, not sure what else to do, coughing at the sharp taste but managing to keep it down. I rather worried I might collapse to the floor right then and there, but instead, I actually began to feel giddy. I laughed. I wasn't even sure at what.

"There you go. Good show. Now that that's done, maybe you'll offer up more than a sentence about yourself." She again took my hand and led me to a nearby couch.

"Scram, boys!" She said cheekily to a group of men occupying the seat. "Mabs has the most scandalous story to dish, and something tells me I best sit down."

They quickly obliged, picking up their drinks and laughing at the scene as they scurried off.

"Mabs, I do hope I haven't upset you. Truly. I can be a bit boisterous at times. It's just my way. You must be when you're an entertainer. Carrying the scene, they call it.

"I once did a show with Spencer Tracy on Broadway when he was just starting out. Of course, neither of us had starring roles. A good thing too—at least for him. Awful performance. I was quite surprised when he later won the Academy Award. Of course, who am I to talk? He went on to fame and fortune and now my best performances consist of throwing parties." She became sullen for a brief moment, although I'm not sure anyone else would have noticed. Even in her sullenness, she had a certain elan.

"Do you know Spencer? He was with a company in Winnipeg for a short time, you know."

I shook my head. At least it was something, even if I hadn't uttered much at this point.

"But of course you wouldn't. You would have been just a tot then, by the looks of you. Twenty-three?" she asked.

"Twenty-four."

"Well, there you are then. And what else can you tell me about yourself, Mabs?"

I felt like I was interviewing for the position of a Harvey Girl. Of course, with Winifred asking the questions, the position would have been as far from that of a Harvey Girl as one could be.

"To be honest—"

She cut me off. "Oh, please do, please do. And don't leave anything out!"

"To be honest," I continued, "I'm rather out of place here." I wasn't sure why I was spilling all my deepest reservations to this woman, but she seemed to have an effect on me. Or maybe it was just the martini.

"I followed Dagny down from Saskatchewan, but I'm afraid I'm seven years too late. Here she is, mingling so effortlessly with all these wonderful people, spending her days lounging poolside at the Bel-Air and evenings at Ciro's, all the while, my evenings are typically spent with an Agatha Christie or Nancy Drew mystery or, if I'm feeling a bit melancholy, John Steinbeck. And the only pool I ever see during the day is the steno pool," I said, borrowing Dagny's joke. I cast my eyes downward. I must have been such a disappointment to this woman. If she'd jumped to her feet right then and run off to talk to someone more interesting, I wouldn't have blamed her in the least.

"Well, aren't you something," she said flatly, then whistled. I wasn't sure if she was disappointed, angry, or impressed. "That is scandalous, dear! You see all these people here?" She waived her hand around the room. "The closest most of them have ever been to reading a Steinbeck novel is seeing Henry Fonda's name on the marquee when they walked into *Grapes of Wrath.* You've got moxie, Mabs, real moxie. You just need to let it out."

"You think so?" I was relieved that she wasn't offended by my sorry little tale.

"I do. I do. Let me tell you something. When I walked into this room, I immediately separated you from the crowd. And not just because you're one of the few people I don't know here. You may not even know it yourself, but you have an air of confidence about you."

I was sure she was putting me on now, but I wasn't at all sure why.

"You see," Winifred continued, setting her martini glass down, folding her hands, and getting more serious, "to be silent while everyone else is blathering on, to listen while others only speak, that is the mark of someone who values her surroundings. You may think you're shy—and perhaps you are—but I think it's something more. I think you're a person who needs to size up the room, to gain a lay of the land before you make your attack, as it were."

She continued. "In the silent film era, we had to listen. More than that, we had to express ourselves in other ways. We had nothing more than the expressions on our face and the way we moved across the room."

I was suddenly very interested in Winifred and all that silent films had to offer. "Do go on," I said.

"It was a wonderful time. Everything was the height of elegance. Films premiered at *picture palaces*." She said the last two words quiet emphatically, popping her *p*'s. "And palaces they were! No detail was left to chance; ornate Corinthian columns covered with gold, curtains of the finest red velvet, stairs on each side of the lobby that extended to the loges—perhaps beyond, even to the heavens! And we didn't have mere ushers, *no*! We called them *service men*! They were every bit as sharp as the finest soldiers in the army." She smiled as she reminisced about this time now passed. I was enamored, picturing it all as best I could.

"We sacrificed, too. I wasn't a part of the filming of *Noah's Ark* back in 1928—perhaps better that I wasn't—but three people gave their lives for that epic. Many more gave limbs and broken bones."

I wouldn't say she delighted in these tragic facts, but the way she spoke of it did convey a sense of pride, of valor, as if these actors had sacrificed for a cause as great as those who fought in war. Perhaps they had.

I thought back to Dagny's earlier remark about the crowd here knowing what it meant to suffer for their work. I wondered if she knew of *this* terrible tale.

"Mabs, you aren't happy in the steno pool." She said it as a matter of fact, not as a question. "That is why you are this way. There is an actress inside you." She pointed her finger at my heart. "There is an actress inside you, desperate to be released. Let her out, Mabs. Let. Her. Out." She emphasized each word of the final sentence, pausing between each.

Now I was truly frightened. Was she right? Did this woman, who I just met, know more about me than I knew about myself? Had she uncovered parts of my soul I didn't know existed?

"My dear, I'm going to be in Los Angeles a while—I find the weather in Savannah this time of year simply unbearable—and I want you to call on me. I want to help you uncover the wonderful actress I know you to be."

"O-okay," I stuttered. What else was I to say?

"Splendid! Now, how about another martini?!" she cheered.

CHAPTER 6
CALIFORNIA, HERE I *AM*

I was fine when it came to cheering up others, not so fine with myself.
— Gene Tierney

I can't say that I transformed instantly after my conversation with Winifred. Who does? One can't simply flip a switch and go from wallflower to wag. But I did open up somewhat and enjoyed myself considerably for the rest of the evening. I even had that second martini. I took it slow, though, not wanting to spend the rest of the night in the bathroom, hiding out of gastric necessity instead of mere shyness.

Dagny, Kenneth, and I made our exit with most of the remaining guests at the rather prudent hour of eleven, which was fine by me since I was growing rather drowsy by then, and the lovebirds dropped me off at my apartment. I was so tired that as I quickly undressed for bed, I gave little thought to the events of the past few hours. Only when I glanced at my wonderful updo in the mirror did I reflect a bit disappointingly that it would be flattened by morning.

The next day, after work, I was a bit confused by it all. I still wasn't sure this life of parties and pleasure in a glass was for me. I decided to take a walk in Hancock Park, hopeful that I wouldn't run into anyone else who would lead me off toward a new existence. I needed time to think, to decompress.

The La Brea Tar Pits are an interesting place. They were formed thousands of years ago and are the exposed seepage of oil formed from the decaying fossils of dinosaurs. Many Ice Age animals became trapped inside them to die, not from suffocation, but from falling prey to predators like saber-toothed tigers and bears. It is a place of death surrounded by life. That contrast never struck me during the few visits I made before, but now it was as clear as the tar pits were murky.

Animals approached these quagmires of peril when they were often covered by a few inches of water, believing they found a spot to quench their thirst. Instead, that salvation was only a mirage. I can only imagine the fear that fell over them just as the sticky goo pulled at their legs. They must have tried to break free at that point, but it was too late. Their struggle was in vain. Then, as they continued their efforts to escape, predators descended to finish them off. Perhaps they welcomed the prospect of a quick, but slightly more painful death over the slow descent into hell that was the alternative.

I shivered at the scene. Perhaps this wasn't the best place to clear my mind, after all. I turned away and began walking toward a more pleasant area of the park to take a seat on a bench beneath a palm tree. I didn't want to think about death. I didn't want to think about anything. My mind had other ideas, though, and turned to the past year. Why had I come so far only to come not so far at all? Was I following Dagny here or was I trying to escape something back in Prairie River? My childhood, perhaps?

I was suddenly struck with a sense of foreboding. No, that wasn't it. It was a sense of *after*boding, if there was such a thing, a dark shadow of a memory from decades before that I couldn't manifest. Nor, I imagine, did I want to. I quickly shook my head, ridding it from my mind.

I had so many decisions before me. Was the acting bug laying latent somewhere deep inside of me as Dagny had said, or was my true-self really still back on the grass-covered plains? If the former, why was I stuck in my present station, not even trying to break free like the poor mastodon who'd been stuck in the tar pits behind me? Was I waiting for a saber-toothed tiger to come devour me, to devour my very soul, or was I content waiting for a slow death by suffocation?

A tear formed in the corner of my eye and started to descend down my cheek. It was enough. "Mabs! You have to do *something!*" I spoke the words out loud, and they startled me. I was outside of myself at that moment.

I wiped the tear from my cheek and vowed to start living my life. I'd come twenty-four hundred miles. Maybe I wasn't sure why. Maybe it wasn't to be an actress. Maybe it wasn't to be a secretary at an advertising firm. Maybe, it was just to escape the monotony of Prairie River. Whatever the reason, I wasn't going to turn back now. I wasn't going to return home to Saskatchewan. I was going to make it here.

"Okay, Mabs. Okay," I said aloud again. *Tar pits be damned!* I was not going to let myself sink into the darkness of obscurity any longer. The sun was shining! The birds were singing! *I was sitting under a palm tree, for heaven's sake!* Nothing but opportunity before me here in California.

It may have been more than a year since the wintery winds started blowing and the snow started to fall back in Prairie River, but at last, I was going to join Al Jolson. *California, here I come!* California, here I *am!* I stood up, smoothed my dress, and set off back to my apartment. I wasn't yet completely full of confidence, ready to tackle anything, but my complacency, my trepidation, were definitely beginning to wane.

Twenty minutes later I was poised in front of Dagny's door. She was my entry into this world. She's who'd opened my eyes fully. She'd be able to help. Yet, I was still somewhat trepidatious. Should I impose? What if she was entertaining

Kenneth? *I should turn around and go back to my apartment.* I knocked gently.

"Who is it?" Dagny called out. It sounded rather melancholy, but perhaps it was just muffled by the door.

"It's Mabs." No turning back now.

"It's unlocked." Still melancholy.

I opened it. Inside, the curtains were drawn closed, and the lights were off. What little light was coming through the cracks between the curtains bathed the room in a soft, but eerie, glow.

"What are you doing, Dagny?" I asked, a bit concerned by the state of the room.

"Just eating figs in the dark." She was lying on her couch, looking a bit like Claudette Colbert in *Cleopatra*. Draped loosely around her body was a deep red, satin dressing gown. Deep red, like the inside of the figs. Deep red, like her lipstick. Deep red, like her eyes.

"Have you been crying?"

"Oh, don't be silly. Heaven's, no! It's just this sunlight. Sometime the brightness is too much. It gives me a headache."

I chose to believe her, although I had my doubts. She was exhibiting the qualities of the lost soul I'd met the previous morning more than those of the girl she'd been at the party later that night.

She sat up just enough to pat the end of the couch then laid back down. I briefly thought about excusing myself and returning to my apartment, but I accepted her invitation.

"Did you have a good time, last night, dear Mabs?" She said the words in the same, lazy way she'd first greeted me the day before, all the while continuing to devour the bowl of fresh figs before her. There was a lustfulness about the way she did so.

"I want to be like you," I blurted out. It was terribly brash of me and not even what I really wanted to say, but the words were already out there, so I continued. "I'm tired of sitting inside my apartment reading Nancy Drew mysteries. I'm tired of watching other people live life. I don't know why I came down here,"—*Did I mean California, or her apartment specifically? I wasn't sure—*

"but I know it wasn't to continue on in monotony. Will you show me, Dagny? Will you show me how to live?"

"I'm not sure you want this life, Mabs. It's not all it's cracked up to be." She continued to speak in a lazy, melancholy way. I wasn't going to be deterred though.

"I do! I do! You told me I had to stop living inside the pages of a book. I'm ready! My life begins today! This very minute!"

Dagny sat up fully and turned on the lamp next to her. In the light, it was now clear that she had been crying. I found myself not caring as I should have, though. At that moment, I was too self-absorbed to care about anything but my own desires.

"Very well, Mabs. But you should know that it doesn't happen overnight. You must work at this life, even if it does seem from the outside to be all play."

"I'm ready! I'm ready!" I was giddy with excitement, or at least I was trying to be. Perhaps my excitement covered for any trepidation I still had deep within me. In retrospect, however, I wasn't ready at all.

CHAPTER 7
MARTINIS AND MINGUS

Making the simple complicated is commonplace;
making the complicated simple, awesomely simple,
that's creativity.

— Charles Mingus

The following week was rather mundane. A typical schedule of typing memos, filing invoices, and fetching lunches. Still a bit nervous about the path I was embarking on, I turned to my childhood comforts of Nancy Drew and a can of tomato soup. It was so mundane, in fact, that I began to fall back into the comfort of monotony and had pushed the desperate scene I'd made at Dagny's apartment out of my thoughts. That is, until she called me that Friday evening. She was all smiles and cheer. Any trace of the melancholy she had was gone from her voice.

"Mabs, I've got just the thing for you! If you're still interested in living life, that is. That party last weekend at Philomena's was mere child's play. Tomorrow night it's going to be strictly eight to the bar. My friend Clio is having a party at her place in Brentwood, and it'll be a real smash!"

I was nearly knocked over by her words. Like I said, I had fallen back into my old ways. But then it all came flooding back and I decided, *why not?*

"O-okay," I stuttered, still in a bit of a daze.

Dagny continued, as effervescent as ever. "Only the best crowd! Of course, Bogie and Bacall usually drop by, as do Rita, and Ronnie and Jane. They usually don't stay long, though.

Making the circuit, I suppose. But they're not all that fascinating anyhow, I find."

Bogie and Bacall? Rita? Ronnie and Jane? I had an idea of whom she was speaking, but the name dropping came so fast that it was hard to keep up.

"Now, you'll really want to meet Maritta. She's an author. Caused quite a stir with her first novel a few years back. Then there's Charlie. He does some amazing things on the bass even if his emotions can erupt at times. *It's simply that he loves his music so much!"* She said this last sentence quite emphatically, as if she were a defense attorney trying to convince me of her point. "And it's his style. He won't take advice from anyone, you see. I do admire that about him.

"Hello? Mabs? Are you there?"

I don't know how long I was silent or even sure why. I think I was still trying to imagine being foisted into a situation where I might be in the same room as Humphrey Bogart.

"Yes. Sorry. I'm here."

"Well, are you going to come?" She sounded a bit impatient.

I must have hesitated a bit too long again, still in a trance over it all.

"Mabs?"

"Yes. Yes, I'm sorry. Bogart and Bacall, you say? Yes, I'll come. Thank you." I'm not sure I sounded convinced. I'm not sure I was convinced. Despite telling Dagny that I was ready, now presented with another party, and apparently one grander than the last, the trepidation had returned. Dagny had been living this lifestyle, growing comfortable around these people, for seven years. I hadn't had seven hours.

"Mabs, we will make a star out of you yet! I'll be by your apartment at two o'clock tomorrow. We have lots to do to get you ready!"

It was a good thing she did show up at two the next day. Even by then, I was still in somewhat of a daze. Whether it was over Bogie and Bacall or just the prospect of having to go to a party and not play the wallflower once again, I wasn't exactly sure.

We pulled up to the gate of a rather large, Spanish colonial-style home. It opened as if it were expecting us, and we drove up the lane.

"Dagny! Kenneth! So good of you to come! And who are you? Charming. Young. Girl." The woman who greeted us said the last three words individually, as if she were playing separate notes on a piano. She was older, maybe fifty or fifty-five, with greying hair cut quite short. Her gown was of a flowing purple and her hand grasped a cigarette in a long holder.

"M-Mabs," I stuttered, quite overwhelmed by the whole scene and feeling, once again, like a bit of a third wheel.

"Well, M-Mabs, you must come in and have a drink!" She turned on her heels and began walking back up the short set of stairs into the house. I wasn't sure if I should have been offended by the way she mocked my stutter but decided there was no malice in her tone. Besides, I certainly wasn't going to let it ruin the evening before it began. I was committed to making a go of it this time, to actually having a ball and not just playing the part of a statue in the corner of the room.

"Clio, that's a simply stunning gown you're wearing! Purple suits you," Dagny exclaimed as she and Kenneth followed behind the woman and I, in turn, followed behind them, looking around me like the proverbial Alice in Wonderland. *Just what lay beyond those doors?* Would it be the Mad Hatter? The Cheshire Cat? *The Queen of Hearts?*

"You like it?" Clio replied. "I find, at my age, I wear what I want. It might be considered a fashion faux pas by some, but I say to hell with them!" She laughed and took a long drag from her cigarette.

How bohemian! While I was the farthest thing from bohemian, for some reason, I was instantly enamored by this woman called Clio. She didn't seem to have a care in the world. She called the shots in her own life, everyone else be damned. Me? I still blushed when I wore a swimsuit to the beach.

As we walked, I took in my surroundings. It was certainly the most opulent home I ever dared enter. Of course, I heard there were estates much larger and grander than this one, but I couldn't imagine exactly how that was possible.

The floors were made of dark red tile with a mosaic of blue waves running around the perimeter, making the whole room appear an island. *Corsica perhaps*, I thought, picturing the only Mediterranean island I could remember from geography class years ago.

The decor was eclectic but still seemed to fit the character of the house and its owner. I glanced over at a large moose head mounted above one of the two fireplaces in the living room. If I didn't know better, I'd say it was enjoying the party as much as anyone else in the crowd.

"You like it? We call him Bullwinkle," Clio said, noticing the direction of my gaze. "A silly name. I don't know what it means. Something that Paul's nephew came up with. The young man is actually writing a television program. *The Comic Strips of Television* he's calling it! Can you imagine such a thing? Personally, I'm not sure if this television idea will ever really go anywhere. Part of the fun of watching a motion picture is the event itself; getting dressed up, going to the movie house, perhaps a drink afterward at the Frolic Room. That reminds me," she suddenly interrupted herself. "You all need a drink!"

She led us through the crowd, weaving our way past an eclectic group of guests representing every age, color, and background one could imagine. It was a delight to see such a variety. It certainly didn't look anything like what I'd seen in the movies.

We stopped along the way as Clio introduced us to her friends. Dagny knew several of them and they engaged in small talk. What movie was this man casting for? What part had this woman just landed? What painting was another working on?

Where had this couple just traveled to? As they all chatted away, I felt myself become more at ease, certainly more relaxed than I had been at Philomena's party. I began opening up and dropping in a sentence here and there. Yes, I worked at an advertising agency. No, I'd never been to Europe or New York. I was partial to summer, having grown up on the often frigid plains of Canada. A half an hour of this and we'd finally reached the bar.

An attractive looking man stood next to it, working a martini shaker in a most exuberant way, as if he was making music with it. Quite uncharacteristically of me, I almost felt like dancing right there. *Almost.*

"Dagny, Kenneth, you already know Charlie, of course. Mabs, this is Charlie Mingus. In addition to being a rather accomplished bass player, he also makes the best martinis in town." Clio put her arm around his waist and gave him a squeeze. "I'm hoping later he'll play some of his wonderfully modern music for us, but for now, I'm sure he'd be delighted to make you a drink."

"Delighted to make music and mix drinks, Clio! Dagny, Kenneth, Mabs, a martini for you folks? Apparently, I make the best in town."

"What's your secret," I asked, a bit playfully, surprising myself. Even though I hadn't yet had a drop of alcohol, I seemed to have made a transformation while on the walk from the other side of the room. Or maybe it wasn't I who had made it, but Dagny.

Not more than eight hours ago, I was as far from this party—this lifestyle—as anyone could be. Unlike the first time getting made over by Dagny weeks before, this time hadn't just uncovered a set of eyelashes I didn't know I had, it had uncovered something else, buried far deeper inside.

"I keep it simple. These days, bartenders are throwing in all sorts of things. Triple Sec, Grand Marnier, Amaretto. Why, I even hear one bar back East adds orange juice! Call me old-fashioned, but orange juice is for the breakfast table. Don't you agree?"

I nodded. Not because I agreed. I hadn't ever thought about it. But how could anyone disagree with this charming man standing before me?

"I don't even add much vermouth; a quick splash and then pour it out. Just enough to coat the glass. It's all about the gin. And only gin!" He was quite emphatic about this last point. "Too many cats starting to add vodka. It's not that I have anything against the Russians. They're great writers. But you shouldn't mess with a classic. Of course, I'm one to talk." He laughed at this last remark, but I didn't get the joke, and my face betrayed my confusion.

"I started, like so many musicians, playing classical music," he said, enlightening me. "At least that was the idea. But I had difficulty reading the notes and, well, a face like this isn't exactly welcomed in an orchestra. So, I've had to make my own way in music. I wouldn't have it any other way now, though. We all need to make our own way in the world. Can't dance for no one. Even Duke. As much as he's done for us negro musicians, Duke is Duke. I want to break out of that scene, create something truly unique." He paused, realizing he hadn't poured my martini, did so, and handed it to me with a faint smile. "But just not with my martinis."

I took the glass and felt the contrasting chill of the drink and the warmth of his fingertips as they briefly grazed mine. I was enraptured by this man. He seemed to know so much about the world, yet he didn't seem much older than I was.

"Well, May Bell." He pronounced my full name like the flower. I rather liked it. It reminded me of my grandfather, who'd sometimes referred to me as such when I was a very small girl.

"A flower as delicate as you shouldn't spend too much time in the corner," he continued. I took that as a subtle, but nonetheless polite, invitation to go mingle as he went about making another martini.

"Mabs! Mabs, darling!" Dagny sealed my fate as she glided over to my side. "Come meet Maritta. She's the one I was telling you about. The novelist!"

"Until later, Charlie!" I waved, as I was pulled away, a tinge of regret coming over me. The truth was, I wanted nothing more than to spend the whole evening in that corner, listening to him.

CHAPTER 8
THE WOLFF WHO CRIED BOY

I let my drinking do the talking.
— Humphrey Bogart

"**H**ere, have a canapé," Dagny said as she grabbed a small morsel from a tray sitting on an end table. "Don't worry. We'll be having a more proper meal soon, but you simply must try one of these topped with foie gras. They're delicious!"

What a whirlwind! I shoved the treat into my mouth and followed it with a large gulp of my martini. It went immediately to my head, so it was a good thing we'd eaten a late lunch, or I'd have to sit down. Not that there was any chance of that happening this evening, at least not until this *proper meal* Dagny spoke of was served.

I've never been one to intensely yearn for a meal—not that one can yearn much for a bowl of soup or even the occasional hamburger—but I suddenly felt quite hungry, both literally and figuratively, in anticipation for dinner. I hoped it would be as grand as I envisioned. I knew I'd have to wait though. Too many of her—*what did she call them? Coterie?*—to meet.

"You must be, Mabs. Darling girl! Dagny has told me so much about you! I'm Maritta Wolff."

She had? When did Dagny have the time to tell her much of anything? We'd been at this party for less than an hour and, but for the last ten minutes, I'd been by her side the whole time. Was it possible Dagny had mentioned me before this evening? Is it possible that she had, in fact, thought of me during the last seven years? I suddenly felt competing emotions of great affection and deep regret. Why hadn't I tried to reach Dagny since moving here? Was she pining away all this time, wishing for the long-passed days of our youth? *I felt like a wicked friend.*

"Oh, stop, Maritta," Dagny said playfully, waving a hand toward the woman. "I really haven't told her anything," she continued, turning toward me. "Only that Charles did a wonderful job with your hair, and that the dress I picked out for you earlier looked simply stunning on your frame."

Now my competing emotions were of regret and shame. The gin in my martini wasn't helping either. Who was this woman I'd met only a few weeks before while taking a stroll down Sunset Boulevard? *Regret. Shame. Sadness. Confusion. Elation?* Yes, I was feeling that too. I was rather enjoying myself at this little soiree, as big as it was. There must have been upwards of thirty people there between the grand living room and the pool deck outside. My head was spinning. Was it only the alcohol, or was I drunk on the bon vivance of it all? I needed to sit down.

"Oh, my dear girl, you look faint! Come have a seat over here, poor thing." Maritta came to my rescue and sat me down on a piano bench nearby.

"You must excuse her. This is only her second party. And can you believe she's been living here in Los Angeles for more than a year?" Dagny laughed, a bit too mockingly.

Had it been in my character, I might have slapped her right then. Of course, even if it had been in my character, I'm not sure I had the sobriety at that moment to do so. I was rather angry, that was for sure. Maybe I was what they called a *mean drunk.* I hadn't ever had enough alcohol to know. Or maybe I was a sad drunk. I felt like crying but somehow held it together and regained my composure.

Against better judgment, I took a large gulp of my martini, finishing it off and swallowing the olive whole. The alcohol rushed through me, and I was glad I was still seated on the piano bench.

"There's a girl!" Maritta cheered. "Carlisle, my boy! Go grab her another! By god, this woman needs a drink!"

I wasn't going to argue. At this point, I wasn't even going to argue with myself. If this is what one did in Los Angeles, then I was going to play the part. After all, this was a town built on playing the part. I just hoped I could hold myself together after another martini.

A man in a dinner jacket hurried over with another drink and foisted it into my hand. Some of it sloshed over the side and onto my dress. *Mean drunk? Sad drunk? Happy drunk?* Now I was a sloppy drunk, or at least I smelled like one, even if I hadn't been the one to cause the spill.

I took another large sip of the drink, then fished the olive out of the glass with my fingers and plopped it into my mouth. I felt a warmth rise from deep inside me and envelop my face. *Was I getting a red nose like those characters in the matinees?* Not that I cared. I suddenly didn't care about anything. *A carefree drunk!* Certainly, that had to be the best kind. I rose to my feet. It was probably a stupid bet that I'd be able to stand, but it paid off.

"Maritta!" I extended my hand in a very proper manner, and she shook it. "You must excuse me. I'm rather new to all this, you see."

"Quite alright, dear. Quite alright. We all have to begin somewhere, don't we now?"

"Better late than never, I suppose," I replied. "But Dagny tells me you're quite the novelist. I must say all I read is Nancy Drew." *Certainly a loose drunk. Why had I spilled that rather embarrassing fact about myself?*

Maritta let out a huge laugh. "You are too much! Dagny, this girl is a hoot! Second party, I think not. You'll put us all to shame by the end of the night if you keep it up."

I was relieved. She wasn't laughing at me. She thought it all a joke. At that moment, I'm not sure it wasn't and went along with it.

Carefree, happy, proud drunk. I enjoyed my new role as the guest of honor. Or at least the guest of honor in this small circle.

"I think Nancy Drew is wonderful," Maritta said, continuing the charade. "Secrets. Clues. What a little minx she must be! But tell me, what are your secrets, Mabs?"

I suddenly realized I didn't have any to tell and became a bit rueful. It seemed everyone in Hollywood who was anyone needed to have secrets, even if Hedda Hopper splashed them all over the page for the world to see the next day.

"I like to walk barefoot on the beach after dark," I lied. It wasn't a sordid tale about going to bed with Errol Flynn, but it was the best I could come up with on the spot.

"Wonderfully scandalous! It must make your feet deliciously soft. I'll bet you drive the boys simply mad," Maritta cheered. I wasn't sure if I was putty in her hands or if she was putty in mine, but either way, I was rather beginning to like the role I was in. I envisioned a director off to my right and a bevy of stage crew racing about. I let out a hearty laugh in spite of myself. What a gay old time I was having!

"But do go on, Maritta. Tell me, what are you working on now?"

"Well, I'm rather thinking of writing about a small-town girl who comes to Hollywood to make it big."

"But then she returns home to make it bigger?"

"Yes! Yes! What a wonderful idea! You should be a novelist yourself."

Actress. Novelist. Bon vivant of the party. Yes, that was me and I'd only been at it for an hour. *Now, for my close up. Aaaaand CUT!* A self-assured grin crossed my face. A perfect take for my millions of adoring fans I had yet to meet.

We continued on chatting for another twenty minutes. More precisely, I continued on chatting for another twenty minutes while the rest of the ever-growing circle around me stood in rapt attention, devouring my every word. I had never been very loquacious, but now the words flowed freely, lubricated by a third martini that had appeared in my hand unnoticed. Somehow, I was in my element. Somehow, that latent actress Winifred had seen inside me was now uncovered for all to see, and I loved it.

"They say if you put a thousand monkeys in a room with a thousand typewriters and give them a thousand years, eventually they'll write Shakespeare. The problem with that is, a thousand years ago, there were no typewriters, and a thousand years from now, there'll be no monkeys." I don't know where this little joke came from. Perhaps I'd picked it up from some magazine. Perhaps it was all my own, but it didn't seem to matter.

The group roared with laughter. A few nodded pensively as if I'd just uttered the most profound bit of prose since Plato's *Republic*.

Then a gong rang out. I'd never heard a dinner gong before and had no idea what it was. Were we about to be graced by the King of Siam? At this point, it wouldn't have surprised me.

CHAPTER 9
SHE WHO MUST BE OBEYED

*Dessert is probably the most important stage of the
meal, since it will be the last thing your guests
remember before they pass out all over the table.*
— William Powell

"**D**inner is served," Clio cheered as she waltzed out of the
dining room. The crowd started making its way toward her,
laughing and chatting as we went.

It was a splendor that could, indeed, have been set for the
King of Siam. Of course, it was set for royalty of a different kind.
Hollywood royalty.

The table looked long enough to land a small airplane on,
although not with everything atop it; candelabras every few feet,
place settings each with more silver and crystal than I knew what
to do with, decanters full of red wine, bottles of white.

Then there was the artwork adorning all the walls. I didn't
know the difference between a Picasso and a Pissarro at that point,
but I knew enough about art to know what was around us wasn't
something that anyone had just scribbled on a cocktail napkin. I
later found out that one of the paintings was, in fact, created by
Picasso.

I was seated next to a charming, older couple, Melvyn and
Helen. I immediately took a liking to Helen. Of course, in my state
of inebriation, I could have taken a liking to an empty chair. Still,
the woman had passion, and like all the women I had met that
evening—Clio, Maritta, even Dagny—she was strong. She was

self-assured. When she told me she was a congresswoman, it didn't come as much of a surprise.

"I really didn't follow politics much until I met Melvyn here. What really set me off, though, was arriving in Austria about ten years ago. The Nazis were running everything. Even though it had been a dream to sing in the Vienna State Opera House, I couldn't do it. We immediately returned to America where I joined the Anti-Nazi League to encourage America to boycott Germany. I have great affection for the Roosevelts. I consider them friends, but I do wish we'd entered the war sooner. Who knows how many lives would have been saved in Europe?"

I'd been telling jokes about monkeys not minutes before, but this woman was serious for all the right reasons. Now, I was the one who was hanging on her every word.

"So, you're an opera singer?" I felt foolish as soon as the words left my mouth. She'd told me about standing up to Nazis and I chose to pick up on the least important part of her whole story. It didn't seem to bother her, though.

"For a short time. I was mostly an actress. Do you know the movie, *She*?"

I shook my head. *Should I have?*

"All the better. A rather disappointing picture. I do wonder how it would have been received had Merian been able to make it in color. Still, the moniker *has* followed me into the halls of Congress. *She who must be obeyed!*" Helen uttered this last line in a low, dramatic voice, then laughed it off.

"Just as long as you don't go up in flames in the end, dear," her husband chimed in.

"Oh, I likely shall. Politics is an infernal business after all." She said this a bit forlornly, as if she'd only just realized it herself, then looked me in the eye. "Mabs, don't ever let yourself get caught up in the zeitgeist of those around you. Always be true to yourself, no matter what."

I wasn't quite sure to what she was referring, politics I imagine. Nonetheless, I suddenly became very sober in every sense. Her words came as a shock, made even more so by the fact that they seemingly came out of nowhere. One moment the conversation was rather light and trivial, then, with this last comment, the gravity was palpable. Was Helen warning me off the shallowness that defined Hollywood? She was, after all, *she who must be obeyed.*

"Oh, don't take Helen too seriously," said Carlisle, the man who'd been plying me with martinis for most of the evening. He was seated to my left, and I hadn't much noticed, as enamored with Helen as I'd been. His jibe was playful, as if they'd known each other for years. Maybe they had. In any case, Helen didn't appear to take offense to it.

"Plenty of time to save the world, but what's the point in doing so if there's nothing left to save?" he added.

"Quite right, Carlisle. Quite right. Don't take me too seriously, Mabs. I'm just a politician who's spent far too much time listening to herself talk." She raised the glass of white wine in front of her in a toast, prompting those around her, including me, to do the same. "To living life!" she exclaimed! *Oh well, one more glass wasn't going to kill me, right?* I briefly wondered how many would and felt grateful that we were about to eat something more filling than a canapé.

And more filling it certainly was! For a girl whose idea of a grand meal was a hamburger at Tommy's, it was a site to behold. I felt like I was at Bacchus's table, although part of me wondered if it wasn't more like a Last Supper—a Last Supper attended exclusively by Judas and his thirty pieces of silver. I quickly banished this tragic thought from my mind, however, as plates were passed.

Although I'd never been to a formal dinner before, I quickly realized this was anything but. No hired help was serving us. We were all passing the heaping plates of food ourselves in a hastily orchestrated circus. The crowd was raucous and informal. The food was raucous and informal! I was reminded of a word my Swedish grandmother would use, *smorgasbord.* The courses of a traditional meal all seemed to be there but were not served in an order that would have pleased Mrs. Post.

The first thing to pass by my plate was caviar. I'd heard about it, of course, but had never seen it, let alone tasted it.

"Looks a bit fishy, doesn't it," the avuncular old man seated across from me said, completely deadpan. Helen snorted, clearly more amused than I was. It was a rather pedestrian joke, I thought. *But my, wasn't I getting ahead of myself? An hour ago, and I would have made him as the cleverest wit in the room!*

"It's quite all right, dear," he continued. "A bit salty, but I think you'll like it. A bit of an acquired taste."

"I'm sure I shall," I exclaimed and following Helen's lead, took a spoonful and dabbed it on the edge of my plate.

Next up was foie gras. I wondered if the man would make some remark about the goose being cooked but decided to beat him to it. "Looks like this goose didn't liver too long."

"Good show, Mabs! Good show!" Helen exclaimed, clapping her hands together, nearly as giddy as a schoolgirl.

More dishes followed: Lobster. Lamb Chops. Rabbit. Something called Navajo Fry Bread that Charlie had made, stating that he'd grown up on it in Arizona. A curious salad made of something called Jell-O that was an unnatural shade of green, leading me to wonder if it was actually something consumable. And chocolate mousse.

I'd had chocolate pudding a number of times and even whipped up some myself once, but this concoction put even the best of it to shame. It was so light I felt I might rise out of my chair upon tasting the first spoonful. A good thing too, because by the time the desserts made the rounds, I was quite sure I might burst.

An early night it was not. After dinner, Charlie treated us all to a performance on his bass. It was simply divine how he handled those strings. The vibrations seemed to reach my very soul. There was more conversation, lubricated by brandy and scotch, and by the time it was all winding down, I was sure my back teeth were swimming in alcohol. My head and the rest of me certainly felt like they were. I was amazed I made it through the evening and, somehow, back to my apartment and bed.

My dreams that night, or what was left of it, were surreal, as if painted by Salvador Dali or Max Ernst. I was floating through a sea of green Jell-O being jiggled by the vibrations of an unseen bass. The heads of people I used to see ages ago—my sister Olivia, my father—and those of people I had met only hours before—Maritta, Charlie, Helen, even the lobster I'd eaten—were all floating around me, laughing at every word I spoke. Or were they laughing at *me*? I suddenly began sinking into the sea of Jell-O. I reached up, hoping one of the phantasms would grab hold of my hand and rescue me, but they had no hands themselves. I began to panic. There was nothing I could do. I was slipping deeper and deeper. I was in over my head. And then I awoke with a start.

My head was pounding. Where was I? When was I? Who was I? I was covered in a cold sweat. I looked down at my body, half expecting it to be covered in green Jell-O. All that covered me was my nightgown though. I barely remembered getting dressed for bed and wondered if Dagny had helped me into it.

Dagny! Yes! Was it just the night before she'd taken me to such a wonderful party where I finally managed to shake off my role as a wallflower and become a blooming bouquet? It all seemed so far off now. A different time. A different place. A different Mabs. Perhaps it was just the night before that I'd finally met myself, finally started living life outside the pages of a book. It had been my stated goal a few weeks ago. Now, still halfway between sleep and consciousness, the foggy haze inside my mind at that moment stirred something inside me. I was more frightened by it than any mystery I ever read. I didn't want to think about it, so I laid my head back on the pillow and willed myself back to sleep and hopefully more pleasant dreams.

CHAPTER 10
POOLSIDE AT THE BEL-AIR

*At one time, I thought he wanted to be an actor. He
had certain qualifications, including no money and
a total lack of responsibility.*

— Hedda Hopper

I awoke again, hours after the dream, thankful that I hadn't been
plagued by any more. I tried to remember the details of the
previous evening. Had I performed well? I remembered people
laughing at my jokes. I remembered feeling more alive than I ever
had. But was it all a dream or was it the nightmare that had awoken
me in the pre-dawn hours? I was still contemplating that a couple
of hours later when my phone rang.

"Mabs! Wasn't last night just wonderful?! You were a real
smash!" said Dagny. She certainly didn't waste any time getting
to the point. "How are you feeling?"

A real smash? Well, that seemed to confirm it. A smile
crossed my face, despite the fact that I'd already made two trips to
the bathroom to relinquish a quite repellent mixture of foie gras,
green Jell-O, and a bottle's worth of booze. *What would the other
three girls who had to share the bathroom with me think? Were
they teetotalers, like I had been until recently?*

"A bit of a mixed grill, to be honest," I said.

"Oh, dear. I should have told you to pace yourself with all
the liquor last night. You were just having so much fun, though!"

"I was, wasn't I? Was I really a smash like you say?" I asked, wanting to confirm her earlier words and my still somewhat foggy memory of it all.

"More than that, Mabs. Helen simply loved your crack about the goose liver, and Maritta can't wait to see you again. They both called earlier to tell me so.

"But there'll be time for that later. I always find the best cure for a night of drinking is a big breakfast and a day poolside at the Bel-Air. Since it's already nearly noon, however, we'll have to settle for some sandwiches. It's not on the menu, but I find if you make eyes at the waiter, he can bring out a fried egg sandwich, which is almost like breakfast. What do you say? Are you up for it?"

I smirked at the irony of her pointing out that I'd missed breakfast when I had silently judged her for having toast at 11 a.m. the first day we met.

"Oh, why not?!" I exclaimed.

"Splendid. I'll be by in half an hour to pick you up. Make sure to pack a swimsuit!"

I hung up the receiver and collapsed back on my bed. Dagny's uplifting news had erased any remaining hint of queasiness and fatigue I still had, and I was ready to lounge poolside at the fabulous Hotel Bel-Air.

I felt a little silly and rather prideful, but I couldn't wipe the grin off my face. I touched my cheeks and let out a slight giggle, then arose from the bed and went about getting ready for what remained of the day. *Almost noon and it was just now about to start!* I shook my head at the irony of it all.

The Bel-Air was everything I imagined and more. Like a veritable Shangri-La. I've heard people joke that films have always been made in color, but the world before the 1950s was actually just black and white. That certainly wasn't the case here. It seemed to be brighter than anything I'd seen before. The water was an unreal shade of turquoise. The lounge chairs were filled with beautiful people in bathing suits representing every color of the spectrum, often all at once. The umbrellas, equally as vibrant, were like a tropical garden adding to the life of the actual plants surrounding them. The stonework on the pool deck completed the scene. It was paradise!

"There's a changing room in there," she said pointing to a building at the far end of the pool. You do remember how to swim, don't you?"

It had been a few years since I'd done anything other than wade in the surf at Santa Monica, and I never exactly did laps in the river back home, but I still thought it a bit of a throwaway comment.

"There are a couple of lounges over there in the sun. Or what's left of it," Dagny said, leading me over to a place on the edge of the shade. I was a bit disappointed that the sun would soon be disappearing behind the palms but knew I'd be back.

We took our seats and ordered some iced teas and sandwiches. I chose to forgo the fried egg in favor of a Club sandwich, and I certainly wasn't going to order anything harder than an iced tea after the night before.

"So, Mabs, tell me about this job of yours. Do you like it?" Dagny asked after a bite of her sandwich and a sip of tea.

"It's okay, I guess. It pays the bills," I said with a shrug.

"That doesn't sound like much of an endorsement."

"No, I suppose it doesn't. I did think I'd be a bit farther along by now, but like I said when we first met, I fell into rather a rut."

"Well, that certainly all changed last night!"

"Yes. Yes, it did, and I can't thank you enough. I admit I was more than a bit apprehensive. To be honest, if you hadn't been so convincing, had you not shown up to help me get ready, I would never have mustered up the courage to attend."

"Oh, it couldn't have been all that!"

"Well, certainly not after I'd had that first martini!" I giggled.

"Well, here's to liquid courage, then!" Dagny said, raising a glass that held none.

"And a whole lot more!"

"Cheers to that. Cheers to that." She paused as we both took sips of our iced teas, then continued. "But do go on about your job."

"Not much to go on about, honestly. I type up copy that the admen dream up, do some filing, grab lunch for them occasionally."

"But why aren't you an adman yourself?"

"Beyond the obvious reason that I'm not a man? Well, there is one woman on the creative staff. Beatrice, although we all call her Bea. *Queen Bee* behind her back on account of the fact that she's one of the managers. But like I keep saying, I just fell into a rut. Never really thought about writing creatively."

"You were so funny last night, though! You're a real wit. And not just the silly pun here and there. That story about the monkeys; that was pure gold. Funny and rather profound. You really should write. Like Maritta said, you should be a novelist!"

"Well, I'm not sure about all that, but I do jot down the occasional thought from time to time." *From time to time* was really more like once or twice a year. Frankly, I thought her suggestion of penning a novel was rather ridiculous.

"See, there you go. Anyone who's ever written a postcard is a writer."

"Hmm. You think so?" Now that truly was a ridiculous statement. A few comments on the local weather to the family back home could hardly be called novel-worthy prose.

"I know so." She took a bite of her sandwich and began chewing. In the intermittent silence, I began to ponder whether she was on to something. Not a novel, per se, but maybe ad copy. I naturally read a lot of what the copywriters were producing and sometimes thought of ways I could improve upon it. Like she'd done before, Dagny soon lent voice to my thoughts.

"I have someone I'd like you to meet."

"Another someone? How many someones do you know, Dagny?!"

"Enough that I'm never without an invite to a party. But really, he's an adman. Maybe you've heard of him? Stan Freberg?"

"Can't say that I have. But I'm just a lowly typist."

"Lowly nothing. I bet you're a regular Agatha Christie!"

"I do love a good mystery," I joked, rather sarcastically knowing I was most certainly not an Agatha Christie.

"Then stop reading those silly Nancy Drew books and start writing one of your own—but a proper book!"

"I'll think about it," I smirked, rolling my eyes ever so slightly.

"You do that," she prodded, rather emphatically, then added, "or you could always try acting. Didn't you say something about it the day we met? 'Escape to Hollywood. Star in your own life.'"

"So, you *were* listening!"

"Every word, Mabs. Every single word."

Had I seen her all wrong? I must have if she'd remembered that phrase that I barely recalled myself. I was suddenly overcome with joy. Maybe she wasn't as shallow as I thought. Maybe Hollywood wasn't as shallow as I thought. I must confess, all I really knew about it I gained from Hedda Hopper's columns, and I suppose that was terribly unfair of me.

Although I'd admonished myself while sitting in Hancock Park weeks before to *do something,* this time it felt different, unforced. I would give Dagny—and Hollywood—a chance. A real chance. No tears. No apprehension. Well, not much, at least.

While I was pondering all of this, the pool boy came over under the guise of seeing if we needed fresh towels but considering we hadn't even dipped our toes in the water yet, I knew he just wanted to get a closer look at Dagny's figure. I certainly wasn't thinking I could hold a candle to her. He didn't even glance at her, though. Instead, his eyes fixed steadily on me.

"Hello," I smiled.

"Hello." He seemed a bit too shy for the surroundings. After all, this was the Bel-Air, not Buckingham Palace. I decided to break the ice for the both of us.

"I'm Mabs," I said, extending my hand.

"Robbie."

"Oh, Robbie! Is that you?" Dagny had been laying back, sunning herself with her eyes closed. "Mabs, this is the charming young man I was telling you about. Robbie Wagner."

Robbie grinned uneasily. He no doubt thought he was as invisible to her as I thought I had been to him and was now elated to learn otherwise.

"Did you come over to freshen our towels, or did you just want to take a look at our legs?" *How forward of Dagny. I loved it!*

"No, ma'am. I'm sorry."

"I'm not your mother, so no need to call me ma'am. I'm Dagny." *My, my, wasn't she the brassy one?* But, again, I couldn't blame her in the slightest. I was just irked that I hadn't been brassy enough to guide this exchange myself.

"Do sit down, Robbie... If you don't have anywhere to be, that is," I said, patting the lounge chair.

He hesitated briefly, his brow slightly furrowed as if he was weighing the proper protocol of the situation, then took a seat.

"Dagny says you're going to go on to do great things. What sort of things might you be going on to do?"

"Well, like a lot of people in this town, I imagine, I'd like to be an actor."

"And what's stopping you?" I felt rather like a schoolmarm, or at least a doting aunt, even though that was not my intention. He wasn't young enough to be my pupil or my nephew, and Dagny had been asking much the same question of me moments ago, of course. Perhaps I was just trying to transfer my own doubt to him.

"In a bit of a rut here, I guess."

"Oh, will you two get on with it. It's like you were made for each other!" Dagny said exhaustedly.

"I was just telling Dagny I was in a bit of a rut myself." I explained. "Perhaps we should break out of our ruts together?"

I could *feel* Dagny's eyes roll back into her head. I didn't blame her, though. What *had* gotten into me? I certainly couldn't blame it on drinks this time. I did have to keep myself from smiling too broadly. This flirting, or whatever it was, was still quite a new experience for me. But I had to admit, it was rather exhilarating. *No more being the snobbish one; now I was the flirty one*, I thought, remembering Philomena's dog skirt.

"I'd like that," Robbie replied.

"Splendid."

"Robbie, would you go fetch us some towels?" Dagny said, interrupting our conversation.

"Yes, ma—, Dagny," he said, catching himself. "Until later, Mabs." He shook my hand rather properly, then ran off.

"Why, Dagny Lundberg! I do believe you're jealous," I exclaimed, in a faux-Southern accent, channeling Vivien Leigh in *Gone with the Wind*.

"Oh, now you're just being cheeky. Come, let's go for a swim."

While we splashed in the shallow end of the pool, Dagny brought up the subject of me breaking out of my life as a secretary, once again.

"You see what you did just then?"

"What's that?"

"How you were with Robbie. Where have you been hiding that girl the past year? The past twenty-four?! You're a natural-born actress, Mabs. You'll see."

I splashed some water at her. "Oh, now really."

"Yes! Really! You're clearly out of your shell and it didn't take but a few weeks. Why, you haven't even had a martini and you're dancing around like the belle of the ball. Cinderella without the need for a glass slipper or a midnight curfew."

"Well, maybe on occasion."

"There. You see? You do have it in you. But come, I'm getting a bit of chill, aren't you? We should get going."

She was right. Where had the time gone? The sun had long since dipped behind the palms and we were now completely in the shadows. Like Cinderella, I had to go to work the next day, too. It might not have been the best job, but at least I wasn't scrubbing floors and emptying fireplaces.

A fleeting thought did enter my mind. If I were Cinderella, who was playing the part of my fairy godmother? Who were my stepsisters? Dagny was basically a stepsister to me. I shook the notion from my head and followed her out of the pool.

As we dried off, I asked her about acting. "Was it hard to get roles?"

"Well, as I said, I'm really little more than an extra. But no. It wasn't that hard to get roles. They're always looking for a pretty face and a buxom figure down at MGM, and you certainly have both. You're a natural. I can see you going far."

I wasn't all that sure she was right, but I resisted the urge to question her opinion like I'd been doing incessantly before. If nothing else, I would at least go down to the lot with her the next time she had a part. Who knows what might come of it? Certainly, a far better time than sitting at home with Nancy Drew.

Honestly, I really needed to start reading something more age appropriate. Maybe I'd pick up something from Raymond Chandler.

CHAPTER 11
GETTING FRESH

It's said in Hollywood that you should always forgive your enemies—because you never know when you'll have to work with them.

— Lana Turner

The next day at work—the next three days, in fact—I found it hard to concentrate. I'm a little ashamed to admit it, but I was beginning to live for the weekend, for whatever party Dagny might drag me to. Not that I needed much dragging the next time.

"Mabs, can you come in here?" It was Beatrice, the *Queen Bee.* I gathered a pencil and a notepad and went into her office. She was sitting on her desk, surrounded by three admen, clearly holding court.

People think men run the show, that men are the reasoned ones and women are all emotion. Here, in this room at least, that could not have been further from the truth. The Queen Bee may not have sat on the throne, but she was definitely the one in charge, a regular Lady Macbeth. Or perhaps, Cleopatra. My mind briefly flashed to Clio, the hostess at the party the weekend before. So many strong female leads are in this town that I'd never noticed. Maybe I'd be one someday. *But my, wasn't I getting ahead of myself?*

"Michael here, says he spied you at the Bel-Air on Sunday. Glad to see you're getting out."

"Yes, ma'am." While I may have been briefly fantasizing about being a leading lady one day, I certainly knew my place in relation to Beatrice.

"But that's not why I called you in here," she said, getting straight to the point. "We're working through some ideas for a Canada Dry Ginger Ale campaign, and I hear you're from Canada, so I wanted your opinion. We're trying to decide between a buck-skinned explorer, you know, one of those fur-trader types, or a Mountie. Of course, this is for the American market, but we really want to convey the mystique of Canada."

The mystique of Canada. There's something I'd never heard before. To me, Canada seemed rather dull. I considered it for a moment. *Explorers or Mounties?* Who would I want quenching my thirst?

"I'd be more taken with a Mountie, myself," I replied after a moment's pondering. "More refined. And more modern. To be honest, I don't think most Canadians picture themselves as wilderness explorers anymore." I had further ideas of how this ad might go but hesitated in voicing them. After all, I'd only been asked the one question. Then I remembered Winifred and her insistence that I had moxie. I decided to continue.

"But why not have a woman dressed up as a Mountie?" I said, beginning to think through the scenario. "I'm sure it'll be ages before there's a chance of that happening, but it would evoke a certain—" I searched for a word. *"Freshness. Canada Dry Ginger Ale. Get fresh!"* I proclaimed as I expanded my hands over an imaginary billboard. "She would have red hair, of course."

When I finished, part of me immediately regretted it, possible moxie or not. Had I been a bit too *fresh* myself? Michael certainly seemed to think so. His eyes widened and his jaw dropped. *Me, a lowly secretary, giving advice to the Queen Bee?* The other men in the room, apparently not as threatened by my entrée into the brainstorming session, nodded in approval. I felt my cheeks blush with excitement. The person whose opinion mattered the most hadn't yet spoken.

"That's simply ingenious! Michael! Why didn't you come up with this? What are we paying you for?!" Now he was even more stupefied and probably a bit jealous. I caught a subtle glare in his eyes out of the corner of my own. I'd have to watch him or I'd be out of a job faster than I could say *Gingervating*, regardless of what Beatrice thought.

"Very well. Thank you, Mabs. That'll be all."

A subtle grin crossed my face as I turned and walked back to my desk. *Moxie!*

CHAPTER 12
THE YELLOW BRICK ROAD

In show business, the saying seems too often true:
It isn't enough to succeed; someone else must fail.
— Gene Tierney

"**M**abs!" Dagny was standing outside the door of my office building when I walked out one day the following week. I hadn't seen or talked to her since our day at the Bel-Air and was eager to tell her about the praise Beatrice had heaped on me. It would have to wait, though.

"Mabs! I have a screen test. You simply must come with me. Can you take a long lunch tomorrow?"

I pondered this for a moment. Beatrice had praised my ingenuity, but I didn't want to appear too cheeky asking for a long lunch so soon after. I desperately did want to see what a Hollywood set was like, though. Maybe I could feign a headache around eleven and ask to go home early. I hadn't taken a day off since I'd started, so I was hoping it would be okay.

The following day, minutes after eleven, I executed my plan, rubbing my temples and letting out a small groan for effect. *Goodness, maybe I* was *meant to be an actress!* I waited a few minutes, hoping Beatrice would notice my performance, then asked her.

"Of course you can go home early, Mabs. If you need an afternoon to rest that brain of yours, you take it."

Maybe the girls in the steno pool had the Queen Bee pegged all wrong. How kind of her to let me go without a hint of protest. I now regretted all the snarky remarks I'd laughed at, even if I'd never made any myself.

"Yes, Mrs. Sullivan. Thank you, Mrs. Sullivan."

"It's quite alright, dear. And, please, no need for such formality. You can call me Beatrice. Or even Bea, if you like."

"Yes, Mi- Beatrice," I replied, catching myself. I turned and walked toward the door. As I opened it and began to exit her office, she called out.

"Oh, and Mabs, there's no need to feign a headache next time. Whether it's a date or just a day at the pool, I don't care. We all need the afternoon off from time to time and us girls need to stick together."

Amazing! What did she see in me to treat me so kindly so soon? Perhaps it was something in my file. She'd just caught me in my little lie and didn't mind a bit. *What a delightful woman!*

"Yes, Beatrice. I'm sorry."

"No need to be sorry. Now run along or you'll be late for whatever it is you're running off to."

I didn't need to be told twice. I quickly grabbed my purse and hurried down to meet Dagny.

"She didn't! You lucky devil!" Dagny exclaimed, giving me a small shove on the shoulder.

"Yes! She said us girls need to stick together."

"Well, I can't argue with that. Come on, let's grab a taxi. You're going to love MGM!"

Love was putting it mildly. I was *head over heels!* I felt like Dorothy, off to see the Wizard.

"So, this is where the magic happens." I knew it was clichéd, but there really wasn't a better way to say it. My eyes could barely take it all in, and we hadn't even made it to the set.

Little carts buzzed passed, carrying cowboys and doughboys. Men pushed racks full of costumes, a complement of armor for an entire Roman division on one, an assemblage of ballgowns for one of those grand spectacles with dancing and top hats on another. Even a pair of camels. The two-hump kind! *What were they called? Drama-something? Or was it Bactrian? Oh, who cares?! This was an oasis of a different kind. And no. It couldn't be. Yes, it was! It was Lana Turner!* I nearly screamed, overwhelmed with glee. I managed to contain it somehow, though, knowing that Dagny would likely be mortified by such a scene.

"Come on, Mabs, we're almost there," Dagny said with a hint of impatience. She'd probably been down here dozens of times—*maybe hundreds.* Her tone brought me back to reality. *But how could this be reality?! Everything that surrounded me was a dream!*

We finally arrived at a side door of a sound stage. I could hardly contain my anticipation for what lay beyond it! I was not disappointed. When we entered, I was transported around the world to a sheik's palace. Palm trees brushed the sky—in this case, a painted expanse replete with stars and a crescent moon. At the rear of the stage, a balcony overlooked a field of painted sand dunes that appeared to stretch on forever. *A dream of a thousand and one nights, indeed!*

Dagny grabbed my arm and tugged me over to a small row of chairs set back from the stage. "You can watch from over here. I know the director from a previous job, so I'll introduce you after I'm through. He won't mind."

She left me and walked over to the man. She kissed him on both cheeks, and then they engaged in some quick conversation. It was too quiet for me to hear from a distance, but it seemed to be limited to pleasantries. Dagny let out a small laugh then walked over to the stage. Two cameras were set up at ninety degrees from each other, facing her.

"Now remember, Dagny, you have been imprisoned at the palace for three weeks, but you have begun to fall in love with your captor," the director called out.

"Oh, my prince, why dost thou so torment me with your charms? Like the cobra, I know thine aims are but a poison in my veins. Yet, I cannot break free from such an enchanting spell. I am enamored by the diamonds thou dost bestow upon me, the pearls that hang from my neck. But damn these pearls! They threaten my very life! I know it! They seek to squeeze the very breath from my lungs, just like that other deadly serpent whose curse is more prolonged than that of the cobra, but no less mortal. I curse *thee*! I curse *thee*, my love. For were it not your desire, I should have perished already." Dagny threw her forearm over her brow and slowly withered to the ground.

My jaw dropped. It was extraordinary, the transformation she'd just made. And she wasn't even in costume! Yet, I could sense something sad about her monologue. Something true. A secret which I'd glimpsed that day, several weeks ago, when she first greeted me on Sunset Boulevard. In this moment, she was not playing Scheherazade. She *was* Scheherazade. *But who was the prince? Would I fall to his curse, as well?*

The cameras stopped rolling. The bright lights turned off. The director spoke. "That was perfect, Dagny. Thank you. We have enough for now. We'll schedule something with your agent for next week."

I was still in a bit of a daze when Dagny walked over to me.

"Well, what do you think?"

"What do I think? That was amazing! I had no idea— honestly, I'm at a loss for words."

"Oh, that was nothing. Just a few throw-away lines. I much prefer comedies, myself. I find them far more challenging. To make people cry, well, all you must do is turn a few screws. Making them laugh? Now that takes real talent. Perhaps I'll get there one day.

"Now, come, let me introduce you to Vincente."

She led me over to the director, who was just gathering up some scripts and stuffing them into a briefcase.

"Vincente, darling. This is my friend Mabs. She wanted to see where the 'magic happens', as she put it," Dagny said, introducing me.

"Splendid! Well, what do you think?" he asked, putting his briefcase back on the ground.

"It truly is magical!" I tried not to gush too much.

"Vincente, Mabs is interested in acting."

"Oh, it's not all that," I deflected.

"Why not?" Vincente asked with a smile. "Turn around for me. Let me look at you."

I followed his cue and turned slowly. I felt a bit like I was acting right there.

"Well, you certainly take direction well. How would you like to be an extra in this picture?"

"Oh my! That would be something." *Was he just being kind or was he serious?*

"Mabs, you simply must! It's so much fun!" Dagny prodded me.

"Well, it would be a bit of a gas," I admitted. "But my job," I added, more to myself than either Dagny or Vincente.

"Don't worry, that's not a problem," he replied. "Most of our extra shoots for this picture are going to be in the evening. And if you can't make it, you can't make it. We pay by the day."

"Oh, it's not about the money." As soon as I said this, I regretted it. I didn't want to appear proud. "I'm sorry. I didn't mean it like that."

"No, of course not," Vincente said. "Our next scheduled shoot is the twenty-fourth. What do you say? Can we expect you?"

"Sure, it's a date," I said, extending my hand. He gave it a hearty shake and returned my smile.

"Fantastic! Wardrobe and makeup at 4 p.m. Dagny will show you where."

I liked this Vincente. He was rather younger than I imagined a director to be, charming, and quite professional. Not at all what I expected. I'd always thought Hollywood was populated by lecherous old men who used the casting process as an excuse to leer at beautiful—and naive—young women all day.

"Your first part! This calls for a drink!" Dagny exclaimed.

Dagny hailed a taxi, and we drove a short distance to a bar called the Retake Room. It was still a bit early for a drink, especially for me, who had only just recently developed a taste for alcohol, but I was so excited by everything that had just happened that I could hardly refuse.

We sat down at a table near the back and Dagny ordered two glasses of champagne.

"Here's to Hollywood, Mabs," she said, raising her glass.

"There's no business like show businesses," I quipped, raising my own glass, then took a sip. I really was floating on cloud nine. Any apprehension I had earlier completely vanished. I even forgot all about what Beatrice said until Dagny mentioned it.

"So, this boss of yours really liked your idea. That's fantastic! Things really are starting to come together for you. But why didn't you tell me sooner?" Dagny asked.

"Honestly, I was so enamored by everything at MGM, I completely forgot all about it!" I laughed.

"It does tend to have that effect on first-time visitors." She took another sip of her champagne and continued. "Mabs the actress and Mabs the writer," she smirked. She certainly meant it as a compliment, but I thought I detected a hint of jealousy or at least self-pity.

"And I have you to thank for all of it, Dagny," I replied, hoping to nip in the bud any reservations she might have.

"Nonsense. I just pushed you in the right direction. You did the rest." I still couldn't tell if it was false modesty on her part or not, but I didn't care. The fact is, she was responsible for all of it.

"No, you've given me confidence."

"It was there all along, dear. I just helped you uncover it."

"In any case, thank you."

"But of course. Do go on about this job of yours, though."

"Well, she called me in because she'd heard I was from Canada and wanted some input on a Canada Dry Ginger Ale campaign, of all things. I gave more ideas than they were looking for, but my newfound assuredness worked."

"That is just such a darling story! Here's to Canada!" she said, raising her glass in another toast.

Three hours and I don't know how many glasses of champagne later we were thoroughly sauced. That I hadn't eaten anything since breakfast certainly didn't help either.

"We should get something to eat to soak up all this champagne," I giggled.

"Too true, but not here. The drinks are good, but the food is terrible. You know what would be absolutely delicious right now? An *enchilada!*"

I snorted at the way she pronounced *enchilada*, enunciating it and elongating the first *a* in a faux Mexican accent. It did sound appetizing though. Mexican food wasn't something I'd eaten much of at all.

Dagny left some money on the table, and we stumbled out of there. On the way out the door, I literally bumped into Winifred Jenkins walking in.

"Why, Mabs Eriksson! What a surprise! It looks like you've taken up drinking with a passion. I just hope that's not all you've found a passion for. Any ineligible bachelors to sleep with yet?" she laughed.

"Winnie!" I threw my arms around her, partly out of affection and partly just to steady myself. She seemed briefly taken aback. Of course, given the prudent state I'd been in the last time she'd seen me, it was hardly surprising.

"Mabs just got her first part. She's going to be an extra in the Scheherazade picture they're filming over at MGM."

"Isn't that fantastic! See, Mabs, I knew you had it in you."

"I'm playing the lead," Dagny quickly interjected. It was a bit odd, since she'd said the part she'd just read for had been a screen test. Did she know something I didn't, or was it bravado on her part? And why was she so quick to interject? Was she indeed jealous of me, of the attention Winifred was paying to me?

"Good for you, Dagny," Winifred's words didn't sound sarcastic exactly, but they didn't sound all that sincere.

"But—" Dagny began to protest before Winifred silenced her.

"Careful, Dagny, remember our arrangement," Winifred said.

Our arrangement? What was that all about? Arrangement over what? I didn't have time to ponder this thought any further as Winifred turned to me.

"Being an extra is nothing to be ashamed of, and I have no doubt that this is only the beginning, Mabs! Moxie, remember? You've got moxie!"

My confidence was suddenly buoyed by her statement. "I suppose I do," I smirked, and for the first time I truly believed it.

"Splendid. Now, don't forget to call me. I've got so much I can teach you!"

"Oh, I will. I will."

"I'm sorry to interrupt," Dagny said, although I doubt she was, "but Mabs and I were just leaving to get some dinner."

"Well, don't let me keep you then. I'm meeting Spencer here for drinks. Ta-ta." I thought I sensed a hint of hostility toward Dagny in her words. She gave us both a quick kiss goodbye on the cheeks and then continued toward the bar.

As Dagny and I walked down the street to wherever she was taking us, I could feel a tension simmering inside her. I chose to let it lie, but a few minutes later, she broke the silence.

"I'm sorry, Mabs. I'm feeling awfully tired. I think I'll just go home if that's okay."

I was crushed.

"O-okay," I stuttered. I thought about asking her what the matter was but sensed it might open up a conversation I didn't want to have. I sensed I might be the reason for her current state.

Dagny waved down a passing taxi and we rode the rest of the way in an uncomfortable silence. I was thankful the driver dropped me off first, but disappointed, not only that Dagny was upset, but that I was missing out on my enchilada.

CHAPTER 13
TUCKER

Creativity is a drug I cannot live without.
— Cecile B. DeMille

That night, I had another fitful rest. I dreamed I was Dorothy, following the Yellow Brick Road to Oz. Playing the part of the Scarecrow was Michael, the adman whom Beatrice had snubbed in her office. Vincente played the Tin Man and Dagny the Cowardly Lion, eating an enchilada. Neither of the witches made an appearance in my dream, but I had a foreboding that the Wicked Witch was out there somewhere, although I wasn't sure yet whose face she would have worn.

All seemed happy until I suddenly felt a string of pearls around my neck. At first, I was delighted but soon began to feel them constricting me. I called out for help but was completely alone in a desert. Two camels passed by, being ridden by Roman soldiers. They laughed at me—the camels, not the soldiers. I needed water. I needed air.

"Papa!" I called out. My father appeared, and I was at once calm. But then he looked down sternly at me and just shook his head in disappointment. "No, Papa, please! Help me!" His face began to recede, and I ran toward him. The sand slowed me down, though, and the more I struggled to reach him, the quicker he disappeared. I looked around me in all directions. Nothing but sand. A thousand monkeys flew all around me. "In a thousand years, there'll be no monkeys! In a thousand years, there'll be no monkeys! In a thousand years, there'll be no monkeys!" They all repeated the words over and over again in a shrill screech that grew louder and louder each time until my ears rang with a sharp pain. "Stop it!" I screamed. "Stop it!"

Mercifully, I awoke, but darkness still enveloped me. Instead of pearls constricting me, now it was my bedsheets. I hugged my pillow in fear and began to weep. I don't know how long I continued, but I must have eventually fallen asleep again because I awoke to the sun glaring through my window. I looked over at my clock. 9:32.

"Oh no!" I said aloud. I was late for work.

"Well, that must have been quite the party!" Beatrice exclaimed. She was smiling though, so I hoped she wasn't too angry with me. "Don't worry. Don't worry. Like I said, 'us girls have to stick together.' Just don't make it a habit. I can only placate Michael so long. You might also want to put on a bit more foundation next time, dear. Those dark circles under your eyes look something dreadful!

"But enough of that. Mabs," she continued, changing tone, "How long have you worked here?"

"A little over a year."

"And what is it you do?"

"I'm a secretary."

"Yes, but what do you actually *do*."

"Type up copy. Sharpen pencils. Fetch lunch, occasionally."

"Talent wasted! I think you can do more, and I want to give you a chance. We have a campaign proposal for an automobile company, and I want to see if that Canada Dry inspiration was a one-off or if you actually have more creativity in you. I can already tell you're at least a step up from sharpening pencils." She laughed at this last phrase as if it were the most ridiculous thing she'd ever heard. "You just focus on sharpening that creative little mind of yours."

My eyes widened, and my jaw dropped. *Just what was happening?* Last week I was filing invoices and bringing pastrami sandwiches into the room, trying not to be noticed. Now, just like Dagny had predicted, I had the chance to be an adman. Or ad*woman*.

Suddenly, Helen's words rang in my mind. *Be true to yourself. Don't get caught up in the zeitgeist of those around you.* I should have been elated at this new opportunity. Most of me was. But I couldn't help feeling like I had weeks ago, like I was about to be trapped in something I'd struggle to break free from, trapped like the bubbles caught inside a bottle of ginger-ale.

"I need your best ideas," Bea continued. "The client is the Tucker Corporation. We did some work for them last year in promoting their new automobile, the Tucker 48, and now they want to go on a full media tour around the nation to continue the buzz. It's quite the automobile from what I've seen. There are some notes and photos on that desk over there," she said pointing to one that had been left empty until now. "The boys are all out playing golf—or drinking whisky—with another client, so it's just you and me this morning."

Off drinking and playing golf while we were stuck in the office? If I hadn't been in such a wretched state, I would have cared more. As I was, the thought of whiskey—or golf, or anything other than the coffee I'd poured, made me want to retch. Somehow, I held myself together.

"Right away, Beatrice," I replied, then went to the desk and began looking through the notes she had laid there. The car was quite extraordinary. It looked nice enough, quite sleek, in fact, but the hidden features were what really made it stand out. It was the *car of tomorrow*, having several safety features like a padded dashboard, pop-out windshield, and, most curiously of all, a center headlamp that turned when the car did.

I looked out the window and tried to think of a good hook to market all of this, but my mind quickly wandered back to the events of the day before. Things had started out so splendid with the visit to MGM—I was even invited to be an extra, for heaven's sake!—but they turned sour so quickly, and I still didn't truly know why.

"Mabs," Beatrice called out. I jumped as the sound of my name wrested me from my daydream—or nightmare, or whatever it was. "Any ideas yet?"

I didn't have any but must have thought quickly under pressure because what popped into my mind at that moment was quite genius, if I do say so myself.

"You tuck your children in every evening, keeping them safe as they dream. Now, make your dreams come true as you tuck the whole family into a Tucker 48, the safest automobile ever designed. Padded dashboard. Rollbar built into the frame. Tubeless tires. Even a center headlight that turns with the car, lighting your way on corners and back home. Pre-order yours today."

"Well, that's simply marvelous, Mabs. How do you do it? The boys should be back from golf after lunch, and we can brainstorm further, but I think you're on to something. Now, speaking of lunch, have you ever had an *enchilada*?"

She said the word rather as Dagny had the day before, although she didn't draw out the *a* quite as much. I wasn't sure whether to laugh or cry as the confused memory of that earlier moment returned. I quickly shook it from my head, trying not to let my personal life cloud my professional one.

"No, I can't say that I have."

"Well, you're in for a real treat then. A Mexican restaurant just opened up around the corner."

The restaurant was delightfully kitschy with paintings of mustachioed men sitting on burros and women plying their wares in a market. An oversized guitar hung on the wall in one corner and an overwhelming smell of spices wafted from the kitchen where another mustachioed man sang to himself while he cooked.

Beatrice and I took our seats in a booth of padded red leather. A basket of corn chips sat on the table.

"So, tell me about yourself, Mabs. Other than being from Canada and occasionally lounging poolside at the Bel-Air, I can't say I know a thing about you," Beatrice said, taking small bites of a corn chip as we waited for our enchiladas.

I told her about how I'd come to Los Angeles on a bit of a whim, how I enjoyed the occasional movie—*who didn't in this town?*—and how I was partial to Raymond Chandler and Dashiell Hammett novels. I didn't make any mention of my past proclivity to Nancy Drew and, whether it was intentional or not, I didn't say anything about Dagny.

When our enchiladas arrived, we dug in. They tasted simply divine! A celebration in my mouth that instantly transported me down to Mexico, even though I'd never been.

Beatrice told me a bit about herself, how she got into advertising, and provided some mentorship on books and articles I could read to improve my craft, even mentioning a few articles by Dashiell Hammett, of all people. It was such a thoroughly enjoyable lunch and unlike the frivolous affairs that tended to take place when I was with Dagny, that I forgot all about her, the way the day before had ended, and my frightening dream. I may have even forgotten I was still a rather unsophisticated twenty-four-year-old, now being tested for the job of an assistant copywriter. The way Beatrice treated me, I felt more grown up than I ever had before, and it buoyed my confidence splendidly, at least for that afternoon.

After our lunch, we returned to the office to find *the boys* still hadn't returned from their golf—or whiskey—outing, so Beatrice and I brainstormed a few more ideas for the Tucker proposal the remainder of the day. Afterwards, I returned to my apartment, my head held high. After more than a year in Los Angeles, I'd finally hit my stride, it seemed. What did the future hold for me now? My mind turned to my appointment with MGM.

CHAPTER 14
EXTRA EXTRA

Everyone should see Hollywood once, I think, through the eyes of a teenage girl who has just passed a screen test.

— Gene Tierney

I had impressed Beatrice with my work on the Tucker proposal. Even Michael had begrudgingly admitted it was good, as did The Tucker Corporation. We gained the account. With that as a win, I had no qualms about asking to leave early so I could make it to the filming of my first—and, hopefully, not last—scene.

As I took the taxi over to MGM, I suddenly realized I was quite nervous. At first, I wasn't sure why. I was just an extra, after all, but was that it? No, I realized I was nervous because I hadn't heard from Dagny in more than a week. *Was she still upset with me? Had she ever been? What would seeing her on the set be like? Would she act professionally and not even mention anything was amiss? Would she even be there?*

When I arrived at the main gate, I realized I had a whole other worry. I didn't know where I was to go! Dagny and I had left the lot without her ever showing me wardrobe and makeup as Vincente had promised. Thankfully, Kenny, the guard at the main gate, directed me to where I needed to be.

While sitting there, along with all the other extras who were being rushed through makeup and wardrobe by a bevy of beauticians, I forgot all about my nerves and Dagny. When we were finished and I looked at myself in the mirror, I nearly gasped.

I hardly recognized myself. There I was, a blonde-haired prairie girl of Swedish extraction, magically transformed into a dark-haired Arabic woman of the harem.

While my eyes were still blue, they had been ringed with heavy makeup that made me appear decidedly Middle Eastern. The silk gown they'd dressed me in hung gently on my frame and was so light it felt like I was barely wearing anything at all. It was also appropriately supportive in all the right places, accentuating my breasts, while leaving plenty to the imagination. It was by far, the most elegantly refined thing I'd ever worn and revealed a sensuality I never knew I possessed. My heart pounded inside my chest. I was enamored with my new look, but being new, still felt somewhat out of sorts, as if it was someone else looking back at me from the mirror.

Us extra girls were taken over to the sound stage where I'd been several days before. Dagny was nowhere in sight. I was pleased, not having to face her. I didn't want to distract her from her scene, and I also didn't want to be distracted. I may have only been an extra, but I wanted to play my part the best I could.

"Take your places, girls!" Vincente called out. Several of the other girls were chit-chatting away and giggling so he had to repeat himself—a bit more sternly the second time. "Please, quiet down. We have quite a lot to shoot this afternoon, so I need you to take your places."

We were all guided by a few production assistants toward marks on the floor near the rear of the set. I was told to sit on a large pillow between two other girls who were similarly attired. I thought about introducing myself, then decided against it, not wanting to incur a scolding from Vincente.

We sat around for what seemed like ages while all sorts of people ran back and forth. Vincente had several of the assistants come up and show him a sheet of paper only to leave again after a moment and a nod. Another was measuring the distance from the two cameras to different spots on the set. Yet more were fiddling with large spotlights that hung above. At first, it all seemed rather exciting, but it did start to drag on a bit after a while. I was relieved when a handsome young man dressed as a prince walked on the set. I didn't recognize him from any other movies, but I assumed he was our star.

"Okay, Monty. We're ready for you."

Monty took his place between all of us girls and the cameras, looked up to the sky, or what would have been the sky, and began to recite his lines.

"What measure of gold would I soon part from to once again hear the beguiling elixir that emanates from her lips? All the alabaster of Egypt cannot come close to the radiance of her skin. I, the Prince of this great land, ruler of all I see, have met my equal and fallen."

"Good. Good, Monty," Vincente said. "Now, I want one of the girls to rise and walk toward him, demure. You, the one with the blue eyes," he said, pointing in my direction. "Didn't I meet you last week? Show me what you've got. Babs, was it?"

I decided not to correct him and rose from the pillow, ever so daintily, and walked toward Monty, my gaze slightly downcast and by hands cupped in front of my waist.

"Wonderful! Wonderful! You've got real talent, Babs! Now, I want you to dance around him. Remind him of the charms he'd be giving up by committing himself to only one woman for the rest of his life."

I'd never been to a Middle Eastern picture before, so I had no idea what to model myself after, but I seemed to do okay as I danced around Monty, my arms twirling over my head. For his part, he played his character conflicted, clearly charmed by me, but also with half his attention seemingly still dreaming of what I could only imagine was Dagny's Scheherazade character.

"Great work, both of you. Now, while you're dancing about charming our prince, Scheherazade is going to walk in on you both. Monty, you are the prince. It's your kingdom so you can do no wrong, but you will respond as if you've been caught in the act, as if you've betrayed Scheherazade. Babs, you will see the hurt in her eyes and will quickly run away and exit stage right.

"Let's take it from the top!" he shouted to the whole set.

A lump formed in my throat as my nerves from earlier returned. *Was this how I was to face Dagny after more than a week?* I had no clue how our relationship stood, but I was determined to not let it affect my part, especially not since I had just been promoted from background dressing to the role of a featured extra. I walked back to my spot and sat down on the pillow. The two other girls seated near me whispered a word of encouragement and congratulations in my ear before we began rolling again.

"Okay," shouted Vincente. "Scene seven, take one. Roll film and—action!"

As he said the last word, a young man, a boy really, with a clapper stepped in front of one of the cameras and slapped down the filmstick. The sharp sound jolted me into character.

I was ready. It was the most peculiar feeling, really. As my eyes subtly moved about the set, taking in the boom microphone, the cameras, the lights, and everything else, the magnitude of the moment hit me. *I was in movie!* At the same time, I somehow felt as if I weren't in a movie at all. Even though I could see all these twentieth-century technologies around me, my mind, my soul, every part of my being, had instantly been transported a thousand years into the past and half a world away.

Monty entered the scene from his mark off camera, repeated his lines splendidly, and then I came down and twirled about once again. Now was the moment of truth. I looked off stage, bracing myself for Dagny's entrance. She didn't make one. Instead, a different woman entered. I was shocked and my face clearly betrayed it. I quickly ran off stage, trying to look appropriately demure. It must have been what Vincente was looking for since he came up to me after the scene had ended and told me I was simply marvelous.

"The camera loves you, Babs. And the expressiveness in your face…you're a natural! I'm going to work you into a few more scenes. Perhaps even give you a line or two if the writers can work something into the script. What do you think?"

My mouth hung open for a moment until I had the presence of mind to close it. I didn't know what to say.

"Actually, my name is Mabs...." It just slipped out, and I realized I probably sounded quite impertinent. Instead of being cross, though, Vincente just laughed.

"Oh, my! Well, I am sorry, Mabs. I hope my faux pas doesn't scare you away."

"No, not at all, Mr.—" I realized I didn't know his last name.

"Minnelli, but, please, call me Vincente." He had a twinkle in his eye as he said it, and I suddenly forgot all about Dagny.

CHAPTER 15
ABSENCE MAKES THE HEART GROW SHALLOW

The first person I ever cared deeply and sincerely about was—myself.

— Louella Parsons

JUNE

A week later, and I still hadn't *remembered* Dagny. Frankly, I barely remembered anything since Vincente had decided to bump me up from being a mere extra to having a speaking part. My mind danced in the clouds.

He had granted me my wish—or perhaps it was his—and I was given a scene with a short line of dialogue. A *throwaway* line, as Dagny called it. Although, unlike the monologue she'd delivered, mine truly was inconsequential to the overall plot of the movie. It was magnificently consequential, though, to the role fate had cast for me on the stage of life. I became the star I hadn't even realized I wanted to be.

"A tea has never been so sweet, yet remained so bitter, when compared to thee, my prince." I practiced the line in front of my mirror over and over, emphasizing a different word each time until I was sure I had it right. I practiced my entrance, my bow, and the look in my eyes time and time again.

It was nearly all I thought about, so it was a wonder I was still able to come up with more inspired copy the next few times Beatrice tested me. Perhaps my daydreaming that the sycamore trees outside the window belonged to some far-off kingdom instead of simply shading a Los Angeles street helped my overall creativity. In any case, after I submitted my fourth proposal for her review, she officially promoted me to assistant copywriter.

Then the day arrived. I'd barely slept a wink the night before despite retiring at the almost unreasonable hour of eight. I awoke a quarter after five that morning, more than an hour before my alarm, as the faintest pre-dawn light began to appear. I went about getting ready, even applying my makeup while knowing full well that it would be professionally done just three hours later. By a quarter to eight, I was standing outside the main gate at MGM. Kenny, the guard, had just arrived for his shift.

"Why, Miss, you're over an hour early," he said, with a smile. "First part?"

"Oh, yes, and I must admit I'm rather nervous."

"You'll do fine." He had an avuncular way about him that immediately put me at ease. He gave me my pass and ushered me through. "Break a leg," he called out as I walked toward the dressing room.

So, I did. I broke both legs and probably my arms as well. I was spectacular! After the first take, I caught Vincente smiling at me and giving a slight nod of proud recognition. Now, far from being nervous, I needed to ground myself. It was only one line, after all, and I knew I still had so far to go before I even came close to being the next Lana Turner or Lauren Bacall. But I could already feel myself getting high on the potential fame. What's more, while just a week before this thought would have given me pause, this time I didn't think anything of it but pure elation.

After that day's filming ended around four, and I was standing with some of the other girls wondering what to do next, the woman who'd been cast as Scheherazade came up to introduce herself.

"Hello, I'm Dorothea Patrick. Although I guess I go by Dorothy now." She extended her hand. "I thought you were simply marvelous."

"Hello, I'm Mabs," I said, taking her hand. I wondered if I'd ever rise far enough in this business for the studio to give me my own stage name. My thoughts turned to what it might be. Would they do a take on my own name? *Erika Mabton? Bella Eriks?* Or would they invent something out of the blue? I'd always liked the name Caroline. Maybe I could put in a request.

"Do I detect a Canadian plains accent?" she said with a slight tilt of her head and a subtle smirk.

"Yes, I'm originally from Saskatchewan."

"No kidding! I'm originally from Manitoba!"

"Well, how about that? We're practically neighbors," I replied, and we both laughed.

"A few of us are going for drinks. Would you like to come?"

"Thank you. Yes, I would."

When we walked into the bar, the same bar Dagny and I had walked into a week before, several of the cast members were already having a gay time, throwing back rum and Coca-Cola, martinis, and whisky sours. These were the stars I'd read about, and now I was a part of their world, even if only in an ancillary way.

Monty, the man cast as the sheik, walked up to me, two drinks in hand. He handed one to me. I thought back briefly to something I'd heard about Arabs not being allowed to drink alcohol. Even though I knew Monty was only playing the part of an Arab, I appreciated the subtle irony of it all. We were all just playing a part on set. *And was this just a set I'd walked onto as well?*

"Salaam alaikum," Monty joked, greeting me with the Arabic salutation. "Babs, was it?"

"Mabs."

"Yes, of course. Mabs. Welcome to the party!"

Dorothy and I became fast friends. Much of the rest of the cast became my friends as well. At least they acted like my friends in this off-screen movie we all seemed to be a part of.

I spent the next three months on a cloud of bliss. I was cast as an extra a few more times and I attended parties far chicer than the first two Dagny had brought me to. Occasionally, though, I'd catch myself wondering what Dagny was up to and what she'd think if she could see me in my new atmosphere. *Would she be pleased? Would she be jealous?*

Of course, I also pondered at times the reason for her absence from my life. Perhaps we had grown too far apart in the preceding seven years and our brief reconciliation wasn't meant to be permanent. I never had time to reflect on the possible reason for very long though. I was always being interrupted by another beau bringing me a drink or asking me to dance and that was just fine by me.

While Dagny had bought me my first party dress, I now had a string of men taking me shopping and spending more on one ensemble than I spent on a month's rent. Some girls may have felt like a kept woman, being showered with all those gifts. Everything was so laissez-faire with this crowd that no one seemed to care though, so I quickly dismissed any thought of my role in a relationship other than to look stunning. I was just an accessory for some of these men, like a tie or a watch, simply a part of their outfits. I didn't care. I was having too much fun.

I must admit, it was fun toying with all the men as well, knowing that I had them wrapped around my little finger. I suppose this was why Dagny did it, and how she was able to lead such a glamorous existence on nothing more than an extra's wages. Her real job was as a flirt. I always stopped short of giving in to their advances though. Oh, they always tried to get me to come back to their homes, but I always rebuffed them with some half-hearted excuse of needing to wash my hair or rehearse my lines.

One particular Sunday afternoon, a group of us went to the Bel-Air to sun ourselves and splash around in the pool. Robbie was there, and I knew he was even more smitten with me than the first time we'd met. In his eyes, I'm sure, I'd *made it*, and he was still stuck in the same rut we both talked about months earlier. Or maybe he wasn't. After all, finding a man to buy one clothing seemed to be much easier than finding a woman.

While a few of us girls were batting a ball around, I happened to look over to the side of the pool and thought I saw Dagny. When I looked back a few moments later though, she, or whomever it was, had disappeared, and I dismissed it as an illusion.

Somehow, wedged into my schedule of late-night soirees at this or that actor's house, or dancing until dawn at the Cocoanut Grove, I managed to keep up with my work at the advertising agency. After all, while these would-be admirers of mine covered all the drinks and dresses a girl could want, I still had to pay the rent. The payments I received for Scheherazade, and the half-dozen other extra parts I worked, made my eyes pop, but those checks didn't last long. Truthfully, all of it and more went to an increasingly expensive makeup habit I'd acquired.

It may have been newfound inspiration from my new way of life. It may have been the elan I was exhibiting. Maybe it was just dumb luck, but not only did I manage with my work, I thrived in spite of myself. I'd even caught wind of a rumor that I was in line to take over from Bea herself. I believed it, even if with the slightest bit of objectivity, anyone could have known that my copywriting skills hadn't improved. I was faking it, acting. The advertising agency was yet another movie set where I only *played* the part of a copywriter for my adoring fans.

CHAPTER 16
AN UNPLANNED NIGHTCAP

Jealousy is, I think, the worst of all faults because it makes a victim of both parties.

— Gene Tierney

SEPTEMBER

I was lying on my couch, dreaming about the next part or the next party in between sips from a martini glass, when I heard a faint knock on my door.

"Mabs…Mabs…are you there? Please answer." Even through the door, I could hear the quiver in Dagny's voice. I laid still, not sure if I should reply. "Please, Mabs. It's me, Dagny. I've been such a fool."

I waited a few more beats, the two sides of my conscious battling inside me. One told me I didn't need her anymore. I'd made it and she hadn't even been by my side to congratulate me. The other side told me I should forgive her absence, or perhaps even apologize myself.

"Okay, then. I understand, and I don't blame you," Dagny sighed. "That day at the bar, with Winifred—Oh, it doesn't matter now. I'll leave you."

I heard her turn to go and whether it was curiosity, compassion, or a need for companionship, it got the better of me and I sprang to my feet. "Wait, Dagny. Don't go."

I flung open the door. She was standing in the hall, halfway to the stairs, halfway turned from me, as if deciding whether the moment had passed and she should just continue on. She turned her head toward me, and I could see the pain in her eyes, a single tear falling down her cheek. I spread my arms, inviting her to come back and let me embrace her. The savior complex I had for her that I thought had vanished was still present, if only faintly.

"Come here, Dagny. Tell me all about it."

"Oh, Mabs." She walked toward me, and I wrapped my arms around her. She buried her face in my shoulder and began to weep. I closed the door behind us and led her over to the couch to sit. "You were always there for me, my sister, my confidante, my cheerleader. That day when you came to the set with me, I may have put on a good act, but it was only for you. What I mean to say is that I know I'm no good in front of the camera. I knew, somehow, that Vincente wasn't going to give me the part. But then he was so smitten with you. I was jealous. I tried to bury it. I tried to be happy for you, but then we ran into Winifred, and it boiled up inside me once again."

"But, why? I was only an extra. Surely, you've had parts far more significant than that." I didn't tell her that I'd been given lines and that she was right, Vincente was smitten with me.

"It's been three months. Why didn't you ever call?" When I said this, I remembered her words from the first day we'd met on Sunset Boulevard. *Always a dinner. Always a day at the beach. Always a screen test.*

"I meant to. I really did. You don't know how many times I've come within a block of here, only to turn around. I don't know if it was jealously or self-pity. Maybe it was both. Maybe I realized you'd already surpassed me in just a few short weeks, and I knew I'd be nothing but a drag on your success."

"Surpass you? Never! How?"

"I saw you a few weeks after we last parted."

"Where?"

"At the Bel-Air. You were having so much fun with your friends—laughing and carrying on."

So, she had been there! I suddenly felt dirty. Like I'd betrayed her. "Why didn't you join us?"

"What would I have said? What would I have done? You've made it now, Mabs, perhaps more than I ever could have hoped for myself."

"Oh, pish. It's not all that." I wasn't sure if my words were truth or fiction. I wasn't sure if I was lying to her or only to myself. "Now, let's get you a drink."

I stood and went to fix us a couple of martinis. *My, my. What three months had brought. Should I cast her out of my life more quickly than she entered? No!* I quickly shook the thought from my mind and walked the drinks over to her.

"You make martinis now?" She let out a small laugh between sniffles as she tried to compose herself after her burst of tears.

"Yes, now drink up. I have a nearly full bottle of gin and all night for you to tell me all about it."

We talked late into the night, the next morning, in fact. It felt like old times, very old times, like when we were girls the summer before she left Prairie River. Of course, it was better than that since our conversation then had been lubricated by nothing stronger than cream soda.

"Do you remember that time your father caught me kissing Willy Johansen behind the general store? He was *so* disappointed in me. I thought for sure he'd forbid me from ever coming over again," Dagny reminisced.

"You told me you were so nervous, it being your first kiss and all." I replied.

"But the joke was on him, wasn't it?! He was so nervous he ended up biting my lip!" We both laughed until tears of mirth had replaced her tears of sorrow.

"Or what about that time the Sunday School teacher was reading from the Old Testament, and I asked her what a whore was?" We both roared with laughter at this memory.

"She turned beet red!" Dagny exclaimed, wiping a happy tear from her eye.

"And then we had to go to the library and look it up!"

Later, when Dagny thought about how her mother would never get to see how she'd turned out and all the moments she'd missed, we both cried more tears of sorrow. We also shared our regrets over not being by each other's sides the past seven years and the past three months.

By the time the first hints of dawn began peeking through the window, it was as if no time had passed, both in terms of that single evening and in terms of our most recent separation. It brought me comfort to have my friend back again.

"Let's never quarrel again, Mabs. Let's never be apart for so long," Dagny said, holding my hands in hers and looking me in the eyes.

"Yes, Dagny. Sisters until the end, just as we were in our youth," I replied. But such are the promises made on little sleep and lots of gin. Would they last? Only time would be the judge.

She fell asleep on my couch around six, and I covered her up with a spare blanket. Retiring to my room, I lay down to get what little sleep I could before awaking in a little more than an hour. I didn't regret the conversation and connection we'd made, but I knew I'd regret the hangover the next morning. Or the same morning, as it was.

CHAPTER 17
FREBERG AND THE MULE

The whole world is three drinks behind. If everyone in the world would take three drinks, we would have no trouble. If Stalin, Truman, and everybody else in the world had three drinks right now, we'd all loosen up and we wouldn't need the United Nations.

— Humphrey Bogart

Having Dagny back in my life seemed to ground me. Sure, I never went back to being the naïf I'd been months before. Spending time with her meant that I was spending less time with Dorothy and the other stars I'd managed to collect, though. We were both fully ensconced in the Hollywood scene now but knowing that we had the connection of our childhood was enough.

Me being back in Dagny's life clearly had the opposite effect on her. She shared that after seeing me so candidly at the Bel-Air, she'd mostly relegated herself to her apartment. Hearing this, I was relieved she was more of a social drinker and wondered what state she may have drunken herself into while alone.

Now, though, having me by her side meant she was ready to start attending parties once again. We didn't waste a moment. Two days later, I'd already secured an invitation to an evening affair at the home of Errol Flynn, the hedonistic adventure actor.

I'd been to some rather fanciful palaces over the last three months with my movie star friends, but nothing prepared me for Errol's estate.

The Spanish-style home sat on the edge of a steep slope above the Sunset Strip with multiple balconies overlooking the pool and the city lights below. When we arrived, the bacchanal was already in full swing. A few women, apparently not content drowning themselves in the copious amounts of champagne that flowed, now splashed around in the pool.

Fortunately, I'd already been anesthetized to such a scene. Had this been my first entrée into evening entertainment in Hollywood, I may have gone running off. All I could think of now, though, was how I was going to join in the fun.

"Well, well, well. If it isn't Mabs Eriksson. And who is that with her? Why, if it isn't Dagny Lundberg! Where has she been hiding?!" I didn't recognize the woman who'd said those words at a volume much too loud, even for the din of this room, nor did I recognize the man and woman she was speaking with. I half expected a silence to pierce the air and for everyone to look over at us. The rest of the crowd was too ensconced in their own conversations, though, and carried on. We walked over to the trio.

"Mabs, it's so good to see you!"

I froze and searched my mind for who this might be but drew a blank. She caught on.

"Alida Valli. Don't tell me you don't remember me. We traded makeup tips in the bathroom at the Cocoanut Grove, then let a line of suitors buy us champagne cocktails until dawn."

"I'm sorry. Perhaps I was more focused on the suitors." It very well could have been the truth for all I know. She let out a laugh and the other two joined in.

"Well, that's okay. It happens to the best of us. In any case, I'm so glad you're here and so glad you managed to drag Dagny along. Where have you been hiding, Dagny?"

"Oh, I've been around. Busy with shoots. You know how it is," Dagny lied. She looked over her shoulder then added, "Excuse me, I'm going to find the bar," and walked off.

Alida, her friends, and I continued making small talk for the next ten minutes. All the while, I snuck glances around the room, looking for someone more interesting. Thankfully, Dagny came to my rescue.

"Mabs! Do you remember me telling you about that adman, Stan Freberg? Well, he's here!" Dagny grabbed my arm and pulled me across the room to a small group of people who were listening to a blonde-haired woman with a German accent.

"… and that is why we simply had to address the Jewish Question. A problem really. A vile race."

"But surely, there were some good Jews in Germany," a man questioned.

"My dear Mr. Weber, you of all people, being a German, should know that there is no such thing as a *good* Jew. We tolerated them for a time, yes, but they simply held too much sway over the culture. Pharaoh could have put an end to it had he not been so weak." She laughed at this last sentence although no one else did. "Herr Hitler was simply addressing an infestation that had gotten out of hand."

It was clear that the small crowd was growing a bit uneasy with this conversation. Yes, anti-Semitism was fairly commonplace in Hollywood, but it was usually referred to with innuendo and subtle nods. After all, Louis Mayer and Jack Warner had given most of the room its start, so it was rather bold of this woman to be going on about such things at a party like this. Communism growing amongst the Hollywood elite in 1948 was one thing, but this?

The woman turned to me.

"Hello, my dear. Margot Schneider." She extended her hand.

"Hello," I said, taking hers briefly. "Mabs Eriksson." Her touch was ice-cold, reflecting her soul, no doubt.

"Eriksson! A wonderfully Aryan sounding name. Are you Swedish? I admire the Swedes, even if they did sit out the war instead of coming to the aid of their Teutonic brethren."

I was Swedish, or at least my grandparents were, but I suddenly didn't feel at all proud of that heritage.

"Certainly better than the English," she continued, not waiting for me to answer. "That Churchill character really fell for the trickery of the Jew in his country. A shame that Chamberlain didn't remain in power. Of course, if they hadn't pushed poor David from the throne, who knows what might have happened."

I don't know why I was even engaging this woman any further, but the only thing that came to my mind was the question of who David was. I didn't know much of anything about British politics or the Royal Family, but having grown up in Canada, I did know there had never been a King David. Did she mean Edward, the downcast looking man whose picture hung in our schoolhouse for a scant eleven months?

"David?" I asked.

"Yes, dear. David. That's what his friends call him. You might know him as Edward. A truly splendid king he would have made, given the chance to rule. I can't say I cared much for Wallis, but she was tolerable enough I suppose—when she wasn't drinking herself into oblivion.

"That was their real undoing. One should be prudent in drink. I, myself, have a small glass of sherry before bed, but nothing other than coffee in small measure or water the rest of the day. Water is the elixir of the gods! One should try to drink at least six glasses per day. Herr Hitler encouraged it for all good Germans. Of course, he would have frowned at the glass of sherry, but we all have our vices, don't we?"

This woman was growing intolerable, and I certainly hadn't come to this party to prepare for a dissertation from anti-Semitic socialites—or sociopaths—on the perceived mistakes of Egyptian rulers or the health benefits of water. Where was this Stan character Dagny had dragged me over to meet? I began looking for a way to extricate myself from the group as quickly and politely as possible.

"But look at my manners," she continued, not letting me get a word in edgewise. Not that I had any desire to. I was beginning to rethink my attendance at this party and dreading that she'd descended on me of all people to talk to. "This is my husband, Heinrich."

"Good evening, señorita," a rather portly and balding man with spectacles said, extending his hand.

"Heinrich, dear, do stop. We're not in Argentina anymore," she chastised him.

I should have left right then with some excuse about having to powder my nose. Or maybe I should have just slapped her across the face, turned on my heels, and left the party. I'm quite certain I wasn't the only one thinking such things. The rest of our little circle would have no doubt cheered me on. Nevertheless, I chose to be diplomatic.

"Argentina?" I asked. At least I wasn't having to say much. My entire contribution to this conversation had been two, one-word questions.

"Yes, dear, we've been living in Argentina for the past three years after your country forced us to leave Germany. The Argentinians are a lazy bunch, but I do rather enjoy the climate."

She paused, rethinking what she'd just said. "Lazy, but for when they quarrel or make love, that is. It's all they seem to be good for." She laughed once again at this last sentence. I wondered if she knew about their two areas of passion from personal experience. Glancing over at her husband, I rather thought so.

"But it is a lovely country, even if the people aren't. You should come visit."

That would be *horrendous*! I knew Argentina was a fairly large nation. I'd met a charming actor a few weeks earlier named Fernando who had just moved to Los Angeles from Buenos Aires. We'd had a very pleasant chat that lasted an hour or more one balmy evening while sitting beside the pool at the Bel-Air. He'd brought a bottle of Fernet with him and mentioned the size of his nation in passing. Come to think of it, he'd mentioned the size of a few things. I knew that if I were to visit Argentina, however, it couldn't possibly be big enough to share with the woman standing before me.

"I'm sorry. I must excuse myself," I said and began walking toward the liquor cabinet, cursing Dagny the whole way. "What a beast!" I muttered under my breath. At least I was able to break free without consequence. She probably hadn't even realized I'd left, her loquacity being what it was.

"Boy, that dame could talk the ears off a corn field! She must have been vaccinated with a phonograph needle."

I turned around. A young man with thick rimmed glasses who had been on the edge of the previous conversation—or should I say monologue—with the Germans, was standing there.

"Hi! Stan Freberg. You had to get away from that awful woman as well, I imagine." He gave a quick wave.

"Charmed," I said, extending my hand. And I was. "Mabs Eriksson. You're funny, you know that?"

"I hope so. That's what they pay me for. And if I ever find out who *they* are, I'm going to tell them I've seen celery better looking than my salary."

I laughed. What a delightful young man. I'd almost forgotten all about wanting a drink until he mentioned it.

"Can I mix you up some poison? I, myself, hardly ever touch the stuff. Dad was a Baptist preacher and scared it right out of me for a time. But now, I'll occasionally have something rather tame, especially if it gives me the chance to engage in conversation with a charming young lady like you." He reached for a bottle of vodka and another of ginger beer and poured a small bit of the vodka into two highballs then topped them off with the ginger beer.

"They call this a Moscow Mule. Usually, it's served in a copper mug, but I won't tell anyone if you don't." He then grabbed a lime, shaved off a couple of slices, and plopped them in the glasses. "Nazdarovya!" he said, handing me one of the glasses, a sparkle in his eyes. He was a bit goofy, and I imagined, a couple of years younger than I was, but I liked that. So many men at these parties were only after one thing. Stan wasn't threatening in the least.

"Naza *what*?" I asked. While he was still carrying the conversation, he was giving me ample opportunity to speak, unlike the *frau*.

"Nazdarovya. It's how Russians toast each other. And they toast each other so often, I hear, they must go through a loaf per day!"

"You're funny," I giggled. "But I already mentioned that, didn't I?"

"That's alright. My only gigs up to this point have been voicing cartoons, so I never know whether I'm getting a laugh or not. I guess I must be, or old Jack Warner would have thrown me out by now."

"You work for Warner Brothers?" Since I'd already met so many actors at this point, it was nice to be asking this question without getting all giddy and starstruck. Plus, at this point, I couldn't have cared less if I was talking to Humphrey Bogart or Clark Gable. Don't get me wrong. I'm sure they were lovely enough men. It's just that the Hollywood set could sometimes be a bore, and it was refreshing to talk to someone who, while he may have worked at Warner Brothers, wasn't a name you'd see on the marquee.

"Some might call it work. I'm having too much fun though," Stan replied.

"If you love what you do, you'll never work a day in your life!" I exclaimed, raising my glass in a toast.

"I like that. I really like that."

"Picked it up off the back of a matchbook." I hadn't, but it seemed like the right thing to say. It had actually been something my father had said to me once. I can't imagine he liked milking cows and farming wheat at just above a subsistence level, but at least he pretended to enjoy it. Maybe he even convinced himself of it. He was a happy man. That's for sure. I had always admired that about him.

I wondered how many of the beautiful people around me were as happy as he was. All their money. All their fame. But to what end? They all seemed to frequently lose themselves at the bottom of a bottle. Not Stan though. Even though we'd just met, I could tell he was different.

He laughed at my quip. Maybe he knew it was my attempt at a joke. Then he got somewhat serious. "If you don't mind me saying, you don't seem to fit in here."

"Perhaps I don't. I'm just a secretary at an advertising firm," I fibbed. I'm not sure whether I was being modest for his sake or for mine. Perhaps some of the old me was returning, and I wanted nothing more than to return to being *just a secretary*.

"Advertising!" He seemed quite excited by this. "I love advertising. Well, as long as one is advertising a good product. You know, President Coolidge gave a speech all about advertising once. He thought it was the most underrated portion of our economic engine. He marveled at it and said it was basically education of the masses."

"Fascinating," I said, truthfully. It wasn't every day you met someone at a Hollywood party quoting Silent Cal.

"You think so?"

"I do! I don't know much about Calvin Coolidge, but he seemed like a nice enough man, and I'd rather talk about him than Rita Hayworth."

"Oh, Rita ain't so bad."

"I'm sorry—" *Had I made a faux pas? Had I just insulted his idol?"*

"No, no." He interrupted me before I could dwell on it any further. "I'm just pulling your leg."

"Oh," I breathed, relieved. I was really beginning to like this Stan character. He didn't seem to belong at this party, and I was beginning to wonder if I didn't as well.

"Tell me more about this advertising gig. I bet you do more than just type up memos and file papers. Heck, you probably run the company!" My, he was a quick study. I wondered if he was just *pulling my leg* again or had already seen right through me.

"No, not all that. I do run out to get sandwiches from time to time." I wasn't sure why I didn't tell him I did so much more than fetch sandwiches. Come to think of it, for the past three months, someone else had been fetching mine.

Furthermore, Stan was probably the one man in the room who wouldn't have been the least bit threatened by my position, as relatively modest as it was.

He laughed at this as well, but I knew it wasn't done in mean spirits. I don't think Stan had a mean bone in him.

"What's your favorite sandwich?" he asked. *Now there was a question!*

"I rather like liverwurst."

"Well, we should grab a liverwurst sandwich sometime."

"I'd like that," I smiled.

"So, what *are* you doing at this party?" He asked. *Probably a better question although one with a far less interesting answer.*

"My friend Dagny dragged me along," I lied a third time. "For moral support, I imagine. Not that she needs it. She definitely belongs." *Why was I so reticent to be up front with him?* After all, I was sure he was being up front with me.

I quickly gazed around the room and saw Dagny over in a corner, a glass of champagne in her hand, making eyes at a man in a dinner jacket and laughing at jokes that couldn't have been nearly as funny as Stan's. She was certainly back to being her old self.

"Dagny the dragger."

"What's that? Yes, I suppose she is," I replied as he regained my attention. In giving her this moniker, he'd just said something profound, even if unintentionally. Dagny had dragged me into all of this until the moment I began dragging myself, and now I was dragging her. I suddenly felt sad. I had enjoyed the first few parties we'd attended, but after falling in with so many stars, they were now becoming more of a chore than anything. And the characters—they might as well have been characters since they all seemed to be putting on an act—were becoming increasingly two-dimensional.

It was as if they all had a group of Poverty Row writers handing them their lines before they walked through the door. It was as if there was a washed-up director standing in the wings telling them how to speak, how to take a drink, even how to raise their eyebrows. I thought back to that day, months ago at Dagny's apartment, when she had warned me that this life wasn't all it was cracked up to be. I'd jumped in with both feet, however, and, to mix metaphors, I'd made my bed and was sleeping in it.

"Now I'm the one who is sorry," he said, sensing my change in mood.

"No, it's okay. I was just thinking of something."

"What's that?" He was genuinely concerned.

"How we sometimes get dragged along in life without even realizing it. How so many of us have life happen to us instead of having us happen to life."

"That's profound. Did you read that on the back of a matchbook as well?"

"No, that one's all mine."

"All the better then." He finished off the rest of his Moscow Mule, and I took it as a cue to finish mine. I'd hardly drank but a sip and downing the rest of it so quickly made me a bit lightheaded.

"Slow down there! It might be a Moscow Mule but that doesn't mean you have to enter it into the Belmont Stakes!"

I laughed and nearly sprayed him with vodka and ginger beer. As it was, a bit dribbled down my chin. I found the moment endearing though. He'd broken the somber mood.

They say time flies when you're having fun. For the first time in more than a month of parties, I must have been having a ball talking with Stan because, before I knew it, the room was almost empty. Nearly everyone had left, including the German couple, thankfully.

"Mabs, I hate to break up a perfectly good party, but it's nearly three o'clock in the morning."

"Is that late or early," I giggled. Dagny was now being the prudent one. Maybe it was the Moscow Mule. Or the second Moscow Mule. Or the third. Or fourth! *Gracious! How many had I actually had?* I suddenly felt famished. She looked at me crossly.

"No, you're right, Dagny. We should go," I sighed. "But truth be told, I'm not ready to go home. I'm feeling a bit peckish, in fact. Is anyone else feeling a bit peckish?"

"Mabs, are you drunk?!" Dagny was clearly shocked by the way I carried myself. After all, she hadn't seen me in such a state for months and back then, she wasn't as sober as she likely was now or seen me exactly like this. At those first couple of parties we'd attended together, the alcohol had certainly made me loquacious, but I'd still remained at least somewhat refined. Now, I was as silly as a Bugs Bunny cartoon. Even I could tell that. Stopping myself, even if I'd wanted to, that was a different matter.

"Oh, come on, Dagny! I'm just having fun," I exclaimed, spinning gayly on my toes and nearly losing my balance. "You're the one who says I never have any fun."

"Very well, Mabel Eriksson. Let's go get something to eat," she sighed, resigned to being the responsible one for once.

"Are you coming, or do I have to handle this one all by myself," she added, looking at Stan rather sternly. He was clearly amused by my performance, especially since he was holding his liquor far better than I.

He snapped to attention and gave her a mock salute.

CHAPTER 18
A BIG STACK OF PANCAKES

Anyone who has a continuous smile on his face
conceals a toughness that is almost frightening.
                                        — Greta Garbo

"I want pancakes!" I blurted out as soon as we seated ourselves inside Stan's car. It was a good thing he'd offered to chauffeur us around since our ride seemed to have deserted us long ago—if we ever had one. To be honest, I couldn't remember how we arrived at the party in the first place. It seemed like ages ago. Hopefully, Dagny really was being the more prudent one at this point, because I was in the least prudent state I'd ever been.

"Well, I know just the place," Stan offered happily.

Twenty minutes later—my stomach, by this point, estimated the time at closer to an hour—we were seated at Du-Par's. I had a giant stack of pancakes sitting before me. The short-term effects of all the alcohol were wearing off, and now I was feeling a bit silly in a different way, like a little girl whose parents had taken her for a special birthday meal.

Stan accentuated the feeling by reciting a little ditty he'd clearly come up with on the spot.
"Oh, for heaven's sake,
It's time for some pancakes.
I like mine with syrup and butter.
When I see 'em on the plate, it makes my heart flutter.
I want some pancakes,
And maybe a cuppa Joe.

You can take your French Toast back to France,
But my pancakes, no, no, no."
When he finished, he gave me a crooked smile.

"That's very clever. Did you just make that up?" I asked, pointing my fork at him in between very unladylike mouthfuls of pancake.

"Nope, read it on the back of a matchbook," he kidded.

"You know, Stan Freberg. You're quite the charming young man." I was smitten.

Dagny yawned. I could sense it was more out of boredom than tiredness. All she'd ordered was her usual side of toast and strawberry jam.

"Dagny, you must try these pancakes! They're simply wonderful!" They probably weren't. After all, how exceptional can a fried bit of batter really be? At nearly four o'clock in the morning though, everything tastes about the same. Dagny waved off the forkful I was forcing on her.

"Suit yourself. More for me!"

Stan decided to chime in again with a joke. "Two pancakes are sitting at a diner, and one decides it's going to flip. It doesn't go so well, and it starts to cry. The other pancake replies, "don't be sad. Syrup!"

Dagny looked at him blankly. I'm not sure if she didn't get the joke or just didn't think it was that funny, but I thought it was hilarious.

"Get it, Dagny? It's like cheer up! Syrup! Cheer up!"

"Mabs, I'm tired. Let's go home," she sighed, rubbing her brow.

I was oblivious. Maybe I was still drunk. Actually, I'm sure of it. But it was something more. I was drunk on the charm of the man seated across from me. I was probably a bit drunk on the pancakes, too. Everything was making me drunk at that moment. I was overwhelmed and loving every minute of it.

"Let's go swimming!" *Yes, I was definitely drunk.* I'd never acted so silly in my life and now I was blurting out every spontaneous thought that crossed my mind. "Do you think the pool at the Bel-Air is still open?"

Dagny rolled her eyes.

"No, silly me. Of course it's not. But I know what is open," I added mischievously. "The Pacific Ocean!" I threw my hands in the air and, in the process, knocked over a glass of water. That was the closest I'd get to swimming that evening.

"Hey! Keep it down over there!" The woman behind the counter gave us a stern warning. I couldn't blame her. As popular as Du-Par's was, at this hour only one other person was there, a blue-collar man who had probably just woken up an hour before and was headed to some factory job. Or maybe he'd been up all night waxing floors. Either way, he wasn't having anywhere near the fun we—or, more correctly, *I*—was having. Dagny was getting quite antsy to go and even Stan, as gracious as he was with me in my current state, sensed the waitress's chastisement was our cue to leave.

"Swimming sounds like a marvelous idea," Stan said, much to Dagny's chagrin.

CHAPTER 19
MRS. HENRY FONDA?

A romantic, I think, picks the rose and is careless with the thorn.

– Gene Tierney

"So, you were pretty smitten with that Stan Freberg character last night. Or should I say, this morning." Dagny was looking bright-eyed and bushy tailed. Of course, it was almost two o'clock in the afternoon, when, for most people, bright-eyed and bushy-tailed was already in the rear-view mirror and they were wondering if an afternoon nap might be in order. I sure could have used a nap at that point, even though I'd only just awoken. Those Moscow Mules had reared up and kicked me in the head. I sat there, staring into my coffee. Dagny sat across from me at the dinette in my kitchen.

"Ugh," I groaned.

"Hungover, are we?"

"You're not nearly posh enough to use the *royal we*, Dagny, so unless you're hungover, too—and you're clearly not… Why is that?"

"Maybe it was that stack of pancakes. But back to Stan."

"Stan?" I said, still in somewhat of a fog.

"Oh, come now. You can't have been *that* drunk! He was the young man you were hanging on all night."

I reviewed the previous evening in my mind. Thick framed glasses. A charmingly crooked smile. Something about Russian bread and the Belmont Stakes. And why did my mouth taste like day-old syrup? Oh, right, now it was all coming together.

"Did we go swimming in the Pacific Ocean?" I asked, furrowing my brow. I smelled my hair for a hint of sea salt.

"No, dear. Thankfully, we skipped that escapade. You didn't make it two blocks after we put you in the back seat of the car. And since when did you snore?"

"That bad, huh?"

"Actually, it was fun to watch. You reminded me of me seven years ago."

"Did I make a complete fool of myself?" I tried to remember if I had been smitten with this Stan character she spoke of, but either way, I hoped I hadn't completely mucked up the evening.

"Well, not a *complete* fool. Truth be told, I think Stan rather liked you."

"He did?" I perked up.

"I gave him your number. I hope that was okay."

"I guess that depends on if he calls or not."

"Oh, he'll call. He'll call."

I took a sip of my coffee. "What about you?"

"What about me what?"

"Last night was your first time out in months. Did you enjoy yourself?"

"Well, certainly not as much as you did, but yes. I had a good time."

"Who was that man you were speaking to?" I asked, more and more of the previous evening coming to mind.

"Oh, you noticed!"

"Just briefly."

"You didn't recognize him?

"No."

"That was Henry Fonda."

"Well, whoever he was, you seemed quite smitten yourself." I knew who Henry Fonda was, and I was rather impressed she'd manage to catch his eye. But I didn't feel like letting on.

Dagny smirked and tried to hide it by taking a sip of her coffee.

"So, you were smitten!" I pointed an accusatory, but friendly finger at her.

"Well, he is Henry Fonda, after all."

"So, did you give him *your* number?"

"I did one better. He invited me to come riding with him in a few weeks."

"Horses? But you don't even know how to ride a horse!"

"Well, I guess that gives me three weeks to learn so I don't make an *ass* of myself," she said, accentuating the pun. We both laughed.

My stomach suddenly grumbled quite loudly.

"Oh, my!" Dagny exclaimed. "Feeling a bit peckish again, are we? I mean *you*", she said, catching herself. We both laughed again.

"Now that you mention it. Do you think it's too late to get an egg sandwich at the Bel-Air?"

"But Mabs!" She placed her hand on her chest and gasped in faux shock. "Whatever would Stan say if he saw you flirting with Robbie Wagner again?!"

I tossed my napkin cheekily at her. "Well, then, what do you suggest?"

"I could really go for a hamburger. Let's go to the Pier. Maybe you could even get that swim in you talked about last night!"

"Hardy har. I think I'll pass on the swim, but a hamburger does sound right."

By the time we got to the Pier, I was positively starving. No wonder, I hadn't had anything to eat in twelve hours. I devoured two hamburgers, several handfuls of French fries, and a chocolate milkshake in short order. Dagny had a hamburger of her own and nibbled on a bit of my French fries but declined the milkshake.

"So, tell me more about this *horscapade* with Mister Henry Fonda," I asked once I'd slurped up the final bit of my milkshake and reclined in my seat, fully satiated.

"Horscapade. Oh, that *is* clever!" I couldn't quite tell if she was impressed by my little portmanteau or was being sarcastic. "It's quite the event, it turns out. 'Mink and Manure' they call it."

It was a good thing I'd finished my milkshake. Had I taken a drink at that moment, I'm sure most of it would have sprayed out my nose.

"Don't laugh, Mabs. I'm serious." She was trying to be, but I could tell she found the words uproariously funny as well, and was doing her best to hold it all in. "It's a group of Hollywood regulars who all travel to Palm Springs and act the cowboy. They'll all be there. William Holden, Don Ameche, Olivia de Havilland, Robert Taylor. Why, Henry even told me that Cary Grant and Clark Gable often put in an appearance."

"Henry? Well, my, aren't you two just a couple now?" I teased.

"Oh, I don't know about all that. He is married after all." She looked off wistfully into the distance. I wondered if she was already planning some scheme to snag him, legally or otherwise. *Mrs. Henry Fonda*, I could imagine her thinking. She shook away whatever thought was in her head and returned to the conversation.

"Can you picture it, Mabs? Saddling up beside Cary Grant and Henry Fonda?"

"Okay, I'll take Cary, then," I sighed, sarcastically.

She looked at me quizzically.

"What? If you are already on a first-name basis with Henry Fonda, why can't I be on a first-name basis with Cary Grant?"

"Very well then. I better book us some riding lessons." She said it as if it were going to be a chore, and I briefly wondered how much she kept up with this life of hers—and, increasingly, mine—for her sake, and how much was just for appearances.

CHAPTER 20
TWO STEPS FORWARD

Gratuitous cruelty borders on the pathological, psychotic, and that becomes uninteresting because there is no choice.

— Konstantin Stanislavski

It had been more than three months since I'd played my little speaking part for the silver screen. For about a month after filming, I eagerly awaited any news from MGM about when the movie would premiere or if my part would make the cut. After that time, hearing nothing, I largely gave up on ever seeing that film on the silver screen. I'd learned that several movies, even big budget productions like *Scheherazade* appeared to be, never made it to a premiere. Of course, part of me dreamed of seeing myself, if even for a scant thirty seconds, up on the screen, but I'd have to be content with the memory of the part I'd played solely in my own mind. Or so I thought.

I was working away at my desk, reviewing some artwork for a Pepsodent advertisement, when the phone rang.

"Hello, this is Mabs Eriksson."

"Mabs, darling, I'm so glad I've reached you! You don't know what I had to go through to track you down! I tried your apartment first, even sent a messenger over, but of course you weren't there." The voice sounded vaguely familiar, but I couldn't quite place it. Some gentleman I'd met at the Cocoanut Grove perhaps? But why would one of them be sending a messenger to my apartment? Then it hit me.

"Vincente!" I exclaimed, perhaps a bit too excitedly. "So good to hear from you! To whatever do I owe this pleasure."

"Well, I'm afraid *Scheherazade* has been scrapped—at least for now—but I'm working on something new, and I wondered if you might be free to play a part in it?"

"Would I?! Of course!" I probably should have played it a bit more coy, but I was too thrilled by the chance to have a part more significant than *uncredited girl at soda fountain.*

"Wonderful! Now, I'm afraid it isn't anything too extravagant, but you will have more screen time than your part in *Scheherazade.*"

"Any time at all would be simply grand," I perked up. All those pent-up desires to be a star that I'd been harboring ever since filming *Scheherazade* came rushing back.

"Marvelous!" He said. "Now, can you come by my office next Tuesday around four? We can go over your role, and I'll give you a copy of the working script."

"Four will be just fine." I'd so worked myself into the good graces of Beatrice by this time that I was sure she'd be fine with me leaving a bit early. She'd have to be.

"I'll see you then. Goodbye."

"Ta-ta!" I hung up the phone and laid back in my chair, a state of bliss overcoming me. *Hurray for Hollywood!*

"Mabs, can you come in here?" Beatrice called. She sounded slightly serious, and I worried that maybe I'd gotten ahead of myself thinking I could skip out on work an hour early. I gathered my notebook and went into her office.

"Who was that?" She asked.

There was no sense in being coy with her. "Vincente Minnelli."

"My, don't you have friends in high places?" I couldn't read her. *Was she genuinely impressed, or did I hint a tone of sarcasm?* "Listen, you do good work here. Some of the best I've seen in my twenty years in advertising. I don't mind if you take the occasional afternoon. God knows I do from time to time. But

I do need you to be upfront with me and not just assume you can leave whenever you want."

"Yes, Beatrice. I'm sorry."

"It's alright. Now, what does Vincente Minnelli want with you? I know it's not your body." She allowed a wry smile to cross her lips at this last sentence. *Did she know something I didn't?*

"Excuse me?" My reply wasn't meant to be insolent, but it probably came out that way.

"Vincente Minnelli is a homosexual, dear. Surely you knew?"

My mouth dropped open. I certainly knew there were more than a fair share of men who leaned that way in Hollywood, but I guess I was still somewhat naive in that department. Truth be told, I was still rather naive when it came to sex in general. The closest I'd ever come was a peck on the cheek, a slap on the rear end and a few vicariously sordid—but not too sordid—details as Dagny recounted her occasional flings. *I'd have to change that.*

Beatrice let out a rather hearty laugh. "Oh, my dear girl! What did you think he was after?" She paused, as if realizing the truth might be more shocking than him just wanting me for my body. "Wait, is that where you were running off to a few months ago? Here I thought you were just lounging around at the Bel-Air! I guess there's more to Mabs Eriksson than meets the eye!"

"Yes, ma'am. I mean—"

"No, no, it's quite alright, as I said. So, what has he promised you? What exactly were you doing three months ago?"

"It started as scene dressing. A harem girl in a Middle Eastern epic he was directing." Beatrice's eyes widened when I said *harem*. "He promoted me to a part with a few lines, but I guess the movie isn't going to be finished after all."

"Oh, I am sorry." Again, I couldn't gauge her tone. She was clearly enjoying the conversation though. "And that was him telling you your career was over before it began?" Now she was being cheeky, and I could feel my face growing red with a hint of anger. I did my best to hold it in.

"No, if you must know, he has another part for me. Something more involved than just a few lines."

"Okay, okay." She dialed it back. I could tell she sensed she'd hit a nerve and didn't want things blowing up any more than I did. "Very well. You take the afternoon for this little hobby of yours." *Little hobby* sounded dismissive, and I felt the anger welling up again, but quickly forced it down. She was still my boss, after all. And she was letting me go. No sense in becoming too entitled, especially if this part ended up being as much a flash in the pan as the last one. "Just do try to remember that the lion's share of your paycheck comes from the work you do here, not the lion over at MGM."

"Yes, Beatrice. Thank you."

"Now, how is that Pepsodent campaign coming?"

"Pearly white." I gave a big, toothy smile. I had to get at least some cheek into this conversation.

"Very well. You know, you might think of a way you can capitalize on this second job of yours and help out some of our clients. Some tie-ups, perhaps? Maybe your character could brush her teeth with Pepsodent. Then I really wouldn't have to justify your early afternoons."

"Yes, Beatrice. I'll see what I can do." I'd give it some thought, but I had to admit, I felt like I'd just gained the upper hand in our little tête-à-tête. I should have been the one asking her for favors. Instead, it was she asking me. If things continued this way, she'd be asking me for Vincente's autograph and a tour of the set. I turned on my heel and left the room before she could say anything else.

The following afternoon, I was at Adrian, Ltd. looking for a new dress to wear to my meeting with Vincente, when who should pass by the window but Winifred Jenkins. She waved excitedly at me then came inside.

"Mabs, darling, it's been ages! You were supposed to call me, you wicked girl."

"Winifred, so lovely to see you." We kissed cheeks. I can't say it was exactly lovely to see Winifred. But it wasn't unpleasant, either. Truth be told, I hadn't completely sized her up the two times we'd met and now, well, I was quite the different person than I had been, especially at our first encounter.

"A little bird told me Vincente has you cast in his next picture. So pleased to hear it. You simply must let me help you prepare."

A little bird? Just who had told her? And why did she always seem to show up shortly after my interactions with Vincente? Something about her I couldn't quite put my finger on made me wary of her invitation, but I decided to accept, nonetheless.

"Oh, would you?!" I poured on a thick layer of enthusiasm

"But of course, dear. And the first lesson," she said, grabbing the black skirt and blouse ensemble I had been considering, "this dress doesn't suit you, I'm afraid. Here," she continued, guiding me over to another section of the shop and handing me a rather sultry looking red dress with a keyhole neckline and slit that ran all the way up to mid-thigh. "Try this on for size."

I went into the dressing room and emerged a few minutes later. I should have felt a little silly, but quite to the contrary, I felt incredible.

I gazed into the full-length mirror and was almost surprised by what I saw. While I knew I wasn't homely, I'd always thought of myself as more pretty than sultry, more the farm-girl I'd grown up as than a knockout Hollywood starlet, but now I could see it. The red dress hugged curves that, until then, I never bothered to accentuate much. The ends of my blonde hair teased the collar of the dress just slightly. My deep blue eyes stared back at me, and I was enamored, like a modern day, female-version of Narcissus.

"It's perfect, Mabs!" Winifred cheered, clapping her hands together in delight. "Something's missing, though," she continued, putting a finger to her lips. "I know. You!" She snapped her fingers at the salesman behind the counter. "Bring me that black fascinator there." The young man walked obligingly over to the hat she was pointing toward and brought it over to me. I put it on and looked in the mirror. A tingle rushed through my body. Lana Turner, Lauren Bacall, Susan Hayward. They all had nothing on me at this moment.

"Yes! Yes! That's it! Mabs, you look stunning!" Winifred shouted, perhaps a bit too excitedly. "Now, there's no time to waste. You quickly change while I pay the bill, and we'll continue your education in my bungalow at the Beverly Hills Hotel." If the salesman behind the counter was at all shocked by this rather sordid sounding proclamation of hers, he didn't let on. Then again, I'm sure he was all too accustomed to such things, working for Adrian.

"Well, it's not much, but it's home," Winifred said flatly as we walked into Bungalow Number Five. I glanced through the French doors out to the private pool on the patio.

"Would you like to go for a swim? I love having a private pool. That way I can swim in the nude," she laughed. I didn't reply, but she didn't seem to notice. "I'll order us some Club sandwiches, and we can get to work."

Half an hour later, we'd both finished our sandwiches and washed them down with double gins-and-tonics. She lounged on her couch, and I sat at her dining table, wondering what would happen next.

"You certainly dress the part, Mabs. But now, we must teach you to *be* the part. Are you familiar with the work of Konstantin Stanislavski?" she asked.

"No."

"Well, he calls it the *system*. Others have referred to it as *Method* acting." *System? Method? Where on earth was she going with this?* "It's a technique of fully becoming the part you're playing. You must be the character you portray, Mabs."

"Okay." I still wasn't sure what her aim with all this was, but it sounded intriguing enough.

"I want to try an exercise with you. Please turn your chair around and face me." I did as she requested.

"Now, close your eyes. You are angry. Who are you angry at?"

I sat there in silence for a moment, my mind drawing a blank.

"Who are you angry at, Mabs?" Winifred asked again.

I was growing nervous more than angry. Something about Winifred held sway over me. I wanted to please her. I *needed* to please her. But to channel anger I wasn't feeling? "I don't know," my voice quivered.

"You do!" she shouted. "Go with your gut! Who are you angry at?!"

"My mother!" The words shocked me. I wasn't angry at my mother. How could I be? She'd always been so caring. She'd been the one who'd turned our little two-room shack of a house into a home, bringing love and comfort to an otherwise cold place. Even when it was twenty below outside and the winter winds howled through the cracks in our house, she brought warmth. How could I be angry at her? Yet, those were the words that immediately sprang to mind when I went with instinct instead of thought.

"Good! Good! Your mother is in front of you. Where is she?"

"She's lying on the floor." *That was an odd picture.* My mother never laid on the floor. She never laid anywhere.

"Why is she on the floor, Mabs?"

"She's drunk." *What was I talking about?* My mother had never been drunk in her life! She was a self-proclaimed teetotaler.

"Good. Now, speak to her!" Winifred barked the final three words at me as if I were a terrier.

"How could you! How could you do this to us?! Papa works hard every day for us! We barely have enough money to buy cornmeal, and you've gone and used it on gin!"

"Yes, Mabs! Let it out!"

"Do you have any idea what the people in town think of you?! Think of me?! And the schoolmistress! They look at us with such pity when we go into town each morning. That is, each morning we're not helping you out of bed!" *I'd never needed to help my mother out of bed. Who was this person inhabiting my body? My mother was caring and gentle and the picture of temperance.* "Papa tries so much to look past your actions, to forgive you. He has his vows to uphold. *In sickness and in health.* I made no such vow, Mother! I can't stay here and watch you destroy this family along with yourself!" I collapsed in tears, doubling over in my chair. The intensity of my emotions ran through me like an icy river, like the icy river that flowed near my childhood home. I screamed, a low, guttural, primal scream.

"Open your eyes, Mabs! Open your eyes!" Winifred was grasping both of my shoulders and shaking me rather violently. Clearly, this exercise of hers had spun out of her control. I opened my eyes and looked around. *Where was I? This wasn't the rustic shack of my childhood!* "Mabs. Mabs, dear! It's alright! You're safe now. Winnie is here. Winnie is here." She pulled me into her chest, her blouse soaking up the tears that were streaming down my cheeks.

"What just happened?" I was shaking, shivering.

"I don't know, dear. I'm sorry. I didn't think I'd uncover such deep-seated emotion just by asking you to get angry." She handed me a glass. "Drink this."

I took the glass from her and swallowed the clear liquid in one gulp. It counteracted the icy sensation that had just been enveloping me and warmed my insides. Calm began to return, and with it, not a small amount of shame. I barely knew this woman in front of me, yet I had just managed to bare a part of my soul I didn't know existed. I had to get out of there.

"I'm sorry, Winifred."

"Don't be, dear. While that must have been difficult for you, you've uncovered a real asset that will benefit you on set."

On set?! I'd just uncovered something, alright, but I didn't view it as an asset. "I'm sorry, Winifred. I have to go." I grabbed my purse and scurried out of the bungalow, desperately hoping no one outside heard my rage. I ran to the taxi stand and was grateful one was waiting there. I needed to get home.

CHAPTER 21
ONE STEP BACK

A shot of brandy can save your life, but a bottle of brandy can kill you.

— Cary Grant

Until I returned home that evening, I always considered myself a social drinker. Sure, I drank more than I should have on more than a few occasions, but it was always in the company of others, and it was always out of a sense of enjoyment. When I got home from Winifred's though, I was a wreck. My body anxiously shook the whole taxi ride back. Thankfully, the driver didn't notice or, if he did, didn't let on.

As soon as I was inside my apartment, I dropped my purse and poured myself two fingers of vodka, paused, then continued pouring two more. I quickly swallowed the lot and poured another half glass. I didn't want to think about what had just happened. I wanted it all to be a nightmare that I'd awaken from the next morning. But to awaken, I'd have to fall asleep. Half an hour and two more glasses later, I did just that right there on my couch. When I awoke, it was dark, and my head was pounding. So was someone at my door.

"Mabs! Mabs! Open up! It's me, Dagny. I need to know you're okay."

I rolled off the couch and crawled slowly to the door. With what little strength I had, I reached up and turned the handle, then collapsed again. Dagny squeezed through the door, stepping over my body.

"Oh, Mabs! What's happened to you?" She kneeled down to my side. "Are you okay? Winifred called me. She said you were over at her bungalow and left rather abruptly after quite the scene. What happened, Mabs?"

I laid on the floor, staring up at the ceiling. The nightmare was still running through my mind. "I need another drink."

"Oh, no you don't. The only thing you're having a drink of is strong coffee." Dagny left me on the floor and went to the kitchen to begin brewing some before returning to my side. She cradled my head in her lap and began caressing my hair.

"Tell me what happened, Mabs," she said softly.

"I was angry."

"Winifred told me as much, but why?"

"She told me to be."

"Winifred told you to be angry?"

"Yes, it was the *system*."

"What *system*, Mabs? Whatever are you talking about?"

"Stan something."

"Stan Freberg? What does he have to do with all this?"

"No, not Stan Freberg. Stan Slavski." A vision of Stan Freberg sitting in Winifred's bungalow suddenly flashed through my mind.

"Stanislavksi? The acting coach?"

"Yes, that's it. Do you know him?"

"Oh, Mabs," Dagny said sadly. "Winifred had you doing a Method acting exercise?"

"Yes, the Method! That's what it was called! My mother—"

"What about your mother? Do you want me to call her?"

"No, she was drunk. Passed out on the floor."

"Mabs, you're not making any sense. You're the one on the floor, dear."

"No, she took all our money and bought gin with it. Papa forgave her though."

"Mabs, you're worrying me. I've never seen you like this. I think I should call a doctor."

"No, don't go! No doctors!" I suddenly felt sick. "Oh, Dagny, I don't feel very well."

"Okay, okay. Let's get you to the bathroom. Can you stand?"

I didn't get the chance. I threw up all over the front of her dress. "Oh, Dagny, I'm sorry." I began to cry.

"No, no. It's okay. Is that all of it? Is there any more?"

"Oh, Dagny, you take such good care of me."

"There, there," she cradled my head above the mess I'd just made. "Here, let's get you over to the couch then get you cleaned up." She helped me lie down, then brought me a towel and wiped my mouth. "Now, you lie right there while I go fetch the coffee, then we're going to figure all of this out." When she returned to my side, she'd stripped off her dress and sat down on the couch next to me in nothing but her slip. I was glad we were good enough friends that she felt comfortable doing so.

Fifteen minutes and two strong cups of coffee later, I'd finally gained some semblance of composure. "What happened, Dagny?" I asked.

"I don't know, dear. I wasn't there," she said gently. "Let's try to figure it out together, though. You said something about your mother?"

As much as I wanted to forget what happened earlier that night, I thought back. "Yes, it was awful, Dagny. She was lying on the floor, drunk."

"But your mother never touched alcohol."

"I know, that's what I don't understand." I paused, then continued. "There's something else."

"What? What is it?"

"My mother had dark hair."

"But your mother has always had blonde hair."

"I know," I said, confusedly.

"You said you were angry?"

"Yes, Winifred told me to be angry. She asked me who I was angry at and that's when my mother appeared on the floor."

"The floor of Winifred's bungalow?"

"No, the floor of our little shack in Prairie River."

"This might sound like a strange question, but was it really your mother who was lying there?"

"Who else would it be?"

"I don't know."

We sat there for a few moments in silence. Was Dagny right? Could it have been someone else? But then why did I call her my mother?

"I think I want to lie down," I said.

"Okay. In your bed?"

"Yes."

"Do you want me to stay?"

"Would you?"

"Of course. Mabs. All night if needed."

"You're such a good friend, Dagny."

"Oh, I don't know about that. If it wasn't for me, you might not be in this mess."

"No, don't say that!"

"Well, it's true. I introduced you to Winifred, after all."

"It's not your fault."

"Okay, okay. Let's not worry about any of that anymore tonight. Here, let's get you to bed." Dagny walked me to my bedroom and helped me change into my nightgown. After she'd tucked me in, the last thing I remember before falling asleep was her singing an old Swedish lullaby I hadn't heard since I was very little, when my father would sing it to me.

Vyssan lull, mina kära små.
I världen glädje och sorger stå.
Mycket ska ni lära,
mycket ej förstå.
Var snara till att giva
och vänta ej att få
när önskedrömmar komma och fara.

I never learned much Swedish as my father rarely spoke it in the house, but for some reason, as I drifted off, the words were as clear to me as if Dagny had been singing them in English.

Fall asleep, my dear little one.
In the world, there is joy and sorrow.
You will learn much,
but much you won't understand.
Be quick to give.
Wait not to get,
When dreams come and go.

I had no dreams that night, or what was left of it. If I had, I couldn't remember them, which was likely a blessing. Dagny gently shook me awake.

"Mabs, Mabs, did you sleep okay?"

"Oh, Dagny, thank you for staying with me. I hope the couch wasn't too uncomfortable."

"It was fine. But how are you?"

"Still a bit of a headache, but I'll manage," I smiled. "What time is it?"

"Seven-thirty."

"I need to get ready for work."

"Are you sure? I did lay out something for you to wear and there's a pot of coffee and a plate of eggs, bacon, and toast waiting for you in the kitchen."

"Oh, Dagny, you are a dear! Thank you!"

"I'm just glad you're feeling better. You're sure you'll be okay?"

"I think so. Maybe I should lay off the vodka for a while though."

"Yes, dear. While I can't believe I'm the one saying so, I think that would be best. You gave me quite a scare last night. Now, I must be going unless there is anything else you need."

"No. Thank you again. I'll be fine." And I was. I even kept to my word and didn't have a drop of alcohol for the next several days.

Probably a good thing, too, because that afternoon, when I returned to my apartment, an awkward looking gentleman with close-cropped hair and thick-rimmed glasses was standing on the sidewalk, skipping about as if in a game of hopscotch.

"Stan!"

"Mabs!" I could tell he was mimicking my exuberant cheer more out of fun than actual excitement, although I knew he was pleased to see me as well. "I tried calling you a few times, but I guess a girl like you doesn't spend too much time at her apartment."

"No, I guess I don't. But it's so good to see you. Won't you come up?"

"I was rather hoping we might take a stroll. It's not every day the sun shines in L.A." He emphasized the rhyming scheme of *day* and *L.A.* The irony of the fact that the sun pretty much did shine every day in *L.A.* wasn't lost on me either. It was charming, and I immediately remembered how pleasant it had been chatting with him earlier that week.

"That does sound lovely. Let me just put my purse away and freshen up and I'll be back down in ten minutes."

"I'll be timing you," he said, looking at his watch with a grin.

When I got up to my apartment, I leaned against my door and felt my cheeks. I knew I was beaming. Stan definitely had an effect on me. And I wasn't the least bit ashamed of it either. Still, I wondered if I was in the proper state. So much had happened in the last few days. In the last day! Vincente was going to *cast* me in something—actually *cast* me—and there was that whole business with Winifred and *The Method* or *system* or whatever it was, and my mother, if it had indeed been my mother. *Was I really in a place to be starting a relationship? And with someone like Stan?*

I knew I would have to choose. A life with someone like Stan or one with Vincente and Winifred and red dresses and parties. From my conversation with Stan that night at Errol Flynn's house, I knew he largely eschewed the Hollywood scene, much preferring an early night with a good book. It had been a fluke that he'd been there at all. Something about it being a personal favor to Jack Warner, him needing an "upright eye" on his biggest star. Stan hadn't gone into it any more than that.

I didn't know what my future held. To be honest, I didn't want to know at that moment. I only knew that, for the rest of the day, it held a walk with Stan.

I freshened up and hurried back down. Stan looked at his watch. "Eight minutes, twenty seconds. Not bad," he joked.

"But who's counting?" I flirted back.

"Certainly not me," he smiled in mock innocence. "Now, why don't you show me around your neighborhood."

"My pleasure." I said, as he offered me his arm and we walked aimlessly around Santa Monica for what must have been close to two hours.

Mostly, we walked in silence, just enjoying each other's company. It was pleasant and, surprisingly at first, not the least bit awkward. I'd grown so accustomed to nearly everyone in my social circles loving the sound of their own voices, it was nice to be around someone who didn't need to jabber away. Especially ironic, really, given that Stan was a voice actor. If anything, all that made me the least bit uneasy was the occasional thought in the back of my mind that I wasn't being myself.

I hadn't told Stan that I was really a full-fledged copywriter. I hadn't told him about my fleeting part in *Scheherazade* or the call I'd received from Vincente. I certainly hadn't told him about what had transpired at Winifred's. Come to think of it, other than a few stories about growing up on the Canadian plains, he knew little about me. And he didn't pry in the least, so I left it alone. I knew the bill would come due soon enough though, and I dreaded that moment. For now, however, we just walked arm in arm.

"How about that liverwurst sandwich?" He said. "If you know a good place around here, that is."

I don't know why him bringing up the topic of a liverwurst sandwich set me off. Perhaps it was the thought that he knew little more about me than the type of sandwich I liked and that was entirely my doing. Or maybe it was the thought of a meat so thoroughly ground down as to be imperceptible as meat and my realization that I, too, was in danger of being run through the grinder in Hollywood and coming out completely unrecognizable. I couldn't do it. I couldn't do it to us, what little of us existed, and I couldn't do it to Stan. The time to choose had come. Although the better angels of my nature were pulling me toward Stan, I somehow knew the devil inside would eventually end up winning out. As much as I was being pulled in that direction, enough of my conscious still remained that I had to set him free.

"I'm sorry, Stan. I have to go." I broke free from his arm. "I really enjoyed our walk and you're a sweet, sweet man, but you and I, we would never work out."

He stared back at me, and I could tell he was a bit dumbfounded and a little hurt. I hated hurting him, but I knew whatever small bit of pain he was experiencing now was far less than what I'd cause him if I stayed.

"Farewell, Stanley Freberg. I will always remember you." I kissed him on the cheek, turned, and walked quickly away. I didn't look back and, after a few steps, quickened my pace. I had to get away before any second thoughts entered my mind.

CHAPTER 22
A FACE LIKE LANA'S

*Smart writers never understand why their satires
on our town are never successful. What they refuse
to accept is that you can't satirize a satire.*
— Hedda Hopper

When I got back home, I shut the door purposefully behind me
and locked it even more purposefully. I wasn't sure what I
was keeping out. Perhaps it was more a symbolic way of
keeping myself in. In any case, there I remained in self-inflicted
solitary confinement almost the entirety of the weekend. Other
than a walk to the beach and a visit to the grocer on Saturday, I
didn't leave. I called Dagny and spoke with her briefly to let her
know I was okay, but ignored the phone when it rang, fearful it
might be Winifred—or Stan—and not wanting to speak to either.

At work, I dug in like never before. I'm not sure if my
newfound sobriety helped or hindered my creativity, but Beatrice
sure seemed to notice.

"You've been awfully quiet the last two days," she said
Tuesday just after lunchtime. "Nervous about your meeting with
Vincente Minnelli?"

I wasn't, but it seemed like the perfect excuse. I certainly
didn't want to tell her about what happened with Winifred. "Yes,
that must be it," I replied, neutrally.

"Well, I'm sure you'll do fine. If you want to leave now
and clear your head on the way to MGM, feel free."

"Thank you. And thank you for letting me go. I'll make sure I'm in bright and early tomorrow morning." I'd like to say that I was pouring it on thick, that I still had hubris when it came to my relationship with Beatrice, but the fact is, I was thankful at that moment. The whole Method exercise and drunkenness that had followed, the painful scene with Stan, all were making me want to reform myself, to be a better person, at least off the set.

"Oh, don't worry about that. You have fun. And break a leg!"

I changed into the splendidly revealing ensemble Winifred had purchased for me and was at Vincente Minnelli office a half hour later.

"Mabs, so good of you to come down. Won't you have a seat?" I was always struck by how much the epitome of class Vincente was. When I was in a room with him, I felt like no one else mattered, that I was resting on a throne. "Let me tell you about this project I'm working on, darling. It's a story about Hollywood. The people who make it run and sometimes run others into the ground while doing so. I like to think it's the best kind of satire in that it's melodrama. But that's perhaps more than you want to know." He grabbed a few sheets of paper and continued.

"The part I have for you is as an extra. Not that you're an extra. Your character is an extra in the movie being made within the movie. She has two different scenes, both played as the lover. Do you think you can do that, Mabs?"

"Yes, I think so," I replied. The truth is, I didn't think at all before the words left my mouth and if I had, I wouldn't have been sure at all. But since this might be my big break after all, I had to say yes.

Vincente handed me the pages he was holding. "You're reading the part of Linda. You walk down the stairs and catch David in the arms of another woman. You're not jealous because you know you're only a fling for him, that this other woman is his true love. You're feeling rather proud of yourself, though, because you've been able to capture him, at least for the night."

I nodded. I certainly had no experience with anything like what he described. At least I wouldn't have to worry about breaking down into hysterics over the Method, though. I read through the character's lines and did my best to picture the scene.

"What's she still doing here?" I said, doing my best to capture the disgust I envisioned would be dripping from this woman's lips.

Vincente read the part of David, speaking to his love interest. "Go on, get out of here."

"The project is done, Joan. You're business. I'm pleasure," I said, arrogantly.

"Damn you, get out of here! Go back to the room!" Vincente cursed at me.

"Oh, by the way, Joan. I watched the movie. You did well." I read this last line as nonchalantly as I could, knowing it wasn't truly a compliment.

"Very good. Very good," Vincente said, breaking the scene.

"You think so?"

"Very much so. I think you'll do splendidly in this part. Now, you're going to have to do a screen test with the producer and some of the other actors. Will you be free again this Thursday afternoon?

"I'll make sure I am. Thank you so much for this opportunity," I gushed.

"You just practice those lines and you should have no trouble at your screen test."

Excited, I kissed him on the cheek and stood to go. As I was leaving, I wondered who would be playing this other woman. "Oh, Vincente, who do you have cast for the other part? The other woman?"

"Lana Turner."

"Splendid," I smiled. And it was, her being the closest thing I had to a Hollywood idol.

When I arrived at work the next day, Beatrice pretended to show restraint, but I could tell she was on the edge of her seat waiting to hear how my meeting with Vincente had gone. If I were to wager a guess, I'd say she was living vicariously through my *little dalliance* with Hollywood. Oh, she pretended not to let on, but I could tell she was enamored with it all.

That's why, the day after that, she nearly pushed me out the door at noon, a full three hours before I needed to leave for my screen test. I definitely had her wrapped around my little finger and was loving every minute of it.

As I walked up to the MGM main gate, Kenny tipped his hat and waved me through like I was a regular. I thought back to the first time I passed into this wonderland, when I'd accompanied Dagny to her screen test. Had it really been only four months? It seemed so much longer.

Then I remembered Dagny and her riding lessons. Wasn't next weekend her outing with Henry Fonda? My, how the past week and a half had flown by! Had she even booked any riding lessons in that time? Perhaps she had and hadn't told me. It was her date, after all. I would just be tagging along, rather uninvited, if I did end up going. I shook the whole business from my mind. While I certainly wasn't going to try Method acting again, I needed to get into character at least somewhat.

"What's *she* still doing here? What's she *still* doing here? What's she still doing *here*? You're business. I'm pleasure." I let the word *pleasure* escape my lips with the feel of silk, then punctuated it with a devilish laugh. I was determined to make Vincente proud and really sell my part in this film to whomever was there.

By the time I had my hair and makeup done and slipped into a sleek, black, mermaid-cut gown, I was ready. I *was* Linda. I'd never felt so confident in my life!

"Good afternoon, Vincente. Good afternoon, gentlemen." I greeted them all with a sultry gaze, doing my best to channel some femme fatale with my eyes half-closed. I could almost hear the seductive notes of a saxophone from one of those movies playing as I walked onto the set. A man and woman, stand-ins for Lana Turner and whomever would be playing the part of David, were there, ready to read their parts of the scene. I took a few steps up a staircase built on set, leaned over the railing, and delivered my lines, then glided sensuously up to the top, my hips swaying as I went, and out of what would have been the frame. I felt ecstatic, and if I'm to be honest, even somewhat aroused by my character.

"She's marvelous, Vincente! Wherever did you find her?" One of the men sitting next to him asked. Another leaned over and said something quietly I couldn't make out.

"That's wonderful, Mabs, darling. Please come back down," Vincente called to me.

I did so, walking as sensually back down the stairs as I'd walked up them. I didn't want to break character. Not because I thought I should continue acting for the men in front of me, but because I didn't want to. I was enamored by my role as this tramp.

"Mabs, Jerry here wants you to read for the part of Joan. Just to give it a try. No pressure. Do you think you can do that?"

The lead? This man, Jerry, wanted me to read for the lead role?! I nearly fell back in astonishment but managed to hold it together.

"Why, of course! I'd be delighted to, Jerry," I said as confidently nonchalant as possible, although I'm sure my widening eyes betrayed my real feelings.

"Splendid! Give her a script," Jerry said to a younger man standing near him. He ran the pages out to me.

"Now, don't worry about memorizing the lines this time, Mabs. Just read from the page as best you can," Vincente instructed.

I looked down at the words. I'd been playing the part of the tramp. Now I'd have to play, not her opposite to be fair, but certainly a character of purer motives. "Oh, David, why don't you come back with me? Life simply isn't a party without you."

The man temporarily cast as David read his part. "I can't, Joan. Don't you see? You're the star now. You belong in front of the camera. I belong here, in the shadows behind it."

"No, don't say that, my dear! I want you! I need you by my side! I need you to help me take that bow. I knew you might be upset with me coming here tonight. But I had to try. I had to coax you…out of the shadows." I paused to catch my breath in the middle of the last sentence. It was unintentional, but after reciting the line this way, I realized how perfectly the pause punctuated it. I sensed the rest of the people on set were impressed by my reading as well.

"Leave me, Joan. Leave me. Enjoy the light without me. You have to. I'm no good for you anymore."

"Very well, then." I said, softly, then turned from him. If I'd been a better actress at that moment, I could have forced a tear from my eye. Perhaps if I could master the Method, instead of it mastering me, I'd succeed. Whatever I did, though, it seemed to have been enough for the men watching me.

"Amazing!" Jerry clapped his hands. "Such range! And that face! Why, she rather reminds me a bit of Lana Turner!"

My mouth dropped open. *Had I really just been compared to my on-screen idol?* Even more incredibly, was I going to take the part meant for her? It was all too overwhelming. I felt lightheaded. I needed to sit down before I fainted. Vincente could tell.

"Mabs, are you okay? Come, have a seat here." He retrieved me from the stage and walked me back to his director's chair. Now I didn't just feel as if I was resting on a throne. I actually was, and it was more wonderful than I ever could have imagined.

CHAPTER 23
ASPIRING ACTRESS,
ASPIRING COWGIRL

*I've often said there's nothing better for the inside
of a man than the outside of a horse.*
— Ronald Reagan

The following day, Vincente rang me at work again. He got right to the point, not even bothering to say hello. "Mabs, darling, I just reviewed the film. The camera loves you even more than we did in person, if that's possible."

"Oh!" I exclaimed, a bit shocked by the suddenness of the call. Once I'd caught my breath, I continued. "That's wonderful, Vincente. What happens next?"

"Well, I'm afraid we can't sideline Lana and put you into her part, as much as I'd like to. Too much in the works already. But I am casting you for the part of Linda. If that all goes well, and I'm sure it will, I'll have something more substantial for you in my next project. Filming starts in just over two weeks, and we should be able to have both your scenes wrapped up in three or four days. I know you work at an advertising agency full-time, but I'm counting on you getting that week off."

"That shouldn't be a problem," I replied. I knew it wouldn't. Far from it, Beatrice would be positively over the moon when she heard the news. When I told her, she tried her best to play it straight, but the huge smile she was trying to suppress said otherwise.

"Well, aren't we going places, then?" she said. I suspected her use of the word *we*, carried a subtle hope that she would be taken along on my path to stardom somehow. I disregarded it. Not that I wished any ill-will toward her. After all, she'd given me my big break in advertising, something I'd never forget, but this new course was mine and mine alone.

★★★

That evening, Dagny called. "Mabs, I've been trying to reach you for days, you scoundrel! Where have you been?"

I realized, while she'd known I'd been with Winifred working on my acting, I'd never told her why. I'd never told her I had auditioned for Vincente's new film and now been cast. It wasn't an intentional omission, but I debated whether to tell her now. I chose to be forthright. After all, she'd cared for me so much the week before, how could I not?

"Dagny! You'll never believe it, and I am sorry I didn't tell you sooner, but it was just confirmed a few hours ago. I've been cast in Vincente Minnelli's new film! Just a small supporting role, but I'm so excited!"

"You haven't! That's wonderful!" Of course, being on the phone, I couldn't tell her expression, but the tone in her voice told me that she was genuinely happy for me and there'd be no repeat of that horrible time months before when she'd been overcome by jealousy. Perhaps, now, she knew her place. Perhaps, now, so did I.

"But I am sorry you haven't been able to reach me. How are your riding lessons coming along?"

"That's actually why I'm calling. Our Palm Springs adventure is next weekend and neither of us has ridden yet. Unless, of course, this part of yours is as a cowgirl," she giggled. I was touched that she'd said *our* Palm Springs adventure, confirming that I was to be included, even though, technically, Henry Fonda had only invited her, to the best of my knowledge.

"No, nothing like that. Quite the opposite, but I'll tell you all about it when I see you. I'm free tomorrow. Of course, I haven't a thing to wear so perhaps we should make a day of it. Shopping in the morning, riding in the afternoon?"

"That sounds like a wonderful idea. Let's meet at my apartment at nine."

"Splendid. See you then." I hung up the phone and smiled. What a life I was beginning to lead! Aspiring Hollywood actress. Aspiring cowgirl. Aspiring...*what else might lay in store for me?*

"Mabs, I know it's only been ten days, but it seems like it's been ages! It's so good to see you." Dagny said as I walked out of my apartment.

"I know! Where has the time gone?" We gave each other a small hug and kissed cheeks. It was a very *Hollywood* greeting and something we never would have done when we were younger, back home in Prairie River. It was terribly affected, but then, so were we.

"Well, let's get *duded up*!" She said, taking my arm.

"*Duded up*! Oh, you *are* funny. Yes, let's!"

We spent the better part of the morning visiting a handful of shops and picking out a few outfits for that day's riding lesson and the adventures in Palm Springs to come. We were tempted by a couple of mink stoles—we were going to something called the Mink and Manure Club after all—but decided on a bit of financial prudence and left them behind after admiring ourselves in the mirror with them on. We both ended up purchasing some silk shirts embroidered with lassos, mine yellow, Dagny's blue; denim jeans; and brown snakeskin boots.

After returning to Dagny's apartment to leave our purchases behind and change into the outfit of the day, we caught a taxi up to the Sunset Ranch in the Hollywood Hills. During the twenty-minute trip, I told her about my upcoming role as Linda and how it had all come about, starting with that first day she introduced me to Vincente Minnelli.

"Mabs, I'm simply delighted for you. I know I acted positively beastly when Vincente took to you that first day, and I'm sorry for that—"

"Oh, please, it's all in the past," I interrupted, dismissing her apology.

"No, I mean it. I just know there are big things in store for you! I will never be a star. The best I can hope for is enough work as an extra to pay the rent, and enough men waiting in the wings to pay for all the rest. That is to say, I don't regret my life. I have a good time. But to know where you're going, and to know I may be able to bask in the glow that will shine from your star, if even slightly, brings me great joy."

She was being honest with me, I knew. But, as had happened so many times before, I wondered if she was being honest with herself. *Did she really not regret her life?* I quickly pushed any doubt out of my mind. It wasn't my place to question, in any case. Besides, we were going horseback riding!

"Welcome, gals. I'm Bert." A cowboy that looked the part of Gene Autry in his earlier years came sashaying up. "Here for a horseback ride?"

"Yes," Dagny smiled. She was clearly smitten, but then who wouldn't be? Any girl who says she isn't in love with a cowboy just isn't being honest. "We're going riding with the Desert Riders in Palm Springs next weekend and neither of us have ridden a horse since we were little. We don't want to make *asses* of ourselves," she continued, repeating her pun from a couple of weeks before.

"Well, okay," he chuckled. "We wouldn't want that to happen. The Desert Riders, you say?" He let out a low whistle. "They are a fine bunch. Got a chance to ride with them myself a couple years back. As a matter of fact, Mr. Fonda used to board a horse here back in the day."

"No kidding?! He's who invited us!" I exclaimed, then realized I spoke out of turn and probably came across as a show-off. If I did, Bert didn't seem to notice. He was probably used to a whole host of stars coming up here.

"Well, isn't that a small world story. Now, follow me, and we'll get you saddled up." He led us over to a paddock where a half dozen horses were running about.

"Miss, I'm going to put you on Leo. She's that Appaloosa over there," he said, looking at me then nodding in the direction of a white horse with brown specks all over her coat. "And you," he said, turning to Dagny, "will be on Shadow, the black horse. Both of these ladies are very tame, perfect for first time riders, so you don't need to fret. I'm going to bring them out of the paddock, saddle them up, and help you on. Then we're going to ride up into the hills." He turned to walk into the paddock then turned back. "One more thing. What you're both wearing is fine for today and looks the picture of Veronica Lake, I'm sure. But you might want to get something a bit more comfortable and a bit less flashy if you're going riding with the Desert Riders next weekend." Dagny and I glanced at each other and smiled a bit sheepishly. I guess we had more to learn about the Desert Riders than we thought.

That realization was further put to the test over the next two hours. We had fun, and the views of Los Angeles below us were stunning for sure. But by the time we were done, our backsides were definitely sore, and we knew, first-hand and all too well, why cowboys walk with their legs so far apart.

"Well, Mabs, Dagny, you both take care. Enjoy your experience with the Desert Riders next weekend, and you come back and visit the Sunset Ranch anytime," Bert said as he helped us off our horses. As we got into our awaiting taxi, we glanced back and saw him tip his cowboy hat to us and wink, the low golden light of the setting sun casting a warm glow on his face. The moment was almost cinematic in its perfection. At least it would have been if my rear end hadn't been feeling the effects of the ride.

As soon as we got into the taxi and began to drive off, I turned to Dagny. "I don't know about you, but my butt is killing me!"

Dagny laughed out loud. "Mine too! I think we need to get a little something to wet our whistles and ease the pain."

"I second that." As I said it, I remembered that I had sworn off alcohol for a while just a week and a half ago. *Ten days was awhile, wasn't it?*

Perhaps it was the fact that it was a social drink instead of me trying to dull Method-wrought emotions. Perhaps it was because Dagny was being rather sober herself. In any case, I behaved myself. After a steak dinner worthy of the cowgirls we now were, paired with a couple of whisky sours, we returned to Dagny's apartment. There I retrieved my outfits—ones I wasn't sure I'd be wearing again after Bert's critique of them—and returned to my own apartment.

"Ta ta, Mabs. I'm so looking forward to next weekend in Palm Springs."

"Me too," I smiled. "Happy trails to us both."

When I arrived back to my apartment, I was exhausted from all that had happened that day. I quickly dressed for bed, then drifted off to sleep. My dreams were wonderful that night, unlike previous ones.

I was riding through the same hills and canyons we toured during the day. Beside me were Henry Fonda, Cary Grant, and Veronica Lake. My horse walked slightly ahead, and I could tell they were all admiring me. They were stars, but I was the biggest of them all.

"You were simply wonderful in your last picture," Veronica gushed.

"Yes, you are a shoo-in for the Academy Award this year," Cary said.

"You must star opposite me—no, I would be delighted to star opposite you," Henry added.

Then I stood on stage at the Shrine Auditorium. Olivia de Haviland was in the audience and somehow, I knew she should have won, but I didn't care. The crowd rose and applauded wildly, even Olivia.

"I'd like to thank Mr. Vincente Minnelli, for giving me my start in pictures. And my friend Dagny, for taking me to my first audition. And so many others, Dorothy Patrick, Sydney Guilaroff. Adrian, of course. And last, but certainly not least, my mother. This is for you, Mother." I held up the gold statuette and looked toward the middle of the crowd where she was seated.

The woman who smiled back was younger than she should have been, and her face was framed in flowing brunette hair. She was not the woman who I'd called my mother for nearly all my life. She was the woman from my Method-induced vision at Winifred's. One would think that my dream might have pivoted into a nightmare at that point, but it didn't. Seeing this woman, who my subconscious was calling mother, brought me a calm confidence. In my dream, I knew I had succeeded not in spite of, but because of her. Any anger I'd shown toward her weeks before was not only forgotten, it was as if it had never occurred.

Winifred was there too, seated front and center. I'd purposely not mentioned her. She gave a subtle nod that no one else could have possibly noticed. She knew she'd created me, molded me into what I had become like no one else. We both knew, however, it had to be our secret. Before I left the podium, a devilish smile, not unlike the one I'd revealed during my audition for the part of Linda, crossed my lips.

CHAPTER 24
MINK & MANURE

In dealing with a girl or a horse, one lets nature take its course.

— Fred Astaire

The next day, my body ached even more, and I was worried I'd be too sore to travel to Palm Springs, let alone ride horses again. All I wanted to do was lay in bed, or possibly a hot bath. *Oh, how I wished my apartment had a private bathroom. Maybe I could take my earnings from my role as Linda and find a new place.*

Thankfully, by the time Friday rolled around, my rear recovered, and my memories were only pleasant ones of riding the trails. It had been delightful being out in nature, even if it was just a scant thirty minutes from the hustle and bustle of the streets of Los Angeles. I'd lived in the city for almost two years and wondered why I'd never taken the time to visit the relative wilds of Griffith Park. Come to think of it, since leaving Prairie River, other than the occasional walk on the beach, my feet had rarely left pavement. I looked forward to venturing out to Palm Springs, an untamed wilderness compared to Griffith Park. I was also intrigued by just what exactly the Mink and Manure Club entailed.

Just after 10 a.m., while daydreaming about this very thing, Dagny called. "Well, are you all ready for our little *horsecapade?*"

"Mink and manure!" I shouted gleefully. "What time does our train leave?"

"One-thirty. We get in just before four."
"Grand. I'll meet you at the station at one."

When we arrived at our hotel—Henry Fonda had booked us a room at El Mirador—I was awestruck. The Byzantine tower that rose above us as we entered transported my thoughts not to Palm Springs, but to the Orient of Scheherazade. Palm trees, of course, were commonplace in Los Angeles, but the ones that surrounded us here seemed so much more exotic. I almost wished I'd packed some long flowing robes and veils for the visit. *If only Rudolph Valentino were still alive!* I imagined him descending the steps, dressed as *The Sheik,* and taking my hand then taking me to his harem.

"Isn't this marvelous?!" cried Dagny, reading my mind.

"A dream of a thousand and one nights," I replied.

"Well, we'll have to do with only two," she smiled. "Come on, let's check in."

We walked into the lobby. Our luggage was already there. With the magic that surrounded me, I almost forgot that the hotel had sent a man to the station to gather our things. I wasn't yet a Hollywood starlet, but I was already being treated like one and I relished in it. A broad smile crossed my face.

"Look, Dagny! They've brought our bags!" She seemed indifferent and I reminded myself that she'd probably been on at least a few trips like this before. I quickly composed myself, not wanting to make a spectacle.

"Miss Lundberg, Miss Eriksson, we have your suite all ready for you," the man at the desk said, raising his hand to signal the bellhop over. "If you'd just follow Douglas here, he'll show you the way,"

When he showed us to our suite, I was in awe once again. The sitting room between our two bedrooms was nearly twice the size of my apartment and appointed with hand carved furniture. The floor was covered in red tile, and the afternoon sun cast its rays through the leaded glass French doors, bathing everything in a warm glow.

"I could live in this room forever," I sighed.

"Well, we only have three hours to get ready for Mink and Manure," Dagny said, bursting my bubble ever so slightly. "But I think that gives us time to order a bottle of champagne. Henry's paying, after all," she added with a wink.

As we sipped our champagne and nibbled on a plate of dates and cheese that arrived with it, Dagny filled me in on what we could expect of the weekend, recounting her conversation with Henry a few days earlier. "Tonight, it's strictly a fashionable affair. There'll be plenty of cowboy hats and snakeskin boots, of course, but thankfully no manure I'm told."

"No bullshit?" I joked.

"Oh, there might be some of that. We are in Hollywood East, after all." We both laughed.

"Not much time to enjoy the room tonight though, I'm afraid. We're being picked up at 6:30 a.m. sharp tomorrow for our ride into the desert."

"Ugh," I moaned, already feeling tired.

"Well, at least we don't have to worry about breakfast. We may be riding into the desert, but we'll eat like kings and queens. Steaks cooked over an open flame, along with eggs, bacon, pineapple, and plenty of cowboy coffee."

"Mm, I can hardly wait," I said, licking my lips before taking another sip of champagne.

"But now we should ready ourselves for the evening ahead." Dagny drained her glass, and we parted ways to our own rooms, each of which had a full bath of its own.

I probably spent a good twenty minutes in the shower, something I never could have gotten away with at my apartment, what with three other girls waiting to use the bathroom and using up all the hot water. Pure heaven! And all the more decadent knowing we were in a desert.

We both spent so much time getting ready, we arrived fifteen minutes late to the Ranch Club. Not that it was a problem. Others continued to stream in far later than Dagny and I.

"Dagny, delighted you could make it," Henry greeted her with a peck on the cheek. "You must be Mabs." He gave me the same greeting. I managed not to swoon. Then he looked over my shoulder and called to someone.

"Hey, Bob! Come over here. This is the gal I told about," he said, calling to someone halfway across the room, then turning his gaze back to Dagny.

I turned my head and came face to face with Robert Taylor.

"Ladies," the heartthrob said with a tip of his black Stetson. Although nearly eight years older than he'd been when he starred as Billy the Kid, he looked as though he were on the set. His mustache was perfectly trimmed, and he didn't have a hair out of place

The evening's festivities continued until well after midnight. Johnny Boyle and his wife, Tani, captured the room, alternating between his famous cowboy ballads and her native Hawaiian tunes. Allen Jones charmed us all with his *Donkey Serenade* and the room roared with laughter when a white horse—in this case, two people in a costume—nudged up to him. Veronica Lake, Don Ameche, Bruce Cabot, and, yes, even Cary Grant were all there.

While I'd spent many an evening mingling with stars equally famous back in Los Angeles, doing so here seemed so much more genuine. No one put on airs. No one needed to impress another. If Hollywood really did exist beyond the facades of the back lots, it was here. No Western sets. No lights. No cameras. Just the action. I felt more relaxed than I had in a long while. Cary found me sipping a Moscow Mule from its copper cup a half hour later and struck up a conversation with me.

"A Moscow Mule. Seems fitting for this evening," he said as an introduction. "Of course, I hear they've all been reduced to eating mules in Moscow these days." His words came across with a hint of lament so that I wasn't sure if this was meant to be a joke or not. Either way, a radiant smile quickly returned to his face. "Hi, Cary Grant," he added, extending his hand.

"Good evening, Mr. Grant. Mabs Eriksson," I replied, taking it.

"Please, call me Cary. Is that a Canadian accent I detect?"

"How keen you are! Yes, it is." While all Cary had to do to draw a woman to him was flash his pearly whites—maybe not even that—the fact that he knew me to be Canadian after a scant six words made me even more enamored. It also reminded me we were both subjects of the Crown and the affinity that went along with that helped too.

"I love Canada. Anytime I'm feeling a bit homesick for England and I can't hop across the pond, I try and get to London, Ontario. Have you been?"

"I'm afraid not. I'm from a dot of a town in Eastern Saskatchewan. It definitely wouldn't remind you of England."

"I'm sure it's quite lovely."

"In its own way." I suddenly felt a pang of homesickness, what with our talk of it and the picture of Prairie River popping into my head. I briefly wondered what my parents and my sister would be doing just then.

"Oh dear. Have I just said something to upset you?" he said, sensing the subtle change in my mood.

"No, not at all. I was just reminded of home."

"Oh. Do you miss it?"

"I haven't thought about it in months, to be honest, so I guess not. Truth is, Saskatchewan feels a world away." I suddenly grew a bit distant myself as I said this. "It's funny, but the girl who lived in Prairie River, well, I don't think I'd even recognize her if she came up to me on the street. But enough reminiscing." I shook my head. "It's nothing I want to think about now. At least nothing a turn on the dance floor won't fix."

"Then, if I may have the honor…." He raised an upturned palm, and I accepted as Johnny Boyle began to play *Twilight on the Trail*. Cary's grace was legendary even then, but as he led me softly and slowly across the dance floor, I was as light as an evening's desert breeze and understood, just like the cowboy in Johnny Boyle's song, what real contentment meant.

CHAPTER 25
SADDLES AND SMOKE TREES

There ain't never a horse that never been rode;
there ain't never a rider that can't be thrown.
— Gary Cooper

By the time we returned to our suite at El Mirador, removed our makeup, and retired to our beds, it was nearly half past one. I briefly debated staying up all night, but my heavy eyelids quickly won out and I was fast asleep before long.

I awoke what seemed like only minutes later when Dagny knocked on my door at half past five.

"Wake up, Mabs! It's time to channel our inner cowgirls!" She cheered, walking in.

"Ugh. I'd rather channel my inner Sleeping Beauty," I moaned, throwing a pillow over my face.

"Okay, okay. I don't know how you can be all sunshine and rainbows after only four hours of sleep, but okay," I chided her.

"Better than lemons and vinegar," she said. I made a feeble attempt at throwing my pillow at her, but it only made it three-quarters of the way to the door. "You missed, dear. And if you don't hurry up, you'll miss Cary Grant!"

This woke me up. I remembered his smile from the night before. He was more radiant than even the sunniest day!

"I hate to admit it, but you're right. I didn't think it was possible to be starstruck after attending as many parties as we have, but *Cary Grant*!" I squealed like a girl half my age, but only for a moment before catching myself and realizing how ridiculously immature it sounded.

At 6:30, we were seated on a bench just outside the lobby, dressed in our embroidered shirts, blue jeans, snakeskin boots, and white Gambler Cowgirl hats. Henry rolled up in a white 1936 DeSoto Custom Convertible Sedan.

"Ready to ride the trails, ladies?"

"Giddy up!" Dagny cheered.

Fifteen minutes later, we pulled up to a corral of horses at the mouth of the Palm Canyon Wash and were greeted by the most peculiar sight. A woman with a deputy's star was seated on her horse and had a man tied up at the end of a rope. They all seemed to be in good spirits, though.

"Not to worry, ladies. This is all part of the fun. This is Pete's official induction into the Desert Riders.

The woman dismounted her horse, walked over to the man named Pete, and planted a kiss right on his mouth. Everyone howled.

After a few moments of this, another man sitting atop a beautiful brown Dutch Warmblood and wearing a sheriff's star piped up. "Okay folks, for those of you who are new," he turned his glance toward Dagny and me, "we're going to be riding up the wash to Smoke Tree Mountain. Don will cook up some steaks, then we'll descend down the Theilman Trail. The whole affair should take a little over four hours. Back in time to get ready for lunch, although I suspect you won't need it after the spread Don has for us."

Everyone started saddling up. The *deputy* led a pair of Morgan horses over to us, already saddled up. "This is Tahquitz and Kewet. Now, they can live up to their names. Tahquitz is the god of thunder and lighting, among other things, and Kewet means *fiesta* in the local Indian dialect. They can be a bit lively at times, but they'll both take good care of you on the trail today."

"I'm up for the challenge," I said, as I put a foot in the stirrup and lifted myself onto Kewet like I'd done it a hundred times before. I hoped I'd be able to continue with such ease over the course of the morning.

Dagny climbed onto Tahquitz, and Henry jumped on a shiny chestnut colored Arabian with a perfect blaze down its nose. The group slowly started toward the wash. Near the front, I spied Cary looking as dapper as ever.

The four-mile ride up the wash was stunning in its beauty and offered so much to take in. Smoke trees and creosote bushes abounded. Rabbits scampered away in front of us. Friendly little lizards scooted from beneath our horses' hoofs. An occasional bevy of quails scurried about. I never would have imagined a desert was so full of life.

It must have been a little too full of life about a mile into the ride. About thirty feet in front of us, one of the horses reared and its rider was thrown off. The other horses around it got a bit skittish, but their riders were able to keep them under control. The rider who'd been thrown started laughing and then everyone around him started laughing with him.

"George took a crupper!"

"Hey! A three-pointer, George!"

"Welcome to the Caterpillar Club, George!"

Took a crupper? Caterpillar Club? My, what interesting phrases they had.

After forty-five minutes or so of riding, we came to the top of Smoke Tree Mountain and the view was nothing short of breathtaking. The air offered a refreshing crispness and the sun, now a good way above the horizon, bathed the valley below in its golden rays. The smell of steaks cooking on an open flame reminded me of how hungry I was.

"Here we are," the Trail Boss called out as he dismounted his horse.

As with the night before, everyone seemed completely at ease. Perhaps even more so. No one feared any writers from *Variety* or *The Hollywood Reporter* up here. We sat around the campfire, some of us at rustic picnic tables, some of us on rocks, and drank strong coffee out of tin mugs and ate our steaks and eggs off tin plates.

"Get enough to eat?" Cary plopped down on the seat next to me, a steaming mug of coffee held comfortably in his hand. Dagny sat at another table, fawning over Henry again.

"Oh, good morning, Cary! Yes, thank you. Nothing like a steak cooked over an open flame."

"Food always tastes better after a good ride. But I'm sure this is all old hat to you, growing up on the prairie," Cary replied, taking a sip of his coffee.

"I'd like to say so, but fact is, we only had one horse. A donkey actually, and a rather pathetic one at that. I suspect he's been turned into glue by now."

"That's a shame." Cary gave a slight frown and sipped at his coffee.

"Maybe, although perhaps not after the hard life he led. Either way, I'm glad I'm not a donkey!"

"Perish the thought. You're only the finest breed of filly."

"You are sweet." It was a rather silly line, but I was flattered by it.

"Well, I'd ask you to dance again, but I don't hear any music. Perhaps our horses can prance back down the canyon together after breakfast."

"It's a date!"

"At the risk of sounding trite, what's a girl like you doing in a place like this?"

"Well, Dagny over there"—I nodded in her direction—"she was invited by Henry. We often tag along together, and I definitely wasn't going to pass up this opportunity. I haven't left Los Angeles since moving there a year and a half ago."

"Well, I'm so glad you did, and my only disappointment is that we haven't crossed paths earlier."

I blushed. *What a charmer! English men definitely were different.* Dagny could have Henry. The rest of the women in Hollywood could have Bogie and Errol and all the other *tough guys.* Just leave Cary for me. "Well, I do hope our paths cross again."

"I'll see to it," he said with a smile. He paused for a moment and the smile turned to a subtle frown as he appeared to be pondering something. "It will have to be some time though. I'm set to leave Tuesday for filming in Germany. I'll be gone for three months, I'm afraid."

"Oh, that is too bad. But at least you'll be closer to England should you miss it."

"Yes, a small consolation. But what if I should miss Los Angeles?"

"I hear Spain is rather similar," I offered.

"But it doesn't have you."

I blushed again. Then any further increase to the heat of this little romance we were enjoying was saved by the bell. Or the triangle, in this case.

"Okay folks, last call for grub," Don called out.

"I couldn't eat another bite," I said to Cary, gently patting my stomach.

"Now," said the Trail Boss, "we have a nice surprise for you all. School's back in session here in Palm Springs, and the high school choir has come all the way up here to fill the hills with their voices."

The morning had already been incredible but what happened next made it out of this world. A group of ten boys and girls started walking out from behind a rock, dressed in matching white shirts, blue jeans, and cowboy boots. As they walked, they began to sing.

"We ride across the shifting sands,
Up to the canyon's spreading fame.
The glory of the world is ours.
Snowcapped peaks and desert flowers.
Oh! Hear the God of Tahquits call,
Oh! Come ye Desert Riders all.
And with the spirit that makes us one,
Arise and greet the morning sun."

Cary leaned over while they sang and whispered in my ear. "This is the *Desert Riders Hymn*. Written by one of the members. It always makes me smile. Although I do miss England occasionally, I do love it here in Palm Springs. I may just move here one day."

The choir continued to sing a few more traditional cowboy ballads and then it was time to mount our horses and return to the valley. I don't know if it was an unwritten rule to not talk on the way back, but no one did. We just enjoyed the peace of our surroundings and each other.

CHAPTER 26
MISS ERIKSSON

I turned my hair dark and have received much better parts ever since.

— Joan Bennett

OCTOBER

A fantasy I could never have imagined a year ago, was now a reality. A dozen stars I hadn't even seen from afar just a few months before, had surrounded me for two days. Top among them, Cary Grant. Sure, they hadn't manifested their counterparts in my literal dream of the week before, gushing over me and my future performance, but some of them knew I was credited with a part in Vincente Minnelli's next picture. That made me, at least in a small way, part of their club, and maybe even earned a modicum of their respect. It was splendid. And the manifestation of this fantasy was just beginning. I was now only hours away from fulfilling that credited part.

I'd now been to MGM many times and knew my way around. When I walked through the gate, Kenny tipped his hat as if I was a regular. Though I'd already acted in a movie—spoken lines even—this was different. I was the *supporting actress*! I also somehow knew, unlike the *Scheherazade* picture, this one would make it to the silver screen.

The feeling was electric as I walked into my dressing room. *My* dressing room! My name even adorned the front of it!

Just a few months had passed since that first audition, and I was on the cusp of becoming a star. I wasn't even sure how it happened. After all, I'd never truly sought it out. It was a fluke occurrence. Being in the right place at the right time, and right it was.

"Good morning, Miss Eriksson. May I take your coat?" The girl doing my makeup and helping me dress smiled at me as I slipped it from my shoulders. "Mrs. Rose has two gowns she's chosen for today's shoot. Let me help you try them on."

It was all so incredible! *Miss Eriksson.* Not since grammar school had I been called that and then it was certainly with different intentions. "I think I'll try on this black and white one first," I replied. She unzipped the dress I'd worn from home that morning then helped me dress in my costume. It was beautiful and sultry. *I* was beautiful and sultry. I admired myself in the full-length mirror. Like the day at Adrian's weeks before, my reflection knocked me out. I pursed my lips, giving myself a subtle kiss, cognizant that there was a wardrobe girl standing two feet away. She probably knew this was my first big role, but I wasn't going to let on if she didn't. "Yes, this will do nicely. I don't think there's even a reason to try the green one on, do you?"

"No, Miss Eriksson. Now, let's do your makeup." Her reply was very demure. Even if she disagreed with me, she wouldn't have said it out loud. I loved it!

An hour and a half later, everything was done. Sydney Guilaroff even came in to personally do my hair, which, in this case, also involved dyeing it black. I thought back. Six months ago, I had my hair styled for the first time before attending my first Hollywood party with Dagny. At the time, I thought it was grand to be coiffed by Charles, who simply studied under Sydney. Now I was having my hair done by the man himself!

"Mr. Minnelli is ready for you, Miss Eriksson," another girl said after knocking on my dressing room door and poking her head in.

"You'll do splendidly, Miss Eriksson," Sydney said, as he helped me rise from my chair and quickly fixed a few hairs into place. I must admit that I was a bit nervous and his words and doting on me were just what I needed. I left my dressing room ready to knock them dead. *Lana Turner, eat your heart out!*

"Ah! There she is. Good morning, Mabs." Vincente smiled. An assistant director came over and led me to my mark, then someone else with a light meter came over to take a reading next to my face. The set buzzed with the activity of a dozen stagehands. They were like a swarm of bees, and I was the honey. Then she walked in.

"Good morning, Miss Turner," greeted the assistant director.

"Good morning, Lana," smiled Vincente as Lana Turner walked over and gave him a kiss on the cheek. Three more voices greeted her as she made her way toward me. This was it! A star I had only admired from my seat at the theater, standing a mere three feet away. I was determined not to gush, to play it straight. After all, while we may not have been equals, we were now colleagues.

"You must be the girl playing opposite me. Lana Turner." She extended her hand, and I took it. The feeling of our palms touching was electric. I was head over heels. Yet, I managed to maintain my composure. Maybe I was destined to act after all.

"A pleasure to meet you, Miss Turner."

"Oh, please, call me Lana. We may all use formalities on set at the beginning, but I believe good actresses must come to know each other more intimately to truly make a scene believable. Even if our characters are not, shall we say, *friendly*."

"Yes. Of course. Thank you, Lana." I wondered if she felt the electricity between us as well or if she treated every other actor this way.

"And here's our star! Good morning, Kirk," Vincente shouted gleefully as Kirk Douglas walked on the set.

"Let's make a movie!" Kirk exclaimed, a determined yet cheery grin on his face. I could immediately tell he was full of energy and an unstoppable drive. I liked Vincente and wanted to please him with my performance, but with Kirk, I knew I *needed* to bring my best.

Our scene together went more splendidly than I ever could have hoped for. I flubbed my first take just slightly. Nothing so bad that it seemed to irritate anyone. The second take went well enough. By the third, we were wonderfully dynamic, and Vincente said so. Still, he asked for one more, just to be sure.

"Okay, that's a wrap," Vincente called out, clapping his hands. You're free to go for the day."

While we were headed off the set, Lana came up to me. "I'm headed over to the Retake Room after I change. Do you know it?" she asked.

"Yes," I nodded, thankful that I'd been there before so I could continue what was becoming less and less a charade and more and more my actual life.

"Splendid. I'll see you there," Lana smiled, then spun and glided off toward her dressing room, leaving me alone for the first time.

While there was the faintest hint of doubt that this might have still been a fantasy, I'd almost fully internalized that it was real life. Of course, if I'd been outside myself, viewing that morning's events like a dream from afar, I'm sure I would have fainted on the spot. Instead, just like Lana, but in no way trying to imitate her, I glided off toward my dressing room as well, with a huge grin on my face that I couldn't contain.

I walked into my dressing room and was briefly surprised, in a pleasant way, by my appearance in the mirror. I really was stunning, even more so with my new black hair.

"Well, hello good looking," I breathed at my image candidly, my wardrobe girl not having returned yet.

A few minutes later, she popped her head in and asked if I needed any help getting my makeup and costume off. *Why not?* I thought. It certainly wasn't every day I got this treatment so I might as well take full advantage of it.

Twenty minutes later, I walked back out the Main Gate, smiled at Kenny as he tipped his hat once more, and waived down a passing taxi.

"Retake Room, please."

"Yes, ma'am," the driver said with a smile. He looked at me in the rearview mirror. After a block, he spoke again. "If you don't mind me asking, I know I know you from some picture, but for the life of me, I just can't place it."

My thoughts wavered. Sure, he was just a taxi driver, but he mistook me for a star, a star who was actually on the silver screen. I contemplated coming clean and telling him the truth, but I was too caught up in the moment. I was, after all, a star, even if my scene hadn't yet premiered to the wider world.

"Oh, that is kind of you to say. It's hard to know what you would have seen me in. There are just so many movies being shown these days, aren't there?" It wasn't exactly a lie. The three sentences, standing alone, were one hundred percent truthful. Who was I to blame if he inferred something different?

"Well, whatever picture it was, I know it was fantastic. I guess I'll just have to keep watching," he replied. Luckily, I didn't have to carry this farce any further as he came to a stop in front of the Retake Room.

I took two quarters from my purse and placed them in his hand. "Well, ta-ta. See you in the movies," I smiled coyly.

"Ta-ta," he replied with a subtle longing in his voice. Sure, he was just a taxi driver, but he was also my first fan.

I walked through the door and had a brief—and rather unwelcome—flashback to the first time I'd been there, Winifred's face smiling rather devilishly at me. I shook the thought from my head. I knew I'd have to face her again someday, but I wasn't going to focus on that now. At that moment, I was about to have drinks with Lana Turner as a room full of Hollywood royalty looked on.

CHAPTER 27
RETAKE

I think the mirror should be tilted slightly upward when it's reflecting life—toward the cheerful, the tender, the compassionate, the brave, the funny, the encouraging, all those things—and not tilted down to the gutter part of the time, into the troubled vistas of conflict.

— Greer Garson

"**M**abs, over here!" Lana waved with a smile. I waved backed and crossed the twenty or so feet to the bar. "I'm so glad you could join us," she said, kissing cheeks. "This is Greer Garson. Do you know Greer?"

I did know Greer, and not just from the movies. I knew her from the week before. She'd been at the Mink and Manure Club.

"Why, Mabs Eriksson! I knew you recently contracted with MGM, but I didn't think you'd already found our secret little hideout. So good to see you again. Did you enjoy yourself at the Mink and Manure Club last weekend? I *am* sorry we never had the opportunity to chat. So many of us there this time, and unfortunately, my filly wasn't in a condition to ride the canyons the following day. Sore muscles, the poor dear."

Contracted with MGM? Secret little hideout? An apology for not seeking me *out?* Apparently, my reputation was grander than I'd imagined! What did these women know that I didn't? Greer was certainly under the impression that I'd signed a contract with MGM even though I'd done no such thing. And just why was Lana inviting me for drinks?

"Mabs, have a seat here, dear," Lana instructed, patting the barstool next to her. "We understand you're new to things and we want to do what we can to help you."

Help me? I'd always heard actresses were incredibly jealous and catty, not willing to give those new on set the time of day, let alone help them. This was almost too much, but I was determined not to let the moment get the better of me.

"Of course," I said, not sure how else to respond.

"Greer here took a quite conventional path and did some very respectable stage acting in Birmingham before being discovered by Mister Louis B. Mayer himself. Me, I was discovered at a soda fountain. Well, we've both experienced our ups and downs but, as you probably know, my personal life has been much more fraught with difficulties. I probably fall in love too easily, and out of it…" She let the last sentence drift off. Why was she telling me her life story? I wasn't sure, but I wasn't going to interrupt her to ask.

"Manipulation, Mabs!" she exclaimed, quite suddenly and vociferously. "Our publicity men think we're stupid. Our business managers treat us like children. Directors are convinced they're gods, and we're just a bunch of marionettes. And the studio! The studio created us! We were nothing but dust and clay before they came along and molded us into what we are today, if you ask them! Maybe they're right. They do own us. That's for sure. Maybe they did create us. Maybe if Billy Wilkerson and Zeppo Marx hadn't found me, I'd have ended up like my mother, a two-bit nightclub singer and alcoholic."

"Two-bit nightclub singer and alcoholic?" I asked, cautiously.

"Well, one outta two ain't bad," she responded with a wry smile, then took the martini glass next to her and downed the rest of its contents, including an olive, in one gulp.

"Those are fifty-fifty odds," she continued. "If only my dad had been that lucky at the poker table. We'd still be living in

Wallace. Probably running the whole damn town." She let out a small hiccup. "But where are my manners? Teddy, get Miss Eriksson here a martini!"

The man behind the bar promptly brought over a glass filled to the brim with the strong elixir Lana was drinking. After listening to her monologue, I needed it.

"Well, here's to beating the odds," I said, toasting her.

"To beating the odds!" Greer chimed in, lifting her own glass.

"Yes, I like that. I like that a lot," Lana said, raising hers, which somehow had refilled itself in that moment. After having gone on a rather fiery rant, Lana's beautiful smile once again returned at these last words. She took a sip and continued, more calmly. "But here I am, going on, probably scaring you half to death, and I haven't let you get a word in edgewise. Of course, I haven't given Greer here much of an opportunity to speak either, but she's English. Their kind don't talk much anyhow. Right, Greer?"

"At least not until I've had another drink!" Greer chimed in. "But do go on, Mabs. How are you liking MGM?"

The floor was mine and I was speechless before these two extraordinary women. I took another large swallow of my martini and let the gin lubricate my mouth and my mind. "Simply wonderful. I do like Vincente very much. He doesn't seem at all like the directors you were describing, if you don't mind me saying. I just hope I can continue living up to his exacting standards. Perhaps I should give Winifred another chance." I said this last sentence as an aside, more to myself than to Lana or Greer. I'm not even sure why. Neither of them probably even knew Winifred.

"Winifred Jenkins?!" Greer exclaimed with a cheer. "A wonderful woman! Why, we wouldn't be where we are without her."

"My heavens! Really?" I replied. I had my doubts about Winifred, but Greer's approval made me think I was being too critical. I briefly wondered if Winifred had run them through the same Method exercises as I'd gone through. Had they fared better?

"Oh, yes. Has she put you through the Method exercises yet?" Lana added, a sly smile crossing her lips.

I visibly swallowed.

"So, she has. Not to worry. It's a big jarring at first but you'll find them invaluable as you progress," Lana continued. "In any case, you do as she says, and your star will rise."

"Oh, I shall. I shall," I nodded quickly.

"But enough of this, girls! Let's end the afternoon on a high note," Greer chimed in. "A toast! To your first role, Mabs!" We all clinked our martini glasses together then downed what little liquid was left.

"Well, thank you so much, Lana, Greer, this has been an enlightening conversation to say the least." As we stood to go, I reached in my purse to pay for my drink.

"Please, Mabs. We have a rule here at the Retake Room. Us veterans pay for the drinks the first time out. When you get your first recognition in the *Reporter*, though, you must buy a round for the whole bar."

"Seems fair enough," I smiled, then put my money back in my purse. The electricity I'd first felt between us hit again as we left the bar and she touched me on the shoulder as we said goodbye.

Months ago, I'd been smitten just to have hair like Lana's. Three weeks earlier, I nearly fainted at being compared to her on set. Now, all I wanted was to mold myself after her as much as possible, to be a star shining bright in the sky.

CHAPTER 28
STAR-CROSSED LOVERS

How does it happen that something that makes so much sense in the moonlight doesn't make any sense at all in the sunlight?

— Lana Turner

The filming of my second scene, which only featured a brief interaction with Kirk and none with Lana, went off well. We completed it after five takes. To be honest, without Lana to play against, it was more of a challenge. She *carried the scene* as Winifred would say. Then it was back to reality—the *old* reality. At least for now.

"Well, look who finally decided to grace us with her presence." I knew Beatrice was being sarcastic—undoubtedly because of her latent jealousy—but it was still a terribly catty thing to say. I had half a mind to slap her. I'm sure I would have if she wasn't the one playing at being in charge. "But, truly, Mabs, how was the *dream factory*? And what have you done with your hair?!" She twirled around gayly as she said this, no doubt trying to envision herself there.

"You know, if you tap those ruby slippers of yours, you might just find out," I said, cheekily. She looked down at her shoes. They were a dull brown. I laughed to myself. *I bet she thought she really had ruby slippers on for a moment. Ha!*

"But my hair, do you like it? They dyed it black for the part, and I think it suits me. I think I'll keep it this way."

"Well, then. Don't you have some cheek to you?!" she, said, choosing to respond only to the first part of my comment and trying to act incensed. It didn't play well on her.

"Come now, Bea. Surely, you're not really cross," I said, suppressing another laugh.

"No, I suppose not," she replied. "But it is good to have you back in the office. Things just weren't the same here without you." I almost felt sorry for her. She was technically my boss, yet I was the one calling the shots.

"Well, it's good to be back then. What are we working on?"

"A new client. Woodbury Soap."

"Aren't they with J. Walter Thompson?"

"Nationally, internationally, they still are, but they want to bring us on board for something very specific, tie-ups and celebrity endorsements. I'm hoping you can use some of those connections you've made over at MGM to help with that. Their man is coming here this afternoon. A Mr. Carlisle."

While she blathered on, my first thoughts were of Greer and Lana. I don't know who Beatrice thought she was—or *I* was, or the actresses over at MGM were—but I wasn't so full of myself that I'd march into their dressing rooms and ask for them to push *facial cocktails*. They might think I was making a crass comment on their beauty! *"A skin you'd love to touch."* *Oh, honestly!* But then she mentioned this man, Carlisle. My mind went immediately to that evening at Clio's five months earlier. *Could it really be the same man who brought me martinis all night and charmed us at dinner?*

"Mabs?! Mabs Eriksson?!"

So, it was him!

"One and the same! Carlisle, so good to see you again," I smiled, walking up to him and extending my hand in a dainty handshake. He leaned in and kissed me on the cheek."

"Beatrice told me we'd be working together but I didn't believe it until you walked through that door. 'Hawking soap!' I said to Bea. 'Surely not Carlisle! He wouldn't get his hands that dirty!" I laughed at the ironic pun I'd just made.

"Well, don't tell anyone, but dear old Dad got me the job. Said I was a lazy bum, and I couldn't just spend my days at the yacht harbor and on the tennis court," he replied with a self-assured grin on his face. "I told the old buzzard that I did no such thing. 'I also spend quite a lot of time on the golf course and at Santa Anita, I'll have you know!' I told him!" Carlisle punctuated his comment with a hearty laugh.

"Oh, Carlisle, you're too much!" I joined in, shoving him gently on the shoulder. "But I won't tell anyone if you don't. This isn't my real gig either. Just finished shooting a picture with Lana Turner and Kirk Douglas," I said in mock seriousness.

"Well, aren't you two fast friends," Beatrice said as she popped into the lobby.

"Yes, Carlisle and I go way back. Met at a little soiree in Brentwood a few months back." I gave him a sly smile.

"Brentwood. Oh, that *is* charming. Well, why don't we go back to our conference room and get some of your ideas down on paper, Mr. Carlisle," she responded, then added sardonically, "at least the ones about soap."

"Never use the stuff myself. They don't call it bathtub gin for nothing," he joked.

"Yes, well," she replied. Her lips curled into an awkward frown, realizing he'd bested her attempt at a joke at his expense.

We sat down in the conference room and for the next hour or so, proceeded to talk about soap, mostly at the direction of Beatrice and one of the newer copywriters in our office who sat in. As for me, I found it hard to concentrate on anything other than Carlisle's charmingly handsome smile and picture-perfect teeth. *Why, he should have been working for Pepsodent, not Woodbury, with teeth like that!*

I'm sure I must have contributed a few ideas during the meeting. I do remember saying something about Lucille Ball and her new radio show. *Favorite husband. Favorite soap,* or something to that effect. I'm quite sure Beatrice thought it was brilliant. I'm also quite sure I rolled my eyes when she said so. Honestly, it was such a bore I couldn't wait to get out of there.

"That was simply ghastly, wasn't it?" I breathed at Carlisle once I had walked him back to the lobby and we were out of earshot of Beatrice. Not that I cared much at this point what she heard.

"Must keep up appearances, I suppose," Carlisle responded. "Better than making the stuff, though. Do you have any idea what goes into soap?"

"Not the faintest. To be honest, I thought soap was just soap."

"Well, it's horrid stuff. Makes you wonder why we put it on our skin. But it seems to work. Of course, the old buzzard seems to think *I* work too!" He let out another laugh. "Look at me, though, going on about soap when I have a perfectly lovely girl standing in front of me. You know what I'd like?"

"I can't imagine," I said, playing somewhat hard to get.

"Enough of this *Woodbury Facial Cocktail* nonsense. I'd like a real cocktail. With gin. And vermouth. How about it? Can I buy a girl a drink?"

"That would be simply wonderful," I said, batting my eyes. "Now let me just grab my purse."

Once down on the street, he hailed a taxi. "Beverly Hills Hotel," he said after we were seated. I'm sure there was no connection between Winifred and him, but I still blanched at his words and the memory of that horrid evening inside her bungalow.

"I do enjoy the Polo Lounge, don't you?" he asked.

"Oh, yes. Very lovely," I said, a bit absently, doing my best to erase from my mind the phantasm of me screaming at my mother—or whomever she was—herself a phantasm, that evening weeks before.

Carlisle started in recalling some regatta he'd been a part of off the coast of Rhode Island that summer, and something about a young congressman named Jack Kennedy. It was all terribly fascinating, and any thoughts of Winifred quickly disappeared.

The thirty minutes it took to get to the Beverly Hills Hotel quickly passed and our taxi pulled up to the red-carpeted entrance where one of the smartly uniformed staff opened my door. It may have been a rather mundane Monday, we may have arrived in a nothing more than a taxi, and I may have worn a simple houndstooth skirt and jacket. Still though, I felt rather glamorous walking into the Polo Lounge clinging to the arm of such a handsome bachelor.

"What do you think of the new pink hue on this building?" Carlisle asked as we entered.

"Oh, I think it's quite charming. Reminds me of a summer sunset," I said.

"Mm." I wasn't sure if the sound that came from his pursed lips meant he agreed, disagreed, or was indifferent. I didn't much care either. At that moment, I would have felt a warm glow about me even if the sun had long since set.

Being that it was a pleasant evening, though, and still warm and clear, we chose to sit on the patio. A waiter came over to take our order.

"Two martinis. Dry. With a twist. Caviar and toast points. That will do for now but leave the menus."

"You really take charge, don't you, Carlisle?" I said, admiringly. He'd been charming that first evening we'd met. But the room had been so filled with other people like Maritta Wolff and Helen Douglas—and my head had been so filled with the effects of all the martinis I had—that I truly didn't notice just how charming he was. Now he was here in front of me, on a mostly deserted patio with nothing to intoxicate me but his smile and the handful of stars that were beginning to appear. I moved my gaze from his and up to the sky. His followed.

"You know, if all these dreadful palm trees weren't in the way, we'd be able see Venus appearing near the western horizon," he said, quietly.

"The goddess of love..." My words drifted off into the ether, perhaps directed at Venus herself more than anyone else.

"I should take you out on my boat some evening. That's always the best way to view the stars. We could sail to Catalina Island. Have you been?"

"That sounds divine, darling. I've only been once, on the ferry, but that was in the light of day." It was divine. I'd just met him for the second time and already he was talking of a moonlit sail to Catalina Island. I slowly returned my gaze from the sky and back to his, but my mind still played in the clouds.

"Your martinis and caviar, madam, sir," the waiter said as he placed our items on the table, breaking my reverie.

"Well, here's to the stars," Carlisle said, raising his glass.

"To the stars," I cheered, fully aware of the double meaning, even if he wasn't.

After we finished another round of martinis and the tin of caviar, Carlisle ordered himself a steak and me a filet of sole. I didn't mind that he ordered for me. There was a fish resting on my plate, but I was his catch that evening.

He continued to talk, mostly about himself and his yacht and his society friends back in Rhode Island, but I didn't mind. I hung on every word that fell from his perfect lips. He could have been reading from a chemistry textbook, and I would have been his, such was the chemistry between us.

An hour later, we finished our meal and Carlisle signed for the bill. Evidently, he had an account at the hotel. We then walked toward an awaiting taxi, and I felt the glamour of holding onto his arm and striding down the red carpet once again. Certainly different than the last time I'd exited in haste and tears.

"Now, you live in Santa Monica, is that right?"

"Yes," I said, a bit disappointed that the evening was apparently coming to a close so soon.

Carlisle paused, perhaps aware of the disappointment in my voice, then continued. "You know, the night is still young, and I have the most wonderful view of the night sky from my patio. Venus has already set, but perhaps we could spot Cassiopeia."

"You amaze me, Carlisle. All this knowledge of the stars. Yes, that would be lovely."

We arrived at his home in Pacific Palisades about twenty minutes later. It was a beautiful art-deco affair. Not as lavish as some of the homes I'd been to, of course, but quite respectable for a man of his station, even if that station—and the house—were clearly inherited.

Around the back and over the rooftops of some homes to the west, I could see the ocean crashing against the shore in the distance—and those stars, although I didn't have the faintest notion which ones were Cassiopeia.

"Oh, your home is simply wonderful, Carlisle. Such a stunning view."

"It will do for now, but what I really need is one nearer the marina. It's such an arduous journey to get to the yacht, you know."

"I can't imagine," I said, truthfully. Part of me knew it was a terribly shallow and conceited thing for him to say, but that made me admire him even more. He was a man who knew what he wanted and wasn't afraid to go out and get it, even if it was with the *old buzzard*'s money.

We walked up the path to his porch and when he dug in his pocket for his keys, I tugged him closer and embraced his arm. "That was a wonderful dinner. Thank you." I was new to romance in nearly every way. Indeed, I'd played at it on the set before I'd even imagined it in reality. Perhaps the acting had prepared me in some way. I channeled my character, Linda, and put any nervousness I had about what was about to happen to the back of my mind.

"My pleasure, darling."

"But we never ordered dessert," I said coyly. Truthfully, I wasn't much for sweets of the confectionary kind.

"I believe there's a bit of leftover tart in the kitchen," he replied while he opened his front door, and we walked inside.

"I was hoping for something a bit more…filling," I said, while running my hand over his chest and imagining what Linda might have said at a moment like this.

He turned his head toward mine, took my chin in his hand, and lifted my lips toward his. "You know, they say gentlemen prefer blondes," he said, a glint in his eye. "I must not be much of a gentleman, because I much prefer you with dark hair." Then he kissed me.

This was it. This was the moment I'd been thinking about for weeks, even before I knew Carlisle would be the aim of my desires. Tonight, the tart in the kitchen didn't matter. Tonight, the only tart that mattered was me.

CHAPTER 29
EVERY DAY'S A
SATURDAY IN HOLLYWOOD

*All alike, you men. You only want the satisfaction
of being through with us first, that's all. So far, I've
had the good fortune of beating you to it. So, I am
heartless.*

— Greta Garbo

I awoke at a quarter past six just as the stars began to fade into
the grayish-blue tint of a pre-dawn sky. A champagne headache
throbbed behind my eyes, but I delighted in it, the dull pain a
physical reminder of the pleasure the previous night carried.
Carlisle slept soundly next to me, his bare chest glistening in the
faint light that began to seep into the bedroom.

I considered rising and going to the window, perhaps to the
kitchen to fix some coffee. The night before hadn't offered time
to explore his home. There'd been no time for anything other than
the feel of his arms as they wrapped around my waist, lifted me
up, and carried me to where I now lay. I felt my neck, then let my
hand work its way slowly down my body, gently touching the
places he had kissed me, arousing memories of what had occurred
the night before.

I imagine many women would fall in love. The first time,
a handsome man, the morning after. A warm glow, a soft light, a
passionate embrace. He knew all the right things to say, and his
touch was a perfect balance of tenderness and strength. At some

point, Sarah Vaughan serenaded us from his phonograph with *A Hundred Years from Today*. It was perfection. Vincente couldn't have directed it better himself. And I enjoyed it, but I was not in love. *Should I have been?*

As if sensing my conflicted emotions, Carlisle rolled over in his sleep and wrapped an arm around my waist. I bristled slightly. It's not that I didn't want to feel him against me again. I just didn't want to feel him now. I gently removed his arm and the sheet that was draped over my body and rose out of bed. He mumbled quietly in his sleep, protesting my absence. I wondered, though, was it *my* absence? I imagined I was only the latest in a long string of girls he invited back to his home with the promise of a starry sky. But I wasn't jealous. Not in the least. I'd have done the same.

I grabbed a blanket that had migrated to the floor in the midst of our passion and wrapped it around me, then walked to the kitchen. I opened cupboards and drawers looking for coffee. It must have made an awful racket despite me trying to keep quiet because, before long, Carlisle appeared.

"Good morning, darling," he said. *My goodness! Even fresh out of bed, his hair in a tousle, and wearing nothing more than a pair of wrinkled pajama pants, he looked irresistible!*

"Good morning. Sorry to wake you. I was just looking for the coffee."

"Never mind that," he said, closing the distance between us and wrapping his arms around my body. I instinctively lifted my face and let his lips graze mine. "Mm," he sighed into my mouth.

I let his lips—and his hands—linger for a moment longer, then broke away. "The coffee, dear?"

"Let's go out to breakfast."

"But I have to get to work, darling," I pouted. "Even if you don't," I added, with a wry smile.

"Oh, that old bird Bea won't mind. Why, you can tell her we were doing product research!"

I snorted slightly at his line, then let him drag me off to his bedroom to *study*.

When I waltzed into the office a full two hours later, Beatrice was waiting for me, hands on her hips and a definite frown on her face. "Just what's the excuse for your tardiness, today, Mabs?" she scolded.

I was on cloud nine after the night, and then the morning, with Carlisle and couldn't care less about her demeanor. Truly, I should have spent the day with Carlisle. She should have been grateful I was showing up at all. "Oh, go chew on a bar of Woodbury, why don't you." The words slipped out without a thought. I knew them to be too brash as soon as I said them, even for Beatrice.

"Well, I never! Some girls have all the luck, but I wonder if it's all worth it. I have the right mind to tell that woman she can shove it—" she exclaimed but abruptly cut herself off mid-sentence and put a hand to her mouth as if she'd said too much already. Then turned on her heel and marched back into her office.

What was that about? All the luck? To tell that woman she can shove it? What women? Me? Some client of ours? I wondered briefly then dismissed the questions from my mind. I decided I'd crossed the line and chose to patch it up by playing it off as a joke. I followed her into her office where she was already seated at her desk, looking quite frazzled and pretending to keep herself distracted by pushing papers around.

"So, you don't like it? For the campaign, I mean."

She looked up, a slightly hurt, slightly confused look on her face.

"We get Tyrone Power and Gene Tierney to team up again as their characters from *That Wonderful Urge*. Instead of tossing perfume bottles at him, though, she tosses soap. We end with a product shot and the announcer stating *'Ladies, you may not be able to clean up his act, but with Woodbury Soap, at least your*

skin will shine!'. We run it between the newsreels and the feature."
I pursed my lips and put a hand on my hip, waiting for her reply.
I was quite impressed with what I came up with on the spur of the
moment, if I do say so myself.

"Why, Mabs! I *am* sorry. I had no idea that was part of a
campaign. It's brilliant!" Her demeanor changed instantly, like a
puppy rebuked by its owner, then quickly forgiven. It was quite
pathetic, frankly. Far from pitying her, I was now rather disgusted
by Beatrice.

"Well, then, I guess my work here is done!" I said,
triumphantly, then turned on my heel, walked out of her office,
right past mine, into the lobby, into the elevator, and out of the
building. I imagined her staring after me as I went, not sure what
to think or do.

When I stepped out onto the sidewalk, I let out a rather
boisterous laugh in spite of myself. An older gentleman passing
by took an exaggerated path around me, only further amusing me.
Now, what to do with the rest of my day?

I walked to the phone booth on the corner, plopped in a
nickel, and rang Dagny.

"Dagny, darling! I feel like we've been terribly missed at
the Bel-Air, don't you? Gather your suit and meet me there in an
hour!"

"Mabs, is that you? What time is it? What day is it?" She
sounded half-asleep, three-quarters upset, and drunk on a fifth of
gin.

"Dagny, are you alright?"

"I don't know." She began sobbing.

"Don't go anywhere. I'll be right over." My sympathy, any
feelings really, for anyone else had waned considerably over the
past few months, but it still remained for Dagny. I hung up the
phone and hurriedly waved down a taxi.

Thirty minutes later, I was at the door to her apartment. My
mind flashed back to the day, six months before, when I'd last
found her in a similar state, eating figs in the dark. I tried the door
and found it unlocked.

"Dagny, what happened?!" She was laying on the floor, an empty bottle of gin next to her.

"He's gone," she moaned quietly.

"Who's gone?" I probed.

"Kenneth."

"That man who accompanied us to those parties at Philomena's and Clio's?"

"Yes," she began sobbing loudly, no doubt being reminded of the gay times she had with him.

"But I didn't think you—what about Henry Fonda?" I said, interrupting myself mid-sentence. I knew mentioning that her relationship with Kenneth had seemed to be superficial at best wasn't the appropriate response for the moment.

"Oh, don't be silly, Mabs. You know Henry Fonda isn't interested in me. But Kenneth! Kenneth! Oh, sweet Kenneth!" she called out, rolling onto her back, and flinging her arms wide. "I thought he was the one."

"But what happened?"

"I happened, Mabs. And, yes, Henry Fonda happened. Burt Lancaster happened. Rory Calhoun happened. That charming bartender down at The Mocambo happened, as did the one at Chasen's. And Romanoff's. And Chateau Marmont. Why, even the young man who operates Angels Flight happened," she said, referring to the boy, not more than nineteen, who operated the funicular railway on Hill Street. I briefly thought about making some bon mot about him giving her a ride but kept it to myself.

Still, while not exactly a surprise, her list was quite a shock. After all, I'd only just been with a man for the first time the night before. "Oh, my," I said.

"Don't judge me too harshly, Mabs." Her words were not a rebuke, but a plea.

"No, of course not. But I still don't understand. What happened to Kenneth?"

"He moved back to Cincinnati. Said his dad wanted him to take over the family business but he needed to settle down with some nice church girl his parents had set him up with. Oh, he was nice enough about it, I guess. Said I'd been a lot of fun and that he'd never forget me. What happened, Mabs? Where did it all go so wrong? Didn't we used to be nice church girls?"

I wasn't sure how to answer. Yes, we'd gone to church, and we were nice enough growing up. There wasn't any other choice in Prairie River.

I sat down on the floor next to her and began stroking her hair. "There, there, Dagny. Surely another suitor will come along."

"Of course one will," she said, a bit angrily. "And another after him and another after him. But I'm just so exhausted caring about what people think. Putting on a show both on set and off. None of it's real."

"Sure it is." Dagny's words scared me. She was making too much sense. She was sounding too much like me—the *old* me of six months earlier. I needed to pull her out of it. "Come on, Dagny. Let's gather our suits and head down to the Bel-Air. We can make eyes at Robbie and drive him wild. We'll get businessmen visiting from Kansas City or Chicago to buy us drinks. We'll get all dressed up—I'll call Charles to come do our hair—and we'll head down to the Cocoanut Grove or Ciro's and dance until dawn."

Dagny sniffed away a tear. "But isn't it Tuesday?" She paused, then continued, a suspicious look on her face. "Say, why aren't you at work?"

"Dagny, dear, every day's a Saturday in Hollywood."

CHAPTER 30
MAI-TAIS AND
HANDSOME GUYS

Well, you know what they say in Hollywood—the
most important thing is being sincere, even if you
have to fake it.

— Cesar Romero

"Well, if it isn't Mabs Eriksson and Dagny Lundberg. Welcome back to the Bel-Air, ladies," Robbie Wagner was positively beaming at the sight of us. I'd borrowed a bathing suit from Dagny, and we looked the perfect pair, sisters but for my new black 'do, which Robbie immediately picked up on. "Mabs, I love what you've done with your hair."

"It suits me, don't you think?" I said, running a hand through my locks. "But tell me, Robbie, what on earth are you still doing here?! Don't get me wrong, I am pleased to see you, but I'd be so much more pleased to see you on the lot at MGM. Dagny, we should make some calls, get him an audition." Dagny didn't respond. I could tell she was still feeling melancholy.

"Robbie, why don't you bring over a couple of Mai-Tais. This afternoon, we're celebrating!" I cheered.

"Right away. What are you celebrating?"

"Being alive, Robbie. Being alive!"

"I can drink to that," he smiled. "Well, I could if I wasn't on duty."

"What time are you off?" I asked.

"Five."

"Splendid. You'll join us for dinner then," I said in the moment, then quickly realized that it would be awkward if he did. Thankfully, I knew the invitation would go unaccepted in any case.

He left to retrieve our Mai-Tais, and Dagny looked over at me. "Mabs, what's happened to you?"

"Why, whatever do you mean?"

"You are a completely different girl than the one I met on Sunset Boulevard six months ago. You are certainly different than the girl I grew up with in Prairie River. Maybe you have been for a while, but I guess I hadn't fully realized it until now." She sounded concerned.

"Isn't it wonderful?" I replied, completely disregarding that concern. "And I have you to thank! You and Hollywood!"

At that moment, Robbie returned with our drinks. "Here's to Hollywood!" I exclaimed, taking both glasses, handing one to Dagny, and toasting the marvelous place we found ourselves in at that moment. Dagny half-heartedly raised hers in response.

"Come now, Dagny. It'll be alright. I promise," I said, sympathetically.

"You really think so?" she sighed.

"Yes! We're going to finish these fabulous drinks Robbie just brought over. We're going to play in that pool over there," I nodded in the direction of the water. "Then we're going to buy ourselves a couple of new cocktail dresses and go out on the town! Why, by this time tomorrow, you won't remember him." I intentionally didn't use Kenneth's name so as not to remind her of him any more than necessary.

"Okay," she agreed, passively.

"And when you eventually do think of him," I added, "it will be with relief. He has to face the rest of his life in *Cincinnati* running his father's business and getting henpecked at home. Meanwhile, you'll still be here. Hollywood!" I cheered again and raised my glass before taking another large sip. "Now, come on."

I grabbed her hand, barely giving her a chance to set her drink down, and pulled her toward the pool.

After another couple of Mai-Tais and half an hour of bouncing a ball around the pool, Dagny finally loosened up. A big smile crossed her lips, and she laughed out of pure joie de vivre. Robbie brought us some fried egg sandwiches around two and we worked on our tans in the waning autumn sun.

"Just think, Dagny. It's probably snowing in Prairie River right now. Isn't it just grand to be living here?" I said, looking over at her. "Sunshine, Mai-Tais, and handsome guys!"

"Yes. Yes, it is." This time I could tell she meant it. "Do you mean Robbie?" she added.

"Well, yes, him too. But no. I didn't tell you, I spent last night with Carlisle."

"So that's why you're so cheery, you tart!"

"Well, there was a tart, but it was me he ended up having for dessert."

"You scoundrel!" She picked up the crumpled napkin next to her and tossed it at me. "Tell me more," she demanded, lust in her voice.

"Oh, it was wonderful, Dagny. He was wonderful. And you should see his…" I paused, letting her mind wander and her eyes widen as I decided how to finish the sentence. "…house. He has a magnificent view of the ocean."

"Oh, Mabs, I'm so happy for you." Her words sounded a bit forced, but sincere, as if she truly wanted to be happy for me but was still pining over Kenneth. I couldn't help but smile. I was happy for me too.

"But we should get going. The shops will close soon, and we simply must find something to wear for tonight!"

"You're right. But let's get one more Mai-Tai before we go. Oh, Robbie, dear!" she called out.

CHAPTER 31
POLKA-DOTS AND PINEAPPLES

If there is one thing that is foreign to me, it is shopping for pleasure. On the other hand, I believe that it is right to honor all those who create beautiful things and give satisfaction to those who see me wearing them.

— Grace Kelly

"Goodness, Dagny! A few hours ago, I could barely convince you to get off the floor of your apartment to have some fun. Now, look at you. Go easy on that Mai-Tai." I wasn't sure when she'd finished the bottle of gin I'd found her with that morning, but I did know both of us were on our third poolside drink and, being that we planned to dine at the Cocoanut Grove that evening, I wanted her to pace herself.

"I'll have you know, I've trained for nearly a decade to be able to down a drink like this," Dagny giggled.

"Very well, then. But we do need to get going."

"Oh, you're right," she pouted, slightly. "It's just so relaxing here by the pool!"

I knew if I didn't get her going soon, she was liable to fall asleep right there on the sun lounge. I would too, the drinks and the warm afternoon sun were draining the energy from me. I pulled her up, we got changed, and soon we were off to Bullock's to pick out some cocktail dresses for the evening.

I don't know what compelled me to do it. It certainly wasn't out of necessity, for I had enough money, but while Dagny was trying on a series of dresses and I was picking through a rack of silk scarves, I came across a black one with white polka-dots that I simply had to have. Perhaps it was for the sheer thrill of it, but instead of putting it aside with a plan to pay for it, I quickly looked around and stuffed it into my purse. A tingle rushed through my body.

"Did you find something you like?" Dagny asked, walking up behind me. I flinched. Had she seen me?

"Oh, yes. Um, I rather like this pineapple print here. Should be perfect for the Grove this evening, don't you think?" I said, grabbing a white, peplum top dress with pineapples and hula girls on it that was within arm's reach. It would have stuck out at the Cocoanut Grove more than Jane Russell's breasts in *The Outlaw*.

"Oh, very funny. I'm being serious though, Mabs. You're the one who was in such a rush to instigate this little spree. I've found something to wear this evening so chop-chop!"

Instigate? Spree? Shopping spree or crime spree? What had she seen? I wondered again but then pushed it out of my conscience.

"Very well then, you help me pick something out."

She did, and we found a sleek, dark red, bias-cut pencil skirt with matching jacket and pillbox hat. I loved it! A pair of shiny red heels and a white blouse would complement it nicely. While it certainly wouldn't stick out like the pineapples, it was an unconventional enough look that I was sure to be noticed. I looked rather like one of those new air hostesses who were beginning to fly around the world! My polka-dot scarf would have to wait for another evening to make an appearance, though.

CHAPTER 32
COLD FISH AND
ERRANT MONKEYS

Deep down I'm pretty superficial.
— Ava Gardner

'd been to the Grove before. I'd even been pulled onto the dance floor and twirled around by Howard Hughes a time or two. But it was always on a Saturday night. Somehow, going out on a Tuesday seemed different. More *scandalous*, even if I had just told Dagny that every day was a Saturday in Hollywood. Somehow, I felt as if I owned the room before I even set one foot through the door.

I surveyed the room and spotted Lana Turner and Ava Gardner at the bar about twenty feet away. "Well, if it isn't Mabs Eriksson. And who is that despondent looking thing standing next to her?" I heard Lana say. I don't know how my ears were able to pick it up from across a room of merriment. I just hoped Dagny's hadn't. She was definitely in much better spirits than she had been that morning, but after lounging by the pool and shopping, she'd backslid slightly. Perhaps it was a latent melancholy, perceptible only to those with an actress's intuition.

I descended some steps, Dagny in tow, and crossed the floor.

"Well, Ava, if there's one thing we both can attest to, it's Artie's tongue on that clarinet reed!" I could hear Lana laugh as I got closer. She'd clearly changed the subject now that we were coming nearer.

"Too true, Lana! Too true! He has to be good for something beyond tooting his own horn, now doesn't he?!"

"Say, we should start a club! We could call ourselves the Six Sisters!"

"I can never remember. Are you number two or three?"

"Depends. Do you count Jane?" Lana said with a laugh, wrapping up her banter with Ava then, without missing a beat, turning to me. "Well, hello Mabs. We were just discussing ex-husbands. I'm sure you'll learn all about that soon enough."

"Oh, do stop, Lana. Let's give the poor girl a chance. You know, I hear Clark Gable is single again," Ava offered.

"What about Jimmy Stewart?!" Lana added.

"He's much too quiet. And too tall!"

"You know what they say about tall men."

"Ahem, when you ladies are through trying to fill my dance card, let me know," I interjected.

"Your dance card?!" Ava roared. "Is that what the girls are calling it these days?! Really though, Mabs, we're just having some fun. Fun is the name of the game on a Tuesday, don't you know?"

"Yes, this is Hedda Hopper's night off. We can be ourselves for a change," Lana added.

"Here's to that old bat having at least one night off a week," Ava cheered, raising a coupe of champagne. She looked at me again and added, "But who's your friend? She looks like she needs a drink!"

"This is Dagny. She's the one who got me into acting," I said, grabbing Dagny's arm and pulling her, quite literally, into the conversation.

"Well, Hollywood owes you a debt of gratitude, my dear," Ava bowed, somewhat mockingly, then grabbed another champagne coupe and foisted it into Dagny's hand. "So, tell me—Dagny, was it?—What pictures have you been in?"

"Um," Dagny hesitated.

"She did a little something with Henry Fonda a few months back," I interjected with a fib, saving her.

"Oh, we love Hank. Don't we, Ava?" Lana said. "Always good for a few laughs at the Derby after a day of filming."

"Excuse me, girls. I need to go powder my nose," I said. I don't know if Dagny was thinking about Kenneth again or was simply overwhelmed by the scene, but I had to snap her out of it—again. "Are you coming, Dagny?" I tugged at her arm.

"Oh, yes, of course," she replied absently, and I carried us off to the powder room.

We were halfway there, weaving in between the crowd, when, out of the corner of my eye, I caught Judy Garland walking up to the microphone. I wasn't going to pay much attention. After all, I'd seen her here before and, at that moment, snapping Dagny out of her melancholy was what I was focused on. Still, as we walked, I couldn't help but hear the words of the song that began to emanate from her lips.

"You're only a baby. You're lonely, and maybe someday soon you'll know," Judy breathed, each word falling away like the last rays of sun on a day you'd rather forget.

Who was the baby? Dagny? Me? I wondered.

"With fate it's no use competing. Youth is so terribly fleeting," Judy continued.

I tried to block her words out of my mind as I looked at Dagny. "Dagny, you told me, several months ago, that I was acting the cold fish. Now it's my turn. Life's too short to worry about the past. There's never been a better time to live for the moment!

"By dancing much faster, you're chancing disaster, time alone will show," Judy continued.

"Now, I want you to go back out there and have some fun! Find a guy to pull you out onto that dance floor, then pull you into his arms," I said, grabbing her by the shoulders.

"Poor little rich girl, you're a bewitched girl. Better beware. Better take care." Judy's tempo began to quicken.

So did my words as I prodded Dagny on. "Let him seduce you. Let yourself be seduced. Do you understand?" I raised her chin and looked into her eyes.

"The life you lead sets all your nerves a-jangle. Your love affairs are in a hopeless tangle. Though you're a child, dear, your life's a wild typhoon!" Judy crescendoed.

"Yes, okay," Dagny nodded hesitantly, a peculiar fear in her eyes.

"In lives of leisure, the craze for pleasure steadily grows."

I dismissed Dagny's fear out of hand and dismissed Judy's words from my mind. Neither of them was going to stop me tonight or any night.

"Cocktails and laughter, but what comes after? Nobody knows."

I knew. More cocktails and more laughter. The party was just getting started and I didn't give a damn about how it was going to end.

"You're weaving love into a mad jazz pattern, ruled by stars and moon. Poor little rich girl, don't drop a stitch too soon."

My life wasn't going to be ruled by stars or moon or Dagny or Lana or Vincente or Winifred or anyone else. I was going to rule my own life now. I was going to rule Dagny's, and the rest of the night, at least, she played her part. Whether to please herself or please me, I couldn't care less. She was distracted and amused and that's all that mattered. At one point, I even caught her laughing obligingly at one of Zeppo Marx's ghastly jokes. I had other matters to attend to though.

"There you are!" Lana exclaimed as I rejoined her and Ava. "We were about to send out a search party!"

"Yes, we thought one of those errant monkeys had carried you away," Ava chimed in. Lana gave her a sideways and somewhat dirty look, apparently not amused by her joke.

"Oh, pish. As you said, it's Hedda's night off. No flying monkeys in sight tonight," I retorted.

"Oh, you are sharp!" Ava replied.

"Lana, aren't you going to introduce me?" A handsome, dark-haired man standing next to her said.

"Why, Pan, you haven't met Mabs Eriksson yet? You should! She's going to be your next star, you know. Mabs, this is Pan Berman."

"Charmed, I'm sure," I said, extending my hand.

"So, you're going to be my next star, are you?" he said, raising my hand to his lips.

"I believe I am, Mr. Berman," I said, confidently.

"She just finished filming Vincente's latest with Kirk and me. A small part, but she played it wonderfully. A crime you haven't signed her yet. Why, if I were her, I'd already be on the phone to Henry Ginsberg shopping my options."

"Well, we can't have that," he smiled. "Why don't you come by my office Thursday, and we'll make sure you have a permanent home at MGM."

"A contract? Why, that would be wonderful, Mr. Berman," I pretended to fawn. Inside, though, I was thrilled. A contract! This was what every man and woman who came to Hollywood chasing stardom aspired to and now it was within my reach.

CHAPTER 33
THE CONTRACT

Hollywood is a place where they'll pay you a thousand dollars for a kiss and fifty cents for your soul. I know, because I turned down the first offer often enough, and held out for the fifty cents.
— Marilyn Monroe

Just after eleven, I blew off early from work. Beatrice had given up protesting me taking an early afternoon at this point. She knew I'd bested her. I was making the company money as long as I provided one golden nugget every few days. That's all it took to placate her. Besides, the men were always leaving for a game of golf or a round of drinks. I was twice the copywriter they were, so why should I care? Truly, I was beginning to feel I could take this job or leave it. I had bigger stars to reach for now.

After a Cobb Salad and a couple of gin and tonics at the Brown Derby, I headed over to my 12:30 appointment with Pan Berman. It was 12:35 when I walked through his office door and a few seconds later when my eyes fell on Winifred seated on a leather couch in the corner. She sipped from a glass of bourbon, her stocking feet kicked up on the table in front of her. I could only hope to have gams like that when I reached her age.

"Mabs, darling. So good of you to join us. I was just telling Pan here how, in the right hands, your star will reach heights loftier than those of Lauren Bacall, Hedy Lamarr, and Myrna Loy combined." She punctuated her statement by circling her non-drink hand in the air, rather like a cattle rustler might circle a lariat.

Pan got up from his chair, walked around his desk, and circled me. Months before, I might have stood frozen, a frightened lamb waiting helplessly to be devoured by this wolf. Maybe it was Winifred's presence in the room that bolstered my confidence, but now I felt like the sheepdog. He could pad around, eyeing my figure as long as he wanted, but he wouldn't dare strike. If any attack was to occur, it would be mine.

"Vincente told me as much, but one can't always trust his judgment, now can he?" Pan smiled. "Looking at you again in the light of day, though, and after hearing all that Winifred has told me, there's no doubt. I'll grant Vincente's wish…and yours, I imagine," he added with a rather patronizing sneer. I held my tongue. If there were any wishes that needed granting, I'd be the one summoning the genie.

Pan walked back to his desk and sat on a corner. I sat down facing Winifred. "You always seem to pop up at the most opportune times, Winifred," I said, my shoulders square and my brow slightly furrowed. I wasn't upset, but I did want to know her secret. She was only too willing to spill it.

She chuckled slightly. "I'm not a piece of toast or a Jack-in-the-Box, dear. I never *pop up*. I've been watching you, Mabs. Guiding you ever since that first evening we met. Oh, yes," she smiled. "Everything that's happened to you since then hasn't merely happened. It's been planned. Vincente, Dorothy, Lana, Greer. Why, I even ensured success at that other little job of yours. Of course, I do have to thank you for making that part rather easy. *Go chew on a bar of Woodbury!* Simply brilliant the way you orchestrated that! Why, I may just call Gene and Tyrone and have them star in that little advertisement of yours."

Of course. I knew I was talented, both as a copywriter and as an actress, but perhaps I'd had too high an opinion of myself. It was beginning to make sense now. So much of what had happened the last few months were fate and fate's name was Winifred Jenkins.

She continued, giving me a deeper look into all that she'd apparently orchestrated. "Naturally, Carlisle is one of mine as well. A charming young man. He mentioned he'd met you at Clio's soiree a few months back and was intrigued. Well, it was only too perfect to put the two of you in the same room again. Do go easy on him though. He may come across as a tiger, but he's really just a tomcat. All talk, but when a fight breaks out, he's off.

"So, yes. I do tend to make an appearance at opportune times, but if you're going to succeed in this town, Mabs, you'll find you need to make your own opportunity." She took a healthy pull from her glass and crunched down solidly on a chunk of ice. The sound reminded me of bones cracking, and I willed myself not to react to the shiver running down my spine.

She was right, though. I knew this was the way it had to have played out. Far from being surprised by her explanation, her words drew me closer, like a hypnotic scent I knew was poisonous yet couldn't be resisted.

Do as she says, and your star will rise. Greer's words rang out in my head.

The dream I had about accepting an Academy Award while Winifred watched on from the front row also came to mind. Funny how the subconscious can know things the conscious mind does not.

"Yes, you know it's true, don't you? Now that you know I know you know—" She paused, looked up at the ceiling and mumbled to herself, reviewing the last six words to make sure she had them right. It would have been funny coming out of any other person's lips. It probably would have been funny coming out of hers if it had been a different place and a different day. Now, however, I didn't find the situation funny at all. Even if I had, I knew enough not to even crack a smile. Pan just sat there, staring rather blankly, as if he knew how this entire scene was to play out. Perhaps he did.

"Well, let's just say we're going to be working together much more closely now. You want your name in six-foot letters over Grauman's. You want your own table at Ciro's. You want your own home in Brentwood or Pacific Palisades. I will make that happen, Mabs. All you have to do is take my hand." The last sentence flowed from her lips like silk, her voice mesmerizing. Her eyes bore into me, an almost reptilian gaze. Now it wasn't a genie that had been let out of a lamp, it was an asp that danced before me.

"Yes, of course, Winifred." The words crossed my lips automatically, without any forethought. I was no longer in control. Perhaps it was Method acting, but it wasn't I who was channeling memories. It was Winifred. She controlled me. Her experiences, even if not known consciously to me, were now my experiences. I was her marionette.

"Pan, you have the contract all ready?" Winifred asked.

He grabbed a clipped together stack of papers from his desk and tossed them on the table in front of her. "What does this make? A dozen this year? You're slipping, Winifred," he said, a chuckle punctuating the last two words.

A dozen what? What was he talking about? I couldn't concentrate. I was too focused on Winifred. She took another drink of bourbon, again crunching down hard on the ice, set the glass down, and picked up the contract.

"I should say not, Pan. I'm just getting started. But this contract," she said as her eyes scanned the pages. "Three hundred dollars a week? Oh, come now. I think we can do better than that. We'll make that five hundred. What do you think, Mabs? Does five hundred dollars a week sound fair to you?"

I didn't know what to say. It wasn't that I was shocked by the numbers—even if the lower of the two was more than I made in a month. It was that I, quite literally, had no words in my mind. Winifred was still in complete control. I sat there, mute.

"No, you're right, dear," she continued. "Let's make it an even thousand. At least to start." She continued flipping through the pages. "No, no, no! This will never do! I need specific language in this contract about her roles, Pan. Only dramas. And the darker the better. We're not turning out the next Judy Garland, by god! Even if she can sing—can you sing, dear? Oh, never mind—I don't want to hear even a hint of her being cast in a musical. And any jokes while she's on screen better be of the deadpan kind that Bogie likes to make." She picked up a pen and scratched out a bunch of lines then scribbled a few notes on the margins of the page. After scanning the last few pages and nodding to herself, she called me over.

"Come over here, Mabs. Come sign your *contract*." The final word was wrapped in darkness. Her face now held a delicate smile. It reminded me of a matronly neighbor who I occasionally saw out walking her black poodle. Was I about to make my own Faustian bargain? I should have ran at that moment, ran all the way back to Prairie River, but I was in too deep. My body refused to do what my mind, my soul, knew was right. The baser demons of my nature were about to defeat the better angels.

At Winifred's words, my body was released from where I was sitting and carried over to the table. I took the pen from Winifred's hand and scribbled my signature on the last page.

"Wonderful!" Pan shouted, clapping his hands together. "This calls for a drink." He pushed a button on his desk and, moments later, a girl came through the door. "Evelyn, champagne," he said to her. She quickly turned around and came back a minute later with a cart carrying three glasses and a bottle of champagne in a bucket of ice. Pan retrieved the bottle and popped the cork. As the pressure from the bottle was released, so too was the pressure inside me. The audible sound brought my mind, my soul, and my body into a new congruence and a smile, a genuine smile, crossed my face.

"This is going to be so much fun!" I said, raising my glass in a toast.

"Oh, yes it will, Mabs. Oh, yes it will," Winifred replied.

CHAPTER 34
CHICKENS OF THE SEA

In Hollywood, gratitude is Public Enemy Number One.

— Hedda Hopper

I breezed into my office just after ten on a Tuesday, having completely disregarded it the previous Friday and the day before. Now that I knew Winifred was in control of my fate even here, I was even more cavalier. I knew I was pushing even Beatrice's patience at this point, but I couldn't care less. I really had half a mind to just quit, but something about the power I had over her, the game I got to play, enticed me.

"Mabs, please come in here." She definitely sounded cross.

I took my time. I set my purse down on my desk and walked over to the coffee pot. I drew out the process of filling my cup with the hot, black liquid. I poured the cream ever so slowly and added sugar by the quarter teaspoon. If I could have added it grain by grain, I would have. I stirred the lot for several seconds then took a few sips. Finally, I walked into her office. Randolph Crenshaw, the president of our company, was sitting in her chair. She stood behind him, posture erect, her hands folded neatly in front of her. Was Crenshaw one of Winifred's puppets as well? If not, perhaps the game was up. I doubted it, but if so, so be it.

"Mabs," he began, "Miss Sullivan tells me you've been providing this firm with some exemplary work." While the words were a compliment, the tone was not complimentary. "But she tells me your schedule is erratic." He paused, waiting for me to offer some sort of excuse or explanation. I didn't, and after the clock in her office ticked through twenty seconds, he continued.

"She tells me you've been working on a project with MGM. Getting some celebrity endorsements for a few of our clients." *What a bore this man was.* I wondered if he was going to say anything we all didn't already know. I again wondered about Winifred's influence over him. Why was he going through this ruse? We all knew how it was going to play out. Another pause. The clock clicked past five seconds this time. He was clearly growing uncomfortable. This was not going at all how he expected.

"Yes, well. Is there anything we can do to help you?" He added after a moment, beginning to fidget in his chair.

"No." I let the word hang in the air. The tension in the room certainly made it thick enough that, had the word been physically manifested, not much effort would have been needed to prop it up.

"Can we adjust your schedule at all? Do you need more time over at MGM to meet with, um, well, these…" He searched for a word to end the sentence, "*endorsers*?" That was certainly awkward. How had this man become head of an advertising firm?

"No."

"Mabs," Beatrice said, trying to break the tension. "We work from nine to five in this office. We take an hour for lunch. If you have business elsewhere, business relating to this firm, that is, just let us know. We'd be happy to accommodate you." Her voice began to quiver slightly. She was clearly trapped. She knew I had connections. She and Crenshaw may have even felt that the ideas I was submitting were so valuable that they couldn't just fire me, but they also couldn't let me waltz in and out of the office anytime I wished. I imagine other copywriters were probably raising a fuss. Then I began to think further about the situation and what the rest of the male copywriters were allowed to get away with.

"Perhaps if I took up golf? Or maybe you'd like it if I spent my time throwing back scotch with the boys?"

Crenshaw squirmed in his seat. Beatrice's eyes darted around the room, looking for an answer that would never come.

"I'm over here, Beatrice."

They were speechless. A couple of cads who were paid to craft words and they were speechless. I was loving this!

"Well, this has been a real hoot, but I have some work to do, so if you'll excuse me." I turned on my heel and walked out the door. As a matter of fact, I did have some work to do, and for them, no less. Not at all because I felt like I had something to prove either. I knew who I needed to prove myself to and it wasn't these two. When the time was right to finally quit, I'd know.

I took my seat at my desk and spent the rest of the day creating a campaign for Chicken of the Sea Tuna. *Chicken of the Sea. Ha! Perhaps it would feature Crenshaw and Beatrice.*

CHAPTER 35
THE WICKED WITCH
OF HOLLYWOOD HILLS

You aim at all the things you have been told that
stardom means; the rich life, the applause, the
parties cluttered with celebrities. Then you find
that you have it all. And it is nothing, really
nothing. It is like a drug that lasts just a few hours,
a sleeping pill. When it wears off, you have to live
without its help.

— Susan Hayward

"**B**ut, really, what's the point of dressing up on Halloween? The better costume would be nothing at all," I said.

Dagny had telephoned me to say she'd heard Errol Flynn was throwing a costume party the next day, wondered if I'd been invited, and if so, asked if she could tag along. Parties at Errol's were often a hedonistic gas to be sure, and I knew I'd end up going, but I wasn't particularly looking forward to it. Besides being boorish, I also found Errol boring. And, frankly, I wanted to tease Dagny just a bit.

"Why, Mabs! Are you saying you want to go *au natural*? Scandalous!" She'd witnessed the changes in me over the past several months, but her words came across, not in mock surprise, but in genuine shock. I think she knew me—the new me—well enough to know it was something I'd contemplate at this point, but not enough to think I'd actually do it. To be honest, she read too much into my response.

"Oh, stop!" I laughed. "I simply meant that wearing everyday clothes would be more of a costume than a witch's hat and broom." Her assumption did make me consider showing up in nothing other than a witch's hat and broom though. Ultimately, however, I opted for the full ensemble. After all, being scantily clad at one of Errol's parties wasn't really that scandalous.

Luckily, it didn't require too much effort to pop over to MGM and have them rummage through costuming for something that fit. When I looked in the mirror, I saw that it suited me perfectly. *Just try and stay out of my way. Just try! I'll get you, my pretty, and your little dog, too!*

When I returned to my apartment that evening, I contemplated calling Carlisle and inviting him along, but then wondered if I should leave myself free. Not free for other men, mind you, though that was a possibility, but free to escort Dagny. It had barely been two weeks since Kenneth had broken her heart, and I suppose I was being sentimental.

Eventually, I decided not babysitting her was the best option, though. Besides, it had been as long since I saw Carlisle, and truthfully, I missed him somewhat—or at least his touch.

"Carlisle, darling! Errol's throwing a Halloween party tomorrow evening. Naturally, being Errol, it'll be delightfully wicked, but it can be dreadful when one shows up alone, so I could use an escort. Won't you join me?"

"Why, Mabs, so good to hear from you! I wondered when you'd call." *What arrogance! I loved it!* "Yes, that sounds, well, wickedly delightful as you say, but I'm afraid I don't have a thing to wear." I was sure that was a lie. He was resourceful. He'd come up with something.

"I'm sure that's not the case. Why don't you pick Dagny and me up at my apartment at half past seven tomorrow?"

"Perfect. And what will you be going as?"

"Why, what else? The Wicked Witch!" I laughed decadently then hung up the phone.

We arrived at Errol's shortly after eight. Things already appeared to be in full swing. Two girls dressed as mermaids and a man dressed as Captain Ahab or some such thing, already splashed about in the pool. *Where else would they be?* I took a second glance and noticed one of them was Dorothy Patrick. I hadn't seen her in ages. I made a note to say hello at some point during the evening.

"How fantastic!" Carlisle laughed. I was sure he'd been to a few Hollywood parties in his day, but this appeared to be the most decadent.

"Well, look what the flying monkeys dragged in! Glad you could make it, Mabs." Ava Gardner came up to us dressed as a WAC Major.

"A little much, don't you think, *Major* Gardner?" I raised an eyebrow.

"Well, someone has to keep order around here. Besides, dressed like this, I might be the only girl that Errol doesn't have the gumption to screw, and that's quite alright with me," she laughed. "And you," she continued, turning to Dagny. "Didn't I see you at the Cocoanut Grove a few weeks ago? Of course, it's so hard to tell who's who with all these damn costumes. Charming outfit, by the way. You're certainly not in Kansas anymore, Dorothy. Where's Toto? Still locked up in Mabs's dungeon?" she snorted at her jibe. I didn't think it was funny and would have put a spell on her at that moment if I were really a witch.

"Ye-yes," Dagny said, clearing her throat nervously. She was becoming unbearable, even worse than I'd been the first time she'd taken me to that party at Philomena's. What did she have to be nervous about? Even though I was quickly gaining on her, she'd still been to far more Hollywood parties than I had.

"I'm surprised to see you aren't dressed as the Scarecrow." Ava continued, turning to Carlisle and letting out a huge, mocking laugh. Her own joke cracked her up so much, it took her several seconds to regain her composure.

"No, he's with me. We tried to find him a flying monkey costume, but the best we could do was this Tarzan getup."

"Me Tarzan. You Ava." Carlisle said, then beat his chest and let out a yell.

"Yes, well. Isn't that nice," Ava feigned, rolling her eyes, then walked off.

"Okay, very good, darling," I said, patting him on the shoulder. "Now, why don't we go get something to drink."

"Tarzan like Scotch and Soda!" *Oh, god! I began to wish I hadn't brought him. What the hell had gotten into him and where was the charming man from two weeks before?*

"Listen, Carlisle," I turned to him and quietly but firmly said, "I'm sure you're a real hit with the kiddies. But you're going to have to knock that off. It's embarrassing.

"Right. Okay. Just having a little fun." He cleared his throat and straightened up.

We made our way past the usual set; David Selznik, Peter Lorre—who didn't really need a costume—Veronica Lake. I spied Winifred in the background talking with some young thing, perhaps her next catch. I wasn't at all surprised she was here. I assumed, going forward, I'd be seeing a lot more of her. Then I saw Stan Freberg. I froze.

"Mabs Eriksson! What's it been? Two months?"

He was all smiles, even more so dressed like a clown. I wasn't laughing. I suddenly wanted to be anywhere but there. I felt like Dagny's Dorothy had a bucket of water poised right above my head and was about to turn me into a steaming pile of rags.

It was easy to put on airs when everyone else was in on the game, when everyone else was dancing about in the Land of Oz. Stan knew my secrets, though, at least some of them. He knew I was just as much playing the part as everyone else at the party, while he was likely the only *real* person there.

"Mabs, it's me, Stan Freberg. I know I look a little silly in this clown suit, but surely you remember me?" He looked equal parts saddened and confused. I snapped myself out of my shock.

"Of course, Stan! So lovely to see you! Yes, that clown suit definitely got me!" I forced out a laugh.

"And you! A witch! I sure wouldn't have guessed you'd show up like that."

"Oh, yes, well. It's just something I got off the MGM lot."

"It's mighty fine. And, Dagny, a pleasure to see you again." He extended his hand. Dagny shook it, Stan seeming to put her at ease. "Tarzan," he said, finally turning to Carlisle. "Glad you could swing out of the trees. We needed another gentleman to class this place up. I say forget these dinner jackets they call *monkey suits* these days. Why not wear a *real* monkey suit?!"

"Edmund Carlisle. Charmed, I'm sure." He kept cool, disregarding Stan's joke and not making any of his own, either. He apparently didn't want to test my patience but, if anything, it made him look all the more foolish.

Stan turned back to me. "MGM you say? You, ah, doing a little work there now?" He put on an air of faux seriousness, as if we were two regulars having a business meeting at Chasen's. His clown get-up made it twice as funny, and I forced myself not to laugh.

"Yes, signed my contract just two weeks ago after doing a little something with Lana and Kirk last month." I knew I had no reason to namedrop in front of Stan. He wasn't the type to care, but somehow, I couldn't help myself. Perhaps I was doing it so those around us could overhear. Not that any of them cared either, really. After all, this was a Hollywood party. For all I knew, Lana was bobbing for apples in the next room while a trio of tarts played pin the tail on the jackass with Kirk. Or, truer to form, Kirk was probably the one doing the pinning of quite a different kind.

We were suddenly interrupted by a frantic scream, "She's drowned!"

We all turned toward the commotion. Captain Ahab was carrying Dorothy Patrick out of the pool. He set her down on the ground, while another man, ironically dressed as a doctor, came over and attempted to resuscitate her.

I know I should have felt more concerned. If something like this had happened a decade ago, back home in Prairie River, I'd probably have prayed for her, but a flash of dark humor was the first thing to pop into my head. *All those scales, all those fins, and she still couldn't swim.* I snorted a laugh, then quickly covered it with a cough and tried to put on a facade of sorrow.

After a minute, Dorothy began to cough up water, and the group around her cheered. A few of them patted the doctor on the back. I looked around and noticed Dagny was gone. I glimpsed again and saw her kneeling over Dorothy, grasping her hand, and saying something that was probably words of comfort. *Dorothy treating Dorothy. Quite the interesting twist.* I also saw the pain, the fear, and the thankfulness in both their eyes. *How odd?* I never would have thought Dagny to be the comforting type, at least not to a total stranger.

"Well, how about that drink, Tarzan?" I said to Carlisle. After all, this was a party. Dorothy was alive. Let's get on with it.

Stan's eyes flashed with shock, a peculiar look for a clown, at least one not starring in an Italian opera or a Shakespeare play. The mood all around was terribly somber and the party had just started. Someone needed to shake things up. I knew that someone had to be me.

I walked over to the bandleader, who had been staring at the scene in shock for the last few minutes, and told him to play *That Old Black Magic*. I don't know what compelled me to do it, but as the small orchestra began to play, I grabbed the microphone and began to sing. It had the desired effect. *That Old Black Magic* cast its spell, and the party took on a jubilant air once again. By the time I sang the second line, all eyes had left Dorothy, who had now regained her composure and was slipping out of her mermaid tail, and were on me. By the time I'd finished, it seemed the crowd forgot all about her and were focused only on me. I'd never felt so alive!

I walked back and joined Carlisle, Dagny, and Ava. Stan had disappeared. All the better. That look of shock veiled in makeup unnerved me.

"Since when do you sing?" Dagny said, her mouth agape, her shock now transferred from Dorothy to me.

"Well, someone needed to liven the mood. Come on, let's get a drink. I'd say we should invite the mermaid, but I think she's had enough already!" I laughed. No one else did.

CHAPTER 36
THE RUSSIANS ARE COMING

If I were well behaved, I'd die of boredom.
— Tallulah Bankhead

NOVEMBER

I chose to make an appearance at the office a few days later. Everyone was chatting about the surprise victory Truman had just pulled off over Dewey. They all appeared to be quite thrilled. I was looking forward to my own surprise victory in Hollywood. It wouldn't be a surprise to me, of course. Just to everyone else.

"Can you believe it, Mabs? Aren't you just thrilled? Who would have thought old Harry would win?" Michael was being uncharacteristically friendly. The whole office had taken on a jovial atmosphere. I went into my office, cracked open a bottle of whisky and took a drink before sitting down and kicking my feet up on the desk. I leaned back and stared up at the ceiling. *My god, this was a boring scene!*

"Mabs, nice to see you." Beatrice's greeting didn't carry even a hint of sarcasm.

"Oh, hello, Bea," I replied flatly, perhaps even a bit forlornly.

"Are you okay, Mabs? You didn't vote for that wet sock, Dewey, did you?"

"I'm Canadian, Bea. Remember? I don't vote. Furthermore, I don't really care about your silly contests. They both seem like wet socks to me. Aren't we supposed to be coming up with advertising campaigns around here anyway?"

"My, aren't you the professional one? Okay, back to work. Any gems bouncing around that brain of yours?"

I had a few gems but none of them were particularly relevant to the advertising world. I chose to throw one out there anyway, just to see how she might respond. "People around here are altogether too happy. We need something to shake them up. Instill a little fear. Make them remember their own mortality and the futility of it all. Turn on the radio, Bea. See if you can't find a dirge for us to listen to."

"What on earth are you talking about, Mabs?"

"Like I said, Bea, fear. Fear is a far better motivator than happiness. If we want the masses to buy makeup, for instance, don't entice them with beauty. Drive them away from ugliness. Want them to buy life insurance? Make them fear death."

"And what about canned tuna?"

"Hunger and the thought of having to slice open a cold fish."

"Oranges?"

"Scurvy."

Beatrice laughed. "You must be joking!"

"I'm not. Who do we have in the queue?"

"Well, a man came by recently. He sells binoculars via mail-order and wants to expand his business. How are you going to strike fear in the hearts of men about binoculars, Mabs?" She crossed her arms and gave me a self-assured grin, confident she'd just bested me.

"Oh, do give me a challenge," I sighed. "Don't you know the Russians are coming? There's a *Cold War* a brewing and it could turn hot at any moment! Why, there could be Russians storming the beach at Santa Monica right now. If you had a pair of binoculars, you could spot the enemy before he spots you!"

Beatrice's eyes widened. I half expected her to run to the window and peer out in search of the would-be foe.

"Oh, honestly, Bea. There are no Russians coming. At least not today. But the public doesn't know that. Call this man. Tell him to up his production. In stores for Christmas and all that. If you like, we can even do a warm fuzzy campaign with a little boy in his pajamas looking out the window through his product, waiting for Santa Claus." I opened the bottle of whisky and poured another glass for myself and one for Beatrice. "Here. You look like you could use a drink."

"Ten in the morning is a little early in the day for me, dear."

"Well, more for me then," I replied and downed both glasses in short order. She just rolled her eyes, turned around and left my office. I kicked my feet up on the desk, leaned back in my chair, and daydreamed about Russians storming the beach twelve miles away.

I was startled about twenty minutes later when my phone rang. "Miss Eriksson, Mr. Minnelli would like to know if you're free for lunch at Chasen's tomorrow at noon."

"Yes, of course. Tell him I'd be delighted." I hung up the phone and my thoughts wandered off to a movie set. Maybe something based on Dostoyevsky or Chekov.

CHAPTER 37
THE MURDER OF
GIOVANNI MARINO

The idea of a star being born is bushwa. A star is
created, carefully and cold-bloodily, built up from
nothing, from nobody. Age, beauty, talent, least of
all talent, has nothing to do with it. We could make
silk purses out of sows' ears every day of the week.
— Louis B. Mayer

always loved lunches at Chasen's. The dark, wood interior, the leather, the smells of broiled steaks emanating from the kitchen. It was, by far, the classiest place in Hollywood.

When I spotted Vincente and he, in turn, spotted me, a huge smile broke out on his face. Behind that smile, though, was a pain I hadn't seen since Dagny and I met on Sunset Boulevard so many months before. He seemed like such a gentle soul. I wondered what was troubling him.

"Mabs, darling, so good to see you," he exclaimed, getting up from a booth situated near the back of the restaurant as I approached.

"Vincente! Splendid to see you as well! How are you?"

"Oh, to be honest—and I'm not sure why I'm telling you this—" he started, collapsing back into his seat with a sigh, "but Judy had another episode this morning. Just dreadful. One of the worst. I don't know how I can go on with it. The greatest pain isn't what she attempts to inflict on me, but the pain I feel knowing she's slowly destroying herself.

"This business is just awful sometimes, Mabs. The way they take these young, impressionable girls from small towns and prairies and mold them, manipulate them into monsters." I knew he was talking about Judy. I couldn't help but see the parallel to my own life though. *Was I destined to become a monster?*

"Oh, goodness! That does sound dreadful. You poor dear," I said, reaching across the table and gently patting his hand. I hoped this would be the extent of it. The whole episode was becoming uncomfortable. He broke down and began gently sobbing. *God, what had I done? 'How are you?' wasn't supposed to be an honest question. Didn't he have a shrink he could spill this too? There seemed to be as many of them as there were actors in this town.*

"I *am* sorry, Mabs. How unprofessional of me." He took out a handkerchief and dabbed his eyes and wiped his nose. A forced smile returned to his face. "Let's get on with it, shall we?"

Yes, let's! I was beginning to think I'd have to go running to Pan, that I'd have to renegotiate my contract to stay as far away from Vincente as possible. Maybe I could be cast in one of Melvyn LeRoy's latests.

"That's quite alright. But I am excited to hear about what you have to say," I said cheerily.

"Oh, it's going to be wonderful, Mabs. My best picture yet. Frances Marion is writing the script. I'd like you to play the lead alongside Gregory Peck. It's a period drama set in mid-nineteenth-century Sicily, *where my grandfather is from.*" He said the last few words with a wistful look in his eye, then paused before beginning again in a more excited tone. "It's love! It's lust! It's jealousy! It's murder!" He ticked off each word with the wave of his hand. His voice intensified with each one as he went on so that the whole restaurant must have heard him by the time he said *murder*. It all thrilled me to no end.

"It sounds just wonderful, Vincente. Do go on." I was giddy.

"You will play a humble farm girl, Luciana Costa. You meet a mysterious man, Giovanni Marino, who travels through your village one day. He is a bandit, a highwayman. You allow him to hide away in your family's stable. Even your parents, your siblings, don't know he is there. He makes love to you in the hay, and you fall in love with him. But then, he says he must go and will return when it is safe to make you his wife. You trust him and you wait and you wait. Months pass and finally he returns." I wondered if this would all be filmed on the back lot or if I'd be lucky enough to gain a trip to Italy out of it.

He continued. "He has somehow made a success of himself, an honest success. He tells you he is sorry, but he has met another woman, and she has been betrothed to him by her wealthy father. He wants you to be happy for him, but you are jealous. You travel to Palermo, where this woman and her family live. You want to talk to her, convince her to release the man you love and who you believe still loves you. You confront her on the street, but she laughs you off. Enraged, you push her into the street, and she is run over by a wagon. In the commotion, you are able to escape. You know you should feel remorse for what you've just done, but all you can feel is excitement! What a thrill to have taken a life. Now she is gone and the man you love is free to be with you at last."

A thrill to take a life? How peculiar. I ruminated on this scene while he continued and imagined myself pushing a woman to her death. It *was* rather thrilling.

"You go to him and tell him what you have done. He is horrified, but you are confused. Shouldn't he be overjoyed that the other woman is now gone? Shouldn't he be thanking you? Your confusion turns to anger. In your rage, you reach for a dagger which is resting on a desk near him and plunge it into his heart. As the final scene fades to black, you begin to laugh."

"Oh, my! That is quite the story." My eyes were wide. I let out a laugh, imagining myself in the final scene. Two men seated nearby turned toward me momentarily before returning to their grilled tenderloins and champignons.

"Yes! Just like that. What a devilishly wonderful laugh," Vincente responded. "This will be big, Mabs. I'm sparing no expense on this production. A month of filming in Palermo and the surrounding countryside."

"Wonderful! Simply wonderful. When do we begin?" I said with a huge smile. I was elated. This is what I'd been waiting for ever since he gave my character a line on that first day of filming *Scheherazade*. I could hardly sit still.

"The middle of January. We will be sailing from New York after the new year. Have you ever been to Europe, Mabs?" I'm sure he knew I hadn't. A big, beaming grin crossed his face as he watched the excitement in my eyes.

"Heaven's no! I've never even been to New York!"

"Then we must leave a few days early. It's my hometown, you know? A marvelous city. I look forward to showing it to you."

"That sounds simply enchanting, Vincente," I said, shifting the vision of my dreams from an Italian countryside to the glittering lights of Times Square.

"But there will be plenty of time to discuss all that later. Right now, I'm famished." He raised a hand and motioned one of the waiters over. "Do you like oysters?"

CHAPTER 38
HAPPY BIRTHDAY, SISTER!

It's important to know where you've come from so that you can know where you're going. I probably chose my profession because I was seeking approval, adulation, admiration, and affection.
— Cary Grant

My schedule was completely open until we departed. The studio would be finishing up pre-production, casting the supporting actors, arranging travel, and designing and building the sets for what would be shot here in Hollywood.

I made the occasional appearance at the office at Winifred's insistence. I'm not sure why she needed me to do so. Perhaps it was part of the contract she'd made with Beatrice and Crenshaw.

I even came up with a rather inspired and humorous advertising campaign for Timex Watches that would be run as a serial in major newspapers. It involved a man who was perpetually either too late or too early for appointments. He'd miss his train and be forced to walk to work. He'd arrive much too early for a dinner party and catch the hostess and her husband in a row. He's a sorry character until someone gives him a Timex for his birthday. He becomes successful in every way possible, culminating in a trip to the racetrack where he wins big.

I made the rounds at the requisite parties. Now a contract player cast as the lead in Vincente's new picture, and one that was already becoming the talk of the town, I was the sought-after guest with all sorts of men and women fawning over me.

I'd heard Dagny had been cast in a minor role—at least what I now considered minor, but I'm sure she thought was the opportunity of a lifetime—and was spending all her time over at Paramount.

Then, without even realizing it, my birthday arrived like a surprise relative I wasn't expecting and didn't much want to see.

The phone rang, and I absentmindedly answered it.

"Happy birthday, Sister!"

"Who is this?" I don't know what compelled me to ask this. After all, I only had one sister. But for the fleeting thought, I'd hardly remembered her at all in the past year.

"Do you have another sister I don't know about, you silly goose?" she laughed.

I paused for a moment. It had now been several months since I'd talked to her, and I had to put myself in the right frame of reference. "Olivia! How are you? I'm sorry. It's not the best connection and my mind was elsewhere," I lied, trying to sound enthusiastically happy to hear from her.

"Were you pining over William Holden?" she laughed again. *Altogether too much laughing.* She was always a silly git.

"No, nothing like that." I'd been pining over Vincente, although pining wasn't the right word for it. Pondering was more like it. Should I tell her about him? Where to begin? So much had happened since we'd last talked that she'd scarcely believe it. The few postcards I'd sent home—it had been several months since I'd done even that—were limited to pleasantries and a mention of my job as a secretary at the advertising firm.

"I hope you're taking care of yourself, getting out. Have you made any friends? We do miss you up here. It snowed a foot last night. Mother strained herself helping Papa with one of the hogs a few weeks ago and has been laid up in bed since. She's almost fifty, you know. I'm sure she'd love to speak with you. Why haven't you called? Or written more? Why, we haven't received more than a few postcards from you since April. I'm rather surprised I reached you. I've tried to call before. Have you received any of my letters?"

"Olivia! God, take a breath!" I thought about just setting the receiver down and letting her ramble on, oblivious to my presence or lack thereof. She'd always been good at carrying on one-sided conversations.

"Oh, I am sorry. It's just so exciting to finally talk to you!" Now she was sounding like a moviegoer one might run into on the street.

It's just so exciting to finally talk to you! I've seen all your pictures. I just loved you opposite Clark Gable. I silently and mockingly mouthed the words. It was hard to believe she was my *older* sister. Then my mind went to her mention of our mother, then to that awful scene at Winifred's months before. I contemplated telling Olivia about it, but it would undoubtedly shock her to no end and just raise more questions. She was brash enough she'd likely tell our father, and he'd end up at my door a week later to drag me back home. No, that would never do. I'd have to just ask her without any backstory.

"Listen, Olivia. This may seem like an odd question, but is Mother really our mother?" I said, sitting up and getting very serious. She went silent for several seconds and it spoke volumes. "Olivia? Are you there?"

"Why would you ask such a thing? Of course she's our mother. Whose mother would she be?" Her words were forced, each sentence punctuated by a nervous laugh. *She* definitely wasn't an actress.

"Olivia, what aren't you telling me? What are you hiding?"

I heard an audible gulp on the other end of the line and then she began to speak, her voice quivering.

"O-okay, you have a right to know, I imagine. And you've guessed as much already. Yes, Mother is our mother." She paused for a moment, probably considering how to continue. "She was there for every important moment of our lives. She was by my bedside when I had typhoid. She was by yours when you got bit by that river otter or whatever it was. She took care of the chores when Papa injured his back. She stayed awake in worry all night when that awful blizzard kept him from returning from Porcupine Plain. A better mother no one could ask for." I heard her sigh on the other end of the line. "Oh Mabs, should I really be telling you all this?"

"Tell me, Olivia. I need to know," I insisted.

"She was devastated when you left, you know, but she knew she had to let you leave," Olivia continued. "She prays for you, for your safety and your happiness, every night." As she continued with this sad tale of sacrifice, her voice became more and more exasperated. It almost made me feel guilty for all my debauchery the past several months. Almost.

"Go on." She was sitting on the most important part, and I was sitting on the edge of my seat with anticipation.

"But, no, in the technical sense, she is not. Our mother, our birth mother, was sent to a mental hospital when I was seven and you were four. You would have been much too young to remember the details or even much about her. But for the fact you asked means something must have triggered vague memories. What happened, dear sister?"

"Why did she go away?" I asked, disregarding her question. Thankfully, she didn't probe further.

"Oh, she was an awful woman. It wasn't her fault, though. I only learned a year ago why. She was from East Prussia and the Great War did things to her, you see. Her village was mercilessly bombarded. Perhaps it would have been more merciful had she perished in one of the many barrages. But then, neither of us would be here, would we?" As she said this last sentence, I wondered if our nonexistence might have been more merciful as well.

She continued. "She managed to escape to Sweden where she met Papa. He says she was quite well for a time. She delighted in making blintzes and would often wear the one dress she'd managed to take with her. Apparently, her family was rather well off. Something happened about a year after they came to Canada, though. Papa was never sure what, but she changed drastically. She was prone to violent mood swings. One moment dancing gayly about the parlor, the next throwing whatever she could get her hands on and cursing him in Polish, wishing she'd never met him, never come to what she thought to be such a desolate place. Sometimes she wished she never survived the war and would walk out into the snow barefoot, wearing nothing but that dress."

It sounded awful and I wanted Olivia to stop talking. I wanted to hang up the telephone, run off to a lonely little bar where no one would know me and drink myself silly. But I couldn't put the telephone down. I couldn't tell her to stop. I needed to know it all. "What happened? What finally sent her to the mental hospital?" I asked.

"It was frightful, Mabs. It was on a particularly cold night with the wind howling outside and the house shaking almost as violently as she was. She grabbed the poker from the fireplace and began waving the glowing hot end wildly about. Papa was afraid she might burn the whole place to the ground.

"You came out of the bedroom and the tip of the poker grazed your forehead, sending you to the ground, screaming in terror. She dropped the poker and rushed to you, cradling you in her arms and speaking to you in Polish. She began squeezing you. Not in a violent way, but nonetheless, Papa was afraid she'd crush you or smother you. I'd never seen him get even the least bit violent before then, and I've never seen him get violent since.

"He rushed over and pulled her off you, flinging her halfway across the room. She screamed at him. She screamed at me. Then she just screamed. And screamed. She didn't stop until she had made herself hoarse, finally collapsing on the floor in utter exhaustion."

By this time, Olivia's voice was quite emphatic, nearly shouting each word. I could feel the terror in her voice, remembering something I'm sure she wished she could block out. I was grateful that I seemed to have managed at least that. I reached up and lightly touched my fingers to a spot above my right eye. There was a nearly imperceptible scar there, no bigger than a grain of rice. When I put on makeup, it disappeared. I hardly noticed it myself and never gave it any thought. Until now.

I shut my eyes, remembering the scene play out. I could feel the searing hot iron of the fire poker burning into my skin. I wanted to scream, but I didn't know what I'd say, so I just sat there in stunned silence, my hand strangling the telephone receiver with all my might. I was shivering. I felt even worse than I did that horrid day at Winifred's bungalow.

"The next day, a man came and took her away," Olivia went on, her voice more somber now. "We went and visited her once about six months after that. I remember the journey took days. It was in Manitoba. They seemed to be taking good care of her, but she was distant, always looking away, a sadness in her eyes. While I was only seven, I sensed there was something wrong and it makes my heart ache even to this day. You're fortunate to have been so young and to not remember any of this."

But I did remember, if only vaguely. My mind recalled a scene of a frail woman who looked much older than she was, wearing an elegant, flowing gown, and sitting in a chair, gazing out a window. The room was sterile, and everything was white. The only thing to look at was that window. A raven perched on a rather large poplar tree just outside. *It's strange the memories we hold deep in the recesses of our minds, somehow suppressing them until just the right moment brings them to light. I could smell the ammonia in that room even now.*

"Mabs? Mabs? Are you there?" My sister's voice was gentle and came to me like a dream while my mind was still present in that room with my mother, gazing out at the raven.

"Yes, I'm here. I'm sorry, Sister, but I must go." I was in complete shock over it all. I didn't feel much else. It was as if it was all happening to someone else and I was a bystander. I knew the feelings would rush in soon enough once I'd had time for it all to sink in. But I didn't want that. I didn't want to feel.

"I just remembered an appointment I need to get to," I said quietly. As I went to replace the receiver, I could hear her telling me not to go, to say something in response, and then, *click*, all was silent once again in the room.

I went to the liquor cabinet and pulled out a bottle of vodka. I'd never much studied the label, but now noticed it was made in Poland. *Naturally. Like mother, like daughter.* I poured it into a glass, but the bottle ran dry after barely a finger. *I definitely needed more than that,* I thought, my brow furrowing in disappointment. I downed the lot in one gulp, set the glass down purposefully on the liquor cabinet, retrieved my coat and purse, then left in search of someplace to finish what I had started.

CHAPTER 39
A GIRL WALKS INTO A BAR

Most people go through life using up half their energy trying to protect a dignity they never had.
— Raymond Chandler

I don't know the name of the bar I found to drown my feelings. I only know it was the first one I came across after leaving my apartment. I don't know how long I was there. I don't know how much I drank. The only thing I remember was the bartender's name, Jill. One doesn't see many women behind the bar. I was grateful for it though. She left me alone and kept the whisky coming. I was also grateful we were the only two there. An hour later, I heard the door open.

"Oh my god, Mabs! I've been looking everywhere. I don't know what compelled me to look here, but I'm so glad I did." Dagny was in tears. "Why are you here? Why are you here alone on your birthday? I was hoping to celebrate with you."

"If you must, plenty of stools, plenty of whisky," I said, speaking quietly to the glass in front of me instead of her.

"No, this doesn't look at all like a place to celebrate." She looked at Jill apologetically as she said it. "And you don't look in a condition to do so either."

I slammed the glass down on the bar and it shattered. Jill didn't say a thing. She just looked on in sympathetic silence.

"Come on, Mabs. Let's get you home," Dagny said, taking me by the shoulders and trying to get me to stand.

"No!" I shouted, wriggling free of her grip. "Leave me be!"

"I will not, Mabs! I will not leave you be!" Her words were firm and scolding. She reminded me of a schoolmarm we'd shared when we were ten. "I don't know what's put you in this state this time, but I promise we'll figure it out together." These words were much softer.

"Oh, you'd like that, wouldn't you?! You'd like to be the savior this time. Well, sister, let me tell you something. Being the savior isn't all it's cracked up to be. See this scar on my arm? You know how I got that? A muskrat! A baby muskrat I tried to save! Or how about this?" I lifted my bangs and pushed my forehead toward her. "I just found out how I got this gem a few hours ago. Can you see it? Can you?! Mother scarred me with a fire poker when she was in one of her manic, drunken rages."

"Your mother never drank," Dagny said, perplexed.

"Oh, you'd think so, wouldn't you? Well, that woman you know isn't my mother. My mother was sent off to a mental hospital when I was four, dontchya know? Damn it, Jill! Give me another glass!" Jill made a motion toward the glasses stacked neatly behind the bar.

"Don't give her a glass, Jill," Dagny said, sternly. Jill froze, unsure who to listen to. "Come on, Mabs. I'm taking you home." She grabbed my arm more firmly this time and pulled me from my stool. I tried to wriggle free again, but Dagny's hand held fast. I was too drunk to offer much resistance, and I begrudgingly followed as she dragged me out of the bar.

CHAPTER 40
MATKA, SIOSTRA

If goodness is its own reward, shouldn't we get a little something for being naughty?

— Lauren Bacall

"Mabs, Mabs. Wake up, Mabs. You're having a bad dream."

I sat up like a shot. The room was still dark but a faint glow from the moon outside my window cast a soft light on Dagny's face.

"Are you an angel? Is this heaven? No, it can't be. There's no way I'm getting into heaven."

"No, Mabs. I'm not an angel and this isn't heaven, but don't say that. You're not going to hell. At least not while I'm here. Now, who or what is *matka*? You kept repeating it in your sleep. You were in quite the frightful state. I must have gone through nearly two rags sopping the sweat from your brow. You mustn't do this to yourself, dear Mabs." Her tone was gentle, not the least bit reproachful.

"*Matka*? Why, I don't know. You say I was repeating it in my sleep?"

"Yes, dear. You were thrashing about something awful." She put her hand to my forehead and gently pushed a lock of hair away. I searched my mind, trying to remember what I had just dreamt. I looked down at the bed. The sheets were in a tangle. I had an awful taste in my mouth and my head was pounding.

"What time is it?" I asked.

"Half past two."

"Have you been awake all this time?"

"I may have nodded off for a few minutes, but I wasn't going to leave you."

My mind returned to my dreams. "It was horrid, Dagny," I gulped. "Olivia told me as much earlier today—or yesterday—but I hadn't allowed myself to picture it fully. My subconscious didn't cooperate. I could hear her screams from the bedroom. It was all in Polish. I couldn't understand it. Just the one word. I came out of the bedroom. She was waving that fire poker around like a mad woman. '*Matka*', I cried. Oh, I was so frightened, Dagny. Then she struck me with the poker. It seared into my forehead. I can almost feel it now. Just awful, Dagny. Just awful."

"I'm sorry, Mabs. I never knew."

"You couldn't have. We didn't meet until we were five. The thing of it is, I didn't know either. Not until Olivia told me. She remembered."

"Do you remember anything else?"

"She dropped the poker and ran over to me as soon as it happened. She took me in her arms but was squeezing me so tightly, I couldn't breathe. I cried out again, although I was muffled by her arms. '*Matka! Matka! Matka!*' Papa ran over and pulled her away. Her screams continued. They were guttural, Dagny, like a feral cat. Then I woke up."

"Oh, Mabs, that's horrible." She put her arms around me, and I began to sob into her breast until I fell asleep.

When I awoke again, a dull light, filtered by gray clouds, was shining through the window and she was still sitting in a chair next to me, asleep. She jerked awake.

"Oh, I'm sorry, Dagny. I didn't mean to wake you."

"No, no, I'm fine. What time is it?"

"Nearly ten. Do you have anywhere you need to be?"

"No, I can stay. Do you want me to make you some breakfast?"

"Would you? You are a dear. I'm sorry, I must have been ghastly to you last night."

"It's okay. It's not your fault. I'm sorry such awful things happened to you. Everything always seemed so pleasant at your home. I always wished I could be part of your family growing up."

"But you were, Dagny. You were. I don't know what I would have done without a friend, a sister, like you."

"We did take care of each other, didn't we, Mabs?" She moved from the chair to sit next to me on the bed and wrapped her arms around me. She made me feel safe.

"Well, that sure was one heck of a way to spend a birthday," I laughed slightly, sniffling and wiping a few tears from my eyes.

"We all have one awful birthday, I'm sure, Mabs. But let's forget about yesterday. We'll make today your birthday." She broke our embrace and looked me in the eyes. A sweet smile crossed her face.

"You know what I'd like to do?" I asked.

"What's that?"

"After breakfast, I'd like to take a walk on the beach. Can we do that, Dagny? Will you walk with me on the beach?"

"Of course."

★★★

After breakfast and a shower, I felt better. The initial shock of learning about my mother had dissipated and I was looking forward to a peaceful walk on the beach with Dagny.

It was a bit of a gloomy day out with a thick blanket of grey clouds covering the sky. I was grateful for it though. I didn't need the sharp contrast of a Southern California sun shining down on me at this moment. I needed the soft light that only a cloudy day can provide. It also meant we had the beach almost entirely to ourselves and that, more than anything, was what I wanted. Just Dagny and me and the few dozen seagulls that glided above us.

While we strolled, I focused on the sound of the waves crashing against the shore and the smell of the salt air. I might not make it to heaven, but this was a good stand in. A few minutes into our walk, Dagny began to softly sing.

"I've traveled 'cross these United States from sea to shining sea.

I've seen it all from the Golden Gate Bridge to Lady Liberty.

From the shores of the Atlantic to Californi-ay,

Each place I've seen in this great big land makes me want to say,

'Oh, I'm proud to be an American, patriotic and true.

'I'm proud to wave our glorious flag, that beautiful red, white, and blue.

'From the purple mountain majesties to the fruited plain,

'This nation that I love so dear, well dear, let me explain."

I let out a slight giggle. "What's that, Dagny?"

"Oh, I'm sorry. Sometimes I absentmindedly start signing some of my lines. It's from the musical I was cast in over at Paramount."

"I heard something about that. Tell me more."

"Are you sure? I don't want to bore you."

"Of course not. I want to hear every last detail." It was odd. Six months ago, she would have gone on and on about news like this completely unprompted. I wouldn't have been able to get a word in edgewise. Now she was worried she'd bore me. She was almost reserved in the way she began to speak about this new role of hers.

"It's quite marvelous, actually. While I'm not the lead, I am a supporting actress alongside Bing Crosby and Joan Fontaine. Can you imagine, Mabs? Bing Crosby."

"That *is* wonderful," I smiled. Her good news took my mind from the thoughts of my mother that kept creeping into my mind, and I was grateful for the distraction.

"At the risk of taking you someplace you'd rather not think about right now," she started, "what's going on with you? Last you told me, you'd signed a contract at MGM. Imagine that," she continued as a bit of an aside. "You, with a contract. Have you been cast in anything yet, *Miss Starlet*?

"Yes, it is rather amazing, isn't it? As a matter of fact, I had lunch with Vincente a couple of weeks ago and I've been cast as a lead in his new film. We'll be shooting on location in Italy in February."

"Oh, Mabs. That is exciting," she exclaimed with delight, stopping in mid-stride, and turning toward me. She grabbed my hands and, had it not been for the subdued atmosphere of the morning, I'd have expected her ready to jump up and down. It lifted my spirits to see her so happy at my news so, as silly as it was, I decided to jump myself.

Then she jumped and soon we were both skipping and running and, soon enough, even dancing along the beach like the schoolgirls we'd left behind in Prairie River so long ago. It must have been quite the spectacle for anyone looking on and it was just what I needed. I was still haunted by the news of my childhood, but this distraction helped to push it to the back of my mind.

After several minutes of this, we'd eventually tired ourselves enough that we slowed back down to a comfortable walk.

"Oh, Mabs, I truly am happy for you," Dagny said once we'd caught our breath. "I must admit, I never thought things would happen this fast for you, if at all, when I dragged you along to that audition so many months ago, but here you are. The sky's the limit for you now, Mabs, and you're going to be a star in that sky."

A muted grin crossed my face as she said this. Yes, the sky was the limit.

CHAPTER 41
WILD RIDE

I don't really know why, but danger has always been an important thing in my life– to see how far I could lean without falling, how fast I could go without cracking up.

— William Holden

DECEMBER

I did my best at keeping thoughts of my early childhood out of my mind and largely succeeded. On good days, I focused on preparing for my new role or taking a walk on the beach. On not so good days, I had a martini or two. Thankfully, I never repeated an episode as bad as that initial one and, much to Jill the bartenders' delight, I'm sure, never set foot in that bar near my apartment again.

Dagny was a huge help, of course, spending quite a deal of time with me, no doubt wanting to ensure that I kept as sober as possible. We kept the party-going to a minimum, instead preferring late lunches and more days at the Bel-Air, even though the pool was now closed for the season. On occasion, she simply came over to my apartment, and we entertained ourselves there.

"I'm so bored, Dagny," I said as we sat, listening to The Mills Brothers on the phonograph. "I want to be in Italy now."

"You will be soon enough. Just enjoy the moment. It's good to be bored sometimes. It's good to just have a relaxing evening in sometimes," she replied, looking up from the back of the record she'd been studying.

"Ha! That's a laugh coming from you. Whatever happened to *always a day at the beach, always a dinner, always a screen test?*"

"I don't know. I guess I'm just not as attracted to all that as I used to be."

"It must be that musical you're in. It must be Bing Crosby. All that wholesome Americana is getting to you."

"I don't think that's it, but so what if it is?"

"We didn't move all the way down here to listen to records. That's what. We could have done that back in Prairie River," I scolded her.

"I doubt it would be The Mills Brothers, though. Anyway, what's gotten into you? Why are you so antsy for adventure all of the sudden?"

"I guess I've just had nothing to do the past few weeks."

"Well, you're the one who quit your job at the advertising agency."

"Did I?" I laughed. "Really, I just stopped showing up as soon as Vincente cast me in his Italy picture. I knew it was coming, or at least something like it, but I suppose a small part of me was prudent enough to hedge my bet and stick around to make sure. Besides, it's not like I was showing up that often near the end anyway." There was another part of it, too. A part I didn't want to share with even Dagny. Winifred was now in control more than I cared to admit, and it was her who told me I needed to stay at the advertising agency until she told me I could quit.

"Is that what it was," Dagny said, pursing her lips and looking at me knowingly as if she were some schoolmarm.

"Oh, don't give me that look," I said, rolling my eyes. "You know, I'll bet Bea's pining away in her office right now expecting me to waltz through her door again. Pathetic really. In any case, I had to. That place was stifling my creativity."

"Ha! That's ironic coming from someone who was a copywriter. Weren't you being paid for your creativity?"

"My talent was wasted on them. Ad copy is so mundane. I was practically turning it out in my sleep."

"So, what are you going to do now then?"

"Well, right now I'm going to finish this whisky sour."

"And then?"

I downed the rest of the drink, crunching on the last bit of ice. I needed to do something. I was getting cabin fever. "I know. I feel like going for a drive!"

"That's absurd! First of all, we don't have a car."

"I know where Carlisle parks his, and he's out of town."

"Second of all, you don't know how—"

"How hard can it be? Come on, we'll just drive down The Strip and look at the glittering lights."

"Well, that does sound fun, but I don't know. What if we get pulled over?"

"Come, now, Dagny. Where's your sense of adventure?"

"I left it at home. At the bottom of my sock drawer," she said with a cheeky smile.

"Ha! That's a good one. Honestly though, don't be such a wet blanket." I stood up and pulled her to her feet. She didn't offer much resistance.

"Well, okay. Just a few blocks and then right back to Carlisle's, promise?"

"Promise," I said, putting my hand to my heart.

We took a taxi to Carlisle's house, and I let myself in with the key I knew he hid under the flowerpot. Dagny giggled. I could tell she was beginning to enjoy this little caper. I was glad she still had a little adventure in her. I grabbed the keys from where they hung in the kitchen, and we went out to the garage. I opened the doors to reveal a 1947 Studebaker Commander Regal DeLuxe convertible.

"That's quite a car!" Dagny fawned and punctuated it with a whistle.

"I know! Come on, let's get in." We walked into the garage and opened the car doors, then put down the top. Carlisle had given me a couple of driving lessons around his neighborhood, so

I wasn't a complete novice. But as we backed out, I had some difficulty with the clutch and heard the gears grind.

"Are you sure you know what you're doing?"

"Quiet! Yes!" I replied, a bit frustrated, but I soon got it, and we were on our way, with the wind in our hair.

"Now remember, we just drive down to The Strip and back. You promised."

I had, but it was such a thrill that I began to have other ideas.

"It would be a shame just to drive it on The Strip. I feel like we need to get the full effect of the wind in our hair. I know! Let drive out to Malibu."

"You're mad, Mabs! It's nearly dark and that's an hour away! Plus, how much have you had to drink?"

"Well, aren't you the matron? I'm fine. Come on. We can watch the sunset!"

"It's already set."

"Then we can stay out all night and watch the sunrise!"

"We're on the West Coast. That's not much of a sunrise," she replied, but I could tell it was a half-hearted protest. She'd resigned herself to my plan. I turned toward the Pacific Coast Highway and Dagny remained silent, nervously fidgeting with the hem of her blouse.

After five minutes or so, I knew she was beginning to relax when she ran a hand through her hair, letting it blow in the wind, then reached both arms up to feel the air press them back from above the windshield. There was still enough light that the road was clearly visible, and we were having a fantastic time.

A few miles in, with the city well behind us and nothing but country road ahead, I began to press down on the accelerator. The hills to the right faded into a blur and the center line nearly disappeared.

"Must we really drive so fast? It's getting dark," Dagny said. I glanced over at her. She had her back pressed into the seat and her fists were balled up in nervousness.

"Oh, Dagny, you really do sound like a matron." I pressed down on the accelerator even harder, and the car took off.

"I just love the feel of the wind in my hair and the smell of the ocean! I feel so alive!" I held my hand out the window and let it glide like the wing of an airplane, floating up and down, up and down. "I feel like I'm flying!" I glanced at the speedometer. We were flying. Nearly sixty miles per hour.

"Please, Mabs, let's slow down. Let's go home. I'm frightened." She shouted, her body tense and her hands tightly gripping her leg.

I pressed down more. Sixty-five miles per hour. Seventy. Seventy-five. While I did ease up occasionally to take a curve, we were still going quite fast, a curve to the left, another to the right. My body was being rocked side to side. I glanced at Dagny. She was clutching her legs tightly but didn't protest any further. She couldn't escape. She was captive, not just physically, but emotionally.

A blind curve ahead. I wasn't paying full attention. Headlights. Dagny screamed. I jerked the wheel to the right, surprisingly unfazed by the truck that passed by us close enough I could feel the wind from it hit me. Unfazed, that is, until the car went off the road and up a slight rise, its front end bucking up like a wild horse breaking its reigns. For a brief moment, I realized the irony of the fact that it wasn't a horse, but horsepower, that led to this event.

Somehow, I managed to hold it together though, and somehow, we'd managed to drive off the road in one of the only spots where certain death wasn't assured.

"Wow! What a rush!" I cried with glee.

"Damn it, Mabs! You almost killed us!"

"But don't you feel so alive?!"

"Be serious!" she fumed. "If we hadn't just nearly died, I'd kill you myself!"

"Oh, I am sorry. You're right. Here, you better drive us home," I said, composing myself and putting an appropriately serious look on my face, even if I didn't feel it.

Then I glanced out the windshield and realized that wasn't going to happen. Smoke and steam rose from the front of the car. Even if we hadn't died, the engine clearly had.

"Oh, damn it again, Mabs! I knew this was a bad idea. I knew I should have done more to stop you." She screamed, not at me so much as in utter frustration, then put her hands to her face and began to cry.

It was now late enough that the chances of another car coming down the highway were growing slim, and we were much too far from any kind of civilization to walk.

After a few moments, she dropped her hands from her face and composed herself. "Come on, Mabs," she said resignedly, letting go of her anger. "Let's put the top up and get in the backseat. We'll have to sleep in the car until morning when another car comes along."

It may have been dark, but it wasn't late enough to sleep, especially for a night owl like me, especially not with the adrenaline still pumping through my veins. But what else was there to do? We put the top up and climbed into the back seat. Dagny closed her eyes. She didn't fall asleep though and a few minutes later she opened them again.

"Mabs," she said gently, looking over at me.

"What is it, Dagny?" I'm sure she wanted to tell me to go to sleep, scold me like the wicked child I was, but just as a wicked child can break any heart with her doe-eyed glance, when she looked over at me, I broke hers. Far from being the scolding parent, she leaned into me and wrapped her arms around me.

"Mabs, I don't know why I'm saying this now, especially after you almost killed us. Perhaps that's the reason, but I feel like you're truly the only one who understands me, the only one who cares. Perhaps it's because you knew me before. Perhaps it's because we both come from a place like Prairie River. Perhaps it's just the silence." She paused for a moment, her words drifting away, then continued.

"But here, alone, nothing but the darkness and the silence between us…" She let this final sentence trail off as if she were not sure how, or if, or why, or when, to continue.

I waited, wanting desperately for her to finish her thought, not so much because I wanted to know what it was, but because I wanted something to distract me from the silence.

Truth be told, I wanted the wild ride to continue. Not just the literal ride that had taken place moments before, but the ride that had been going on the past few months. It was simpler that way, not having to think, not having to feel. I began to realize what Dagny must have loved about the Hollywood scene before I entered her life. Then I wondered what had happened. Why had things changed for her? Why had things changed for me?

I remembered a script Dagny had read to me once, for a part she never got. What was the line? *Thinking is overrated. Live for today. No, not even the day! The moment!* It was a cheery line. Everyone jumped in a pool, dressed in their finery, but she'd delivered it with sadness. Recalling it made me sad now too.

"What is it, Dagny, you can always tell me." I hugged her close to me. I wasn't just humoring her. I wanted her to know I really did care, especially since I had nearly just killed us both.

"I've been with so many men these past several years. It was always for want of being loved, truly. But for a few, like Kenneth, it was always just for the night. And he turned out to be little more in the end. Or maybe it was me." I saw a tear sparkle in the moonlight and run softly down her cheek.

"I never saw any of them again," she continued. "At least nothing more than a glance across a crowded room. They wanted it that way, I know. But strangely, if I'm being honest with myself, so did I. The idea of love was always more comforting than love itself. The night turned to dawn, and I left them in an empty bed."

"That's nothing to be ashamed of," I encouraged her, but I knew she felt that way. Somehow, over the last few months, we'd traded characters. She now played the part of the gentle lamb while I'd become the lioness.

"Love doesn't happen like it does in the movies. Sometimes I wish it did. Then again, isn't that why things always fade to black?" She paused and let her gaze fall upon the faint light that made the horizon, far out at sea, barely visible. "Fade to black. Fade to black. It would be so easy. A happy ending." But we both knew what she was talking about, and we both knew it was anything but.

She was silent. I heard a coyote howl off in the distance and it sent a shiver through me.

"Dagny?" She didn't answer. She had fallen asleep, the poor little lamb. I ran my hands gently over her hair and then, soon, so did I.

CHAPTER 42
AULD LANG SYNE

It was a fête worse than death.
— Barbara Stanwyck

A car eventually came by just as dawn was breaking. The driver, an elderly man on his way to fish, gave us a ride to Malibu where we called a tow truck. By midday, the car had been repaired. We drove—very slowly this time—back to Carlisle's and parked the car back in his garage. He'd be none the wiser, or so I hoped.

Three more weeks passed. Dagny had more than forgiven me and promised not to breath a word of our caper to Carlisle, and I was appropriately penitent, vowing not to drive again. I'd also managed to suppress memories of my birthday and my birth mother. I'd seen two letters arrive postmarked from Prairie River, but promptly tore them up and threw them away, not wanting any news from my past to provoke me further.

Dagny was invited to Christmas dinner at Bing Crosby's house and invited me along. It was a rather intimate affair with just his family and a few of us untethered souls. The eggnog flowed freely, but other than that, it was a very tame afternoon. After eating, we played charades by the fire, and one of the other actresses pressed a surprisingly shy Bing Crosby into singing *White Christmas* for us, naturally.

Two days later, Dagny helped me pack and rode with me to the train station to board the *Super Chief* to New York.

"Oh, you'll have so much fun in Italy! I just know it," she said. "Maybe you can bring me back some leather boots. I heard there's a shop there run by a man who used to live right here in Los Angeles. I think he used to make shoes for Gloria Swanson. Salvatore something or other." She gripped my shoulders and smiled at me as we stood on the platform. I recalled the day I said goodbye to her at the train station in Prairie River. This time, I knew I'd see her again soon.

"Best of luck with your musical, Dagny. I'll be sure to write, and I'll see you in February. By then, we'll both be stars!"

"Yes! Isn't it grand!" We kissed cheeks and then a porter came and grabbed my luggage. As the train pulled out of the station, I looked out the window and saw her wave goodbye.

Traveling only coach class up until then, I enjoyed having a larger drawing room all to myself. Not that I spent much time in it. Most of the two and a half days were spent with some of the other cast and crew in the Navajo-themed lounge or dining cars with their turquoise and copper accents. We were waited on by Harvey Girls as we conversed with our fellow stars and other celebrities. We dined on fresh trout, New York steaks, and Malossol Caviar. We drank Châteauneuf-du-Pape by the gallon. All the while, the dulcet *clickity-clack* of the rails beneath our feet kept tempo.

All of this was but a preview to what awaited when we arrived in New York. Grand Central Station was indeed grand, but I had to be content with just a glimpse. We were immediately ushered to an awaiting limousine by an army of porters, then whisked off to the Plaza Hotel.

During the next two days, Vincente, true to his word, took me around to all the landmarks; the Empire State Building, Times Square, the Statue of Liberty—the words of Dagny's little show tune briefly entered my mind—and shopping at Saks and Macy's. He showed me some of his old haunts as well, and we dined at Tavern on the Green.

Then it was New Year's Eve. I'd never even been awake at midnight on the last day of the year, let alone ushered in the new one surrounded by partygoers blowing horns and throwing streamers. What wonders the year 1948 had brought!

At 9:30 on the last night of the year, after dinner at the Palm Court, Vincente knocked on my door, ready to escort me— me and the rest of the stars of his upcoming production—off to the fête of the year. I'd purchased a gown at Saks the day before, special for the occasion. It was a mermaid-cut of navy-blue satin adorned with an array of sequins that really accentuated my figure. The hairdresser from the hotel had come to put my hair up. He was no Sydney Guilaroff, but he would do. My look was completed with a string of pearls Tiffany's had loaned to Vincente. While I knew I was not yet a star in the strictest sense, when I looked at myself in the mirror on the way to answer the door, I was in my element. I was born to wear couture. It's a shame I'd be playing a peasant girl once we reached Italy. After tonight, my gown would have to wait to make its next appearance. I had no doubt it would.

"So, where are you taking me this evening, Vincente?" I asked as I slid my arm around his elbow.

"Babe is having a small get together at her St. Regis penthouse," he answered, matter-of-factly, as if I should know.

"Babe?" I probed.

"Yes, forgive me. I forget that you wouldn't know many of the New York set. Barbara Paley, née Cushing, one of the *fabulous Cushing sisters.*"

I shook my head. I really had no idea who he was talking about but went along with it.

"Everyone calls her Babe," he continued. "She worked for a short time at *Vogue*, married Stanley Mortimer, divorced, then married Bill Paley last year. I guess that covers the lot of it. Your typical East Coast socialite. They're all rather interchangeable, to be honest." He said these last words not with contempt or even pity, but as someone might refer to the weather. I wondered why we were attending this particular party. Were these Paley folks insufferable inspirations for Vincente's next picture, or were they entertaining enough to join in greeting the new year? I guess I'd find out soon enough.

We arrived at the Paley's penthouse just after ten with the party in full swing. I didn't recognize a soul—none appeared to be actors—but I certainly recognized the type. As Vincente had said, they were interchangeable with many of the socialites I mixed with back in Hollywood.

The living room was rather quaint compared to many I'd been in. It couldn't have been much more than fifteen by twenty feet in size and was decorated in a Louis XIV-style with ornate chairs and tables and drapes of gold and white. It seemed rather quotidian really. I assumed everyone in New York society decorated their homes this way. So much for this Babe Paley woman being a fashion icon. She was stuck two and half centuries in the past.

"Just dreadful, isn't it, dear? I'm having it all ripped out next month and bringing in Billy B to make some sense of it. Hints of North Africa and the Ottomans. Maybe a little of that Indian calico. I do so love the Near East, don't you? Hi! Babe Paley, welcome to our little New Year's fête." She extended her hand, and I shook it.

"Hello. Mabs Eriksson. To be perfectly honest, all I know of the Near East is flying carpets and I imagine those would be terribly unsafe on these floors. I don't know much more about interior decorating either. I'm only an actress. I decorate myself with each new picture." It was false modesty, but Babe seemed to appreciate my words.

"Ha! Yes. You're staring in Vincente's next picture, aren't you?"

"So good of you to notice. I am. But, say, where can a girl get a martini around here?"

"Right over there," she said, pointing to a bar in the corner. "But tonight, we're all drinking French 75s."

"Bien súr," I replied as I walked off toward the bar. I was stopped in my tracks.

"Why, Mabs, no one told me you'd be here this evening."

I'd given up being struck by Winifred's surprise appearances. Perhaps it was the fact that I was out of my element, on the opposite coast. Perhaps now that I had some notion of what drove my anxiety that night at her bungalow, I could break free of the grasp she seemed to have on me. She may have been instrumental in getting me to where I was, but hadn't I come far enough now? In any case, I didn't want her to spoil this evening and far from being under her spell this time, I actually felt emboldened and ready to size her up.

"I'm sure that's not true, Winifred." She wouldn't get a hold of me this time, to get a hold of my mind, *my soul.*

"Oh, but it is! It is!" she lied. "Why, Babe only called me last week. I was back in Savannah with Auggie. He does so like to spend Christmas in the South. I think it's odd, personally. Then again, spending it anywhere outside of New England seems sacrilegious to me. No snow. No fir tree. No yule log. It just doesn't have the proper air to it, now does it?"

"No, I suppose not." I rolled my eyes. I wanted her to get to the point, whatever it was. "You were saying? About Babe?"

"Oh, yes," she continued, focusing back on the crux of her story. "As I was saying, Babe called me last week and said she was throwing a New Year's bash. Well, it had been a while since I'd reconnected with so many of my friends up here, so I thought, 'why not?'"

"Yes! Why not?!" I cheered mockingly, throwing a hand in the air, and plastering a faux grin on my face. "Only one problem, Winnie."

"What's that," she asked, a bit confused.

"You don't have any friends!" I laughed.

"You know that. I know that. These people don't," she said, getting very quiet and very serious. "You listen to me, Mabs." She jabbed a finger at my chest, pursed her lips, and narrowed her eyes. "Don't think for an instant that you're going anywhere without me. I may not be boarding the *Vulcania* next week, but I'll be sailing with you every leg of the journey, and I'll be with you once you get to Sicily too. Just remember that."

I forced a laugh loud enough to gain the attention of those around us. I did my best to sound entertained. Inside, however, I was terrified of her words. *How could someone come across so threatening in such a delicate way?* I could probably take her in a fight, after all. *Or could I?*

"Oh, Winnie, you are a hoot! *I don't think I could stand another Russian winter here!* What a crack up! I'll have to remember that one!" I leaned into it, inventing a punchline to a joke that was never told in order to fool myself as much as anyone around me.

Winifred stood there stern faced. I went around her and straight to the bar, doing my best to stifle the nervous shaking in my hands. It wasn't a French 75 I needed now, but a French 150. And fast.

The bartender quickly mixed one up and I drank it down even faster.

"Slow down there, toots! Don't you want to be awake for the stroke of midnight?" he asked, quite impertinently for someone who was quite clearly the help.

"Listen, Mack, I don't know who you think you are, but you better watch your lip. I've never been awake to usher in the new year, I'll have you know, so why should I start now? Gimme another one of those French 75s. In fact, gimme two."

He'd been looking at me with a slightly smug little grin on his face, but it suddenly shifted to a frown and his gaze went to my right. I turned around. Vincente was there.

"Mabs, are you alright? This man isn't giving you trouble, is he?"

"No, sir. No trouble, I swear. Another French 75 coming right up, Miss," the bartender said, scrambling frantically to make the drink.

"No, no, that won't be necessary," Vincente replied, gently raising a palm toward the bartender then turning to me. "Mabs, come with me." He said it firmly enough that I knew it was not a request but a demand. He grabbed my arm and ushered me into a hallway. "Mabs, what's wrong? I can't have you acting like this before we've even left for Naples. I need to know I can trust you. This business can be rough. I need to know you can handle it."

I sobered right up at his words. While I was obedient to Winifred out of some sort of fear, I wanted to be obedient to Vincente out of respect and adoration.

"Yes, Vincente, I'm sorry. There won't be any more problems," I said respectfully, like a child who'd just been scolded for tracking mud inside the house.

"Good, now take this." He pressed a turquoise and crimson colored pill into my palm then handed me a glass of what appeared to be a gin and tonic. "It will calm your nerves."

I put the pill in my mouth and washed it down with the drink.

"Now, this is a New Year's Eve party! Go enjoy yourself. Make some friends. At least for the night."

So, I did. At least as much as possible knowing Winifred was lurking somewhere in the background. I did manage to avoid any sight of her for the rest of the evening though, almost making me wonder if our earlier encounter was an apparition. Vincente's magic little pill also helped me to relax.

I spent the rest of the night chatting with C.Z. Guest, Barbara Hutton, and Gloria Vanderbilt. I was intrigued by C.Z.'s stories about her short time in the Ziegfeld Follies. *And Gloria Vanderbilt!* Well, what does one say about Gloria Vanderbilt? All that money and class to match. I took mental notes. *Oh, to be a swan.*

Then a few of the staff began handing out glasses of champagne and the countdown began. When the clock struck midnight, I was suddenly twirled around and found Gloria's lips on mine. It was shocking, to say the least. I'd only kissed Carlisle up to that point, so I didn't have much to compare it to, but it wasn't entirely unenjoyable. Still, it wasn't really romantic either. It was just a rather anonymous fit of new year passion.

"Oh, excuse me, dear!" she said, when she saw the shocked look in my eyes.

"Quite alright," I gasped, regaining control of my breath. "It's New Year's after all. And you're certainly now one acquaintance I won't soon forget, *Auld Lang Syne* and all that." I smirked at her, then raised my glass of champagne in a toast before drinking it down in one gulp. 1949 was off to quite a start.

CHAPTER 43
PEP PILLS

An American may speak love with his lips; the Italian must say it with his eyes.
— Rudolph Valentino

JANUARY 1949

After ten days aboard the American Export Lines' *Vulcania*, another day in Naples, and another taking the train down the west coast of Italy to Sicily, I was quite exhausted.

I'd like to say the journey across the Atlantic was one big party, but I remained in my cabin, fighting off seasickness most of the voyage. Still, I did manage to take a few turns around the ship's deck and marveled at the expanse of an endless sea in every direction.

I thought, too, about my parents making a similar voyage in the opposite direction some thirty years before. This led to thoughts about my mothers, both the one who bore me and the one who raised me, my father, and the lie I'd lived under for so long. Part of me was homesick. Part of me wanted never to return.

I considered sending a letter when we reached Naples but couldn't imagine how to explain it all. Not the turmoil I felt about my past nor the nervous excitement I felt for my future. Maybe just a postcard would do. But what would I write?

Greetings from Italy, Mama and Papa! I'm a murderous Italian whore now. Much Love, Your Daughter (The Other One)

No, that would never do. Best I just leave it alone.

The day after arriving in Palermo, we filmed the scenes of *Sicilia! Sicilia!*—the working title of the film—that took place there. Not much was needed to transform one of the streets into the nineteenth century. There was still a fair amount of rubble left over from the war, but Vincente had found an area that provided a convincing stand-in for what it must have looked like a century before.

Frances Marion had reworked some of her original ideas and expanded on the script, setting the story during the tumultuous days of the Sicilian Revolution. Instead of a mere bandit, my lover was now a revolutionary. The woman I end up pushing into the path of an oncoming horse cart, played by Gloria Grahame, was not his betrothed, but the daughter of one of the Bourbon military officers stationed in Palermo. I'd gone from being nothing more than a jealous peasant to a woman with a purpose. Still, Vincente wanted his dark ending, so he had my character eventually stab my lover after she felt his commitment to him—and the revolution—was not sufficient enough. I loved the new direction. It allowed me to play a strong woman, one that I felt was very similar to my own blossoming personality.

"ACTION!" It was a little odd, starting filming in the middle of the story, but I'd read the entire script between fits of nausea on the voyage over, rehearsed some of my lines during the two days of relative calm as we steamed between Gibraltar and Naples, and felt prepared enough.

I knew nothing of the Sicilian Revolution and not much more about revolutions in general. But I did my best to employ the Method and channel whatever revolutionary tendencies I had inside me. In reality, I'd never considered fighting for the cause of the *little guy*. Then again, wasn't *I* the little guy in some sense? And I'd made it, really made it, grasping the crown at this very moment.

"Maria Elena, you claim to care for us, the peasants, the farmers, the laborers! You show up at the orphanages when it suits you, but I see through you. It is all an illusion! You disgust me, you and your—your father and his men! I spit on you! *Ptuh! Ptuh!*" It was invigorating, delivering that first line. I felt like Luciana was the character I was born to play. When I'd played Linda, it was with a more subtle sensuality, my lines delivered like the satin of my dress. I knew that wasn't me. Now, I was alive! My words were as colorful and rough as the costume I now wore.

"You miserable creature! How dare you speak to me that way! Ever since King Ferdinand granted your kind certain freedoms, you think you are special. You are not! You are not qualified to clean my shoes with your tongue!" Gloria matched my temper, albeit more subtly. We were well paired, I thought.

"I wouldn't care to lick your shoe if my life depended on it! You watch yourself. Your day is coming! All of you! Your day is coming! We will have our victory, and the ruling class will rule no more!"

"Ha! I laugh in your face, poor *picciota.* Now, be gone!"

"CUT! Okay, good. Both of you," Vincente said. "Now, let's do another take. Mabs, really play up the disgust you have for the ruling class. Gloria, pull back a bit. You certainly have equal disgust for this lower-class of would-be revolutionaries, but at this point the first shots of the revolution have not been fired, so Luciana is hardly worth your time. And ACTION!"

We reshot the scene another four times until Vincente had what he wanted and then broke for lunch. It was a simple, yet delicious affair of *pasta al norma*—pasta with eggplant—and *pesce spada alla ghiotta*, which was a swordfish grilled over hot coals.

There was a festive atmosphere about the town, due, no doubt, to all the locals witnessing a Hollywood production. It was also so much more down to earth than Los Angeles or New York. Surprisingly, I found myself touched when a little girl came up to me with a bouquet of poppies.

"Per la lattanta!" she said with a smile. I had no idea what she was saying but smiled back and waved a thank you as she skipped away, singing to herself.

I amused myself the following hour by walking around town and finding myself in the *Mercato di Ballarò*. It was a stage play all to itself with the merchants being the actors, performing for all who walked by as they encouraged passers-by to try their goods.

"Bollito magro! Bollito magro!" Again, I had no idea what they were saying but I loved it. That is until the aromas from all the stalls became too overwhelming to my senses. Strong scents had never affected me before, so I wasn't sure why I was suddenly feeling a bit queasy. I swallowed hard, trying not to let it overcome me, and wiped a bead of sweat from my brow. Perhaps it was being in a new place. Perhaps it was still the effects of travel. Perhaps I had been skewered by the swordfish I'd just had. I sat down on the street and held my stomach. It couldn't have been alcohol. I hadn't had a drop since Naples. *Why was I feeling so awful?*

Luckily, moments later, one of the grips strolled by, noticed me, and rushed to my side. "Miss Eriksson? Are you alright?!"

"Not so much. I need to go back to my room."

He helped me up and walked me several blocks until, at last, we'd made it to the hotel. I felt horrible. Not just physically, but the second shoot of the day was to begin at 4:30, less than an hour away. "I'm so sorry. I don't think I'll be in any state to do our next scene. Please tell Mr. Minnelli."

Two hours later, I was awakened by a knock at my door. It was Vincente.

"Mabs, are you alright? No, a silly question. Of course you're not."

"Oh, Vincent. I'm so sorry. I'm not sure what came over me. I was walking through the market and suddenly fell ill. Perhaps it was the fish? Is anyone else feeling ill?"

He came over and sat on my bed. "No, Mabs, no one else is ill." It was not a reproach. It was well known that stars would sometimes feign illness in some sort of power play over the director, but Vincente knew my star had only just begun to rise and I wouldn't pull that stunt, especially so soon. I think he also knew I genuinely wanted to please him.

"Oh," I groaned. "I'm so sorry to throw off your shooting schedule."

"Nonsense. These things happen. We plan for them. You're in a new place. You've been traveling for days. It would be hard on anyone. You rest and we'll start fresh tomorrow afternoon.

Unfortunately, the next morning I didn't feel much better. They called in a local doctor, but he didn't know what to do, so finally, with the hour approaching and not wanting to fall yet another day behind schedule, Vincente gave me a pill. This one wasn't turquoise and crimson like the one he'd given me in New York, but plain white and round. I swallowed it with a glass of water and laid back down. Within about ten minutes, I felt wide awake.

"How are you feeling?" Vincente asked.

"Amazingly well! I'm ready to work!"

"Wonderful!"

I washed my face and got back into my costume. Half an hour later, we were back on the street, ready for the next scene in the low golden light of the setting sun.

When I went up to Gloria, I could feel her disdain. She barely looked at me and when she did, her brows furrowed, and her eyes shot daggers. Was she upset by my performance the day before? Or maybe she thought me unprofessional, holding up the production schedule.

I tried not to let it bother me. I decided, if anything, this is what her character was feeling too, so it would make for good chemistry between us. *Sulfur and saltpeter.*

"ACTION!"

"You again? You miserable cur. You know you don't belong in town. Go back to your mountain *topaia* and let me never lay eyes upon you again!" I wasn't entirely sure if she was speaking to me or my character. I played into it.

"It is you who should leave!" *Yes, what made Gloria so special?* She wasn't exactly a star either. Just a two-bit floozy who played a string of two-bit supporting parts. "My family has been on this island since Magna Grecia. You're just a transplant from France." I spit on her face. It felt natural in so many ways. I didn't mean to spit, at least not on her face, but I told myself I was selling the scene to the fullest.

She wiped it from her eye and glared with intense hatred at me. I knew, this time, she clearly wasn't acting. "You bitch! You spit on me!"

"CUT! Gloria! What on earth are you doing? You know that's not the line! We can't have that kind of language on set!"

She immediately snapped out of it. "Oh, I'm sorry Vincente, I guess I just got caught up in the scene." She flashed him a curt smile then glared at me again.

"Okay, let's take it again from the top. ACTION!" Vincente shouted.

We played the scene again and it was still spirited, but not quite as much, even though I did spit on her again. The second time, she managed not to react except as her character was written.

"How dare you, peasant!" She lunged at me, and we began to struggle. The horse cart came into the scene, and I shoved her in front of it. I hadn't meant to. I was just overcome once again with the reality of the scene we were playing so that I wasn't *playing* at all. I was fully Luciana and acted as she would without a thought. Luckily, the horse reared up and Gloria rolled out of the way.

"What are you doing?!" she screamed at me. "Vincente! She's mad! She wasn't supposed to shove me like that. What sort of show are you running here? I could have been killed!"

"Wasn't that the idea?" I said, looking down at her in the dust, my hands on my hips and a half smile curling my lips.

"You're crazy! Downright crazy! I'll never work with this woman again!" she shouted, turning toward Vincente. She got up, dusted herself off, and stormed off the set.

"That was incredible! John, tell me you got all that!" Vincente exclaimed, looking at the cameraman.

"Every bit, boss. Every bit. We can edit Gloria's fall with the shots of the stunt work later and it should turn out splendidly."

"Now, Mabs," Vincente said, turning to me and softening his voice. "That was wonderful acting. I dare say it didn't even appear to be acting, but we do need to be more careful. We've just started filming, so I have several more scenes to shoot with Gloria. I am glad that little *pep-pill* I gave you did the trick though. Are you still feeling well?"

"Oh, yes, Vincente. I've never felt better! Thank you. And I am sorry. I will try to contain myself in future."

"Very good. Okay, folks! That's all for today. Go enjoy yourselves the rest of the evening. Although don't enjoy yourselves too much. We leave bright and early tomorrow for Camporeale."

CHAPTER 44
THE SHEEP AND THE GOATS

Inside of all the makeup and the character and makeup, it's you, and I think that's what the audience is really interested in...you, how you're going to cope with the situation, the obstacles, the troubles that the writer put in front of you.
— Gregory Peck

The next morning, someone began banging on my door at 6 a.m. It was far too early—and I hadn't even stayed out late with the rest of the cast, drinking grappa, and singing along with an old man and his mandolin. I sure could hear them though. It would have sounded delightful if I hadn't felt ill again after the effects of the Vincente's pill worn off. What *was* wrong with me? Whatever it had been, it was even more pronounced as I opened my eyes.

"One hour until we depart for Camporeale, Miss Eriksson," a young man's voice called from behind my door. *Ugh! An hour. I'd never make it.*

I raised myself up in bed and was suddenly overcome with nausea. I leaned over and just managed to hit the bedpan on the floor next to me. *How wretched!* I reached for the glass of water on the bedside table and did my best to wash my mouth out. That's when I saw another of Vincente's magic *pep pills* lying there. I quickly swallowed it along with the rest of the water in my glass and laid back down. Sure enough, like the day before, I felt much better after about ten minutes.

I quickly dressed, ran a comb through my hair—luckily wardrobe and makeup would make me genuinely presentable—and, amazingly, was outside ten minutes before a rickety old bus pulled up. The *Sicilia! Sicilia!* Express was here to take us to Camporeale.

The roads were terrible, and I thought I might be sick several times along the journey with all the jostling about. As it was, a few of the other cast members did lose their breakfast out the windows. Perhaps had I eaten any, I would have joined them.

A journey of not more than thirty miles, a distance that would have taken less than an hour back in Los Angeles, ended up taking us more than two. Still, the countryside was rather pleasant.

We passed by terraced vineyards and peasant farmers herding goats. Women, undoubtedly much younger than they looked and carrying water jugs, passed by us going the other way. A time or two, we stopped for wagons being drawn by donkeys. It sure was a world away from the parties and nightclubs of Los Angeles.

It reminded me of my childhood. For the first time in many, many months, I was homesick for Prairie River. I missed Papa. I missed Mama, the one who'd raised me. I even missed Olivia and her silly charms. I missed Dagny, but not the Dagny I now knew, not the Dagny I'd met on Sunset Boulevard. I missed the Dagny I'd said goodbye to at the train station almost eight years before.

"Good morning, Mabs!" Gregory Peck plopped down in the seat next to me, interrupting my memories with that charming voice of his. We hadn't talked much on the ship during our Atlantic passage, and he'd been gone from the set the last two days. I imagine he wanted to go over our lines or build some sort of chemistry before we began shooting. "Forgive me for saying so, but you look a bit forlorn. Is everything alright?"

"Oh, yes," I said, turning my gaze from the window and quickly wiping away a small tear that had formed in the corner of my eye. "I was just thinking of home."

"Los Angeles?"

"No, Los Angeles could never be home." I said the words without thought and realized how candid I was being, even with myself. "I'm not sure Prairie River, Saskatchewan is anymore either, though. *You can't go home again.* Isn't there a novel by that name?"

"Yes, I believe there is, although I can't say I've read it or know anything about it. It does sound like a reason to be forlorn though."

"Yes, it does, doesn't it? Then again, if we can't go home again, the only way is forward. We must greet the next day with open arms and let it embrace us fully!" I said, throwing my arms as wide as I could, given the cramped space we were in.

"My, that was sure a quick turn around," he smiled.

"No sense in being melancholy. No good can come of it. Besides, aren't I meant to make love to you in the hay in a few hours then stab you to death tomorrow?!" I gave him a coy, flirtatious smile.

He laughed. "Yes, yes you are. So, let's make the best of the time we have left."

Camporeale was a relatively small town at around 6,500 residents, but still more bustling than I'd imagined. Perhaps the nicest thing about it was it had escaped any damage during the war and still resembled fully its nineteenth-century charms.

This is where most of the filming would take place, so we would call it our home for the next week. Surely, many of the scenes could have been filmed back on a sound stage in Hollywood, but Vincente wanted the realism that could only come from filming as much as possible on location. The fact that his ancestors had come from the island likely had a lot to do with his desires too. After we'd settled into our rooms and freshened up from the journey, he called the whole cast and crew together and addressed us.

"As many of you know, this story, while fictionalized, is deeply personal to me," Vincente began, standing atop a horse-cart and addressing the entire cast and crew gathered before him. "My grandfather and great-uncle were among the very revolutionaries you all are portraying. Their struggle for freedom was real. But like so much of history, the lines between good and evil, black and white, are seldom as clear as we wish them to be.

"The central theme of this film beyond the revolution itself, the love story turned sour between Giovanni and Luciana, may never have occurred in reality," he continued, joining his hands together then ripping them apart as if to symbolize a love affair broken. "But my vision with all this is to show how the chaos of a revolution, the blurred aims of those involved, can manifest themselves personally. We are not angels. We are not demons. We are only a mix of the two being constantly pulled between the two competing fates. What appears to be so clear one day can be clouded by love or lust the next, be it a noble love manifested in patriotism, or a baser, more animalistic lust between man and woman, woman and man."

He turned his gaze to look directly at Gregory and me. "Mabs, Gregory, the crew will be scouting locations and setting up shots for the remainder of the day. I want you to take this time to get to know not just each other's characters, but each other's true selves as well. I'm not completely convinced of this Method Stanislavski talks about, but I do agree with his idea that the person you are is a thousand times more interesting than the best actor you could ever hope to be. He's said that you must never lose yourself on the stage but act always in your own person as an artist. Make your scenes real. Play truly."

He returned to looking at the entire crowd. "Now, for the rest, you have your work, so let's get to it!" With that, he hopped down from the horse-cart and went over to speak with the cameraman.

We followed his advice. We broke away from the crowd and spent the afternoon somewhat in character, somewhat as ourselves, hopefully melding the two together as one. We found a rustic *osteria* and ate lunch. We worked out our backstories. We walked around the town and ventured into the surrounding fields to watch the goatherds and shepherds tend to their tribes and flocks.

"And before him shall be gathered all nations; and he shall separate them one from another, as a shepherd divideth his sheep from the goats; And he shall set the sheep on his right hand, but the goats on the left." Gregory uttered these words with an intense solemnity as he gazed out at the pasture. They sent a chill through me. "Matthew, Chapter Twenty-Five," he added.

"Do you often quote scripture?" I asked, a bit perplexed by it all. He had clearly strayed far from character now. At least I never had the impression that Giovanni Marino, a mountain bandit, would ever say such a thing.

"No, not often. I'm not sure what made me recall that passage other than seeing these sheep and goats before us."

"Well, you certainly know your chapter and verse."

"I once considered going into the priesthood. I suspect I knew, deep down inside, that I'd never be holy enough though. Perhaps we can honor God through our work on this picture."

Now there was a peculiar thought! "The Gospel of Vincente?" I mused.

"Something like that."

"Giovanni Marino as Jesus. Luciana Costa as Judas. And Maria Elena is who? Mary Magdalene?" I was intrigued by Gregory's idea, even if I thought it wasn't what Vincente had intended.

The next day, I took yet another of the pep pills first thing and, thankfully, wasn't plagued by any nausea. We began shooting right after breakfast. The establishing scenes, Luciana working at her family's small farm, followed by her first encounter with Giovanni, took the whole day.

Our on-screen love affair blossomed, especially given the work we'd both put in the day before with our characters' backstories. There was even a scene where Luciana's sister finds out about Giovanni and vies for his attention. While I'd certainly never competed against my own sister for the affections of a boy or a man, I'd competed with her over silly things and pulled from those experiences. It helped that the girl playing my sister, an Italian actress who was cast, played the part as a bit of a git herself.

The following day, we shot the big climax, the murder scene, in a barn filled with hay. There were multiple cameras set up around the space. Vincente had, indeed, spared no expense on this production. The crew ran about taking light readings and measuring distance to our marks. When all seemed ready, Vincente said the magic word I now tingled with anticipation for every time we shot a scene. "ACTION!"

I channeled Luciana once again and spoke my line. "Gio, you have no doubt heard now that Maria Elena is dead. It was me! I killed her! And I'm not ashamed. I'd do it again. We can be together now, don't you see, my love?"

"Oh, Luci, what have you done?! Yes, I loved you. I still do, it's true. But so much has happened. This terrible revolution. What is it all for? And now you've gone and turned yourself into a murderess. I had so hoped you wouldn't be scarred by that fate." Gregory balled up his fists in frustration.

"What is it all for?! Gio! It was you who pulled me into the fight! It was you who showed me what living not just for love but for country meant. How could you throw that all away now that we are so close? So close to victory. So close to that love. What is it all for? It is for us! No longer will the Bourbons dictate our future. No longer will my own family dictate our future!"

"No, Luciana, I'm sorry. I can't go on. I thought I was prepared for the fight, but I don't have it in me. I was a bandit, a rogue, but I realize now it was all a façade. You can surely continue the struggle without me. I won't fault you that. But I must go. This revolution is not for me. I have no stomach for it any longer. I have no stomach for death."

"Then you are a coward! A sheep! But also, a goat. All the sacrifices we've made, and you leave them on the altar intact? Would Cain have been so foolish?"

"Perhaps you are Abel then. Perhaps you will gain the blessing of Providence, while I am forced to wander in the wilderness. Be that my lot, I will accept it." He dropped his head in despair.

"No! You mustn't! We are meant to be together! To fight side by side, not as kin but as lovers, lovers of each other, lovers of this island, lovers of our nation's fate!"

"It is done, Luciana. I must go," Gregory began to step back from me. "Godspeed in your struggle, which I thought once was mine but is no longer. My only struggle now is that of a man forced to wander alone forevermore. I leave you now." He began to turn to go. I felt the anger rise within me. I was fully Luciana. He was Giovanni.

"You will not! You will stay!" I rushed to him, but he pushed me away.

"Get away, Luciana! Leave me!"

"No!"

He pushed me and I fell back. There, just within reach, an awl rested on the ground. I was more enraged than ever. More enraged than I'd been opposite Gloria a few days before. Not just my character, but me, Mabs. I felt the fire burning inside me. My entire body was hot. I could even feel it behind my eyes as they glared at him. This was no longer the Method. It was something beyond. I grabbed the awl, rose to my feet, and rushed at Gregory. Giovanni. Had Vincente not yelled *cut* at that very moment, I shudder to think what I might have done.

"Mabs, that was wonderful! Such passion! I was completely enthralled. Splendidly played." Vincente clapped. The whole crew clapped. Is this what acting was? *No, it was so much more.* I crumpled to the ground and began sobbing uncontrollably. The awl fell from my hand, and I doubled over, an intense pain growing inside me. Not the pain I'd felt the day before, something even baser, something that seemed to be ripping at my very soul.

"Mabs! What is it?" Gregory rushed over to my side. I buried my face in his chest and heaved repeatedly as wave after wave of emotion overtook me. Vincente joined him.

"Are you alright? You're not hurt, are you?" Vincente pulled me gently away from Gregory to make sure I hadn't injured myself.

I was hurt more than I think I'd ever been before, but my wound was much deeper than any he could see.

"It doesn't appear that you're injured," Vincente said, prodding my sides ever so slightly.

Gregory pulled me back into his chest. "Mabs, you mustn't be so upset. You played the scene better than I've ever witnessed in all my years of acting."

I couldn't stop. What was I becoming? What had I already become?

"Okay," Vincente said, turning to the rest of the crew, "that's all for today." Then he reached in his pocket and pulled out a bottle of the pills he'd given me on New Year's Eve, the crimson and blue ones. *Crimson for the blood that flows from the heart, blue for the blood that flows back.* I swallowed two along with a glass of water someone else brought over and then fell into darkness.

When I awoke again, I was in my bed in the little room that I called home in Camporeale. It was the next morning. A fog still clouded my mind. *What had happened? Had it been another dream? Was Gregory okay?* I looked up. He and Vincente were both there, standing near the window and speaking in low whispers.

"Mabs, I'm glad to see you are awake." Gregory crossed the room and knelt beside the bed. "How are you feeling?"

"Oh, Gregory, I'm so glad to see you, to see that you are alright." Luciana had left me and taken part of the reality of the last day with her.

At this, a puzzled look crossed his face. "Of course I am. But it is you we are worried about. You are feeling better now?"

"Yes, I think so. A bit of a fog. Forgive me, I don't know what came over me."

"Think nothing of it. It was an emotional scene. You were just caught up in it. It happens sometimes. It can be painful, but fantastic. You will see when you view yourself on screen. It was truly amazing. I must admit, I wondered how it would be, cast opposite you but I needn't wonder any longer."

"I was really all that?"

"All that and more." Vincente walked over and stood behind Gregory. "But you rest up now. We have some war scenes we need to shoot today with some of the supporting cast and extras, so no need to trouble yourself with anything but rest. I'll have someone bring up your meals and anything else you need."

"Thank you, Vincente. You are a dear."

"Think nothing of it. The next three days we will film the remainder of your scenes, much less emotionally taxing than the last, and then you will have all the time you need to recover on the trip back home." He brushed a lock of hair from my forehead, kissed it softly, and laid me back down. They both left the room and moments later, I fell asleep once again.

CHAPTER 45
LA LATTANTA

If only those who dream about Hollywood knew how difficult it all is.

— Greta Garbo

FEBRUARY

With the help of the pep pills, I managed to make it through the final days of filming in Sicily and the two weeks of travel back to Los Angeles. I wasn't feeling much better though, so Vincente had made an appointment for me to see a doctor the day after we returned. I didn't make it.

I was unpacking when the most intense physical pain I'd ever felt pierced my stomach. I felt like my insides were being ripped out. It was so severe that I fainted, collapsing to the floor. I don't know how long I was out, but when I came to, my thighs and the floor between them were covered in blood. I shrieked.

Oh my God! I was dying! Visions of my father and my sister flashed through my mind. So, too, did conflicting visions of my mother, the one I had known most of my life, and faint ones of the woman who'd given birth to me. I had to get to the phone. I had to call someone. Tears streamed down my face. I didn't want to die. Not like this.

I pictured the La Brea Tar Pits, not as they were now, but as they were in prehistoric times. I was sinking into the abyss, all the while praying a saber-toothed tiger would come finish me off quickly.

I don't know how I managed to make it to my telephone and dial the operator before collapsing again, but the next thing I knew, I was in a daze and being lifted onto a gurney in my living room. Then back into darkness before I finally came to in a blindingly white room that smelled like bleach.

Halfway conscious, my mind returned to my early childhood and the visit to my mother—my birth mother—in the asylum. Then, strangely, to the dirty coffeeshop on Sunset Blvd. the first day I met Dagny. *Bleach can cover up all sorts of ills, but does it ever really eliminate them?*

"Dagny? Dagny? Are you there? I wish that man would hurry up with our tea and toast." I said, still in a dream state.

"Mabs, I'm here! I'm here! You want tea and toast? I'm sure we can get that for you."

My dreams were more lucid than I expected. It almost sounded like Dagny was right there beside me. "Dagny? Is that you? Is that really you?"

"Of course it is, dear. I came as soon as I heard." I felt a hand press into mine and I returned to full consciousness. She was there! In the flesh!

"Oh, Dagny. It is you!"

"Yes, Mabs! I'm here! You gave us all quite a fright."

"Us all?"

"Yes. Vincente and Winifred are in the waiting area. We tried to ring Carlisle but there was no answer."

"Oh, I don't care about any of them, especially not Carlisle, but I'm so glad you were the first person I saw when I opened my eyes." I remained silent on Winifred, but the fact was, her being down the hall sent a chill up my spine. I furrowed my brow. "What happened? Why am I here?"

"Perhaps I should get the doctor," she said, looking behind her, then back. Something in her eyes betrayed her. She knew why I was there. *Why couldn't she tell me herself?*

"No, Dagny. Don't go. Tell me." I grabbed her arm. I didn't want to be alone, and I had to know what was going on.

She swallowed and tried best to cover the worried look in her eyes by forcing a smile. "Oh, Mabs, I'm so sorry. You've lost the baby." Tears welled up in her eyes and one trailed softly down her cheek.

Lost the baby? What was she talking about? Surely, I wasn't pregnant. The possibility immediately sobered me up but instead of being somber at the news, I let out a sharp laugh. It sent a pain through my stomach. I winced and quickly brought myself back under control. "What baby? I don't have a baby! What are you going on about, Dagny?"

The worried look returned to her eyes. "You mean…you didn't know you were with child?"

She was serious. I got serious as well. Suddenly it all made sense. The sickness on the boat that never left once we reached Italy. The near fainting in the market in Palermo. Perhaps even my violent reaction during the scene with Gregory Peck. I remembered, too, the little girl who brought me flowers. *Per la lattanta.* Of course! *For the baby!* How perceptive. How could she have known?

"Oh. Wow." I said softly. I laid back into my pillow and stared at the ceiling. I didn't know what I was feeling or even should feel. Was I happy to have been a mother if only for what? Two months? Was I sad to have lost the child? Was I relieved to not have to think about raising a child? Or the other alternative. I'm sure MGM had access to *procedures*. They seemed to be almost a rite of passage amongst actresses in Hollywood, but I'd also heard some horror stories.

Should I tell Carlisle? Suddenly, I was quite relieved no one had been able to reach him. Probably best I keep it quiet. After all, I didn't think of us as serious in the least.

"Are you okay, Mabs? I mean, I'm sorry. This must be an awful lot to take in all at once. Is there anything I can do?"

"I'm not sure what I'm feeling, Dagny. If I'm to be honest, I feel rather outside myself, like all this is happening to someone else, and I'm watching it up on screen. Perhaps they'll make a movie about it someday." I let out a small chuckle. "I know that must sound crazy."

"No. No, that doesn't sound crazy. Mabs, I'm sorry." Dagny began to cry.

"Whatever do you have to be sorry for?"

"Oh, Mabs, it's all my fault. I led you into this life. Perhaps it would have been better had we never met again last spring. Perhaps it would have been better had I never entered that *Fame and Fortune* contest. God knows my life hasn't turned out to be all that glamourous, and now I've gone and spoiled yours too."

"Nonsense, Dagny. My life is wonderful!" It was lie I was telling myself as much as I was telling her. At that moment, how could anyone think it was wonderful? But, maybe, if I said it enough times, I could convince myself of it.

"I couldn't ask for any better. So I had a miscarriage. These things happen every day." Even as the words left my mouth, I knew they were yet another lie, but it was a lie I was choosing to believe myself. "Think about it. I just got to go to Italy! I'm going to be a star. Grauman's Theater! The red carpet!" The words came out in quick succession, each one brighter than the one before. Life would be wonderful even if I had to act it out for myself alone.

"It's like you said, *all the good fortune, none of the regrets*. And, while your star hasn't risen yet, I'm sure it will. Besides, look outside. It's February and the sun is shining on palm trees. Back in Prairie River, they must be buried under three feet of snow."

Dagny got up and walked to the little window and pulled back the curtain. "Oh my god! Mabs!" She cheerily gasped. "You'll never believe this, but it's actually snowing!"

"Oh, now you're definitely putting me on. It doesn't snow in Los Angeles."

"No, I'm serious. It's snowing!" It brought and immediate change to her mood. If something as unbelievable as snow in Los Angeles could happen, maybe life really was wonderful after all. More than that, it was as if the snow had washed clean the specter of death that had just hung over the room. It even raised my spirits slightly. I sat up further and went to join Dagny at the window but was overcome with faintness when I tried to stand, so I laid back down. I'd have to take her word for it.

"Don't try to stand. You lie back down. Sunbeams or snowflakes, rain or shine, I'll be by your side. I promise you, Mabs." It sounded like something from another one of her musicals, but as corny as it was, it made me feel loved. She rushed back over to my bedside and embraced me.

"And I'll be by yours. Sisters to the end, right?" I gave her hand a squeeze.

"To the end," she smiled, squeezing back.

Just then, the doctor walked in with Vincente in tow. "Best we let the patient rest, Miss Lundberg. We should be able to release her tomorrow, and then you can have all the time together you want."

Dagny pressed her hand into mine a final time, then ran the back of the other one gently over my forehead. "I'll be here tomorrow to take you back to your apartment. Goodbye, Mabs."

Vincente walked over and sat in a chair near the foot of the bed. "Now, don't you worry, Mabs. This sort of thing happens all the time. It's just fortunate that it happened here in Los Angeles, and not while we were in Sicily or, worse yet, aboard a ship in the middle of the Atlantic. I've called Howard Strickling, our *fixer*, and he's going to make sure none of this makes the papers. In fact, outside the three of us and your friend Dagny, no one need ever know."

I thought again about the little girl in Palermo. *She knew*. I nodded my head in agreement. "Yes, Strickling. The papers. No one need know."

"Now, you get some rest," Vincente continued. "I need you back in the studio by next week to film some final scenes and do some reshoots. It should be a fairly light schedule and won't last more than a few days. Then, come April, we'll be all ready to release this film—and your star—to the world." He smiled gently as he said it. I smiled back.

Yes, I'd been dealt a setback, but I was still on track to achieve the dream. I was sure of it. Vincente and the doctor left, turning off the light as they went, and I drifted off into a literal dreamland.

I wish I could say my conscious mind's insistence on things being wonderful translated into my dreams, but it was just the opposite. I'd certainly had some frightful nightmares in the past, but this one was terrifyingly macabre.

I was aboard an ocean liner, on the deck and looking out at the vast ocean before me, except that it wasn't an ocean of water, but snow. It collected in huge drifts and blew about violently, like some of the fiercest blizzards I remembered from my childhood. The ship came to a stop, and I disembarked with scores of other passengers onto a beach covered in palm trees. Goats and sheep ran around. They all seemed to be laughing. *"Lattanta! Lattanta! Lattanta!"*

Then, I was in my mother's room at the asylum. A fire was raging in the fireplace and a line of six iron pokers were lined up against it. The raven that I remembered from my childhood visit to that asylum flew from the poplar tree and landed on the sill outside her window. Instead of the face of a bird, though, it was the face of a baby. My mother, who now looked strikingly like an older me, rose from her chair and walked to the window. She opened it and let the raven hop onto her crooked arm.

"What do you think, Mabs? She looks cold," my mother—myself—said, then turned to the bird and began stroking its head, which still carried the face of a baby. I watched in horror as she carried it closer and closer to the fire. I knew what she was about to do, but I couldn't watch. Nor could I turn away.

"No, please don't," I begged.

"But this is what you want, Mabs. This is what you've always wanted."

Suddenly, the fireplace turned into the entrance to Grauman's Theater, a red carpet extending from its doors. I looked down at my feet and saw I was standing at the other end. The raven beckoned to me, along with six goats to my left and six sheep to my right. I began to walk toward them when the carpet disappeared from beneath my feet. I was now standing on one of the pep pills I'd thought of as my salvation these past few weeks.

"Go on Mabs, embrace the flames. Feel their warmth. They're calling to you," a voice from behind me urged. It was Winifred's. I took a step and then found myself falling through the darkness. I just kept falling and falling. I was frightened but strangely accepting of my fate. After all, it isn't the fall that kills you. It's the sudden stop at the end.

One would think I might awake with a start, gripped by fear. Instead, I slowly opened my eyes to find myself in the darkness of the hospital room. A strange calm embraced me.

CHAPTER 46
REFORMED TRAMP

You find out who your real friends are when you're involved in a scandal.

— Elizabeth Taylor

The hospital released me the next morning at eleven, and Dagny was there to greet me. An orderly wheeled me out to the waiting room in a wheelchair. I felt it entirely unnecessary. Dagny had brought a fresh set of clothes. I had taken a shower. I felt refreshed. I even looked different when I gazed at myself in the mirror. My hair had grown out and was now showing more of my natural blonde than the black I'd been dyeing it for the past four months. *I'd certainly need to fix that.*

"Mabs, how are you feeling today?" Dagny said softly, even solemnly. She wore a long wool coat and a face to match, with the corners of her mouth turned up in a sympathetically forced smile. I hated being the object of pity, especially when I was feeling the exact opposite of pitiful. *Why was she acting so somber? Had someone just died? Oh, yes, of course.* I silently chuckled to myself at the irony of my thoughts.

"Never better!" I said cheerily. "I'd be even happier if I didn't feel like a spectator at my own funeral. Now let's go get something to eat. I'm starving! The food in this place is the pits."

"Alright," she replied, her smile softening a bit and a sparkle appearing in her eye. "A burger at Tommy's then?"

"Heavens no! Let's celebrate!" I leapt out of the wheelchair at the word *celebrate*, almost as if it were part of an act, then took two steps toward her, grabbed both her hands, and twirled her around in front of me. "I could really go for some lamb chops at Romanoff's. And you look in desperate need of a martini."

"My goodness! Mabs, whatever's gotten into you?"

"Perhaps it's not what's gotten into me, but what's just left!" I said, making a rather macabre joke.

Dagny just stared at me, quite clearly stunned.

"Oh, I'm sorry, Dagny. That was in poor taste, wasn't it? But do remember, I didn't even know I was carrying. I never had the chance to bond with the baby, so why should I feel any sense of loss? Besides, for the first time in a month I haven't awoken with nausea. If you knew what it was like, you'd agree that's reason enough to be cheery." It was a lie, the first part at least. Far from being indifferent, I was relieved not to be carrying a child. Had I known from the beginning, I wouldn't have felt any different.

"Well, when you put it that way," Dagny took both my hands and squeezed. A smile crossed her face. "Romanoff's then. And martinis." I knew she still wasn't convinced but was doing her best to go along with me.

"But enough about me," I said as we took our seats at a table in the center of the room. We hadn't requested it, but it was perfect. I wanted to be seen. I caught Alfred Hitchcock out of the corner of my eye. He was dining with what appeared to be a couple of studio executives in the back. At a booth underneath the muraled wall the restaurant was famous for, Joseph Schenck cozied up next to some platinum blonde tart who was spilling out of her dress and clearly didn't care. Veronica Lake was seated a few tables over, giggling over some boy a few years her junior who I didn't recognize. We nodded at each other. Tallulah Bankhead, not one to care in the least what convention demanded, was cooing at her lover of the week—or evening—a girl half her age.

"You're sure you're okay then?" Dagny said. She clearly didn't seem the least bit interested in being seen by any of our fellow diners. We might as well have been in the restaurant alone, the complete lack of attention she gave to anything or anyone around us.

"Yes, I'm feeling wonderful. I'll be simply over the moon once I get a martini in me! But you? Cheer up, for heaven's sake. It's been weeks since I've seen you. I want to hear all about it. Weren't you working on some musical before I left? Something with Bing Crosby, wasn't it?"

At this, she perked up. "Oh yes. It's grand. I think I've finally found my niche. I simply adore musicals. Who knew? After a few lessons with a voice coach, it turns out I can sing." I thought she might break out in a number right there, but she stopped short, for which I was grateful. Being seen is one thing. Being a spectacle is another. "They're just so much fun. And that Bing Crosby is a regular laugh riot."

"That's truly marvelous, Dagny," I smiled. I so wanted her to be happy and she'd worked at it for so long, but I also wasn't quite sure about this new demeanor I was witnessing. She'd been carefree, even shallow, for so long, I couldn't see the reason for the shift. Then again, my demeanor had shifted 180 degrees as well. "And what about your love life?" I added coyly. "Are you still seeing Henry Fonda."

"Oh, no. I've strictly sworn off married men. There is someone though." She paused and gave a wistful smile, looking up at the ceiling and bringing her hand to her chest. "He's marvelous. He was in the war, you know. A true hero. He's doing stunt work now. And he's so down to earth."

Our martinis came, and we toasted each other's blossoming careers. Over lunch—Dagny had a quite sensible Waldorf Salad, and I had my lamb chops—we caught up on the last two months. I told her all about Sicily and Gregory Peck but skipped over my fits of hysteria and my newfound reliance on the variety of pills that kept me sane.

She went on about the musical, remembering some of the funnier moments on set with Bing Crosby. I asked her about any parties I'd missed, and she confessed to only attending two rather tame affairs in the past month or so, one being a mandatory studio party that sounded like an awful bore.

"I just don't see much point in them anymore. It's all rather vapid, to be honest. As a matter of fact, this is the first stiff drink I've had in three weeks. Bill and I—that's his name, Bill—we'll occasionally share a bottle of wine over dinner although, quite often, we leave it half full on the table when we leave."

"My, aren't you on the health kick then? No drinking. A Waldorf Salad. I leave you alone for a month and a half and come back to a changed woman." Of course, I'd begun to see the change in her even before I'd left for Italy, but now it had seemed to run its course, and she was fully grounded in this new sobriety. I played my comment off innocently enough, but inside I was a bit disappointed, irritated even. Who would be my accomplice now? I'd have to rope her back in. No, this new wholesome play wouldn't work at all.

"I know," she giggled. "Isn't it splendid?"

"Well, I'm not sure *splendid* is the word for it. I hope you'll find at least the odd moment to sip drinks poolside at the Bel-Air or come with to one of Clio's parties. Why, they'll all think you've fallen off the face of the earth."

"Oh, let them. Besides, maybe I have. I do feel it's all been rather heavenly," she smiled. I looked down and noticed her martini glass was still three-quarters full. *Heavenly. Hmm.* Clipping the wings off this angel sitting in front of me might prove more difficult than I thought, but I was determined. She may have been a reformed tramp, but she was still a tramp, nonetheless.

"Well, it's still early enough. I say we go sun ourselves at the Bel-Air right now. What do you say? It's been ages since we've toyed with Robbie," I laughed.

"I didn't tell you! Robbie must have finally taken your advice. He's no longer working at the Bel-Air. They told me he's giving acting a go."

"Well, that is nice to hear, but I will miss him fetching us Mai Tais and fried egg sandwiches."

CHAPTER 47
MAD JAZZ PATTERN

Unless you really understand the water, and understand the reason for being on it, and understand the love of sailing and the feeling of quietness and solitude, you don't really belong on a boat anyway. I think Hemingway said one time that the sea is the last free place on earth.

— Humphrey Bogart

The following day I stayed home. I felt fine but the doctor had strongly recommended I rest. Dagny had been a dear and brought over plenty of groceries and prepared dinner for me ahead of time, so all I had to do was put it in the oven. I napped some. While awake, my mind did drift to thoughts of my pregnancy. My baby. I didn't want to focus on it though. I turned to by bookshelf for distraction and read a book I found on my shelf.

"On an evening in the latter part of May, a middle-aged man was walking homeward from Shaston..." began *Tess of the d'Urbervilles.* I quickly became enthralled by the protagonist and the struggles she faced. Her story wasn't a complete parallel to my own, but I did see similarities; leaving home, a parent who'd died, a jilted lover. I thought of Stan Freberg. Of course, he wasn't a lover, and I'd been the one to push him away from anything resembling a relationship before it could begin, but somehow, my mind made the connection.

By the time I reached the final phase of the novel, I was riveted and applauded Tess when she murdered Alec for betraying her. This had not happened in my own life, to be sure, but it reminded me of my part in *Sicilia! Sicilia!* I thought back to that moment when I'd nearly stabbed Gregory Peck with the awl. It had felt so natural, yet I'd crumbled under the emotion of it all. Would I eventually meet my Stonehenge? My Wintoncester Prison? *Was I already there?*

As I reflected on the novel I'd just finished, I heard a knock at my door. *It must be Dagny, here to check on me. What a friend she was, a sister. A real Liza-Lu to my Tess.* I went over to the door and opened it.

"Mabs! When were you going to tell me you'd returned? I'd heard a rumor and had to see for myself."

"Oh! Carlisle. Well, isn't this a pleasant surprise." I made a confused frown before quickly forcing a smile. *Pleasant* wasn't what I immediately felt upon seeing him in my doorway, but I settled on the word, nonetheless.

"You look like hell, darling. Can I come in?"

He was right. I'm sure I did look like hell. I hadn't showered since leaving the hospital and I was wearing a pair of pajamas. Still, it was rather presumptuous of him to greet me that way. Nonetheless, I stepped back and let him in.

"I only just got back Monday. I must have contracted some kind of bug while traveling and was in the hospital until Wednesday," I fibbed. As I looked at him, I reflected on the fact that the *bug* I'd contracted had come from him, not my travels. *God, he was handsome. I bet our baby would have been a knockout.*

"Oh, you poor thing. Feeling well now though, I assume?" He said the words as if any illness I'd experienced had been entirely my fault and probably didn't amount to much more than a papercut. *He certainly was sure of himself.*

"I know just the thing to lift your spirits. Get dressed in something comfortable, trousers if you have them. I'm taking you sailing." *That was quite an invite.* I wanted to hate him, but I couldn't resist his charms. Then he doubled down by an inviting me on his yacht. It almost erased any irritation I felt over his arrogance.

"That sounds smashing. Why don't you fix yourself a drink and I'll be out in fifteen minutes."

The fresh ocean breeze buffeting my face and blowing through my hair did wonders for my state. Any lingering fatigue I'd had from resting at home the past two days was swept away by the wind and carried out to sea.

I'd only ever been out on the water once before, several months earlier when a bunch of us from MGM had taken the *SS Catalina* over to Santa Catalina Island. This was quite different. We were so close to the water, and the sailboat being propelled along by the wind felt natural, even passionate. Of course, the passion was also aroused between us as Carlisle gave me the wheel, standing behind me and guiding my hands as I steered.

Once we were out aways, he dropped the sails and let us drift. He went below decks and fetched a simple picnic of roast chicken, bread, cheese, and figs. We washed it down with a bottle of champagne.

"What are we celebrating?" Carlisle asked.

"Being alive!" I replied, then added as somewhat of an afterthought, "and my first lead in a movie."

"Well, that is grand," he said, filling our glasses before raising his. "To life and to the movies!" We clinked glasses and each took a sip.

"I have one more to add," he said, taking a seat next to me. "To love." *To love?* My heart skipped a beat, not out of glee but out of shock. Maybe even a small amount of nervousness. *Where was he going with this?* I didn't need to wait long to find out.

"Mabs, it's no secret that I've been with my share of lovers. I've had a great deal of fun and many of them have been appropriate matches. Or at least my father seemed to think so. He's been pestering me more and more about settling down. Since I'm nearing thirty, I must start to think about it, mustn't I?" Carlisle paused and gazed out to sea for a brief moment then looked back at me with a warm concern in his eyes.

"I'm sure this is all coming as quite a surprise, and I'm certainly not about to get down on one knee and propose or anything like that, but I was hoping you'd consider taking whatever this is we currently have between us and making it more serious."

I was stunned. *Yes, it had come as quite a shock!* Until now, I'd only thought of myself as one of his part-time lovers. Occasional flings to entertain ourselves. I was even quite sure there were other women, perhaps even more serious than myself, that he'd been courting. I thought of our baby and what might have been. I even started to wonder about the possibility of bringing a child into the world. *Was this Fate's invitation to a life of domesticity? Did Carlisle know something? Had he had some kind of paternal premonition? No, that was too much to fathom.*

"My goodness! Yes, Carlisle, this is quite a surprise. I'm glad you didn't get down on one knee. I certainly wouldn't have been at all prepared for that." I paused and thought some more as I gazed out at the setting sun and sipped my champagne.

Now that my star was rising in Hollywood, I assumed the studio would begin pestering me about *settling down* as well. I'm sure they'd want to match me with one of the eligible stars, if possible, but surely Carlisle was a good match. Old Money New England family. Dashingly handsome. A house in Pacific Palisades. This yacht. He certainly met all the criteria.

I wasn't in love with him, but we were passionate together. Perhaps it was the champagne or the sunset. Perhaps it was knowing that I had carried his baby for even a short time. Perhaps it was the scent of the ocean or the scent of his aftershave. Likely, it was a combination of it all.

I drank the rest of the champagne in my glass with one swallow then looked at him with a demure smile. "Of course, Carlisle. I think that would be wonderful. Let's show the world what a team of Mabs Eriksson and Edmund Carlisle can do." I wasn't at all sure it was the truthful answer, but I knew it was the one expected of me.

"Wonderful, darling!" He refilled our glasses, and we toasted again to our *official* relationship. As the sun dipped below the horizon, he leaned over and kissed me.

In the following weeks, between me shooting my final scenes on set, we made our relationship very public in every way possible. His society connections and my rising star ensured we were invited to all the proper functions, charity galas at the golf club, private boxes at Santa Anita, and black-tie events at industrialists' homes. If William Randolph Hearst and Marion Davies had still been entertaining at their estate in San Simeon, I wondered if we'd even have been invited there.

Of course, we were also seen at all the usual spots together, the Cocoanut Grove, Ciro's, a few premieres at Grauman's. It was enough to make one's head spin, even if I'd already experienced so much. We even made it into Louella Parsons' *and* Hedda Hopper's columns twice. Furthermore, it was a good distraction from any passing thoughts of my miscarriage and what might have been.

On one uncharacteristically quiet evening alone, my mind returned to a time months before at the Cocoanut Grove with Dagny. *Cocktails and laughter, but what comes after, nobody knows.* Now I knew, and it was something grand, but was I spinning my life into a *mad jazz pattern?* Would I end up *dropping a stitch too soon?* It was a fleeting thought that I dismissed with a martini and one of the calming pills that I now always had easy access to through the studio. I no longer even needed to ask. I downed both in short order and soon drifted off to a dreamless sleep.

CHAPTER 48
THE WARRIOR POET

The closer we come to the negative, to death, the more we blossom.

— Montgomery Clift

MARCH

It's not that I was purposely ignoring Dagny. Far from it. We'd tried to get together a few times in the past month, but with her still working on the set of *America: The Musical*, me doing my final shoots on *Sicilia! Sicilia!,* all the social functions we were both attending with the new men in our lives—and let me tell you, men are exhausting!—we never connected until the day the swallows came back to Capistrano.

Carlisle had been invited to a society gala at the Los Angeles Country Club to raise money for something about Berlin and airplanes and Russians. I hadn't a clue about any of it, but that really wasn't the point of these things anyhow. I invited Dagny and Bill to join us. I was greatly looking forward to seeing her again and finally meeting her new beau.

Carlisle and I arrived shortly before they did and seated ourselves at a table near the dance floor they'd set up in the main dining room. An eight-piece orchestra was playing Glenn Miller's rendition of *When the Swallows Come Back to Capistrano*, naturally, and as the vocalist started in about his love coming back to him, Dagny and Bill entered the room and walked toward us.

Like everyone else in the room, including Carlisle and me, they were dressed formally. She and I wore sequined, off-the-shoulder gowns; mine dark yellow, hers light blue, and the men wore dinner jackets.

"Mabs, thanks for inviting us. This is Bill," she said. I shook his hand, and then he turned to Carlisle and introduced himself. The whole encounter was almost as formal as the dress, and I wondered why. It hadn't been that long since I'd last seen Dagny, yet it was as if we were meeting for the first time in years. Was it the setting? Were we all just acting stiff because that's what one does at the Los Angeles Country Club? I'd been there twice before for similar events, but it had never really been my cup of tea. Maybe we'd both changed so drastically in the past few months that now, with everything surrounding the miscarriage behind us, we really were strangers once again.

My mind returned to our encounter on Sunset Boulevard nearly a year prior. *What had I thought then? Something about saving Dagny from herself?* I'm not sure if I'd succeeded or even tried, but the tables appeared to have turned. She was acting more domestic than I ever could have imagined. At the very least, she was in what appeared to be a genuine relationship with a genuine man. While Bill was a stuntman over at Paramount, if he had been the doctor or engineer I'd imagined her with at our first meeting in that dingy café, I wouldn't have thought twice.

On the other hand, I was barely even playing at being domestic and certainly had no interest in doing so beyond what might further elevate my rising star.

"So, Bill, tell us about yourself," Carlisle started, obviously trying to size him up.

"Not much to tell, really. I'm a stuntman over at Paramount. It's a job, although a far cry from where I expected myself to be, and certainly no match for the real thing." I immediately caught on that there really was *much to tell* even before he punctuated his statement with those somewhat mysterious words, *the real thing.*

He played aloof, reserved, but I sensed it was his way of warning Carlisle not to push the matter. While Carlisle was dealt his good looks in spades, and he could put on the appropriate air of sophistication when necessary, as his type always could, he was out of his element here. Worst of all, he didn't even know it. Bill was not *sophisticated* in the Hollywood or Newport, Rhode Island sense and that gave him the advantage. He'd probably never set foot in a Country Club and didn't care in the least if he ever did again. Bill was truly confident in his own skin, whereas everyone else in Hollywood was putting on an act both on screen and off. All this should have thrown Carlisle off his game, but he wasn't perceptive enough to notice.

"The real thing, eh?" Carlisle's follow-up question sounded innocent enough, but I'm sure we all sensed the challenge behind it. I discreetly squeezed his hand under the table, hoping he'd back down. Although, it was in vain, Bill still didn't rise to the challenge.

"Bill was in the war," Dagny offered.

"Not now, Dagny," Bill said gently, patting her hand between his.

"The war! Well, a real-life hero seated in front us. My admirations, sir." I hoped Carlisle would come off as genuine with the compliment, and we could leave it at that, maybe get up and dance, but I knew it was another challenge and so, too, did Bill and Dagny.

"Dagny, don't you just love the golf course? I've been taking lessons, you know. It's a real gas!" I interrupted, trying to change the subject.

"Have you now? Well, we'll have to put together a foursome sometime," Dagny replied nervously, catching on to what I was doing. It wasn't enough. Carlisle and Bill held each other's gaze with steely emotion.

"They say you've never really lived in a country until you've nearly died in a country. If that is true, then perhaps the only place I've ever lived is Egypt." Bill shifted his look between the three of us, relaxing a bit as he began his story.

I'd never met a fighting man before. I'd met a few that had been in the army or navy, of course. Some had even been overseas during the war. But the man sitting across the table from me, with his clean-shaven face, closely cropped hair, and a suit that that fit him more like a soldier's dress uniform than anything I was accustomed to at the parties I attended, was the bona fide thing.

"Felt the sting of battle and smelled the putrid odor of death, eh?" Carlisle said, sounding a bit too much like Hemingway for his own good.

Bill needn't have even continued, for my sake at least. Everything about him beyond his words told me volumes. Despite how he carried himself—the assuredness he exuded with his dress and upright posture—I suspected there was a wound inside him not even the best surgeon could heal. I could see it in his eyes. I'd grown familiar with people's eyes since I'd started acting and could now see whatever it was they were trying to hide. Everyone always says the eyes are the windows to the soul, but no one ever takes the time to look through the glass. Perhaps it is because they are afraid of what they may discover. Perhaps it is because they are afraid of what they may reveal in their own. Whatever the case, he was the first *real man*—in every sense of those words—I'd met in months, and I was drawn toward him.

He continued. I imagined it was catharsis for him. He'd probably kept it bottled up inside. After all, it's not the sort of thing one talks about at fancy-dress galas. Now that he'd started, though, the story flowed from his lips like spring water into a parched desert valley. "Death is not a sporting man. He never bothers to strike when we look him in the face. Instead, he prefers to sneak up from behind. And so it was when the two of us did battle on this day."

He had a certain poetry to his speech, much more Steinbeck than Hemingway. I could see why Dagny—the reinvented Dagny—was attracted to him. He was the best of men, the rare type that is the warrior poet. I instantly knew that this quality was what had led him through the war and to this point right now, here, in front of us.

"We'd already made it through some of the most intense barrages of the war at El Alamein," he continued. "We pushed Rommel back, deep into the desert and were in pursuit, headed toward Gazala. To say I was self-assured of victory would not be accurate. No, I was not that cavalier. After all, I had seen far less than anyone around me. But I did have a sense of calm despite being close enough to death that I could taste the angels' tears.

"To say that my future had been sealed the moment that Messerschmitt appeared in the distance would be too harsh. In reality, it had been sealed the moment I left America to join the British in their fight against Hitler. Perhaps even sooner. Perhaps it was the moment Hitler invaded the Rhineland.

"You see," he suddenly grew quite pensive, "no one can ever know how much of the path he walks is of his own making, and to give in to such fatalism is not only imprudent but rather tiresome as well. A man must do his best to live in the moment, not gazing forward, not gazing back.

"When that ship left the dock in Southampton on its way to carry us on our two-month voyage around the Cape of Good Hope—I've always found irony in that name—and on to Suez, I didn't think to wonder if we'd ever return to those verdant shores, if we'd ever dream the dreams we once thought mundane."

His eyes grew misty. I looked at Dagny. She was captivated by his words, and I could see the hint of a tear begin to form in her eyes as well.

Carlisle must have tired of it all and was now talking to another man twenty feet away, demonstrating a tennis stroke. Let him. I didn't care. Sure, we were lovers, but only as far as the Society and Hollywood sets were concerned. It was all very public, and we still had fun together once the lights were dimmed, but beyond that, we were two separate souls leading two separate lives. That is, if either of us had souls left.

I looked back at Bill, and in that moment the room with all its gaiety—the clinking of champagne glasses, the giddy laughter of young women amused by something so unimportant it would be criminal to even mention, even the light of the moon that danced in the sky outside the window—it all just disappeared and the three of us were left alone. I was suddenly very uncomfortable being there. I felt like a misplaced shoe in a closet full of matching pairs.

"You know, it's funny. I can almost hear the sound of the drum and the bugle beating out *The Road to the Isles*." Bill gazed off at what I could only assume were those distant shores that flooded his memories.

"I don't find it funny at all, dear," Dagny replied, running her hand lovingly over his arm. "I know I've never heard it before, but right now, I can almost hear it too." Her mouth formed into the sweetest smile I'd ever seen, a combination of Donna Reed and Shirley Temple. She was happy, genuinely happy, and I was happy for her. Almost.

The silence passed between us for the next few moments. I felt I should leave, perhaps make a beeline for the bar, but my feet wouldn't move. Bill held sway over me as much as he did over Dagny.

He had made her a better version of herself. Even more than that, she'd met him just as her old self had started to emerge from beneath the shell of frivolity, and his presence in her life had helped with that renaissance. He'd helped her uncover some long-buried character that hadn't seen the light of day in nearly a decade. Part of me ached for that sort of connection. I knew I'd long since made my decision though.

Dagny may have been carried away for a time by the Fates, but she had always been at their mercy, a dandelion seed carried by the wind and planted wherever she was dropped. I, on the other hand, had gone in with both eyes open and my feet planted at least somewhat firmly on the ground. Or so I told myself.

I want to be like you, Dagny! I thought back to that day at her apartment and the moment before it at the Tar Pits, when I'd first given in to the dream of Hollywood.

Come over here, Mabs. Come sign your contract. The day at Pan Berman's office with Winifred.

A thrill to take a life. Lunch with Vincente at Chasen's where he'd bestowed upon me the part of Luciana. Yes, a thrill to take a life, indeed. Would the man in front of me agree? After all, he'd likely taken more than a few.

The man, Bill, interrupted my thoughts. "How discourteous of me! Here we are at a splendid party full of good cheer and I'm recalling the past. And after I've just finished saying we must live in the moment. I am sorry. Please, let me lighten the mood by getting you both a drink." He was suddenly all smiles, any hint of sentimentalism gone from the air. A pity. It was one of the few moments of truth I'd experienced in months. In a town where everyone is paid to be someone else, and the fiction on the screen melds so easily into the reality off of it, real truth, unvarnished truth, is a quality rarer than gold and twice as valuable. Ironic that it would come not only from an actor, but an actor who played an actor.

"No, please, don't be sorry. I enjoyed your story, darling," Dagny insisted, lightly touching his shoulder. "But I will take that drink," she added. "If it's alright with you though, instead of something cheery like champagne, let us drink to the memories of those who have gone before us, those men you once called comrades."

"That sounds like a capital idea." He leaned over and kissed her on the cheek. "Now let's just hope the bar has a decent single malt on hand!"

I definitely needed a drink after all that, but I wasn't going to raise my glass to some far-off band of Scotsmen in tartan and tams. To hell with them and their road to wherever it was. I wanted Bill, or at least a man like Bill, to take me in his arms and make me feel loved, truly loved. I knew that wasn't going to happen though. At least not tonight. The best I could hope for was a night of passion—if you could call it that at this point—with Carlisle.

"Are you going to join us, Mabs?" Dagny said, interrupting my thoughts. She put her arm around Bill's elbow, and they started for the bar.

"No, I don't think I will. But you two have fun. It was splendid catching up with you."

"You're not leaving already, are you? Why, we've only just arrived!"

"I'm sorry, Dagny. I must go. Another time, perhaps." I didn't leave her a chance to respond as I spun on my heel and marched off toward Carlisle.

"Come, Carlisle, we're leaving."

"Whatever for? We only just got here. Why, I haven't even finished my first glass of champagne!"

"If it's a drink you need, there's plenty at my place, and that's not all," I said with a devilish smile as I grabbed his arm. "Take me home."

CHAPTER 49
UNQUENCHABLE

The things we ignore often come back to us in our sleep.

— Gene Tierney

For a man who'd just been promised anything he wanted when it came to me, he didn't drive very fast. And, when we got to my apartment, he didn't move any faster.

"What's gotten into you, darling?" he asked as he took my key and unlocked the door.

"Nothing yet. Maybe that's the problem," I said coyly.

"You haven't had much to drink. At least I didn't see if you did, so I can't imagine why you're acting so peculiar," he pondered out loud as if it were some Marlowe mystery to solve.

"Oh, get off it, Carlisle. I want to take you to bed, and you're standing there like one of the Katzenjammer Kids. Well, this ain't no comic strip, Bud. It's just you and me." He was right. I was acting peculiar. He was also right that I hadn't had much to drink. What he didn't know was that I'd discreetly swallowed a couple of pep pills on the drive home.

"No, this won't do. This won't do at all. You're making no sense. I'm leaving now, Mabs. I'll ring you in the morning. By then maybe you'll have snapped out of whatever three-ringed circus you're presently part of."

"Okay, you go, Carlisle! You go running off to Daddy, to *the old buzzard*! He'll surely know what to do, right? Pathetic," I sneered, my hands on my hips while I continued to shout at a volume loud enough the three other girls on my floor could no doubt hear me.

"All you men are the same. Only good for one thing and when it comes time for that you run. Maybe Tallulah Bankhead is right. Yes, that's what I'll do. I'll find myself a woman. It's nearly 1950 now. That sort of thing will be all the rage any day now! Maybe I'll call Gloria Vanderbilt. At the very least, she knows how to ring in the new year!" If it was a scene I was playing—and I wasn't entirely certain at that moment it wasn't—it was to an empty theater. Carlisle had slammed the door behind him to leave my words echoing off nothing but my own four walls.

I took the pins out of my hair and kicked my heels off, then mixed myself a martini and toasted my image in the mirror before downing it with a couple more pills. This time the ones to take me down. *Crimson for the blood that flows from the heart, blue for the blood that flows back. Crimson for the lust left unrequited, blue for the shadows that fade to black.*

Soon, I too *faded to black*. No energy to make it to bed, I fell asleep fully clothed on my couch. My martini glass tipped from my hand, draining its remaining contents onto the floor.

As I slept, my subconscious was carried a few miles away and almost a year prior to Sunset Boulevard and my first meeting with Dagny.

"Hello, Dagny, where've you been all my life?" Our roles were reversed. I was now the distant soul, she the naïf. Or was she?

"It won't work this time, Mabs. I won't fall for it," she said, crossing her arms and pursing her lips.

"But what about Maritta and Charlie? And Clio? What about fried egg sandwiches poolside at the Bel-Air? What about Winifred?" I pleaded desperately.

"I don't know. Perhaps you should ask her yourself."

"Moxie, Mabs! You've got moxie!"

I turned around and saw Winifred standing there, two martini glasses filled to the brim with a mixture of the crimson and blue pills that brought me down and the little white ones that pepped me up. "Go on, dear. Take your medicine."

Suddenly I heard the whine of an airplane buzzing through the sky. I looked up and saw what must have been the Messerschmitt Bill had spoken of.

"Come on, Mabs! We have to run. El-Alamein is just over that hill. I can't carry you, though. You have to make it on your own." I felt a hand grab my arm and turned to see Bill.

"CUT!" I twirled around again to see Vincente Minnelli sitting in a chair. "Now, Mabs, I want you to *actually* kill him this time. Take the awl and drive it into his heart."

"Whose heart, Vincente? Whose heart do I drive it into?" I replied, confused.

"Why, your father's, of course. And Carlisle's. Aren't they one in the same? Isn't it your father who is keeping you from ascending into stardom? Into the heavens?"

"The heavens! That's a riot, Vincente!" It was Lana Turner. She was standing with Winifred and Ava Gardner, and they were all laughing at me.

"You don't need to do this, Mabs. You don't need to save me. Let me go." I was suddenly by the river back home in Saskatchewan. The muskrat I'd tried to save as a child chattered at me.

"Big diamonds, Mabs! Big diamonds!" We were back in the dingy coffeeshop now, the elegantly dressed woman walking past. Unlike the reality of my consciousness, this woman carried a newborn.

"Look at our baby, Mabs. Isn't she a knock-out? It's all about good breeding stock, you know." Carlisle was now seated next to me in the booth. "Just a shame that you can't be part of her life. What shall we name her? Winifred? Luciana? No, I've got it. We'll name her Dagny. That way, you'll know she was saved, even if it wasn't by you."

"Listen! I can hear them playing *The Road to the Isles*! We're saved, Bill! We're saved!" Dagny—the adult Dagny— shouted at Bill as the Messerschmitt buzzed around us above the desert, and I held the baby tightly. She continued shouting at Bill, ignoring me. "Leave her! She's gone. Both of them are. We can't save her. We can only save ourselves!"

I looked down at the baby in my arms. "I'm sorry, Dagny. I'm sorry I couldn't save you." I began to weep and with each tear, the valley surrounding me began to fill until I was aboard a sailboat, Carlisle's sailboat, floating in an ocean, no land in sight, no one there but me and the baby. The wind began to howl, churning up the waves.

"Look, darling, we're saved! Water, and so much of it! We'll never thirst again!" I said to my baby. She held her gaze on mine. I reached over the side of the boat and cupped some water into my hand. I held it to my lips and took a drink but quickly spit it out when I realized it was poisoned with the salt of my own tears.

"Oh, sweet thing, I've done it again and now we have nowhere to turn. No safe harbor from this storm. No oasis in this desert." I held her close to me as the storm rocked the boat violently and waves crashed over us. The tempest continued with the fury of a deity who'd been betrayed, smashing into us on every side. I knew we would drown, and I resigned us to our fate. I closed my eyes and rocked the child—my child—in my arms.

When I awoke, I was holding something tightly in my arms, and I could hear the crashing of the waves and smell the saltiness of the ocean in the air. The sunshine shone brightly around me. *We'd made it through the storm!*

"Oh, Dagny, my sweet girl! We're still alive!" I looked down expecting to see my baby and was shocked that all I held was a throw pillow. My soul emptied. Where was my baby? She just had to be there.

I began to sob. "No! No! Why did you take her away? Why? She was all I had. She was the only thing to live for, and now she's gone. She's gone and it's all my fault!" The tears continued to flow from me as they had in my dream the night before, but instead of filling a valley of despair with an ocean of tumult, they only filled me with rage. With each breath and subsequent wail, it was not the waves that began to beat against me, it was my very soul, consumed by an unquenchable anger that a thousand years of sorrow-filled tears could never extinguish. It was not my fault my baby had been torn from my womb before I'd ever known her—and I was sure she was a girl—but whose fault was it? I pounded my fist on the back of the couch and screamed.

CHAPTER 50
A LIFE OF DEATH

There is no terror in the bang, only in the anticipation of it.

— Alfred Hitchcock

APRIL

Carlisle didn't call the next day, or the day after that, or the day after that. I suspect he thought me mad. Perhaps he didn't have the courage to tell me to my face or even over the phone. For all I knew, he packed up his nice little house, sold his boat, and done as I'd screamed at him and ran back to New England and Daddy. I was perfectly fine with that too. If I never laid eyes on him again it would be too soon.

I recovered some from the dream I had and the trauma it brought to my consciousness but some of those awful visions still remained seared into my waking mind. While I wasn't sitting around making a list of who I wanted to meet my vengeance, my anger was constantly burning just below the surface. Anger at losing a baby I never knew. Anger at losing a life that could have been. Anger at all that life had become. Yet, it was the life I'd chosen. I knew that on some level even if I didn't want to admit it to myself.

So, no more sunshine and rainbows for me. I was a dark storm cloud casting a shadow over everyone else's bright California day. I wore a permanent scowl on my face and walked with a purposeful gait in every step I took. My demeanor must have caught the eye of someone who thought it would provide a good vehicle for something dark because, a few weeks later, I found myself sitting across from Alfred Hitchcock in a booth at Chasen's.

True to the legend, when I arrived, the table was already covered with food, a shrimp cocktail, some stuffed celery, a rack of lamb, a baked potato, and a heart of palm salad.

"I'll have the roast prime rib from the cold buffet and a half avocado, please," I told the waiter as I took my seat.

"No!" Hitchcock said abruptly, raising a palm toward the waiter. "She will have the squab and a French endive salad with Roquefort dressing." *I would, would I?* Well, no one says no to Hitchcock, so I simply nodded at the waiter to go ahead with the order.

"Cold meat disturbs me. Ever since I was a boy. Never could stand the sight of it. Eggs as well. The shape is unnerving," he explained. *He was unnerving. Who's disturbed by an egg?*

"Vincente mentioned I should speak with you about a part," he said, quickly getting down to business. "He said you were good in his Italian picture that just wrapped. But it was someone else, one of the assistant directors I overheard on the lot last week, who convinced me. He said he saw you take on a very real, but subtle anger in the last month. He said it even permeated through you when you were off set, as I imagine you have been for a few weeks now." My body tensed at his comment. *Was it really that obvious?*

The sight of him stuffing a cold shrimp into his mouth only made it worse. He reminded me of a mythical creature, devouring the souls of the damned. I just sat there, staring straight ahead, saying nothing.

"I have just the part for you. It's dark, very dark. It involves a woman driven mad by her desire to reclaim innocence. The harder she strives for the lost purity of her youth, the greater the perversion of her future. She seeks to erase all connections to her vices, but in doing so, only compounds them." He finished the sentence and continued to peer at me.

Did he know something more about me than he was letting on? It seemed eerily perfect. I looked around half expecting some macabre dreamscape to cloud my vision. *Was I having another nightmare?* Were those awful shrimp on the table going to jump out of the glass and start dancing around to a chilling scherzo? I blinked my eyes twice in quick succession, forcing myself to see the reality in front of me. At that moment, the waiter brought over my squab.

I shook off any doubt I had in the reality before me and put on the air I knew Hitchcock was looking for. It wasn't difficult. "I'm always interested in a life of death, Mr. Hitchcock. Sign me up." I picked up my knife and drove it into the bird on my plate without looking down, without blinking an eye.

"Splendid! Now, if you haven't tried the sabayon here, you must. It's to die for." I chuckled at his choice of words. When I'd devoured my squab, I did order the sabayon, savoring every decadent spoonful. *A life of death. Yes, indeed.*

When I arrived back at my apartment, I saw a telegram waiting under the door. It was an invitation to an intimate little dinner party Vincente and Judy were holding at their home the following week. My mind turned to Carlisle. What would people say if I showed up without him? Should I call? Try to patch things up? I surely wasn't about to apologize, and I couldn't imagine he was either.

I unlocked my door and went inside, then poured a gin and tonic, sat down on the couch, and stared at my telephone. Perhaps if I stared long enough it would ring. I slowly sipped my drink. And then it rang! It startled me and gin spilled from my glass. *It couldn't be, could it? No.*

I placed my glass on the floor and walked over to the telephone. I stared at it as it rang once more and then picked it up. "Carlisle?"

"No, Mabs, were you expecting him?"

"Oh, hello Dagny," I said, my voice falling, although I'm not sure why. I wasn't actually disappointed that Carlisle hadn't called. Maybe I was just disappointed that I'd think such a silly thing.

"You don't sound pleased to hear from me. Is something wrong? How are you and Carlisle? You know, you both left in such a hurry from that party a few weeks ago and I haven't heard from you since."

"No, no. It's not that. Everything's fine," I lied. "In fact, I was just waiting on him to call. He was going to take me down to San Diego for the weekend."

"Oh, that is wonderful. Although I was calling to see if you'd like to do some shopping and have some lunch with me tomorrow. But if you're going to San Diego, well, I certainly can't get in the way of that."

"No, shopping and lunch sound splendid." It did sound like a good idea at the very least. I knew I needed to see Dagny again, for her sake as much as for mine. "It'll be like old times. Maybe we could even have a Niçoise salad at that place we went after we ran into each other last spring. Can you believe it's been almost a year?"

"It has, hasn't it? It's certainly been quite a ride. Did you ever think you'd be starring in a Hollywood movie in so short a time?"

"And you, *Miss Domesticity*! All settled down with a responsible man. Hardly even drinking anymore."

"I guess both of us have changed quite a bit."

"I suddenly feel quite sentimental, Dagny. I think lunch and shopping and some reminiscing about the last year is exactly what's in order. Shall I come by your apartment around half past eleven tomorrow?"

"Yes, that'll be perfect. I'll see you then."

No sooner had I hung up the phone did I hear a knock at my door. "When it rains it pours," I muttered to myself as I crossed the room and opened the door.

"Well, Mabs Eriksson. You *are* still alive. I thought maybe you'd run off and failed to tell me." It was Winifred. Her brow was furrowed, and she held her hands on her hips. A pillbox hat sat atop her head, tilted forward. She caused a chill to run down my spine and I froze. Indeed, the whole room seemed to drop in temperature, but I tried not to show my nervousness or fear or whatever it was.

"Hello, Winifred! So nice to see you. I've been meaning to call. Did you hear? Alfred Hitchcock is casting me in his upcoming film."

"Of course, dear. You forget, I know everything that's going on in this godforsaken little town." She forced her way past me and over to my liquor cabinet where she poured herself a bourbon, then went to sit on my couch. She motioned for me to join her. "This place of yours really is ghastly. Why ever are you still here?"

"Where else am I supposed to be?"

"Well, the red carpet, for starters. Are you ready for your premiere tomorrow night?"

My eyes widened in shock. *Was that tomorrow? I wasn't ready!*

"Oh, I'm just toying with you, Mabs," she laughed, then took a sip of her drink. "It's not for another few weeks. I just wanted to see how you'd react. It does show me that you need someone to manage the day-to-day details of your life though. Clearly, you're at a loss. But don't fret too much. It happens to all you girls. Most of the men too, really."

"But—"

She cut me off. "I've set you up with an appointment to meet some men who are going to help you manage your life. You're a big star now. Or at least you soon will be. Monday afternoon you'll be meeting your business manager, your agent, and your publicity man. They're going to take care of anything you need. All you have to do is show up on set and show up in public with that charming beau of yours. You were planning on calling him, weren't you? Something about a weekend in San Diego? And, of course, that dinner party at Vincente and Judy's."

My mouth dropped open. Had she been reading my telegrams and listening at the door while I was talking to Dagny just moments ago, or did she have another way of knowing everything that happened in my life and in my mind? She smiled and started to gently nod her head, motioning me to do the same. Then I remembered my lunch with Dagny.

"I was going to—"

She cut me off again. "Oh, yes, that friend of yours, Dagny Lundberg. I must admit, I misjudged her. I thought she'd be more fun. Seems she's fallen in love with the wrong type of man though. Some war hero, isn't he? Oh, well, can't win them all. But I don't want you seeing her anymore. She's doing nothing but holding you back now."

"She's my friend!" I protested rather forcefully. "If it wasn't for her, I wouldn't even be here!"

Winifred's open hand stung as it crossed my cheek. I staggered back and tears welled up in my eyes. "I can't! I just can't!"

"You can and you will, Mabs. But tell you what, I'll make a deal with you. You invite Dagny to your premiere. She can even bring that *soldier* of hers with her." She raised her lip and flared her nostrils at the word *soldier*, showing her disdain for him and his erstwhile profession. "But that's it. No more. If I could only get her to go back home to Saskatchewan." She said the last sentence more to herself than to me, then quickly shook her head.

"Now, I'm off!" she said cheerily after a beat. She set her drink down and stood up. "You're to be at MGM at one o'clock sharp Monday afternoon for your appointment. And I do mean *one*. You're not waltzing into this one late, even if you may technically be the one in charge." She marched to the door and opened it. As she parted, she called over her shoulder, almost as an after-thought. "Ta-ta! Enjoy your weekend in San Diego." I knew it wasn't an after-thought though. I had to call Carlisle. I had no other option.

CHAPTER 51
EXACTLY WHAT I WANT TO DO

If you want a happy ending, that depends, of course, on where you stop your story.
— Orson Welles

"Hello, Carlisle. It's Mabs. I've been an utter fool." I didn't believe the words and I detested the sound of them coming from my mouth, but I had to say them. Carlisle had become too much a part of who I was. Or at least who I was supposed to be, even to the extent of being the father of my baby.

"What do you want, Mabs?" His voice was utterly devoid of feeling. I might as well have called the operator.

I gritted my teeth. So, this is how it was going to be. "I'm sorry I acted so strangely last time we saw each other. I was hoping we could, well, mend things."

"I don't know, Mabs. I need a woman who I know will act appropriately."

"Oh, please, Carlisle. Give me another chance!" I was pleading now, not because I wanted another chance from him but because I knew I needed another chance from Winifred. It was pathetic but it had to be done.

"Hmm. Very well then. What do you propose?"

"I was thinking we could go down to San Diego for the weekend, stay at The Del. I promise I'll be on my best behavior. It'll be a chance to set things right, start over, as it were." I balled up my fist, digging my nails into my palms. The thought of a full weekend away with Carlisle was enough to give a girl hives.

"Hmm, a weekend away would do us well. Okay, I'll pick you up at nine tomorrow morning."

"Oh, thank you, Carlisle! You won't regret it." My words went unheard as the click of his receiver on the other end of the line rang in my ear. The fact that I hadn't needed to say them made them even more contemptuous in my mind. *Bastard!*

★★★

The next morning, I was ready and waiting outside with my luggage at 8:55. I knew if I'd remained inside my apartment, I may not have ever left. I went back and forth about taking a pill to relax me that morning and ultimately found the willpower to refrain, a decision I hoped I wouldn't regret later. I *was* going to be on my best behavior, at least until I could come up with some other solution. Maybe the studio would pair me with someone else. I'd have to put in a word. I certainly needed out of *this,* whatever *this* was.

"Good morning, Mabs." Carlisle's greeting was pleasant enough as he grabbed my luggage and threw it in the trunk of a new light blue 1949 Chrysler Windsor Highlander convertible. It wasn't exactly warm, however.

"New car?" I asked, stating the obvious.

"Yes. Long overdue. The Studebaker was acting up. Plus, if the clothes make the man, then it follows that the car makes him even more."

"I guess I can't argue with that. It is stunning," I said, being perfectly honest. Clothes, cars, cocktails. At this point, they were all accessories that made us who we were. Truthfully, Carlisle and I were really just accessories to each other. "Lovely weather for the drive down," I added. *My goodness! I'd resorted to commenting on the weather now!* If the mood didn't change soon, this would be a ghastly journey and a ghastly weekend. I felt inside my purse as Carlisle opened the door for me. My hand grasped the two bottles of pills. *No! I must resist!* I squeezed them, willing myself not to give in to temptation.

We rode in relative silence for the first two hours. The top was down so we had the excuse of not wanting to shout over the wind. Once we crossed the San Diego County line though, the mood changed. Perhaps Carlisle had grown tired of the uncomfortable silence and decided to give in.

"So, your big premiere is in a few weeks. Your call didn't have anything to do with that, did it?" He kept his eyes glued to the road ahead as we cruised at a rather fast sixty-five miles per hour.

He'd caught me. What to do now? I couldn't very well jump for it. Even if I could, what would I do then? Hitchhike back to Santa Monica? Call Winifred to pick me up? I shuddered at the thought. She might very well end up throwing me into the ocean on the way back. Should I continue to play the wounded lamb yearning for his forgiveness or come clean and tell him it was all for fame and fortune? Convince him that if he hooked himself to my star, he could rise higher than his New England socialite friends ever imagined? It was all about his ego. Of course, it was also all about mine. *But how to play him?* I decided for the former. After all, he probably thought himself too important for Hollywood. He was Old Money, after all.

"No, of course not, darling!" I poured it on thick. A shame the cameras weren't rolling. "The truth is, I've been beside myself the last three weeks. I don't know what got into me before. Sometimes I just want you so much, Carlisle. Sometimes I just *need* you! Yes, I went a little crazy, but only crazy for you!" *Wow! Was that ever over the top!* Hopefully not too much so or he might think I was mocking him. I began to cry softly for good measure. Fortunately, my bet came through. I really shouldn't have doubted myself or him. His ego was indeed much bigger than his intellect, and my performance was one for the ages.

He pulled the car off to the side of the road. The roar of the wind coming over the top of the windshield was replaced by the roar of the waves to our right.

"Mabs, darling, I had no idea. Honestly, I thought our relationship was all for show. You know, people like us—well, love is not often in our vocabulary. With all the people watching, it's hard to know what's for them and what's for us. Are you telling me you truly love me, Mabs?" He looked at me with doe-eyes. I wondered if he, too, might turn on the tears. Of course, the cynic in me wondered if he might be putting on an act as well. If he was, I was okay with it. We could love each other, or we could pretend to love each other. It was all the same to me.

"Yes, Carlisle—Edmund, that is. Yes, I love you," I replied, addressing him with his given name for the first time.

He took my hand and raised it to his lips. Then he kissed me. It had all worked out. I hadn't needed any pills after all. But now I'd have to keep up the act.

That evening we ordered room service and dined on our private balcony overlooking the beach. The salt air mixed with the smells rising up from our wonderful dinner of Lobster Thermador and champagne. A dessert of chocolate soufflé, coffee, and amaretto, their blissful tastes and scents mixing with the soft light of a rising moon, made for a powerful aphrodisiac between us. At that moment, I really was crazy about him. This time, however, my lustfulness didn't scare him away, and we made love long into the night.

The next morning, he was all smiles, and so was I. As we breakfasted in the Crown Room, I reached across the table and held his hand. He'd been right. A change of scenery was just what we needed to rekindle the romance we'd shared months before. *Could I really be in love? Might this actually work out? Had I become the character I was trying so desperately to play the day before?* I dismissed the thoughts from my mind not because I didn't want to entertain them, quite the opposite. I wanted nothing more than to be in love with Carlisle. *Edmund.* My thoughts shifted to his given name. For now, however, I just wanted to enjoy the moment and not think of what tomorrow might bring.

I did briefly think about our baby that never was and wondered if I should tell him, but again quickly dismissed it. *No, now was not the time.* Likely, there never would be, but I certainly wasn't going to spoil the morning. As if confirming this dismissal, a wood stork that was preening itself on the beach just outside our window flew away.

The rest of the day was equally sublime. We walked barefoot along the beach, picking up shells as we went, had a wonderfully pedestrian lunch of fish and chips, and rented a power boat in the afternoon and cruised around the bay.

"How about dinner at La Maze this evening," Edmund suggested after we had docked the boat, referring to a steakhouse that was frequented by the usual cast of Hollywood stars. For the first time that day, I froze. It was as if a wall had come crashing down. I didn't want to go back to Hollywood or anywhere near it. The short time away from it all, the distance, the new surroundings, all these had done something to me. I wanted to live this real-life screenplay we'd been experiencing forever, or at least until I knew I had to return.

"No, darling. I don't want to think of Hollywood tonight. I just want to be normal for one more evening." I took his hand in mine and gently squeezed it. He squeezed back.

"Then how about Mexican? We'll get lost in Old Town and have tamales at Ramona's."

"That is exactly what I want to do," I smiled.

CHAPTER 52
HELPLESS, HAPLESS,
AND HOPELESS

Press agent—a man who hitches his braggin' to a star.

— Hedda Hopper

The rest of the weekend with Edmund was all I could have hoped for. Pure enchantment. On the drive back to Los Angeles, though, I was overcome with a crushing sense of foreboding. I somehow knew it wouldn't last. Something would come between us and ruin what otherwise could have been a fairytale ending. Something or someone.

Months, even weeks before, I would have looked forward with glee to an appointment introducing me to my business manager, agent, and publicity man. It meant I had arrived. To be cast in a film was now just a silly, childhood dream shared by millions. Now something was coming to pass that most girls didn't even know existed. I'd have a trio of men at my every beck and call. *So why wasn't I thrilled?* Perhaps I knew all too well that it was not they who would be my servants, but I who would be theirs.

I arrived at MGM a full thirty minutes before my appointment. Kenny was there to greet me as usual.

"Good afternoon, Miss Eriksson," he said, tipping his hat. "Excited for your big premiere in a few weeks?"

"Good afternoon, Kenny. Oh, yes, of course!" It wasn't a lie, but it wasn't exactly the truth. I was already torn at the thought of having to act in a completely different sense, not for the camera but for reality. After I walked down that red carpet, I knew I'd never be alone again.

"Well, enjoy your remaining days of relative anonymity and calm," Kenny replied, as if reading my mind.

"Thank you, I will." *Would I be able to enjoy them?* I surely would try.

I walked into one of the boardrooms that had been reserved for our meeting. Winifred was already there, seated at the head of the glossy, dark oak table. I saw her reflection in it before I saw her. A pitcher of water and six glasses was arranged in the middle along with an urn of coffee, six cups, and a tray of cookies. The subtle aroma of coffee filled the room, and I thought back to dessert a few nights prior. This time, the scent was not in the least enticing though. Instead, it smelled bitter.

"Have a seat, dear. So good of you to be on time. The men will be here any moment. Why don't you have a cup of coffee?"

"No, thank you."

"Have a cup of coffee, Mabs," Winifred insisted sternly.

"Yes, ma'am." I poured myself a cup and took a sip. It even tasted bitter. *Why was she so insistent on me having coffee? Was she going to be ordering my every move down to the smallest detail now?*

Three awkward-looking men came bumbling into the room. They were almost comical, but I wasn't laughing. Two were balding, while the third had a mop of curly hair. One of the bald men wore wire-rimmed spectacles and a toothbrush mustache. The curly-haired one's necktie was knotted in a half-Windsor and slightly askew.

"Well, if it isn't the troubled trio, Helpless, Hapless, and Hopeless," Winifred said in greeting. "I'd ask how you are but I'm sure I already know. Now, why don't you three have a seat before you break something."

They all went for the same chair across from me, bumping into each other before sorting themselves out and each taking a seat. Winifred looked toward the ceiling and rubbed the bridge of her nose in exasperation. At least their ridiculous entry had taken her attention off me, if only for a moment.

"Mabs, this is Harold, Henry, and Bert. Not sure why you won't just ditch the casualness and go by your full name, Hubert, but very well."

"Good afternoon, Miss Eriksson, a pleasure to finally meet you," the one in the middle smiled crookedly. "I'm Henry."

"Can it, Hank. She won't remember which of you is which by tomorrow. Heaven knows I can't."

"Yes, Miss Jenkins."

"Mabs, as I mentioned last week, these men are going to, well, ahem, *help* you manage your affairs. They're not that great at it, frankly, but it's the best the studio was able to do for now. We'll find a better team in due time."

I wasn't sure whether to laugh, gasp, or stare blankly. I knew Winifred had gall, but my, this was taking it to a whole other level to insult them so blatantly while they were sitting there. That is what they got paid for though. They were nothing but a bunch of sycophants. Perhaps that's why they were so awkward, reduced to servitude of a point they could barely dress themselves. *And I thought I was a slave!*

For the next hour, the three men, along with Winifred, went over the business of being a star. Henry, my publicity man, would be making sure I got into *The Reporter*, *Variety*, and *The Los Angeles Times* for all the right reasons and, when necessary, stayed out of them for all the wrong ones. He'd make sure Hedda Hopper and Louella Parsons said enough nice things about me and that I'd always have a good booth at the Derby or Ciro's. He briefly questioned my politics, wanting to allay any concerns that might arise from the HUAC Committee, but he let it go when I mentioned I knew nothing of politics. He made some comment about the Canadian Prime Minister, Louis St. Laurent, being a staunch anti-communist and then we moved on.

Harold, my agent, blathered on and on about all the superb parts he was going to help me get. He seemed the most sure of himself out of the three and clearly loved the sound of his own voice. I was grateful when Winifred cut him off and Bert—or Hubert—started talking about my finances. He had an avuncular quality, and I immediately took a liking to him. He was soft-spoken but confident, and I felt I'd always be safe as long as he was around. He told me he'd be taking care of all my day-to-day expenses, and that I'd be given an allowance of two hundred dollars a month to spend how I chose. Far from feeling trapped by this, it felt rather freeing, not having to worry about rent or groceries. Even my wardrobe would be taken care of.

"And now that we have that out of the way, I've got a surprise for you, Mabs. Come with me," Winifred said, rising from the table. Henry, Bert, and Harold all rose with her and quickly scurried out of the room.

I followed Winifred down the stairs and outside to an awaiting dark blue Packard Limousine. She saw me gawking at it and answered the question I was probably going to ask. "No, dear, this is not your new car, but it will be available to you whenever you need it. I have something better though."

We got into the spacious backseat and as the car headed out of the main gate, I saw Kenny wave. He had a rather sad smile on his face.

The driver took us west to the ocean and then headed north until half an hour later, we entered Pacific Palisades. I wondered for a moment if Edmund was in on all of this and we were going to his house. We passed by the turnoff to his street though, and continued to Chapala Drive, coming to a stop in front of a white house with a quaint looking front yard divided by a brick path running up to its front porch.

"Welcome home, Mabs," Winifred said with a smile. "It's not technically yours, of course, but this is where you'll live and entertain as long as you work for MGM. It's fully furnished, and I've taken the liberty of buying you a whole new wardrobe. Oh, I did have a girl from the studio pick out a few of your old pieces— that chic little outfit that makes you look like an air hostess, and of course that scarf you nicked from Bullock's, a few things from

Sicily and New York too. I've burned the rest. I knew you wouldn't mind."

She was right. I didn't even think to mind. She could have told me I had nothing but a closet full of burlap sacks and I'd still be thinking about nothing other than the house. Even if it wasn't technically mine, even if I'd already experienced quite a bit of luxury during the past few months, this seemed different. As I walked up the brick pathway to the front door then opened it and went inside, I thought back to the little shack I'd grown up in. The whole thing could have fit in the living room. My body tingled with giddiness.

I rushed around the house, opening doors and marveling at each room. I ended up in the kitchen and opened the refrigerator. So much food! I was accustomed to eating out now more than I probably should, so my refrigerator was usually quite bare. Plus, I'd only ever been a good enough cook to heat up a can of soup or make a fried bologna sandwich. Now, with this magnificent kitchen, I might have to learn. Or hire a chef. *Would the studio pay for that?*

"A maid will come on Tuesdays and Fridays to tidy up. Of course, if you are hosting, you can also have her come the morning of. If you need help preparing any meals, one of the chefs from the canteen can come by to teach you. They are even available to prepare refreshments for any entertaining you may do as well," Winifred said, joining me in the kitchen. *That answered that, then.*

"I'll leave you to explore. What few personal effects you have are being delivered later this afternoon. The girl who is bringing over your other wardrobe items will help you unpack and put things away. Ta-ta, dear. If you need anything, don't hesitate to call." And with that, I heard the door shut behind her. I was now alone.

It was an odd feeling. Sure, I'd lived alone in my apartment, but it was so cramped, and one could always hear someone next door, above, or even out on the street. I'd been rather close to the action in Santa Monica. Now I was in a neighborhood of well-appointed homes. It was so quiet.

I looked around the living room again and spotted the phonograph. *That's what I needed. Some music would fill the void.* I thumbed through the records on the shelf and pulled out an Andrews Sisters album. I set the needle down and exotic horns began to fill the room followed by the trio's melody as they sang *Bei Mir Bist Du Schoen.* I danced about the room, grabbed an apple from the counter to snack on, and didn't stop dancing until I heard a knock on the door. It was the girl from the studio.

She was wonderfully helpful organizing my things. I watched her place my collection of records on a shelf by the phonograph. She hung a painting of a cathedral I'd purchased in Sicily on one of the empty walls in my dining room. My makeup went into my bathroom. The few dresses and coats Winifred had deemed worthy went into the large closet off my bedroom. When she had finished, she prepared my dinner and departed just before seven. Alone again and so early. Whatever was a girl to do? I knew Winifred had forbidden me from seeing Dagny again. I struggled back and forth with myself, like an addict who knows she shouldn't indulge but must. If Winifred found out, there'd be hell to pay. Maybe I could get away with it. Just this once. And, of course, Dagny wasn't a drug. Far from it. While once I'd sought to save her from herself, I knew that she might be my only saving grace one day. So, I picked up the phone and called her.

CHAPTER 53
RED CARPETS

Trouble is a part of life, and if you don't share it, you don't give the person who loves you enough chance to love you enough.

— Dinah Shore

The phone just rang and rang, but there was no answer. After a good minute, I gave up and replaced the receiver. It really shouldn't have troubled me so. After all, Dagny was often out of her apartment. I had often been out of mine. There was nothing peculiar about it. Yet, it did trouble me. I needed her.

I again thought about Winifred. She was always one step ahead, always looking over my shoulder even when she wasn't there. She knew when I stole wardrobe accessories. She knew when I made cheeky comments about soap to my former boss. I was frightened. Furthermore, Dagny wasn't even home. What would I do? Sit at her doorstep until she returned? So, I gave up, took one of the crimson and blue pills to relax me further, and climbed into bed.

I slept through the night, no dreams or nightmares plaguing me and, just after dawn, awoke to the sound of a sparrow outside my window. I should have been delighted. I had it all yet was empty. I decided to ring Dagny again. Winifred be damned. This time Dagny answered.

"Good morning, Dagny."

"Mabs, he's dead!" she wailed.

"Who's dead?"

"Bill! There was an accident on set. Oh, Mabs. What am I going to do?!"

My heart sank. Somehow, I knew this wasn't a chance accident. I didn't know how or why but too much tragedy was surrounding me. I swallowed hard and pushed the questions to the back of my mind. Dagny needed me at this moment. I had to go to her. "I'll be right over. Don't go anywhere."

I called a taxi, and a half hour later was at her door. I went right in, not bothering to knock. She was in her bedroom, her face buried in a pillow, sobbing. I sat down next to her and stroked her hair. Suddenly, all the problems, the emptiness I'd felt the night before, didn't seem to matter.

"For the first time in my life, I was truly happy, Mabs. We were talking about getting married, raising a family. Now, I just don't know what it's all for."

"I'm so, so sorry, Dagny. I have no words. I won't try to think of any. I'll just sit by your side as long as you need me to. I'll just sit by your side as you've done for me so many times in the past. Sisters to the end."

"Thanks," she said softly. After several minutes, her breathing slowed, and I could tell she'd fallen asleep, but I didn't leave her side. It comforted me to be there just as I hoped it comforted Dagny.

Through it all, everything that had taken place over the course of a year, the ups and downs, the times together and the times apart, we'd strengthened the bond that formed in our childhood. I didn't know what the future held for either of us, if stardom would be our lot or if we'd both eventually settle down and raise a family, but I knew she'd always hold a place in my life, and I'd hold a place in hers.

A week later, there was a funeral. While Bill hadn't been a well-known stuntman, it was still somewhat of a Hollywood affair with a few of the bigger names he'd worked with attending to pay their respects. I kept an eye out for Winifred, fearful she might spoil the day, but even she knew enough to keep her distance and allow me to grieve with my friend, I think.

Winifred had said she'd give me one last chance to see Dagny on the red carpet. Ironically, the carpet running down the aisle of the church was red, so perhaps this satisfied that exception, even if it was more of a final curtain than a premiere.

"Bill got a chance to see some of the early cuts of the musical," Dagny said after everyone left the funeral and we were sitting alone in the front pew, Christ gazing down on us from His cross. "He said I was wonderful and looked to be having so much fun. I can't imagine he knew he'd have an accident, but some of his last words to me now seem so much more important. He told me to never give up on my dreams. At the time, I knew he was referring to the dreams of stardom, but now I just don't know. Are those still my dreams?"

"Do you want them to be?" I said softly, holding her hand.

"Perhaps. I probably shouldn't make any rash decisions at a time like this. I'm just glad that filming is over. Honestly, I'm not sure I'll feel like going to the premiere next month."

"The premiere," I said, more to myself than to Dagny, thinking of my own in less than two weeks.

"Oh, that's right. Yours is soon too," Dagny replied, picking up on my thoughts. "Oh, I do so want to attend, to be there to support you."

"Are you sure?" I thought about Winifred's warning not to see Dagny anymore. Would she still allow for her previous exception? I knew she'd be there, so I couldn't very well hide Dagny's presence from her.

"Of course! Wouldn't miss it for the world."

MAY

The day I thought I'd been so looking forward to for almost a year had finally arrived. So why did I feel like I was about to walk down the red carpet at Bill's funeral ten days earlier, rather than the one in front of Grauman's?

Charles came over to my house and did both Dagny's and my hair. I reflected on how things had come full circle in the time since he'd first done our hair at Dagny's apartment. Then, I'd fancied myself like Lana Turner. Now, my star was quickly rising and would soon overtake hers as Vincente Minnelli's newest *It* girl.

"Well, Mabs, your day has finally arrived. I'm so pleased for you." Of course, Dagny was still mourning Bill, but I suspected the sadness in her voice had another layer to it. I know I felt it.

"Yes, I suppose it has. I'm certainly a long way from that day you dragged me along to MGM." I matched her tone not out of sympathy, but empathy for the both of us. She'd lost the love of her life. I'd found what I once dreamed was the love of mine. A knock came at the door. I forlornly rose to answer it.

"Mabs, darling! It's your big day! Are you ready to wow the world, my little starlet?!" It was Carlisle, being far too exuberant for anytime and especially this one. I put on a cheery smile. I'd have to soon enough for all those gathered at Grauman's, so I might as well start now.

"Oh, grand, Carlisle! Just grand!"

"There's the spirit! Let's go show them what a real star is."

"Yes. Let's!" I was all levity and mirth on the outside, but inside my soul was heaving. If ever there was a time for a pep pill, now was it, but it was too late. They were still my little secret, at least from Carlisle. I'd have to power through all on my own this evening. It would be horrid.

A black 1949 Cadillac limousine was waiting in front of my house, the setting sun glistening off its chrome trim.

We headed toward Grauman's along Sunset Boulevard, and as I gazed out the window, the past year literally flashed before my eyes. There was Brentwood and the road to Clio's house. Next up was the Los Angeles Country Club, and a night both Carlisle and I would just as soon forget. The Hollywood Hills blurred past, and I thought of Errol Flynn's house, witness to the first time I met Stan Freberg, and the last time I broke his heart. Chateau Marmont, Dagny's apartment, the little café where I first ate raw tuna. Finally, the corner where it all began thirteen months before, the corner where I met Dagny for the first time after seven years. First seven years, then thirteen months. Was that the Fates' way of telling me my luck was about to run out? I didn't have time to ponder it any further.

The limousine pulled up in front of Grauman's, its large Chinese pagoda-like structure towering overhead and its twin lions guarding the entrance. Searchlights lit up the sky around us. A hundred flash bulbs exploded as photographers jostled to capture the moment. I stepped out of the car. A throng of fans pushed at the velvet ropes. Young girls called my name, fawning over what it must have been like to act opposite Gregory Peck. Reporters asked how I liked Sicily, and what my next film was going to be. I was close to losing my composure. It was all too overwhelming. I wanted to jump back in the limousine and have it race me back to my house, no, to my apartment. Then I felt a hand on my back. Dagny had stepped out of the car and was steadying me.

But where was Carlisle? I looked around and noticed he was waving to the crowd. His arrogance knew no bounds, and it was growing tiresome.

Then Gregory Peck appeared in front of me. "Good evening, Mabs. So good to see you again. Are you ready to go in? Are you ready for our premiere?" His voice called me back to reality, back to the part I had to play. I remembered our afternoon together in Camporeale before filming began, our lunch at the *osteria*, walking through the fields and gazing out at the sheep and the goats, he quoting Scripture. Dagny gave me a slight nudge. I took his hand. It was time to greet our fans. As we walked along the rope line, I shook hands and signed autographs. Somehow, I was soon lost in the moment and enjoying myself to some extent. A genuine smile crossed my face.

"Ciao, amici!" I greeted them in what little Italian I knew. Then we were inside, and things were somewhat quiet once again. After we took our seats, Carlisle to my left, Dagny to my right, the lights dimmed, and we saw Vincente walk onto the stage.

"Buena sera! Good evening, friends, colleagues, fans. As you may know, the picture you are about to see is one I've dreamed of making for many years. It is loosely based on some family history. My grandfather and his brother fought in the Sicilian Revolution. Although they weren't successful in that struggle, it was their loss that eventually led to my gain. Indeed, it led to my very life, for I would not exist had my grandfather not met my grandmother here in America.

"We never know what the future will hold. What can seem like bad fortune in the present may only be prologue to a brighter future, if not for us then for our posterity." He paused for a moment then, clearly off script and a bit quieter, "Of course, the reverse can also be true." He straightened up and continued.

"So, I hope this picture, and the wonderful actors and actresses I was so pleased to direct these past several months, will entertain you. But more than that, I hope they will inspire you. Inspire you to create your own revolution, whatever form that may take, and inspire you to stay true to your passions and to yourself. And with that, on with the show!"

Bad fortune leading to a brighter future? Good fortune leading to a darker one? Revolution. Inspiration. Truth. Which one was I destined for? The image of myself came on the screen, and I was immediately confused by it all. That wasn't me. The girl on screen had been transformed into someone else. Yes, she was a poor Sicilian peasant girl and I'd been a poor Swedish-Canadian farm girl, so our stations were the same, even if our complexions were not. But now I was living in a house three sizes too large for me. I was riding in limousines and dining on steak and lobster and caviar. What was it the old man had said to me at Clio's party? *A bit fishy. An acquired taste.* Is that what my life was now? Something I once was wary of, but now devoured with abandon?

I don't remember watching the rest of the movie. I don't remember much of anything that happened during the following two hours. All I remember was the lights coming on and Dagny turning toward me.

"Oh, Mabs, you were wonderful! I know I've been melancholy these past two weeks. God knows I have every reason to be. But tonight really cheered me up. It was so grand to see you on screen. Congratulations, Mabs." She leaned over and hugged me. *Cheered her up?* I hadn't remembered the last two hours, but I did remember the last several months. I'd stabbed Gregory Peck, Giovanni Marino, to death with an awl. How was that cheery?

The next three weeks were spent promoting and celebrating the new picture. Some of us reprised our roles as voice actors on NBC Radio's *Screen Directors Playhouse.* We toured the country, even taking an airplane to such far-off cities as Dallas, New Orleans, and Miami.

I kept my promise to Winifred—I had no other choice—and refrained from seeing Dagny again. It was terribly lonely, but it was somewhat bearable, being distracted with flying all over the country.

When I wasn't on the promotional circuit, I met with my agent and reviewed scripts for the next part MGM would send my way. Now that I was their newest rising star, they were working me relentlessly. The pills I took were almost a necessity now, as I had to often arise by five and occasionally even earlier.

Every minute of my life was planned. Even Carlisle had to phone my secretary to schedule an evening with me. After having to do so three or four times, he eventually gave up, and I never heard from him again. Such is the fickleness of romance. Not that I cared much. I was too busy to care.

Though you're a child, dear, your life's a wild typhoon! I remembered the words Judy Garland sang that night at the Cocoanut Grove. I'd tried so hard to turn Dagny back into what she had been, back into what I'd become. Now she had escaped, and I was the one trapped. I wanted so desperately to help her find what she had lost the day I met her on Sunset Boulevard, to help her find herself. Perhaps I had, but in the process, I'd lost myself. The sunset had turned to night for one of us, while turning to sunrise and light for the other. It was all too much, but until the sun rose again for me, I'd be lost, searching in the darkness.

CHAPTER 54
FADE TO BLACK

Hollywood was always heartbreak town, though most of the world fancied it to be Shangri-La, King Solomon's mines, and Fort Knox rolled into one big ball of twenty-four-karat gold.

— Hedda Hopper

JUNE

After another month or so of going a thousand miles an hour, eighteen to twenty hours per day, I cracked. Not significantly, mind you, but enough that the doctor was called in after I fainted one day while rehearsing lines, diagnosed me with exhaustion, and ordered me home to rest for the next five days. He preferred two weeks, but there was no way I was getting that much time off.

I must have slept twenty hours that first night. The next day, I wasn't necessarily exhausted in the clinical sense. At least I didn't feel I was. But I still wanted nothing more than to lie in bed and do nothing.

Around five, hunger getting the better of me, I looked in the refrigerator. While it was full of food, the only thing that looked appetizing was a bowl of strawberries and a bottle of milk. I grabbed both and returned to the couch. My mind was utterly devoid of any thought and that was fine with me. I didn't have the energy to think. I looked over at the hardwood floor and focused on a small crack between the boards. *Was this what complete boredom was?* The ceiling fan turned slowly above.

I must have fallen asleep at some point because I awoke with a start when I heard a knock on the door.

"It's unlocked. Come in," I replied quietly. I didn't have the energy to care who it might be.

"Mabs, what are you doing?" It was Dagny. She was clearly concerned.

"Oh, hello Dagny," I said lazily, only half paying attention. "So good of you to stop by. I'm just eating strawberries in the dark." The scene seemed familiar, and then I remembered that day so long before when I'd come in to find her eating figs in the dark.

She rushed over to my side and knelt down beside the couch.

"You shouldn't even be here," I told her, awakening more and opening my eyes fully.

"What do you mean? Do you want me to go?" She didn't sound hurt, just confused.

"No!" I turned and looked at her, desperation in my eyes. Now fully awake, I suddenly realized how much I'd missed her the past month, how much support I gained from her presence. "Don't go! Please, don't ever leave. It's just that—I mean— Winifred said I couldn't see you again. But I can't, Dagny, I just can't."

"I won't leave. Oh, Mabs, it's all my fault. I should never have introduced you to that awful woman. I should never have pushed you. I'm so, so sorry."

"She has a power over me," I continued. "I just can't—I don't know—" I didn't know how to finish my thought. I put my arm over my face and sobbed. "It hurts, Dagny. It hurts."

"I know. I know. She had that power over me too, but I wasn't as strong as you."

"What do you mean?" I stopped sobbing for a moment, wondering at her words.

She sat down on the couch and looked me directly in the eye. Her lip began to quiver. She began to sob as well and I knew she had something to tell me, something she'd been keeping inside for months. She turned her gaze downward, apparently not able to face me with the words that were to come next.

"She demanded someone in return. I didn't know what to do. Then you showed up on Sunset Boulevard. I hadn't seen you in years. I'm so ashamed. I didn't care about you. I only cared about saving myself."

I should have been angry with her, but then hadn't I lapped it up like a kitten at a bowl of milk? And hadn't Dagny tried to warn me off at least a time or two?

"That day at the Retake Room when we ran into Winifred. I should have been stronger at that moment. I should have warned you then. I'm just so sorry. You were truly always the stronger one and I took advantage of that. I thought you'd be able to take it. I thought the sacrifice was worth it. I'm just so sorry. I should have told you sooner. I shouldn't have been such a coward. But then you were having such a wonderful time. Traveling to Italy. Starring in a movie. I thought maybe you *had* made it." She lifted her gaze slightly.

"But you did warn me, Dagny." I had to forgive her. I had no other choice, seeing her there before me. As weak as I was in the moment, I knew I had to be her savior, even if that meant sacrificing myself. After all, it wasn't her fault any more than it was mine. We had both been pulled into Winifred's world. I had just been pulled deeper. "You warned me, and I didn't listen," I continued. "I wasn't ready. I just wasn't ready."

We embraced and after our tears subsided somewhat, Dagny spoke up again. "Thank you, Mabs. Thank you for saving me. Now it's my turn though. Now I have to be the strong one." She looked into my eyes again and composed herself.

"Up until two days ago, I was going to leave you. I thought I'd lost you long ago. Then I heard about you fainting on set and had to come see you. Thank God I did. Seeing you here like this, I know it's not true. I know I haven't lost you. It seems the girl from Prairie River I left on that train platform nearly a decade ago is still in there." She pushed a finger into my chest.

"You think so?" I replied.

"I know so. Do you think you can do it, Mabs? Do you think you can leave this all behind and come with me?"

"I don't know." I was so confused. Could I really do it? "There's so much here. This house. My career."

"Is it worth it?"

"I don't know. I just don't know," I said again. My head hurt with the competing thoughts that were tearing me apart.

"I know it's a big decision," Dagny replied, stroking my cheek. "Don't think about it now. I'll stay. I'll stay until you are ready. I promise I won't leave you now. Sisters to the end, right?"

"Oh, thank you, Dagny. Yes, sisters to the end." I hugged her tight.

"Come now, you just rest," she said, slowly stroking my hair. "I'm not going anywhere. Just rest. Just rest." Her gentleness calmed me. I laid back down, resting my head in her lap until I drifted off to sleep.

For how long, I don't know. I faintly remember the sound of a car engine and headlights briefly shining through the window. What happened next is a bit of a jumbled mess.

"Mabs, I've come to check—What are *you* doing here, you miserable little bitch?!" Winifred said, seeing Dagny. She had let herself in and caught us. She walked over to the couch, her heels clicking loudly on the hardwood floor. "I *told* you, you were not allowed to see her anymore," she said to me while grabbing Dagny by the arm and flinging her across the room. She grabbed my face in her hand and squeezed. "I'll punish you later," she screamed, dropping me back on the couch. I hid my face in the cushion, terrified.

"Now, *you*!" she screeched, turning toward Dagny. "You could have been my finest work of art. But no, you had to turn *sensible*. Musicals with Bing Crosby. Ha! That's not even a name. It's a sound. Ridiculous! That's all well and good. You can't win them all, but you won't take Mabs. She's mine, remember? You gave her to me! I should have started with her actually. She was always the weaker one, but I guess my charms just aren't what they used to be."

"No, Winifred! You won't! You won't take her! Just leave us both alone! We're leaving you! Leaving this place!" Dagny shouted at her. I slowly turned my head toward them and peeked through my fingers. Winifred had her back to me as she walked toward Dagny and slapped her hard across the face, sending her to the floor. Dagny cowered, slowly trying to inch away like a fly caught in some web. Winifred had backed her into a wall though. She had nowhere to go.

"You should have gone back to Saskatchewan when you had the chance. I should have ended you when I had the chance. Well, no time like the present." Winifred jumped on top of Dagny and began slapping her face back and forth. "You should have listened. You should have obeyed! You could have been the star. You could have risen to the heavens. Now I'm sending you to hell!"

Dagny continued to cower, taking blow after blow from Winifred. She didn't seem to have the will to fight back. Not only had Winifred pinned her physically, she'd pinned her emotionally.

"Please don't," Dagny whimpered. "I promise. I'll go now."

"You had your chance. Even after I killed off that beau of yours, you stuck around." *So, Bill's death wasn't an accident!* I always knew Winifred to be evil, but an actual murderess?!

"Now, just let it happen. Embrace the darkness," Winifred said softly. I was in horror as I saw her wrap her hands around Dagny's neck and begin to squeeze. Dagny struggled to break free, but Winifred had her pinned down. I had to do something. I had to help her. *But how?* Looking around the room for the answer, my eyes set upon the awl resting on the bookshelf. *Yes!* I'd brought it back with me from Sicily.

Suddenly, the passion I'd felt playing Luciana welled up inside me. Her spirit overtook me and my whole being was that of a nineteenth century peasant girl caught up in bloodlust. It wasn't acting. It wasn't even the Method. As I watched, Winifred continued to squeeze Dagny's neck. Dagny was still struggling but she was beginning to slip into unconsciousness. The fire inside me burned hotter and hotter. I grabbed the awl and approached Winifred. As I raised the weapon, ready to plunge it into her back, she turned around.

"Mabs, what are you doing?" She looked at me, not a hint of fear in her eyes. My actions hadn't had time to register with her. The blade came down straight into her heart, like a stake ending the life of the blood-sucking vampire she was. As it entered, only then did shock cross her face. Her eyes grew wide with a combination of fear for the fate that would soon overtake her and confusion over the betrayal I knew she must have felt.

While my actions had come from a desire to save Dagny, now that they'd run their course, I realized the passion that came from within was born out of revenge and utter hatred toward the woman standing, now crumpling, before me. She'd taken my soul. Now I had to take hers.

"Yes, Winifred, you're dying now, and it's all by *my* hand," I said, looking into her eyes. "You have no control over me anymore. No control over Dagny or Edmund or Vincente or Lana or any of the other marionettes you've pulled the strings of for too long. I've broken free, broken free from those strings, broken free from your web."

She was fading fast. She really should have been dead already, but she was a strong woman and refused to die. Her eyes were filled with disbelief, disbelief that I'd killed her, disbelief that I was lecturing her in her final moments.

"I don't know what the future will hold for me or anyone else," I continued. "But I know now that it will be ours. We will make our own destinies. I'm no longer going to play the role of an actress in somebody else's version of my life. I'm going to take a seat in the director's chair now, and everything from here on out will be filmed in one take because that's all we get in life. Indeed, all the world really is a stage, but from now on I won't be acting in it. From now on, it will only be reality."

The life finally flickered, then faded completely from Winifred's eyes, and her body went limp. I looked over at Dagny. She was still conscious and now, free of Winifred's hands, she was curled up on the floor, shaking.

"Dagny, are you okay?" I rushed over, sat on the floor beside her, and put my arm around her back, pulling her close. She shivered. "It's okay, Dagny. She can't hurt us anymore."

Dagny just sat there, shaking, fear still burning in her eyes.

"Oh, Dagny, I lost myself to Winifred and to the lights and the glamour. I lost myself to Hollywood but then you came back. You saved me, Dagny."

Like so many young girls had in the years before, and so many more would in the years to come, I'd been pulled in by the dream, yet awoken to find a nightmare. Somehow though, the Fates had decided to spare me. With Dagny's help, I'd found the strength to escape.

Perhaps it was the cold winters on the open plains of Saskatchewan. Perhaps it was some strength passed down from the mother I'd never known. Whatever it was, I had recalled the savior within me, and saved not only Dagny from a physical death, but even more importantly, myself from what surely would have been a spiritual one. *What does it profit a woman to gain the whole world but lose her soul?* I was grateful that I'd never need to find out. MGM could have the car. It could have the fancy clothes, the jewelry, the makeup, the house, and the Red Carpet. It could even have my name and image up on the silver screen. I had something far more important.

Dagny looked over at me, her eyes still wide. "What—what now?"

"Let's go home, Dagny. Let's go home to Prairie River."

THE END

EPILOGUE
THE LETTER

I realized I didn't want to go back to Hollywood anymore. It was a shallow, dog-eat-dog world. I didn't want that in my life. So I felt content staying in Kansas.

— Karolyn Grimes

Many decades later, Dagny passed away after a long battle with cancer. Amongst her things was a letter she had written to me shortly before that fateful night I took Winifred's life to save hers, a letter she'd never given me but had clearly felt important enough to hold on to for all these years.

I'd done my best to bury that memory, as best as anyone can do with such an awful scene, but as I began to read, it all came flooding back.

Dearest Mabs,

"I was gazing at the stars tonight, and I began contemplating how large the universe is and how small we are in comparison. I realized, all these people chasing fame in Hollywood, trying to impress producers, leading men, even the pool boys at the Bel-Air, well, what's the point? In the end, none of it matters. I don't want to impress anyone anymore, Mabs. I just want to be myself, the self I knew so many years ago back in Prairie River. I want to go home, Mabs.

That might seem terribly pedestrian to you and everyone else in this crazy, shallow town where not just the buildings on the back lot are facades. I want reality back in my life, though, no matter how dull it might be.

And I'm not wasting another moment. I'm catching the train north the day after tomorrow. I don't expect you to come with me. You seem to enjoy this life. Ironic, isn't it? You seemed more suited to life back home while I couldn't wait to leave and now, we find ourselves in the same roles, only reversed.

I'm sorry you followed me down here, Mabs. I'm sorry I pulled you into the web I'd spun for myself. If I could change places with you, I would. In a heartbeat I would. But salvation is something you must accept freely. Salvation is an open invitation, not a kidnapping.

Maybe you'll follow on in time just as you followed me down here. But if you don't, if you remain here, I wish you all the happiness in the world and please know that I will always love you. You took care of me when we were little, Mabs. You even took care of me here when I should have been able to take care of myself. Those sacrifices have been more costly to you than I ever thought or wanted and I'm just so sorry.

Goodbye, Mabs. May you find the stardom you've been seeking. Moreso, may that star be a light guiding you back to what really matters.

> *Always your friend,*
> *Always your sister,*
> *Dagny*

DISCUSSION QUESTIONS

1. Who is the main hero in the story? Who is the main villain?
2. Which character would you most like to meet? Which one do you most despise?
3. Mabs has significant character swings throughout the story. What causes these? Does Mabs ever truly come to know herself?
4. What does An Acquired Taste mean in the context of the novel?
5. Dagny goes out of her way to help Mabs get into acting. Why does she do this? How does Mabs feel when she gets a bigger part than Dagny? How does Dagny feel?
6. Partway through the story, Mabs begins to be wary of Winifred. Why?
7. In Chapter 30, Dagny tells Mabs she is a completely different girl than the one she grew up with. How does Dagny feel about this, especially considering she introduced Mabs to this lifestyle?
8. In Chapter 41, Mabs says the line "Live for today. No, not even the day! The moment!" is delivered by Dagny with sadness. Why does Mabs remember this line and what does it say about her internal struggle at this point in the story?
9. In Chapter 46, Mabs seems quite happy considering she's just lost a baby. She even makes dark jokes about it. Why does she have this reaction?
10. In Chapter 53, Mabs has achieved everything she had once dreamed of. Why is she sad?

AUTHOR'S NOTE

While the overall plot of this novel is entirely a work of fiction, it is set in a historical time and place with several historical characters appearing throughout. To be as true to reality as possible, I read several books and articles, watched movies and documentaries, and listened to radio shows, and podcasts. Some of these provided specific information, while others served as background to inform me of the zeitgeist of Hollywood in the late 1940s. I encourage readers who are interested to engage further by reading or watching the works listed online at AcquiredTasteNovel.com.

There you will also find a readers guide that gives definitions or more information on historical characters and literary references, historical photos I collected from across the internet while researching the novel, and photos from a trip I took to Los Angeles to visit locations mentioned in the book.

ACKNOWLEDGEMENTS

I have written several short stories, poems, and essays. I've also hosted two radio shows and produced other creative works, so creativity is not new to me. This, however, is my first novel. It was quite an undertaking, and besides the authors and creators of the many books, articles, podcasts, movies, and documentaries I consulted, I am deeply grateful to the following people who provided moral support as well as specific feedback during the writing and editing process.

To my wife, Rosie, who helps support our family in a myriad of ways. Without you, I never would have had the time and motivation to attempt this endeavor.

To my mother, Vera Detour, a writer in her own right and an award-winning one at that. Growing up in a home with books and watching her read and write instilled a love of the written word at a young age.

To the members of the North Idaho Writers League, who listened as I read new chapters of this book nearly every week. Because of your invaluable feedback on pacing, character development, and everything else that goes into writing a novel, I am a better writer. Specifically, I need to further acknowledge the late, great Larry Telles, a wealth of information when it comes to Hollywood; Sarah Vail; and Anna Goodwin.

To Amber Laura, Alicia Lynch, and Angie Paxton, my beta-readers who provided detailed feedback on the second draft.

To the staff at the Margaret Herrick Library and the Culver City Historical Society, for research assistance in looking at hundreds of photos from Golden Age Hollywood and sharing your own stories from that era.

To Phil Bevis, a long-time friend, and owner of Arundel Books and Chatwin Press in Seattle, who has always encouraged me to write.

To Kristi Brown, a voracious reader, who outside the members of the Writers League, was the first person to read this book while it was being written and provide helpful feedback.

To Michelle Mendoza, Steve Corda, and Shelley Dudley, my long-time friends and radio show co-hosts and writers themselves, who helped me foster my creativity over many years.

To actress Karolyn Grimes, best known for her role as Zuzu Bailey in *It's a Wonderful Life*, for helping to inspire my love for Golden Age Hollywood and being just a truly great soul in general.

To Suzanne Holland, my editor, for making sure all my commas were in the right place, and correcting my grammar, tense, and continuity errors, and made further suggestions related to pacing and word choice.

To Gary Schneidmiller, who spent time retrieving information on The Desert Riders at the Palm Springs Public Library.

To David Roni, Mayra Villegas, Miguel Macias, and Jason Tang, who palled around Los Angeles with me, exploring countless locations, some completely obscure, that are mentioned in this novel.

To the staffs at the Hotel Bel-Air, The Beverly Hills Hotel, The Frolic Room, Du-Par's, and Miceli's for providing excellent service and indulging my questions about your establishments.

To Benito and the rest of the staff at The Sunset Ranch, for giving me an amazing experience riding the trails of the Hollywood Hills, and Jin, captain of the beautiful wooden sailboat *Charming*, who took my friends and I out for a beautiful sunset cruise off the coast of Santa Monica.

To Bitterroot Mountain Publishing House, that helped make this final manuscript a published reality.

And finally, to you, my readers. If a word lands on a page and no one is around to read it, does it truly exist?

www.ingramcontent.com/pod-product-compliance
Lightning Source LLC
Chambersburg PA
CBHW030632020726
47493CB00006B/1675